A MILKWOOD MURDER

THE PUCCINI CONNECTION

SAM BOND

Cover art by Kim's Cozy Covers

BOUND PUBLISHING / AUSTIN, TX

For Eddie Carter

With innumerable thanks to Lisa Warne-Magro

ACKNOWLEDGMENTS

With thanks to my daughters, Olivia and Tess, for keeping me grounded. My friends for being such a wonderful substitute for family, and to my writing groups, Pen & Fork and Sit Down Shut Up and Write, with a special shout out to Jo Richner for keeping me accountable — daily.

Thanks to Deanna Roy who is always a generous fountain of knowledge and keeps me from beating my head against my desk.

I must also thank my talented cover artist, Kim who, like Josie and myself, also comes from Surrey. Kim took my idea and ran with it, plus she was a complete joy to work with.

Finally, a big thank you to all my first readers: Lisa Warne-Magro, Kathleen Trail, Karen MacInerney, Kasey Pfaff, Stephanie Hudnall, Holly Green, Melissa Fong, Kristi Floyd, Claire Fahey, Sue Cleveland, Tara Cherry, and Eddie Carter. Thank you all for taking the time to give such thoughtful feedback. It makes me abundantly happy to have such avid readers in my life.

"Lesser artists borrow. Great artists steal." - Igor Stravinsky

"When words fail music speaks." - Irena Huang

"Why, why, Sir, why do you pay me back like this?" - Tosca

TWO NATIONS DIVIDED BY A COMMON LANGUAGE

First: Like Josie, I am an expat who has lived in the US for many years. This book is therefore written with American English spelling with one exception — the word mum! Just can't bring myself to spell it as 'mom.'

Second: There are many colloquial English terms within The Puccini Connection. I figure my readers are smart enough to understand words like 'pavement' and 'biscuit' when used in context.

WHO'S WHO IN MILKWOOD

The Monroe Family
Josie Monroe: expat, pianist and main protagonist
Finolla Monroe: Josie's artist mother
Giles Monroe: Josie's father
Imogen Bentley-Driver: Josie's stepsister
Charles Bentley-Driver: Imogen's new husband
Hugh Monroe: Josie's stepbrother

Barton Hall Estate Residents
Belle DeCorcy: Lord of the Manor's daughter
Lord Max DeCorcy: Lord of the Manor
Quentin Young: local composer
Tillman: butler
Mrs Elsie Crackenthorpe: housekeeper

The Police
Detective Inspector Adam Ward: Josie's childhood
boyfriend
Detective Sergeant Helen Winterbottom (Frosty
Knickers): Adam's colleague
Fitz: Desk Sergeant
Police Constable Davis

Milkwood Residents
Rose Braithwaite: Josie's aunt
Peter Lacey: Rose's lodger
Bonnie Curry: next-door neighbor
Magna Carter: owner of Crumbs
Irene Bloggett: owner of Irene's Milk Jug
The Witches of Milkwood: the aforementioned Bonnie,
Magna and Irene
Elgar: Rose's cat
Petruska and Carl Llewellyn: publicans at The Dirty Duck
Susan Ludlow: owner of Waspits
Dan Ludlow: Susan's teenage son
Wendy Williams: owner of the riding stable
Duncan Fitzpatrick: Wendy's husband
Gurminder Singh: classmate of Dan and works at Naans
Reverend Charles Greene: vicar at St Ethelred's
Florence Greene: wife of Reverend Greene
Philip Upton: curate at St Ethelred's
Petra Ainsworth-Browne: local busybody and equestrian
Darcy Blythe: also a local busybody
Lucy Lewis: stablehand
Ivy Lewis: mother of Lucy and one of Josie's pupils

Others
Daisy Pond: visitor from Australia
René: dress shop owner
Douglas Stapeleton: receptionist at Padfoot & Strong
Edwina Padfoot: solicitor at Padfoot & Strong

Josie's Pupils
Georgina Lewis
Poppy Ledbetter
Elsie Walker
Charlotte Wentworth
Timothy Larsdale
Ralph & Alfie Stapleton
Owen & Ophelia Hadleigh

Notable Mentions

Lady Hannah DeCorcy: Belle's mother
Grif and Terry Ayles: troublemakers
Jimmy Gilroy: Josie's childhood friend
Holly Drinkwater: Milkwood resident and *persona non grata*
Mrs Ackerman: Josie's neighbor in Austin, TX
Horace: Josie's budgerigar

DON'T GET LOST - A MILKWOOD MAP

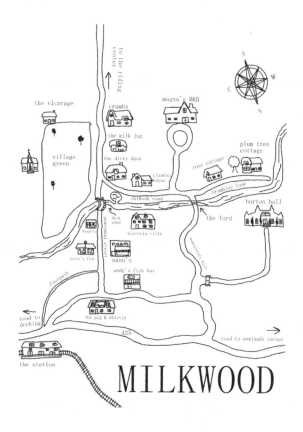

1

I love you," slurred the Scotsman. "I want to marry you."

"That's awfully nice of you," I murmured, trying to dislodge his whiskers from my ear. "But I don't think we've been introduced."

Honestly, this was so typical. I'd been dating now for three years and not received so much as a backwards glance. However, I return to the UK and suddenly I'm freaking Marilyn Monroe. Well, actually, I'm Josie Monroe. I'm a woman of a certain age, with a lot less pout, a lot less hair and way less sex appeal. At least that's how I'd considered myself in Austin, Texas, where I'd spent the last twenty years. Now it seemed I'd morphed into a sex siren worthy of my namesake.

A cool breeze whistled along the corridor as a reveler exited into a typical summer night in England—i.e., a few degrees above frigid.

"Wash your name?" the Scotsman continued, his bloodshot eyes now locked on mine, his hand creeping up my leg.

"Um!"

"I love dat name. Dat's a bootiful name," he whispered to my cleavage.

Now, I might be imagining it, but the Scotsman seemed to be shrinking. When he'd first intercepted me on my way to the loo he'd been, at a guess, 250 pounds and hovering around six feet. I was five foot seven and my self-proclaimed would-be second husband was now several inches shorter than me and getting shorter by the second.

I realized too late that my admirer's feet were giving out beneath him. Don Hamish, as I'd started to think of him, was nonchalantly sliding down my rose satin ball gown, his stubbly chin snagging the material I'd been assured by Finolla complimented my dark brown hair and pale blue eyes. Personally, I thought the color brought out my rosacea, but I'd learned a long time ago not to argue with my mother. This dress cost more than I'd earned in the past month and I wasn't about to let some drunken Scotsman ruin it. I gave the Kilted One an almighty shove and he toppled like a caber at the Highland Games.

I thought about leaving the unconscious lothario where he fell, but that seemed a tad uncharitable. Instead, I scooted into the bathroom and found the fluffiest towel possible to stuff under Don Hamish's head. I'd almost finished when who should appear at the end of the passageway but my mother, Finolla.

"Josie," she hissed, beckoning me towards her. "This is no time for having fun. Your sister's about to toss the bouquet. Come on! This might be your final chance."

And that's how I found myself in my second embarrassing scenario of the night. Me and my rose-colored dress, battling for position amongst a sea of eager twenty-somethings. Truly, kill me now, which is what the bouquet almost did when it hit me on the forehead, taking me down to floor level.

"Honestly, Josie," said Finolla, abandoning her empty wine glass on the table. "I don't know how these things happen to you."

"Um!" I said, clutching the recently acquired ice pack to my temple.

"Why can't you be more like your sister?" said Finolla, gazing at Imogen, currently floating across the ballroom in a rustle of silk. She was nestled against the sturdy chest of her new husband, Charles Bentley-Driver, and seemed to be singing the words to a Celine Dion song I was pretty sure I hated.

I would like to have pointed out that Imogen was a half-sister from my father's side, but—as Finolla was known to say—know when to pick your battles, and never pick them with her.

"Why don't I get you another glass of wine," I said, discarding the melting ice and rising to unsteady heels.

My words were lost on a waft of Chanel, as some French film star, a bridesmaid at Finolla's third—no wait, fourth—wedding, tottered towards the table with outstretched arms.

My father had been Finolla's first and longest attempt at matrimonial bliss and somehow their tempestuous relationship had morphed into a friendship that defied logic. This was something else I'd failed at with Ryan, the insanely good-looking Texan who was now my defunct husband and the ruination of my once on-track life. I'd tried to explain how it's hard to remain friends with your ex when he develops a midlife crisis and goes missing for three years, but to hear Finolla tell it, I just hadn't tried hard enough.

Finolla was currently knee-deep in a combination of French and generous hand gestures. Figuring I wouldn't be missed, I headed to the bar. My half-sister's wedding reception was located in a seventeenth-century moated castle that my father had hired at a cost that would pay the rent on my Austin apartment for an entire year—maybe two. It was cold and drafty and the plumbing was a bit iffy, but it was a castle, a word that always bodes well on glossy wedding invitations.

The lights were flickering low and there were so many clusters of yellow roses adorning each table that you could easily imagine you were in Covent Garden circa Eliza Doolittle. I circumnavigated the frivolity, trying to avoid tripping over the three video cameras capturing the happy couple as they crooned about how their hearts would go on. Ick!

I pinky waved as I passed my father, currently cornered by a local cabinet minister. He raised his glass, and I thought briefly about going in for a rescue mission—but only briefly.

I glanced around the ballroom chock-full of up-and-coming men from the City and Imogen clones, each girl taller and thinner than the next with stick-straight blonde hair and Stella McCartney dresses. I should mention that the closest I've ever got to owning anything by McCartney is a Beatles greatest hits album and that was second hand with a rather noticeable scratch during the chorus of "Eleanor Rigby."

In case you hadn't guessed, traveling from the States to attend Imogen's wedding had not been my idea. To be blunt, I was there at the insistence of my mother, and when Finolla insists it's easier to give in and hope you don't end up in prison, in hospital, or worse, on the front page of the *Daily Yell*.

Indeed, it's amazing how persuasive Finolla can be. Even more so when she books first-class tickets from Austin to Heathrow, texting all the pertinent details. I wouldn't go so far as to say it was bribery, because Finolla and I had already covered this topic ad nauseam, my mother assuring me that bribery was only for those who were unable to negotiate well.

"My friends are starting to think you're in jail," Finolla had said on a rare phone call. "It's been an absolute age and it just won't do."

"That's not true," I hedged. "I was there for Hugh's christening."

"Oh, did I tell you? Hugh's going to be Charlie's best man."

"Really?" I asked. "Imogen's brother? Isn't he a bit, er, young?"

"He's twenty-one," my mother replied. "And you've not seen Imogen since..." Finolla racked the database of her mind in the hope of pinpointing a year or, failing that, a decade.

I'd not seen Imogen since she'd visited Austin several years ago when she'd had sex with every man I knew, several men I didn't know, and a couple of women just for good measure. One could only hope she'd put all that behind her. If not, it was going to be a volatile and short-lived marriage and one that would most definitely give the British tabloids their money's worth.

Weaving in and out of the tables, I was within spitting distance of the bar when I heard my name. This was puzzling, as I knew approximately ten guests and, with the exception of my father, none of them particularly liked me. I turned to see the aforementioned Hugh sprawled nonchalantly over a wingback chair.

If I had to use one word to describe Hugh it would be "confident." If I was pressed to use two, I would add "charming" quickly followed by "cocky." With his tie pulled rakishly to one side, he was all foppish hair and raffish smile, with a trust fund thrown in for good measure.

I could practically hear the sharpening of talons, as a bevy of England's finest prepared to do battle—the battle being who was going to have the privilege of bedding Hugh for the night. If he was anything like his sister, there might be several contenders.

Hugh was obviously not calling me over—from the angle he was facing he didn't even know I was there. The only other explanation was he was talking *about* me. I began to move away, but I heard my name again and, come on, who can resist listening to what's being said about them? Answer: Happy people, that's who.

"Josie? I guess she's not bad," said Hugh, cradling a snifter of brandy. "Course we barely know her. Some big scandal when she was barely out of school. Like mother like daughter, if you ask me."

"Oh, Hugh, you are awful," said a dark-haired woman whose forehead was so abundant she reminded me of a mare we'd once owned named Whinny. She threw her head back and laughed. I may have imagined it, but it sounded decidedly like a neigh.

"She's an odd duck," continued Hugh. "Not a patch on her mother of course. But one does one's best to be cordial. Of course, there was some talk about her being gifted when she was young. Nothing came of it, mind you, and now she's in the South doing something weird in the boondocks of Texas."

I wanted to tell him that Texas might be south geographically, but it was not considered by Americans as "the South" and Austin was *not* the boondocks. It was the freaking state capital, for goodness' sake. I decided this probably wasn't the time. As for the "doing something weird" comment—well, I'd just let that go.

"Why on earth would anyone go to Texas?" said Whinny, saying the word 'Texas" like you might say the word "lice."

"Like I said. Wasted her youth on some brash American," replied Hugh, as if there was no other type.

"Ugh!" said Whinny, who really needed to work on her resting bitch face.

Hugh swilled his brandy. "And now she's a music teacher! So dreadfully provincial."

"No!" said Whinny, as if Hugh had revealed my penchant for operating electric chairs. "How utterly dreadful."

"I heard her husband ran off with some Brazilian model," said a blonde in plunging scarlet.

I took a breath. If people were going to gossip, I really wish they'd get their facts correct. The woman was Argentinian and I use the word "woman" loosely, seeing she'd barely encountered adolescence.

"I heard the husband was quite gorgeous," said Scarlett. "No surprise she couldn't keep someone like that. She's definitely no Finolla."

"Not *the* Finolla?" said Whinny. "We have one of hers next to the Rubens. Is it really true that she—"

"The one and only," interrupted Hugh. "In fact, she's here too."

The conversation was interrupted with a loud whoop as the music took a decidedly Bollywood turn. Ah, the ubiquitous flash mob of jealous best friends masquerading as bridesmaids. Could this become any more clichéd?

I'd heard enough. Eavesdropping on myself was bad enough. I certainly didn't need to hear gossip regarding my mother. For one, there was so *much* gossip where Finolla was concerned, it could take all night—heck, it could take decades. My mother was the woman who made Mick Jagger look like a choirboy. Something she'd said he most definitely wasn't, after a brief encounter at a London nightclub back in the eighties.

I decided to put all thoughts of Hugh and his posse out of my pinot grigio addled brain. Who were they to judge what I did? I enjoyed my job. Teaching was rewarding. It could also be exhausting and soul destroying, plus it didn't pay well, but I was getting off topic.

Reaching my destination, I fished into the top of my pink satin gown for a twenty. The bar was currently packed with men who'd reached that point in the festivities when it was easier to prop up the bar than talk to their dates. I wedged myself between a Steve Jobs lookalike and someone who looked remarkably like Samuel Jackson and patriotically waved the Queen in the general direction of a harried-looking handsome bartender.

In spite of not being my mother I have it on good authority that I am not unattractive. In fact, in my day I could party with the best of them, especially if the party was over by ten—nine on a school night. However, if there's one thing I've learned as I approach middle age it's that unless you are young, pretty or preferably both, it is extremely hard to catch the bartender's eye unless cash is flaunted like a stripper's G-string.

The twenty worked and ten seconds later a very nice chap named Paul upended a bottle of pinot into a glass so generous it could have housed a couple of goldfish and a plastic castle.

I felt someone nudge my elbow and turned to find Finolla directly behind me. Finolla may be twenty-plus years my senior but she had no such problems getting space at the bar. Like the proverbial Red Sea, the crowd parted leaving Paul so enamored that he immediately dropped a wine glass, shattering it to smithereens.

"Clumsy," said my mother, wagging a finger provocatively in his direction.

Paul reached forward and swept away the shards, a move he would quickly regret. The blood was instantaneous and so was my nausea.

"Cluck a duck!" I exclaimed, as I covered my mouth and stumbled from the carnage.

Five seconds later Finolla spun me round. For a millisecond I imagined my mother was checking to see if I was okay, then reality kicked in, and I realized my stupidity as she dangled her iPhone in my direction. "Your aunt," she said, with undisguised dislike.

Of course, Finolla could also have said "my sister," "Aunt Rose," or just "Rosetta," but Finolla and Rose had a relationship that vacillated between mild dislike and unabashed loathing, with a dash of malice thrown in for good measure. My mother believed my aunt to be a manipulative, conniving cow and that was on a good day. Aunt Rose chose not to say what she thought of Finolla, which was probably just as well.

Aunt Rose was not as glamorous as Finolla—who was? In fact, she was about as unlike my mother as possible. It was incredible how two sisters had emerged within twelve months of each other from the same womb. Actually, it was so incredible that the rumor was my grandmother had returned to the hospital to check that a mix-up had not occurred.

Whereas Finolla was tall and willowy, Aunt Rose was petite and voluptuous, which may have been where the angst started. Finolla, who had been given so much in the looks department, got precisely zero in the bosom area. "Standing behind the door when they gave out the tits, darling," was what my mother always said. It didn't improve matters when, by the age of fourteen, it was obvious which of the two I took after.

The only thing the two sisters had in common was their artistic nature—Aunt Rose a piano prodigy and my mother a sublimely talented landscape artist. While Aunt Rose was playing at Carnegie Hall, Finolla was hosting her debut show in Soho. Can you even *say* the words "sibling rivalry?"

By twenty-three Finolla had met my father and given birth to her only child—me. Finding it exceedingly difficult to party at night and raise a child by day, my mother promptly dumped all child rearing responsibilities onto her soon-to-be-ex. By the time I'd reached five she'd disappeared completely, absconding with some minor European count to his chateau on the Rhine.

It was around this time that I started spending my summers with Aunt Rose, as my father divided his life between raising a daughter, a job on the stock exchange and dating Lady Lavinia Davenport—mother to my half-siblings, Imogen and Hugh. Without doubt, summer holidays in the Surrey village of Milkwood were the highlight of my childhood.

I found a quiet spot and wedged myself into a corner.

"Hey, Aunt Rose. It's Josie."

"Josie, posie, pudding and pie," came the familiar voice down the phone.

"The one and the same," I responded.

I'd called my aunt on landing at Heathrow, but only reached her voicemail. I had two days left in the UK and hoped to spend these with her. I'd been worried that her lack of response meant I'd be obligated to remain on the Welsh border with Finolla and the rest of the unhinged Monroe family. Not that Shropshire was a disagreeable county, far from it, but I longed to be two hundred miles south, enjoying my beloved Milkwood, with the added benefit of being as far away from the Monroes as possible.

"Just received your message," said Aunt Rose. "I'm in the Peak District. The reception's not at its best when you're in a limestone valley. Anyhow, I'm cutting my trip short. I assume you're going to be seeing your favorite aunt before you head back to the depths of depravity?"

I once again took this to mean Austin, Texas, and decided it was probably not the most opportune time to say how much I loved my adopted home.

"I'll catch an early afternoon train and should arrive at Euston around five and Milkwood by seven," I said, imagining the warm scones and jam that would be waiting for me.

"Perfect," said Aunt Rose. "I'm adding you to my schedule as we speak."

Aunt Rose had always been a stickler for schedules and the memory of her monogrammed leather-bound notebooks made me smile.

"As long as the M1 isn't at a standstill I should be there in plenty of time. I'll wander along to the station and meet you."

"You don't have to do that," I replied.

"My pleasure, it's not every day I get to see my favorite niece, and besides, I have something exciting to tell you."

I smiled. The last time Aunt Rose told me she had something exciting to share it turned out she'd adopted a new kitten. All of Aunt Rose's cats (and there had been many) were named after English composers. If I remembered rightly this one was a brown tabby by the name of Elgar.

"I'm looking forward to it," I replied, but Aunt Rose was gone. The connection was dead.

2

The door whooshed shut, and with an abrupt jolt we were off. I had discarded the grandeur of the night before and wore a pair of boot-cut jeans, a V-neck tee, and my trusty Vans. My hair was tied in a low ponytail and I was devoid of makeup. Situation satisfactorily back to normal.

There was a hold-up somewhere around Watford and my Euston-bound train limped into the station almost an hour late. I hopped onto the descending escalator and boarded the Victoria line heading south and gave thanks it was the weekend. Navigating the London Underground was bad enough on a Sunday afternoon, I don't think I could have coped during weekday rush hour. There were several things I missed about living in the UK: being able to get a decent cuppa and having a local chippy being the two most important. However, public transport was something I'd happily forsaken in exchange for four sturdy wheels and copious amounts of air conditioning.

I plonked down into an empty window seat and watched the greyness of London subside as rows of terraced houses gave way to trees, fields, and finally undulating countryside. Now this was something I did miss. There was something about the English landscape that filled my heart with joy. The utter lushness of it, for one, was enough to warm my sterile British heart. Austin had many fine parks and an expansive greenbelt, but being so hot for most of the year it never occurred to me to go outside and traverse them. In Austin I gave thanks to the inventor of the air conditioner. In England I gave thanks to Mother Nature.

I watched the scenery slide by and thought about the past few days. Imogen's wedding had not been completely atrocious. Nevertheless, it was a relief to leave Shropshire, my family and the amorous Scotsman behind and proceed southward to Surrey, to the place I felt most at home—Plum Tree Cottage.

In usual Finolla fashion, my mother had promised to drop me off at the station, but a late night dalliance with some Archduke saw my mother disappear as quickly as a flash flood in Texas. When she failed to show at the designated time, I'd left a hastily scribbled note, hailed a taxi and made my own way to the station.

I wouldn't know if Finolla received the note until I flew home to the US. My cell had no reception in the UK and it seemed an extravagance to purchase a phone to use for just one week, or to ask my carrier to turn on international roaming. To be honest, I liked being unreachable—something my former husband would have read great meaning into. For one thing it meant that I got to take in my surroundings opposed to taking in the luminescent screen currently mesmerizing each one of my travel companions. I will admit, I worried for both the mental and physical health of the younger generation. I also feared for their spines, which were going to be hunched over like question marks by the time they turned fifty.

The train slowed and I recognized the outer suburbs of Dorking. Three more stops and I would be there.

It had been way too long since I'd seen Aunt Rose. Commitments in the States, plus my reluctance to answer questions regarding Ryan, made returning to my homeland an unattractive prospect. This meant Aunt Rose and I had lost touch over the years. There were Christmas cards and Aunt Rose never forgot my birthday, an event primarily ignored by Finolla, who seemed to regard my birthday as less of a celebration and more of a relentless reminder of her own steadfast demise. Aunt Rose also sent me the occasional classical music magazine, in which she would write scathing comments in the margins with regard to new recordings and rising soloists. Her remarks on the six best bagpipe tunes of all time had caused me spit out my tea with laughter, and her sardonic wit on the talent of a local composer had made me happy I'd stuck to teaching.

I was looking forward to seeing my aunt and luxuriating in the idyllic hamlet where she lived. Milkwood was situated in a particularly picturesque part of England's green and pleasant land. From its thatched cottages to its duck pond, it was one windmill away from perfection. I had vivid memories of summers of blackberry picking, lazy afternoon picnics and cricket on the village green. Then, of course, there was the infamous summer when Jimmy Gilroy and Adam Ward hung a rope swing over the Tillingbourne. It was exceptionally warm for the season and the rope swing provided hours of pleasure, although to be fair, most of it consisted of us sitting on the bank daring each other to take a swing.

I winced as I recalled a local girl who'd stumbled across our happy band and on refusing to have a go was tossed fully clothed into the Tillingbourne. Oh my stars, kids could be cruel. In America it would be cause for suspension. Back then it barely raised an eyebrow. I probably wouldn't even remember the incident if the unlucky child hadn't hit a submerged rock causing her to split open an eyebrow. This, in turn, caused me to throw up, beginning my lifelong fear of blood. If I remembered correctly the kid got off lightly with eight stitches, whereas I endured the nickname "Puke" for the rest of the summer.

The two boys lived on the nearby estate and were always up for adventure. Adam and Jimmy were rough and tumble and suited my tomboy nature far better than the village pony set. That's not to say I didn't enjoy riding. What I didn't enjoy was the relentless competition in who owned the most expensive jodhpurs or who'd skied at San Moritz the previous Christmas.

By my teenage years Finolla's work was in high demand and she drifted back into my life as if she'd never left. Trips to France, Spain and Monaco ensued and we were not only skiing in San Moritz, but had access to a condo, season passes and a zealous ski instructor named Sven.

I smiled as I thought back to those days. Adam was all gangly and uncoordinated with curly dark hair and intelligent eyes. Jimmy was the good looking one, broad and stocky with eyes so blue you could imagine you were gazing into a cloudless summer sky.

We'd been the best of friends until we hit our teenage years and then, as was to be expected, hormones kicked in, dynamics changed and summers became a whole lot more complicated. I hadn't thought of either of them in years. Now I was surprised to find myself hoping I would bump into them over the next couple of days. I jogged myself from the memory. Both boys were what my father would call "trouble" and in reality they were probably doing time in Pentonville.

I felt the train slow and my heart give an unexpected lurch. Grabbing my suitcase, I started towards the exit and seconds later stepped onto a platform festooned with flower baskets. I paused for a second, breathing in a heady mixture of freshly cut grass and cow manure. Ah, the joys of the country. At close to 8:00pm on a Sunday night there was only one other person disembarking further along the platform and I turned and followed them towards the wooden pedestrian bridge that linked the northbound side to the southbound.

The figure ahead of me was dressed in pale flowing trousers and a colorful summer smock. She was moving at quite a clip for her age as she hung a left and trotted down the steps towards the car park. By the time I reached the stairs she was already at the bottom and, as a shaft of light illuminated her profile, I gasped.

I hurried down the steps and into the forecourt, but the woman had disappeared like ice cream on a Texas summer day.

3

I strode through the carpark and gazed around. Two things struck me. First, there was no sign of the lady from the train. Second, there was no sign of Aunt Rose. This was unusual, as Aunt Rose was a stickler for time. I spotted a phone box and headed towards it. There were two ways to reach Aunt Rose's cottage and I didn't want to go one way, only to find she'd chosen the other.

Opening the door I inhaled the pungent odor associated with all English phone boxes—stale urine and mold. If I am honest, it was a surprise to even *see* one of Britain's iconic red phone boxes these days. In Shropshire I'd not spotted a single one. However, this was Milkwood and one of its delights was its reluctance to change. I gingerly grasped the headset and inspected it for nastiness before holding it three inches away from my ear. I pulled out a scrappy piece of paper containing way too many digits and dialed the number. The English double ringtone echoed through the receiver and I thought I was about to hit voicemail when someone picked up.

I moved the phone even farther from my ear, as music blasted through the speaker.

"Aunt Rose?" I yelled.

"Josie? Is that you?"

I raised my voice even louder, as an overenthusiastic soprano wailed in the background. "Yeah, I wanted to let you know that I'm—"

"What are you doing here? We just spoke."

I frowned. "I've come to see you. Remember? We chatted yesterday."

"Wait! You can't do that—" But before I had a chance to say anything else the phone went dead.

I replaced the headset on its cradle and stepped out into the fresh air. Could Aunt Rose have forgotten I was coming to stay? I tried to do the arithmetic in my head. Finolla was twenty-three years older than me and Aunt Rose was one year older than Finolla. Not exactly young, but in today's world—not super old. Had Finolla neglected to inform me that Aunt Rose suffered from memory loss or Alzheimer's? Surely not. I hated to admit it, but I was certain my mother would not hold back in telling me if anything negative happened to her sister.

I waited for the Number 32 bus to trundle past before darting across the road. Following the A25, I strolled along the pavement until a well-worn gap in the hedge presented itself, allowing me to squeeze through. This was the shortcut into Milkwood and, as long as it hadn't been raining, was the preferred method to reach the village.

Milkwood was situated in the middle of the picturesque Vale of Holmesdale in the county of Surrey, approximately twenty-five miles south of London. It housed roughly three hundred upstanding citizens and was the type of place where you loved your neighbor, held grudges against your enemy and tried your best to out-sing both of them in church on Sunday.

The path took a sharp right and I followed the overgrown lane that hugged the banks of the Tillingbourne—location of the infamous rope swing episode. Sidestepping a bunch of overgrown nettles, I emerged onto Peacemeal Street. It wasn't much as high streets went, but it was home to a cluster of shops that had always had a surprisingly busy customer base. The nearest supermarket was located in Dorking, but Milkwood's store owners, unlike so many other small businesses, managed to survive.

I wandered along the road and past the village's one charity shop. Threads was situated at the far end of the parade and rubbed shoulders with more lucrative stores such as Naan's, our Indian takeout; Waspit's, the corner shop; and Crumbs, presided over by the inexplicably named Magna Carter. As a child, I'd often wondered if it was thoughtless naming on the part of her parents or an unfortunate choice of husband. I'd never had the guts to ask the formidable Miss Carter, whose sticky buns were as soft and fluffy as she was hard and rigid. I was happy to see the familiar stores, as well as Milkwood's two pubs, the whimsically named The Dirty Duck and The Pig & Whistle, which bookended the string of shops.

I crossed the low bridge connecting South Milkwood to North and took a sharp right along Unthank Road. I could hear laughter coming from The Dirty Duck and a cheer, most likely from the village green where, if weather permitted, cricket matches were held on Sunday afternoons. A wicket had doubtless been scored— the last one of the evening, if the encroaching gloaming was anything to go by.

The cluster of shops gave way to square, tidy villas, and I hastened along the street, anxious to reach Plum Tree before dark. I passed The Gables and Clandon House on my left and Wisteria Villa and Mill View with their ornate twisted chimneys on my right. I don't think there was a single address in Milkwood boasting a traditional road and number—an utter nightmare for delivery vans or first-time guests. There was nobody to be seen other than a teenage boy hurrying along the opposite side of the road, hoodie up, head down, and I marveled at the utter quietness of it all.

I came to a sharp bend in the road where the tarmac became submerged by the Tillingbourne. Cars were either forced to traverse the eight-foot-wide stream or attempt a thirty-three-point turn. I'd seen equal amounts of both over the years.

Keeping the Tillingbourne to my right I puttered down the aptly named Brambley Lane. Plum Tree Cottage was located at the westernmost part of Milkwood, at the end of a lane better described as a glorified mud track for nine-tenths of the year. With nettles and blackberry bushes on the right and only two cottages situated on its left, the narrow lane dead-ended into a brambly thicket. The scantiness of its girth found many a tourist reversing back up the potholed track—often destroying copious amounts of the hedgerow and, on one memorable occasion, Bonnie Curry's wooden gate, three garden gnomes and an ornamental wishing well. Mrs Curry, Aunt Rose's only neighbor, was about as happy at the destruction of her garden as a turkey the week before Thanksgiving.

I'd always found it interesting that the home preceding my aunt's was named Rosewood; because of this my aunt often found herself receiving mail for her neighbor and vice versa. You would think this constant toing and froing would have forged a friendship between the two—you'd be wrong. Aunt Rose never married, never had children and liked to keep to herself. Her most charitable comment in regards to her neighbor was that she knew how to grow a good marrow. Actually, in a village whose gardens were judged as rigorously as Saint Peter might judge one's soul, this was quite the compliment.

Rosewood was set back roughly twenty yards from its repaired gate and, in the fading light, I could see the lace curtains twitch. Bonnie Curry was situated at the window, and no doubt news of the prodigal niece's return would be all over the village by dawn.

My attention was diverted from the Curry residence to the hedgerow, as I heard a rustling followed by a hiss. A cold shiver rippled along my spine. Did England have snakes? Nothing too poisonous, if I remembered correctly—you just had to be alert for adders, and they preferred woodland and scrub. I eyed the overgrown hedgerow—not comforting. I decided it was probably a fox or a badger but, nevertheless, decided to stop dillydallying.

As I grew nearer to Plum Tree any rustling was drowned out by a sound of the manmade variety. Puccini, if I judged correctly, as the doleful tones of *Turandot's* Liu blared through the trees.

I rounded a slight bend and the nineteenth-century cottage swam into view. I wrestled with the metal gate and stepped onto an uneven cobblestone path weaving its way towards a pale sage front door. Reaching the entryway, I gave a sharp rap, but there was no way anyone could hear me over the bellowing music. "Signore, ascolta" was one of my favorite arias, one I'd requested to be played at my funeral. However, currently I could do with the volume being lowered, if not turned off altogether.

I knocked again and then tried the handle. Bingo—like most homes in Milkwood, Plum Tree was rarely locked. I poked my head into the foyer before stepping inside and letting my bag drop to the floor. The familiar scent of jasmine mingled with wax polish filled my nostrils and I inhaled deeply. I had been away too long.

"Aunt Rose?"

There was no reply. In front of me loomed a wide staircase and to its right a dark hallway leading to the kitchen. Directly off the foyer were three firmly shut doors. The door in front of me I knew was a coat closet and the double doors to my left led to a spacious sitting room. I decided to choose the door to my right—doorway number three, from which vestiges of light seeped onto the flagstone tiles. This was Aunt Rose's study and where she spent most of her time playing her beloved piano and giving the occasional lesson to Surrey's most aspiring young musicians.

I clutched the brass handle and twisted. The door swung silently open, causing the light from within to spill into the dimly lit foyer. I stepped inside and stopped. Aunt Rose's Steinway dominated the majority of the room. An unlit fireplace loomed on the far wall and a bookshelf overflowing with music clung to the left. An uncurtained window dominated the right and a generous aspidistra bloomed from a substantial flower pot beside the door.

I hurried towards the bookshelf, found the CD player and located the volume button. The music had been so loud that even when lowered phantom notes echoed off the walls. Turning, I surveyed the room. It was exactly as I remembered, but from this side I could see two things not visible from the door: hidden behind the piano lay an upturned footstool and, more worryingly, the crumpled body of Aunt Rose. No wonder the line had gone dead.

Aunt Rose lay face down, her arms stretched above her as if in surrender. I rushed to her side and sank onto the rug. I didn't want to move her in case she'd broken something. What was the rule when someone had an accident? Something like ABC? But damn, what did the acronym stand for? American Broadcast Company? No that was wrong. Airway, Bones, Concussion? First aid had never been my forté. I had a fear of blood bordering on the phobic and I was downright frightful with anything biology related.

"Aunt Rose. It's me, Josie." There was no response.

I scrambled onto my hands and knees and lowered my head. "Don't move. You've had a nasty accident and hit your head." It was then I saw the blood seeping between my fingers. I sprang backwards and held my hands aloft.

Initially, all I was aware of was crimson droplets coating the palms of my hands. I had just taken in this troubling fact when the study door burst open, revealing a figure looming in the doorframe. A figure holding a shotgun.

They say when you're about to die your life flashes through your mind. All that ran through *my* mind was an overwhelming urge to throw up. The figure moved forward and recognition dawned. It was Aunt Rose's next-door neighbor, Mrs Curry. She lowered the gun and pointed an accusing finger in my direction.

I heard one word before I pitched into oblivion. "Murderer!"

My eyes opened and I gazed into an unfamiliar face. The face was young and exceptionally round with dark almond eyes and a charcoal black bob. I shut my eyes and reopened them. The face still loomed in front of me.

It took me a few seconds to remember my location. I was in the UK. In Milkwood. At Aunt Rose's cottage. Then I recalled the rest. I shifted to my knees, whereupon the round-faced person placed a hand on my shoulder.

"If you could stay where you are, please madam." The words were short, sharp and filled with as much compassion as a packet of crisps.

"But my aunt," I said, glancing at Aunt Rose's unmoving body. "She fell."

"Yes, madam, we know."

"And there was…" I lifted my hands. The blood coated my hands and I felt a rush of nausea sweep over me.

"There she goes again," said the voice I recognized as Bonnie Curry's. "Pretending to be all distraught, she is."

I glared at the rotund woman filling the doorway. I'd always thought the name 'Bonnie' was an unfortunate choice for the sharp-mouthed Mrs Curry. The woman did not have a bonny bone in her body. It was like naming a baby Grace before discovering the child possessed as much finesse as a pig on a pogo stick.

"Actually, she really is quite pale," said Round Face. "Madam?"

My eyes swam into focus and I realized that Round Face was flashing a business card in my face. It took me a second to realize this was not just a concerned citizen but a member of the Surrey Police Constabulary. My eyes darted towards Mrs Curry. I wanted to bring the Detective Sergeant's attention to the fact that Bonnie had obviously lost the plot and should probably be arrested on the spot, preferably without her shotgun. But the DS seemed utterly oblivious to the presence of the deranged woman lurking near the aspidistra.

I beckoned the DS closer. "She has a gun," I whispered. I mean, I know I'd spent the last two decades in Texas, but guns never failed to make me nervous.

Mrs Curry raised the shotgun. "Protection! You never know what could be hiding in the bushes."

She really was out of her mind. Milkwood was most likely the safest village in all of England, if not all of Europe.

"Please put the shotgun away, Mrs Curry," said the DS.

Bonnie Curry, adorned in tweed skirt, pink cardigan, and sturdy footwear, reluctantly leaned the gun against the wall.

The immediate problem of the gun taken care of, I turned my attention back to Aunt Rose. "Have you called an ambulance?" I asked.

"Backup has been called," replied the DS.

"Backup? But my aunt needs an ambulance. She needs to get to hospital."

DS Round Face cut her eyes towards Bonnie.

It was then I remembered the last words Mrs Curry had said before I'd hit the deck. She'd called me a murderer and for me to be a murderer that meant Aunt Rose had to be dead. But she couldn't be dead. I'd only just spoken to her.

The realization that I was sitting next to a dead body hit me fast and furious. I scooted to my feet and stumbled towards the door. Bonnie Curry held out an arm which I easily sidestepped, shoving the ungracious neighbor towards the aspidistra as she attempted to detain me. Dashing into the foyer, I flung open the door and hurled myself into the darkness and, more unfortunately, into the person who'd just stepped onto the welcome mat.

My hand shot out to steady myself and I gulped in breaths of fresh air. Alas, it was too late, as I threw up all over the shirt of the badly timed visitor.

"Cluck a duck." I hunched over, wiping my mouth with the back of my hand.

The visitor reached down, raised my chin, and looked me straight in the eyes. "Bloody hell, Puke, is that you?"

It had been forty minutes since I'd thrown up and my hands had barely stopped trembling. I was perched on a wooden tree swing, one hand gripping the rope, the other nursing a cup of lukewarm tea. I raised the cup to my lips and took a sip. Yuck. It had been laced with several teaspoons of sugar. Sweet tea—the prescribed remedy for those in shock and something this unsweetened tea drinker could not stomach.

I peeked over my shoulder. Round Face, or Detective Sergeant Winterbottom as I now knew her, was wedged in the kitchen doorway, no doubt keeping an eye on me. What did she think I was going to do, make a break for it? Okay, so maybe I didn't have the best track record in that department, but I'd not been trying to escape, just attempting to get outside before I lost my lunch.

Of course, throwing up over the pristine shirt of a childhood friend had not been my plan—but such was life. Turns out, my previous partner in crime, Adam Ward, was now on the other side of the law. The boy who'd nicked Mars Bars from the village store, cow tipped Farmer Dale's prize Herefordshires and chucked unsuspecting children into the Tillingbourne was now a DI in the Surrey Police. Who'd have thunk it? Not me.

It had not been the reunion I'd hoped for—me staggering out of Aunt Rose's cottage to heave last night's Chateaubriand all over his chest, but then again, to quote Finolla—life's a ditch, try not to fall in it.

Now I sat listening as the undertaker backed his hearse along Brambley Lane presumably taking Aunt Rose with him.

I automatically raised the cup to my lips before smelling the sweet concoction and tipping the contents onto the grass. I didn't hear the approaching footsteps, but swinging around I found Adam standing a few paces behind me.

It was hard to tell in the dimly lit garden, but from the little I'd seen of him in the cottage, Father Time had been kind. Gone was the squat, acned youth of my teenage years, replaced by a stocky, well-built man, with no hint of the rascal he'd been as a youth. With mouse brown hair and warm brown eyes, he was no oil painting, but there was a kind of rugged handsomeness combined with a confidence that made him more than attractive.

It had been an awkward few moments, as Adam identified me as Rose Braithwaite's niece and not, as was being suggested, some vagabond who'd broken into her house and tossed her into the fireplace.

Adam had then retired to the downstairs loo to strip off his shirt and I'd trudged into the kitchen, accompanied by DS Winterbottom, to wash my hands and rinse my mouth.

In the next forty minutes I'd been witness to the goings on by sound only. Puccini's Greatest Hits had been silenced and I'd been ushered into the garden while the paramedics did whatever paramedics do.

Adam strolled around to the front of the swing and squatted at the base of a nearby ash. He wore just a vest and a pair of jeans and I was reminded, once more, of my embarrassing faux pas.

"I see you've never got over your fear of blood."

I couldn't argue with this, but felt slightly irked that my childhood friend's first words to me pointed out my most embarrassing character flaw. What happened to "so sorry about your aunt, Josie? You must have had such a shock, Josie? Come here, Josie, let me wrap you in my strong arms and make it all better." Okay, scratch that last one, but you get the picture.

"Obviously not," I said, not trusting myself to say more.

Adam suppressed a smile, which made me want to reach out and wallop him. Now, I am not a violent person, but everyone has their limits. I dug my heels into the ground and interlaced my fingers. My hands were starting to shake and I didn't want to show any further weakness.

"It seems your aunt tripped on the rug and had an unfortunate landing."

"Unfortunate," now there was a euphemism. "So can I assume I'm no longer a suspect?" I'd like to think I kept the sarcasm out of my voice, but I'm pretty sure I failed.

"Yeah, sorry about that. We've had a spate of break-ins and petty theft around this area. Hence Mrs Curry's slight overreaction."

"Overreaction? I'm lucky she didn't shoot me."

"You're from Texas. I'm sure you must be used to that."

I narrowed my eyes. "How do you know I'm from Texas?"

"The baggage claim tag on your luggage says AUS."

"Oh!"

"I *am* a detective. It would be nice to think I could actually detect once in a while." Adam sank back against the oak tree. "Plus, your aunt did mention you'd been living in Texas for several years. That helped."

I wasn't sure what to think about Adam and Aunt Rose discussing where I was living. I'd have to reflect on that later.

"So I guess you were planning on staying over?"

I nodded.

"I'm thinking you probably don't want to stay here tonight. Actually, I'd caution against it."

My eyes widened. Where *was* I going to stay? Milkwood wasn't exactly known for its thriving hotel chains and I was pretty sure the last train to London had come and gone. I believed there was one B&B in town and The Dirty Duck rented out a couple of rooms, but neither held much appeal. I hated to say it, but right now I wanted to be with friends or, failing that, family. Unfortunately, the only family member within a two-hundred-mile radius was being driven through the village to the nearest morgue.

"Don't worry. I think I have a solution," Adam said, as if reading my mind. "I have a place in..." Adam trailed off as DS Winterbottom's steely voice cut through the summer air like a cleaver through butter.

"Excuse me, sir, but they want you to know that they're all done."

Adam scrambled to his feet. "Winterbottom..."

My inner fourteen-year-old self tried not to titter.

"...you rent a flat in the village, right?"

"Yes, sir. Above the antique store."

"One bedroom or two?"

"One bedroom, sir."

"Does a police salary stretch to a couch, these days?"

"I do have a couch, sir," said Winterbottom, reluctantly.

"That'll do. Monroe here's not fussy where she sleeps."

Both DS Winterbottom and I stared at Adam in disbelief.

"Excuse me?" I said, my cheeks warming.

Adam gave me the type of look I would give a pupil who told me the dog ate their homework. "You need somewhere to sleep and Helen here has a sofa going spare." Adam's seriousness disappeared as he broke into a grin. "Seems like a match made in heaven."

$$\flat$$

Thirty minutes later my reluctant host, DS Helen Winterbottom, and I were ensconced in her first floor flat staring at each other like a conductor views a particularly troublesome soloist.

This was the first time I'd gotten a proper look at the sergeant. At a distance her face did not look as round. Her dark Asian eyes were devoid of mascara and her black bob was cut with precision. In fact, it seemed everything about Helen Winterbottom was precise. Her figure was trim, her voice irritatingly spare, her flat resembling a bachelor pad rather than the abode of a twenty-some-thing copper.

She did, indeed, have a sofa, but it was not the type one might envision a young woman owning. Instead of soft and fluffy with hints of Laura Ashley, the couch was leather with chrome legs, looking more like an instrument of torture than something you would snuggle down on for the night. Helen Winterbottom's decorating taste was best described as minimalist modern - a curious juxtaposition considering the flat's decidedly nineteenth-century bones.

To say the furnishings were sparse was an understatement. The walls had no art and the kitchen was all counter space with not a coffee maker in sight. There wasn't even a TV, for goodness' sake.

DS Winterbottom—I wasn't ready to think of her as "Helen"—had immediately marched into the kitchen and poured herself a glass of water before disappearing into her bedroom. Seconds later she'd reappeared holding a pillow and a plaid blanket that looked less like an item of bedding and more like a rug you'd throw down and have a picnic on.

"Here," said DS Winterbottom, depositing them on the sofa. "Bathroom's second on the left."

And with that she turned and walked back into her bedroom where I heard the barely perceptible sound of a lock being turned.

6

Liu, the *Turandot* slave girl, had abandoned her traditional Chinese costume. Instead she wore Bonnie Curry's tweed skirt and fluffy pink cardigan while sitting atop an aspidistra singing "I've Got a Lovely Bunch of Coconuts." Suddenly, Liu reached into the potted plant and produced a shotgun. She raised it to her shoulder and said one word: "Murderer!"

My eyes flew open as I lurched skyward, promptly falling off DS Winterbottom's leather sofa onto an unforgiving floor.

It was pitch dark, but then I remembered I was wearing a sleep mask. I plucked it off and glanced at my watch—3:24am. That didn't make any sense. It took me a couple of seconds for my brain to compute that I was looking at Texas time. As I was only in the UK for a week it had hardly seemed worth changing the time. I quickly added six hours and got an approximate English time of 9:24am. No wonder it was light. Daylight had crept over the horizon a good four hours ago.

I disengaged my legs from the blanket, wiped away a slither of drool and clambered to my feet. Traipsing over to the window, I gave the utilitarian blind a sharp tug. The blind zipped upwards giving me a view of a typical summer's day in England. Practically idyllic, if one ignored the storm bank of clouds and steady drizzle.

I turned and surveyed DS Winterbottom's apartment. The dreariness of the day did not improve its demeanor. If anything, it made it worse. It was then I saw that DS Winterbottom's bedroom door was open. Ambling over, I peeked inside. I was greeted by an immaculately made bed (the girl could have been in the army), a desk with a humming computer, and a stack load of weights—not a Winterbottom in sight. I strolled over to the bedside table and grasped the only non-utilitarian item in the room, a 5 x 7 frame, and almost dropped it in astonishment. The image revealed Adam and Helen at a black-tie event. Their foreheads were practically touching and they were laughing heartily. So this was how it stood. I felt a little knot in my stomach that I put down to hunger.

Further inspection found that DS Winterbottom was neither in the bathroom nor hiding in the airing cupboard. Dang! She must have left for work and I'd slept right through. I drifted into the open plan kitchen and peeked inside the fridge. I should point out this was something I would never have done before living in the US I'd always been shocked when American friends strolled into my kitchen and opened my fridge. It felt akin to having someone pulling open my bedroom drawers and rifling through my knickers or, as we would say in the States, panties. It still felt a little like snooping to open the fridge of a stranger, but heck, I was hungry.

Turns out I needn't have worried about invading DS Winterbottom's privacy. The fridge was as bare as her flat, containing a loaf of olive bread, sparkling water, skimmed milk and a jar of peanut butter. It was as if DS Winterbottom had taken a trip to Sainsbury's and deliberately stocked her entire fridge with items I wouldn't touch with a ten-foot barge pole.

It was then I saw the note. It was printed precisely in capitals and attached to the door with a red pillar-box magnet—by far the most whimsical and colorful item in the entire flat. I removed the note and read:

Gone to work. Report to Dorking Police Station at 1:00pm to give statement. Don't be late and lock up.

Scrunching up the note, I tossed it towards the rubbish bin and missed. I raised my arm and studied my watch. I had over three hours to get to Dorking, but first I had more pressing concerns.

Fifteen minutes later I was dressed in my last clean outfit: jeans, sneakers, and a plain tee. My hair, still damp from the shower, had been drawn back in a ponytail, and to prove I was making an effort I'd plugged in a pair of gold hoop earrings and smeared on a trace of lip gloss.

I folded the blanket, left it with the pillow on the sofa, and draped the moist towels on top of the washing machine door. Then, before I left, guilt made me retrieve the scrunched-up note and place it in the rubbish bin. I pulled on my jacket and looped my handbag diagonally across my shoulder. Grabbing my suitcase, I plodded towards the exit. I gave the door a good tug to make sure it was locked before trundling down the stairs and onto the High Street in search of grub.

It was now 10:00am and my stomach sounded like a whining toddler. I couldn't blame it. If memory served correctly, the last thing I'd eaten was a cheese and pickle sandwich, hastily purchased from a dubious sandwich shop at Euston. That had been over twenty hours ago. I turned my back on The Pig & Whistle and had trotted past the butcher's, the baker's and the duck pond when I stopped in my tracks.

I would recognize that smell blindfolded. That was the smell of a good English fry up. My eyes zeroed in on a cafe with windows as steamy as a Ford Focus with a couple of teenagers on the back seat. The sign above the door proclaimed it to be Irene's Milk Jug.

The drizzle was now upping its game to full-fledged rain and puddles the size of swimming pools formed along the gutters. The last thing I needed was to ruin my only pair of sneakers. I waited for a lone car to tootle past before stepping into the road and, with my head down, I followed the smell of bacon.

The door gave a high-pitched jingle as I barged my way into the warmth of the tea room. If I'd been a dog I would have given myself a good shake. Seeing I wasn't a dog, I plumped for taking off my jacket and squeezing out the end of my ponytail.

Across the room I saw three women clustered like witches around a cauldron—okay, make that a platter of scones, but you get the picture. I smiled, but only the elderly lady gripping the platter smiled back. Two of the women I recognized instantly. On the right, wearing an impregnable wall of tweed, stood Bonnie Curry, her arms crossed defiantly across her ample bosom. With her short frame, wide girth, and masses of curls, she reminded me of a less magical version of Professor Sprout from *Harry Potter*.

Standing on the left was the lady I assumed was the proprietor, Irene. She was a petite soul, with a face that casting directors would clamor for, with hopes of selling anything from Bisto to Bovril. She sported faded red hair and pink cheeks and wore a floral apron around her modest waist. However, the smile she gave was quickly erased as the final woman stood heavily on Irene's sensible lace-up brogues.

Of the three it was the woman standing on Irene's foot who was the most striking. It may have been near on twenty years, but I'd recognize that dour demeanor anywhere. The proprietor of Crumbs, Magna Carter, was tall, slim and had a confidence reminiscent of a headmistress—but not in a good way. She must have been seventy if she was a day, but she was strikingly beautiful if you ignored the scowl. With cropped hair and an immaculately tailored pantsuit, she reminded me of Helen Mirren. There was no doubt in my mind that Magna Carter was the woman who ruled this roost.

I sidled over to a window seat and pulled out a couple of chairs. I placed my luggage on one and sank into the second. Grabbing a menu I perused my options:

C HOP AND C HIPS

S AUSAGE AND C HIPS

S ALAD AND C HIPS

Really? England may have progressed in leaps and bounds with its culinary fortitude, but there were still certain backwaters where the residents believed everything was better with chips. Irene's Milk Jug seemed to be such a place.

I turned over the menu and located several breakfast items. That was more like it. My eyes flittered back and forth until I found what I was searching for. A Full English, consisting of Lancashire sausages, English bacon, baked beans, mushrooms, grilled tomatoes, and my old friend, fried bread. All that was missing was black pudding (also known as blood sausage) and, for reasons that should be obvious, something I'd never developed a liking for.

I scanned the price list. £10.99. A bargain, and one my shrinking cash flow could just about absorb. To be honest, my budget for a week in the UK had been pretty meagre. When I was in Shropshire my expenses had been taken care of by my father. I'd assumed that once I'd reached Surrey there would be a similar arrangement, with eating out kept to a minimum. With Aunt Rose dead I was going to have to do some serious rethinking. I had thirty-six hours before my plane departed for Texas. I would have to be frugal.

I took a deep breath. This was the first time today I'd thought about Aunt Rose. Guilt flooded through me. She had been my favorite aunt, but I hadn't seen her in almost two decades. I blamed my lack of compassion on my overwhelming hunger and vowed to wallow in some quality grief as soon as I'd eaten.

I assumed everyone in the village must have heard about Aunt Rose. A death in the village—even of someone well into their three score years—was news. In fact, I wouldn't have put it past Bonnie Curry to have gone door to door announcing my aunt's death like the proverbial town crier. I had a brief vision of Bonnie's frizzy hair tempered by a tricorn hat, her tweeds enveloped by a long wool coat and a bell firmly lodged in her hand, dinging and donging to her heart's delight.

I waved my menu trying to get Irene's attention. Irene attempted to place her platter of scones on the table but Magna was having none of it. Irene stared helplessly across the great divide—or, in this case, two oblong tables stacked with condiments.

"We do not serve murderers," said Magna. "Irene here runs a respectable establishment."

"Oh yes, Magna," said Irene, nodding, her Scottish brogue coming through. "That I do."

"I'm not a murderer," I replied, glaring at Bonnie Curry.

"That's not what Bonnie here's been saying," said Irene, her lilting voice apologetic as her cheeks turned the same color as her hair.

"She tripped," I said. "It was an accident."

"Tripped did she?" said Bonnie. "How come she never tripped before? That's what I'd like to know."

We all digested this ridiculous question and I, for one, decided it was distinctly unanswerable. Why does anything ever happen to anybody? Surely we go through life one step away from disaster. The double decker bus that zooms past the second before you step off the pavement. The pressure cooker exploding the moment after you've left the room—I may, or may not, be talking from firsthand experience with that last example. Cooking was never my strong point.

"Does this mean I'm not going to get any breakfast?"

Magna folded immaculately manicured hands across her pristine pant suit and gave me a look I deemed to mean "not on your nelly."

"I'll take that as a no," I said, ignoring my belly as it wailed in protest. So near and yet so far, it seemed to say.

"We don't need your type around here," said Magna, sniffing.

My type? What the heck did she mean by "my type?" Was there a ban on music teachers in Milkwood? Did she mean Americans? Expats? Women with blue eyes and a penchant for Puccini?

I corralled my bags and lumbered towards the door. My stomach was already growling with confusion; one more look at a buttered scone could send it over the edge. I would leave with dignity, with my head held high. It was all going brilliantly, until I stepped off the pavement and got blindsided by the proverbial bus.

7

Turns out, although the vehicle was red and shiny, it was not a bus, and yes as the old adage goes, I didn't see it coming. Okay, this may or may not have had something to do with me looking in the wrong direction but the next thing I knew there was a screech of brakes, a blast of horn and then I was sailing through the air like I'd been catapulted from a slingshot. Where she'll land nobody knows. Except some part of me did know, and seconds later I was proven correct, splash landing into the deepest, dirtiest puddle Milkwood High Street had to offer.

Hoisting myself to my knees, I once again resisted the urge to shake like a dog, as I realized I was not alone. A pair of tan-colored boots entered my line of sight and I followed the boots skyward to see sable leggings and an immaculately tailored ivory blouse. Finally I reached the apex. A tumble of angel blonde hair cascaded around my observer's shoulders, framing a face that would have been considered pretty, if not for the fact that it was exquisite.

The vision squatted before me, a frown crinkling her brow, which I noted had a tiny scar. "Heavens to Betsy. Are you alright?"

My nose-dive had knocked the breath from me and all I could manage was a pathetic "Erm!"

"Stepping into the road, like that. I could have killed you."

Whereas instead you just tossed me into the air like a matador in a bullring, I thought to myself.

"And goodness knows if you've done any damage to Roger."

I glanced around in search of another set of feet. Finding none I felt compelled to ask. "Who's Roger?"

"I mean he's old. A product of the 50s. You could have inflicted some serious damage."

I may have spent a significant portion of my life living in Texas, but I am still English and our default, when in situations like this, is to say two words: "I'm sorry."

The words must have come out with more of a Texas twang than I'd intended. Although in Austin I am known as being as English as Mary Poppins, over here my slight American accent identified me as an expat within seconds.

"You're not American, are you?" the blonde said, cocking her head to one side.

This was more difficult to answer than one might imagine. I was born in England, but I'd spent the last twenty years of my life stateside and the last five as a US citizen. I wasn't sure what that made me. I settled on, "No."

"Oh. I thought I detected a slight—never mind. You're all Bristol fashion and ship shape now."

Amazingly, I was. Somehow I had crash landed without a single scratch. Unfortunately my clothes hadn't fared as well. I gaped at my sopping jeans and a top that could have won a wet tee-shirt competition. It was then I spotted my suitcase—lying in the middle of the road like a canvas speed bump. Unfortunately, I then spied the tractor barreling past the duck pond. Alas, the tractor had as much intention of stopping as a running back did for the opposing linebacker, leaving me to watch in disbelief as my suitcase was steamrollered by humongous, mud-sodden wheels.

"Oh dear! Was that yours?"

"Of course it was mine. What do you think it did—drop from the sky?"

"Oh! That *is* unfortunate."

There was the understatement of the morning. I scurried over to the former suitcase and scraped what was left of it off the ground. My meagre selection of clothes had burst from its innards and lay scattered across the tarmac. A crowd was gathering by the duck pond and a couple of children were starting to point.

I felt tears prick my eyes and I willed them not to drop. I would not cry in front of a total stranger. I would wait until I reached somewhere private, preferably somewhere with a bumper box of Kleenex and a large bottle of pinot.

"Here."

I turned to find the rest of my clothes being handed to me. "You'd better go home and change."

Easier said than done. I'd locked DS Winterbottom's apartment behind me and posted the keys through the letter box. Irene's Milk Jug wasn't exactly a welcoming bastion of congeniality, and Aunt Rose's cottage had recently housed a dead body. And what was I going to change into? This was the last set of clean clothes I owned.

The look of despair must have shown on my face and I felt a warm hand on my shoulder. "It's okay. Come with me. I live around the corner."

It was either traipse up the High Street in search of a public toilet or go with the person who'd just run me over. As a torrent of rain slapped me in the face I made an executive decision and squelched towards the car.

And what a car it was. A gleaming red sports car with chrome wheels, a cream interior and a boot that barely accommodated my flattened suitcase. I opened the door and hesitated, looking at the immaculate interior and my less than immaculate jeans.

"Oh, don't worry about that. It's leather. The dirt will come right off."

I needed little persuasion, and seconds later I'd limboed my way into the luxurious interior and buckled my seat belt.

"I'm Arabelle, by the way. Arabelle DeCorcy, but you can call me Belle, everyone does." Belle stuck out her hand and I wiped my mud-spattered palm on the knee of my jeans before reciprocating.

"And you are?" said Belle, ramming the car into gear.

"Oh, sorry," I said. "I'm Josie. Josie Monroe."

The car leapt forward and kangarooed a couple of times before stalling. Belle regained her composure. "Sorry about that. Roger can be a little temperamental."

Well, that explained who Roger was.

"You're the one who discovered the dead body."

"The dead body was my aunt," I replied coldly.

"Heavens to Betsy," said Belle. "I'm so sorry. That was incredibly thoughtless."

"It's okay. We used to be close, but I hadn't seen her in a long time."

"But it must have been dreadful," said Belle, putting Roger in gear and accelerating past the duck pond. "Were you alone in the house?"

"Only for a second. Mrs Curry followed me in thinking I was up to no good and now she thinks I've murdered my aunt."

Belle hesitated briefly before saying, "It *was* an accident, right?"

Once again the village bush telegraph had done its job. "Yep, she tripped. The weird thing is I must have been on the phone with her when she did it."

Belle took a corner way too fast, mounted the pavement and missed the bright red post box by millimeters. "Wow! Did you hear anything?"

I thought back to the night before. What had I heard? "Music and…" And what? Something had been wrong—but what was it?

"No dying words?"

I shook my head and focused on an oncoming holly bush. It was weird being in the passenger seat and not having a steering wheel in front of me or, more importantly, a brake pedal.

Belle hooked a sharp left, careening through ornate metal gates before hurtling along a wide driveway lined with mighty oaks. I'd been so busy hanging onto my seat I hadn't paid attention to our route. Therefore, it was with surprise when I viewed the familiar outline of Barton Hall emerge from behind a cluster of century-old oaks.

I gazed at Belle in disbelief. "You live here?"

"I'd hardly take you back to someone else's home now, would I?" Roger screeched to a halt, causing sprays of shingle to shower skyward.

I clambered from the car and gawked at the celebration of late Elizabethan architecture spreading east to west like the Great Wall of China. Barton Hall—oh, the memories. Oh, the drama. Oh, the second Belle realized who I was.

8

I hauled the remnants of my suitcase from the boot and scrunched across the driveway. Intimidated? Not me. For a house (okay mansion) I'd never been in before you could say I knew Barton Hall exceedingly well. I could not have been more than seven or eight when I discovered that the extensive grounds backed onto the end of Aunt Rose's garden. If the Tillingbourne ran low it was a hop, skip, and a splash across three stepping stones, a wobbly log, and a questionable mound of shoal and you were on Barton land and all the wonders it beheld.

The number of times I'd trespassed through acres of England's finest landscaping were too many to count. However, although I'd viewed Barton Hall from a distance, I'd never actually been inside the sixteenth-century abode. And if I'd ever dreamed about entering, I had never envisioned myself looking like something the cat dragged in while doing it.

As I approached the entryway the door eased open and an elderly man in dark morning suit stepped onto the flagstone patio.

"Good morning, miss." The man's left eyebrow rose imperceptibly as his steely gaze roamed over my disheveled appearance.

"Oh hello, Tillman. This is my friend, Ms Monroe."

"Yes, miss."

"She's come to have a bath."

"You don't say, miss."

Belle grabbed my hand, yanking me through the door and into a paneled entry hall. I quickly took in my surroundings. Coat of arms—check. Tapestry—check. Suit of armor—double check. Flippity flip flops, forget Barton Hall, this was Barton Castle.

Belle's footsteps echoed on the wide wooden boards as she clip-clopped across the entryway towards an ornate sweeping staircase. She flicked back her long blonde hair and gave her butler a winning smile. "Tillman, do you happen to know if Mrs Crackenthorpe is in the building?"

"Yes, miss. I believe she's in the ballroom."

Belle wrestled my suitcase out of my arms. "Would you be so good as to give her this? I've no doubt she'll be able to work wonders."

Tillman stepped forward and Belle dropped my flattened, muddy suitcase into his outstretched arms.

I mouthed the word "sorry" and trudged up the Cinderella staircase feeling extremely guilty.

Reaching the second story, Belle hooked a right, flung open the fifth door on the left and beckoned me to enter.

I stuck my head inside before slowly introducing the rest of me. The door clanged shut, and I found myself amidst a sumptuous bathroom resembling something I assumed you might find in the Palace of Versailles. I eyed the sunken bath, the various Molton Brown products and the mounds of fluffy white towels, and decided there were worse places to be.

I peeled off my bra and knickers and lay them on the heated towel rack to dry. The rest of my clothes I folded neatly and placed on a chair. There really was no salvaging them. I removed my watch and ten minutes later I'd washed the last of the mud down the plughole and felt as close to clean as I was going to get.

After giving myself a good toweling I replaced my watch and returned to the radiator. The light material of my bra made it a quick dry, the utilitarian cotton knickers not so much. Oh well, I could go commando for a few hours until Mrs Crackenthorpe had done her worst. I liberated an oversized bathrobe from an ornate hat stand before scooping up the pile of puddle-soaked clothes and heading back into the hallway. I glanced both ways. There were as many doors to my left as there were to my right, giving me a fifty-fifty chance of going in the correct direction. It was at this point I wished I'd asked Belle how many people were currently in residence. As far as I could remember, Belle had two older brothers and as I trundled barefoot along the hallway I sincerely hoped they were not residing here.

A door yawned open and an arm flew out and tugged me inside. I turned to see Belle with a glass of bubbly in each hand. Belle thrust the glass towards me and nudged the door shut. Holding her glass high she clinked the glasses together before downing a huge gulp.

"Erm!"

"It would be a terrible waste if you didn't," said Belle. "Besides, you've had a dreadfully rough twenty-four hours."

I gazed doubtfully at the elegant fluted glass.

"Besides, it's not every day you find a member of your family collapsed in the fireplace and, you know, dead."

Belle's forthright manner made it hard to take offense. I took a sip and immediately felt the bubbles fizzle down my throat and explode up my nose. I stifled the impulse to sneeze as I inspected Belle's bedroom.

The room was airy and light, with high ceilings and ample windows. It contained a queen-sized bed and a dressing table displaying tiny bottles lined up in a perfect row. In the corner was a plush wingback chair and a matching ottoman upholstered in tiny peach flowers. Lush silk curtains cascaded from the windows and the floor was shielded by a shaggy cream rug. Like Belle, the room was immaculate.

I searched for somewhere to put my disastrous clothing and gingerly placed the pile of sodden clothes on the wooden floor. Strolling to the window, I contemplated the parkland below. So lush. So English.

"Does everyone in the village know Aunt Rose is dead?" I asked.

Belle poured herself another glass of bubbly and plopped onto a puff of crisp, white duvet. "You've met Bonnie Curry, right?"

I nodded.

"Then I'm afraid the chances are pretty high."

"Yeah. Stupid question." I meandered over to the bed and stuck out my glass. Belle refilled it to the top and I sank down next to her.

"What do the police think?" asked Belle, cocking her head to one side.

"Adam thinks she tripped and fell."

"And you? What do you think?"

I met Belle's dark brown eyes. "I have no reason to think she didn't."

Belle upended her glass and not wanting her to drink alone I took a healthy sip. For the first time since finding Aunt Rose's body I started to relax.

"How do you know DI Ward?"

"Childhood friend," I said, hoping to change the subject. The less we talked about Adam the longer it was going to take Belle to figure out the connection.

I checked my watch. "I'd better get going. Do you think your Mrs..."

"Crackenthorpe," said Belle, filling in the gap.

I smiled.

"Sounds like some kind of monster from Greek mythology, doesn't it?" said Belle. "As a matter of fact, I believe she hails from the Peloponnese."

I started to laugh. "With a name like Crackenthorpe?"

"Married a Lancashire man. Divorced him soon after, as a woman such as Mrs Crackenthorpe is wont to do, but she kept the name."

"Well, do you think your Mrs Crackenthorpe might have managed to salvage some of my clothes?"

"Honestly? No. So I thought these might do instead." Belle slid off the bed and glided towards the plump ottoman. "Here." Belle looked me down and up before raising a couple of hangers. "Five foot seven? Size twelve?" She nudged a pair of strappy leather sandals towards me. "Size seven?"

Wow. She had me pegged. I upended the rest of my bubbly and slipped off the bed. The hangers contained two of the most beautiful dresses I'd ever seen. I ran my hand over a short-sleeved dress in pale pink with buttons marching down the front. The fabric appeared to be a type of polyester which I soon reassessed to be silk. The second was a cream shift with a border of flowers growing along the knee-length hem.

"They're beautiful."

"They're yours," said Belle, twirling towards me before tossing them onto the bed.

"But I—"

"Do you have a better plan?" Belle indicated my mud-soaked clothes, weeping onto the floor.

I shrugged. "I guess not. But just until I—"

"Really, Josie. They never get worn. Take them. You can wear one now and have the other as a spare."

My eyes cut to the dresses. I would never in a million years buy anything so opulent. Well, maybe if I was invited to the Queen's garden party, but that didn't happen too often when you lived in Austin, Texas.

"I even probably have some spare underwear."

I raised my hand. There were limits. Underwear I could buy while in Dorking this afternoon. It wasn't ideal, but it would have to do. I pulled off the robe, seized the pink dress, and slipped it over my head. Belle passed me the sandals and I slipped them on.

"Gorgeous. No really, you scrub up beautifully."

"Did you know my aunt?" I asked, doing my best not to twirl like an eight-year-old as I admired myself in Belle's full-length mirror.

"Oh yes," said Belle. "She was absolutely frightful."

I turned and stared. "Excuse me?"

"Gosh, did I say that out loud? I mean I hardly knew her, but you must know what people thought?"

"Enlighten me."

"It was well known. I mean, I thought you knew. I mean...gosh, she was horrid."

Two seconds later I was out the door and hurtling along the landing. I didn't need to listen to this rubbish. Aunt Rose was wonderful. She was kind and intelligent and was one of the best pianists this side of the English Channel. What did this jumped-up little society girl know about my aunt? Absolutely nothing, that's what.

I tore down the stairs and sped towards the exit. I had my hand on the latch when a booming voice made me stop in my tracks.

"And where do you think you're going?"

Slowly I turned. Standing at the bottom of the stairs was a handsome grey-haired man in a pair of burgundy corduroys and a crisp blue shirt holding a shotgun.

Not again! I raised my hands. Surely one death in twenty-four hours was enough. Did there really need to be two?

"Who the blazes are you and what do you think you're doing here?"

His accent was deep and gruff, but could not disguise the fact that the man had never attended a state school in his life. This must be Lord Rex DeCorcy, Belle's father.

I attempted to answer but all that emerged was an indecently loud hiccup.

Lord DeCorcy took a step forward and frowned. "And what the blaze! Are those my wife's clothes?"

"Your wife's clothes?" I said, in disbelief.

"That's what I said, girl!"

I was speechless. Speechless if you don't count three hiccups in quick succession.

Lord DeCorcy lowered his gun and shook his head. "I've heard of some dash rotten things in my time, but you, ma'am, have to take the biscuit. What type of lowlife steals a dead woman's clothes?"

9

I took advantage of the lowered gun and turned and fled. I was happy to find it had stopped raining. Not so happy realizing I'd left behind my bag and my purse. Everything but my misappropriated clothes.

No worries, I would figure this out later. Right now I had to get away from Barton Hall and into Dorking. I studied my watch and did the math. It was gone noon. I had less than an hour, no money, and I was at least two miles away from a bus stop. Great. Just great.

I raced along the driveway towards the gates and freedom, silently giving thanks I was not in a James Bond movie. No Dobermans chasing me, no villains taking potshots and, most importantly, no automatic gate closing capability. I was fifty yards from freedom when I realized I had given thanks too soon. With a metallic clang the towering gates started to shut.

I took off running, but physical activity was never my forté. Give me a Mozart sonata or a Chopin prelude and I was your girl. Running, jogging or even a brisk trot—not so much. The gates clinked together and I glanced behind in case I'd imagined the Dobermans into existence as well. Thankfully not.

I knew there was a secondary way out, through the woods and over the stream, but that would mean doubling back and time was not in my favor. Either side of the gate was a five-foot wall topped with spikes protruding like disgruntled porcupines. There was no way I was going to make it over the wall without ripping both myself and my falsely acquired dress to pieces.

Suddenly, I heard Belle calling my name. I gave the gate the once over. It was flat at the top and there were several footholds within the intricate design. I am not one for impetuous decisions, but the next thing I knew I was halfway up one side and had my tummy wedged across the top. It was when I kicked my leg over that problems arose.

I peered down to see one of my strappy sandals entwined on a curlicue. "Cluck a duck!"

"Puke—is that you?"

Crispy pancakes! Surely this couldn't be happening again. I mustered my most nonchalant tone. "Hi, Adam. How ya doing?"

"Better than you, by the looks of it."

I gave the reluctant sandal another tug. No joy. It was then a gust of wind swept in and lifted the treacherous silk up and into the air.

"Whoa!" said Adam, taking a step back.

"If you were any kind of gentleman you would look away," I yelled, trying to flatten the dress without losing my balance.

"Whatever gives you the impression I'm a gentleman?"

I gave the sandal one almighty tug, the strap gave way and the momentum, combined with an errant hiccup, sent me tumbling downwards. Two seconds later I landed in the arms of DI Ward. Adam held me for a second longer than he needed, and I breathed in a heady scent that did something wobbly to my insides. I'd always been a sucker for musky cologne. The last time I'd been in Adam's arms he'd been experimenting with Brut. This was definitely an upgrade.

I gazed into Adam's warm brown eyes and for a second my entire abdomen did a bit of a samba.

"Could you?" I nodded towards the ground.

Adam grinned and lowered me onto the driveway

I glanced towards the gate. Belle was speeding towards us. I had nothing to say to the person who'd insulted the memory of my aunt. Turning, I spied a white Volvo idling at the curb.

"Need a lift?"

I grabbed Adam's arm and propelled him towards the driver's side.

"So that would be a yes?" said Adam.

Yanking open the door I practically thrust him behind the steering wheel. I dashed around to the passenger side as the gates swung open.

I sank into the seat. The car did not move. I stared at my childhood friend.

"Seatbelt?" said Adam.

"For cluck's sake," I muttered, wrestling the belt across my slightly worse for wear dress. "Satisfied?"

In response, Adam put the car in gear and we sailed away from Barton Hall, leaving Belle DeCorcy standing in the lane waving my purse.

"It's good to see you, Josie."

I pursed my lips.

"I mean I wish it had been under better circumstances."

"What were you doing at the DeCorcys?" I asked, letting out another hiccup.

"Josie?"

"What?"

"Have you been drinking?'

"No! Well..."

"Josie, you know I used to piss it up with the best of them. In fact, there was one memorable incident behind the bicycle shed with Holly Drinkwater and a bottle of Irn Bru, but I digress..."

I hiccupped again. Jiminy Cricket, could my body betray me in any more ways? First, I'd flashed my undercarriage to half of Surrey and now Adam was under the impression I was a lush.

"It's just gone 12:30," said Adam. "Do you really think you should be—"

"Don't you dare judge me, Adam Ward. Wait, what did you say?" I peered at my right wrist. 6:38. I tried to figure out the math and failed.

"I said, do you really think you should be—"

"No. I mean, the time. What time is it?"

"If you want to be precise, it's 12:38."

I cut my eyes to Adam. He was trying his best not to smile. I hated to ask, but it couldn't be helped. "And how fast can you make it to Dorking Police Station?"

Adam flipped a switch and a siren blared to life. "I could be wrong, but probably quicker than if you take the bus."

10

Twenty minutes later, the white Volvo swept alongside the red-brick building that housed Dorking Police Station.

If I'd regretted drinking *before* I got in Adam's car, it was nothing compared to the regret I had after, as I made a mental note to Google "temperance movement" once back in the States. I had never been a heavy drinker, not even in my twenties. Alcohol made some people fun; it made me sleepy. I was not a happy drunk. I was a drowsy one.

The journey had taken roughly half the time it should, and included overtaking a lorry full of sheep, a bus full of senior citizens and, most notably, a hearse and the fifteen cars in its wake. The half bottle of bubbly I'd misguidedly consumed made several attempts to reappear, and it was only sheer bloody mindedness, that kept Belle's Prosecco swishing around my stomach and not all over DI Ward's dashboard.

I wanted to question whether the use of sirens and copious overtaking was legit, but my overriding need to be on time silenced my moral outrage. I decided to keep my mouth shut and my hiccups on mute.

Adam cut the flashing lights and pulled into a designated parking spot three spaces from the door. Detective Inspector Ward was definitely up and coming.

"12:58, exactly," said Adam, strolling around the car to meet me.

I sprinted towards the entrance and gave the wood paneled door an almighty heave. I wasn't sure what to expect, I mean this was a police station, you could get all types, but what I didn't expect to see was the three clowns who stood in an organized, if rather colorful, queue. They were dressed in baggy trousers, checkered waistcoats and voluminous bow ties. Their shoes were of the extra-large variety and on their heads sat three bowler hats with the smallest clown possessing the largest and the tallest possessing the teeniest. Their noses were crimson and their hair varied in color from marmalade to magenta. Opposite them was a ballerina clutching a Chihuahua, a strongman in a leopard-skin leotard, and a muscular man in exceedingly compact tights. Each stood statue still, silently gazing at their counterpart.

Adam didn't break stride as he took my arm, escorting me towards a middle-aged man with ruddy cheeks and one too many doughnuts on the girth. "The circus came to town," he said, in an accent originating from somewhere a lot further north than Surrey. "Something about a missing mascot."

Adam acted like the presence of three clowns and assorted circus personnel was normal and, for all I knew, it was. "Fitz. This is Ms Monroe, here to give a statement in regards to the death of her aunt, Miss Rose Braithwaite."

Fitz nodded curtly in my direction before returning his gaze to Adam. "Could I have a word, sir."

Fitz and Adam had their word and I did my best not to eavesdrop. Thirty seconds later the door to the side of the admissions desk buzzed and Adam ushered me through. "Third door on the right, Monroe."

So we were back to Monroe. I guess it was better than Puke.

I entered a room, barren, save for a scarred wooden table and four minimally padded chairs. I had flashbacks to Helen Winterbottom's flat and wondered if she'd been in charge of decor.

I dragged out a metal chair, wincing as its protesting legs traversed the linoleum. Sinking onto cold hard steel, I watched as Detective Sergeant Winterbottom entered the room and tugged out the chair opposite. She wore her usual no-nonsense, down-to-business expression and I decided I wasn't going to waste a smile. Adam lounged in the corner and I wasn't going to waste a smile on him, either.

"I'll start with the good news," said DS Winterbottom. "Mrs Curry has kindly decided to not press charges."

"Charges?" I asked, incredulously. "For what?"

"Assault and battery," replied DS Winterbottom.

"For cluck's sake. Are you kidding me?"

"I don't kid."

I could believe it.

"The woman threatened me with a shotgun. How on earth can she be charging *me* with assault?"

DS Winterbottom shuffled her notes. "Something to do with being, and I quote, 'upended into an aspidistra.'"

I glanced towards Adam. "I may have given her a slight shove, you know, to get her out the way."

Adam was trying not to smile and failing.

"Oh come on. I was about to throw up."

"Yeah, funnily enough, I remember that part," said Adam.

DS Winterbottom continued reading from her notes. "It took Police Constable Davis and two ambulance men to retrieve her. According to Mrs Curry, her second-best cardigan may never be the same."

Winterbottom opened her mouth to speak, but Adam got there first. His smile was gone and he was all business. "Josie. We received some preliminary information back and I'm sorry to tell you that there's a good chance that Rose did not die how we initially thought."

My eyes swept back and forth between the two.

"Josie? Do you understand what I'm telling you?"

I wasn't sure. Something to do with Aunt Rose. Something to do with her death. My head was cloudy, my mind on pause which I swear had nothing to do with the earlier half bottle of Prosecco.

"Miss Monroe," said Detective Sergeant Winterbottom, staring at me with undisguised dislike. "Your aunt was murdered."

11

Two hours later I was back on the streets of Dorking, trying to figure out how to get back to Milkwood without any money. I was seriously thinking about hitchhiking when the bus to Guildford pulled up beside me and squealed to a stop. A bunch of schoolboys tumbled off and kept on tumbling—there seemed to be no end to the plethora of teenage acne and wayward ties. I glanced towards the queue and registered at least ten people waiting to board. I decided to put my morals on hold. Before I had time to question said morals, I'd squeezed past a youth in a scruffy blazer and crammed myself into a seat behind a rather voluminous woman with a pushchair.

I was not the type of person to break the law, which made it all the more ridiculous that I had been all but accused of murder. The way DS Winterbottom told it, I was practically a trained killer with nothing on my mind but murder. There were only two things in this world I was willing to kill. Flies and mosquitos. Everything else was off limits. For goodness' sake, I was the only person I knew stupid enough to catch and release cockroaches. The thought of me killing my aunt was preposterous.

The doors hissed shut and the number 32 lurched into Monday afternoon traffic. I stuffed Adam's business card into a pocket and thought back on the past few hours. As DS Winterbottom had tossed out question after question, I found myself retreating. It was bad enough that Aunt Rose was dead. The realization that she was murdered made it unbearable—surreal. I tried to recall our last conversation. Puccini at full blast had made it difficult to make out exactly what Aunt Rose had said, but if I remembered correctly she was confused. She had thought I wasn't coming. I tried to conjure her exact words, but they wouldn't come.

My mind returned to Dorking Police station and I ran through the previous couple of hours of hostile questions and loaded insinuations, but one thing I remembered more clearly than anything else was an aside I had overheard DS Winterbottom whisper to Adam when I'd returned after a bathroom break. Words I was obviously not meant to hear. "Rose Braithwaite was a nasty piece of work."

I wrestled my mind away from Aunt Rose and started prioritizing. Number one on the agenda was to retrieve my belongings from the DeCorcys. Second was to cancel my flight back to Texas. That had been another surprise. Because Aunt Rose was murdered, and because I was found at the scene, it meant I'd been asked not to leave the country, the county, and, if at all possible, the village. It was the summer, and schools in Texas had months of vacation stretching ahead of them, so I had some wiggle room, but it certainly wasn't what I'd planned or budgeted for. Lastly, I was going to have to figure out where I was going to stay. DS Winterbottom took great delight in informing me that Plum Tree Cottage was off limits until after 9:00pm. She also dropped hints suggesting there wasn't a hope in Hades that she, or her sofa, would host my sorry behind for another night—a suggestion that was plenty fine with me.

The bus rounded the corner and I spotted the familiar avocado green walls of Milkwood's Railway Station. Standing, I dinged the bell and the number 32 stammered to a halt. Promising myself I'd pay double next time, I alighted onto the pavement and headed towards the lane I'd strolled so happily along not twenty-four hours previous. I'd barely covered a dozen paces when the blast of a horn made me leap roughly two feet off the ground. I spun around and there was Belle in a blur of Roger-red hurtling towards me.

Belle hopped the curb and I took a hasty step back before my toes became the next casualty of her appalling driving.

"Oh, hello. I've been searching for you everywhere," said Belle, rolling down the passenger window.

"I had an appointment."

"With Snookums?"

"Snook who?"

"The cute copper," said Belle, smiling.

I chose not to answer.

Belle held up my handbag in one hand and a Waitrose plastic bag in the other. "This was all Mrs Crackenthorpe could rescue," she said, with an apologetic shrug. "I'm afraid the suitcase didn't make it. Dead on impact, according to Mrs Crackenthorpe."

I leaned through the window and grabbed my possessions. Belle didn't let go. "And, Josie. I'm sorry about what I said earlier. Mummy always said I was blunt as a box of biscuits. It's by far my worst habit." Belle cocked her head to one side. "Okay, maybe not my worst."

"Maybe drinking before noon?" I suggested.

"Gosh, no," said Belle, "that doesn't even feature in the top ten. But Josie, it was thoughtless, and I'm sorry. Friends?"

Belle released her hold and I extracted the bags out of the window and placed them on the ground. She stuck out her hand and, not wanting to be churlish, I grasped her palm and gave it a good shake.

"Can I give you a lift back to the village?"

I shook my head. "What makes you think I'm going back?"

"I guess with this now being a murder—"

"How do you know that?" I asked. "I only just found out myself."

"Oh, you know," said Belle, dismissively. "Gossip gets around. Besides, it's the biggest thing to hit Milkwood since Winterbottom got drunk at the church Christmas party last year and snogged Snookums."

I slung my handbag over my shoulder and scooped up the plastic bag—it was very light. "Well, *this* gossip is about my aunt's murder. And I, for one, do not think it's amusing." Turning, I stomped down the path and would have executed a spectacular *adieu*, if I hadn't tripped on a wayward tree root and ploughed into the ground for the second time that day.

12

Fifteen minutes later, I hobbled up the steps of The Dirty Duck and sank into a booth. It was around 4:00pm and the place was near empty. One elderly gentleman cradled a pint by the unlit fire and another patron was wedged into one of the many nooks and crannies on the far side of the pub. Piccadilly Circus it was not.

The pub was a squat, sixteenth-century, timbered building that protruded into Peacemeal Street at an angle normally reserved for drunkards and isosceles triangles. It had been the hub for village locals for hundreds of years. With low ceilings, comfortable furniture and a well-used, and no doubt out of tune, piano, it was charming, cozy and an American tourists dream.

I rummaged into my bag and retrieved my purse. It would have been sensible to check everything was in it, but Belle DeCorcy was many things—annoying, an appalling driver and abominably rich —but I figured if there was one thing she wasn't, it was a thief.

I extracted two crisp twenty-pound notes and a scrunched-up tenner. It would be enough to get me through the next couple of days and then I'd have to resort to my debit card—never an attractive proposition.

My stomach had been growling for so long now that it had invented an entire language. I hoped the server at The Dirty Duck would not have the same issues the Witches of Milkwood had exhibited over breakfast. Maybe they wouldn't know who I was? Yeah, right.

I approached the bar, inhaling the smell of stale beer and fried food in equal measure. My stomach gave off a particularly grue-some yodel and, as if in response, a barmaid strode through a side door and slammed a bottle of ketchup onto the counter.

She was in her early thirties with spiky black hair and dark kohl ringing her eyes. Her lips were the same red as the ketchup bottle and her pale face gave the impression of not getting out much. She was roughly the same height as me and wore a vivid purple top and skin-tight jeans. A badge on her lapel identified her as Petruska.

"You are zee niece of Rose, correct?" The accent was Eastern European. Romanian? Polish? It had been a long time since I'd heard such a dialect and I found it hard to place.

So much for anonymity. I shrugged. "Guilty as charged. You knew her?"

"She play piano here every Friday night," said Petruska, pointing at the upright. "Sometime she play the violin, but we ask her to stop, as it scare the children."

I had a million questions to ask about this, not least what chil-dren were doing in a bar on a Friday night, but Petruska had not finished.

"Of course this is before we had to ban her."

"You banned Aunt Rose?"

"Zis is correct."

I was stunned, but before I could get in a follow-up question Petruska continued.

"And you are zee one who find her."

It was more of a statement than a question. I nodded.

"Zat must have been a large shock."

"You can say that again."

My stomach interrupted our discourse with another impressive gurgle. "I'm sorry. That was me. I haven't eaten in...well, actually, I can't remember the last time I ate."

Petruska reached under the bar and produced a menu. "Here. You look at zis."

The menu had a picture of an extremely scrappy duck on the

front bathing in a murky-looking puddle. I pried open the sticky pages and scanned the contents.

SHEPHERD'S PIE AND SEASONAL VEGETABLES
STEAK AND MUSHROOM PIE AND CHIPS
CURRY AND JASMINE RICE

Ah, how I missed English cuisine. My throat started salivating at the thought of a decent pie. My eyes then fell on the small print. Serving from 5:00pm to late. I stared despondently at my watch and added six hours. It was 4:22 pm.

"Ignore zat," said Petruska. "We make zee exception."

I smiled, pathetically.

"Just not go making habit of it," she continued.

For one second I wondered if she meant ordering food out of hours or finding dead bodies. I decided on the former.

"I'll have the pie and chips and a large glass of pinot grigio please."

"Which one?"

"Erm!"

"Which pie? Zee steak and ale, steak and kidney, steak and mushroom, steak pudding, steak—"

"Steak and mushroom will do nicely," I said, clarifying.

Petruska tapped my order into a computer screen, took my money, and tossed over a packet of smoky bacon crisps. "Here. To be going on wizz. I go tell Carl to start cooking."

I took my drink back to the table, opened the crisps and crammed a handful into my mouth. Finolla would have been appalled, but I'd learned that what Finolla did not know would eventually get back to haunt me. Right now I didn't care. Two minutes later and the maroon-colored bag was flat and I could finally think straight.

I had two phone calls to make. Rooting around in my purse, I pulled out several pound coins, a couple of fifty pence pieces and a dozen twenty pences. I dropped the change back into my purse and hoped it would be enough.

Not seeing a phone, I abandoned my meagre belongings and

headed outside. If I remembered correctly there was a phone box located across the street and, if I was super lucky, it would work.

I yanked open the iconic glass door and, after inspecting the headset for disgustingness, I unraveled the cord, pulled the receiver to my ear and inserted several coins into the slot. I decided to make the easy call first. Unless someone strode into Dorking Police Station tomorrow and confessed to murder, there was no way I was making my flight. After a quick call to directory inquiries I was soon on the line with a very sympathetic Glaswegian named Bob. After explaining my circumstances, I was done with the first phone call. The second would not be as easy.

I reached into my bag, pulled out yet another scrunched-up piece of paper and dialed.

Maybe it had been the shock of finding Aunt Rose, but it had only recently occurred to me that I hadn't contacted my mother. True, she and Rose were in what you would call a "complicated relationship." Okay, they hated each other. But they were still sisters. Surely that counted for something? Regardless, someone needed to let her know and unfortunately that someone was going to be me.

The phone rang once, twice before I heard Finolla's husky voice cut through the crackle.

"Mum, it's me."

"What on earth do *you* want, Josie?"

I inhaled a deep breath. "It's Rose."

"Don't tell me. She's run off with a sailor. Wait—not a sailor, that would be *way* too blue collar. A cellist?"

The normal flippant Finolla.

"Mum...she's dead."

Two minutes later I padded across the road, past the stocks that I hoped were there for show and into The Dirty Duck. In ten minutes the pub had gone from being empty to heaving. For some inexplicable reason it seemed everyone, their mother and several grandmothers had suddenly become extremely thirsty.

I had read in books where someone enters a room and the place goes as silent as the "g" in gnome, but I'd never experienced such a phenomenon—until today. I made no eye contact and scuttled over to what was left of my bedraggled belongings. A second later Petruska plonked down a plate containing the best-looking steak and mushroom pie in Christendom in front of me. A plume of heady goodness circled from a tiny indent in the center and the aroma almost knocked my nonexistent socks off.

"Thank you so much," I said, unfurling my knife and fork and placing the napkin on my lap. "Erm, do you have any salt and pepper?"

"Ah not again," said Petruska, her face clouding.

"Erm—"

"Zee condiments. Zey are missing—again! I zink somebody is playing zee trick." Petruska went to a far table and grabbed a couple of fat brown shakers and dropped them onto the table. "Soon we will have to start chaining zem to zee tables."

Petruska turned and surveyed the patrons watching us with undisguised interest. "You never seen pie before?" she asked, her arms expansive around her head in a very non-British way. "Let zee girl eat in peace." She shooed her hands at them and reluctantly the residents of Milkwood went back to their huddles and their chatter resumed.

I can truthfully say that I inhaled every piece of that steak and mushroom pie. One minute it was there and the next it had vanished, leaving nothing but a puddle of gravy in its wake.

I angled my knife and fork together across the empty plate, a symbol recognized by waiters throughout the British Isles to signify you were finished. This was not the case in the US, and it always frustrated me when American waiters asked if I was done when, to me, it was perfectly obvious that I was not. I'd added this to my list of Englishisms I was convinced Americans should adopt, along with roundabouts and L plates for novice drivers. It was never going to happen, but a girl could dream.

My thoughts turned back to my conversation with Finolla. I hadn't known what to expect, but the unadulterated grief that had poured through the receiver was not what I'd have taken bets on. My mother had sobbed. An extraordinary emotion for a woman who disapproved of so much as a wayward sniffle.

Draining my glass, I glanced at my watch. I'd been told by Adam that I could access Aunt Rose's cottage any time after nine. Initially, I'd thought there was no way I'd return to where so recently there had been a dead body. But as the day progressed my thoughts had changed. To be honest, I'd decided to stay at the cottage for one primary reason—money. Unfortunately, there was no way I could afford to stay anywhere else. The thought of returning to the "scene of crime" did not thrill me. However, unless I wanted to spend the night on a bench by the duck pond there didn't seem to be much choice.

Deciding I needed another drink, I garnered my courage and strode towards the bar. The residents of Milkwood were well into their second round and the chatter was bordering on raucous. Surprisingly, the two original patrons still sat separately from the rest of the group—the old man staring dismally into his pint, the other patron remaining stubbornly anonymous in an under-lit corner.

I maneuvered my way to the bar, pulled a tenner from my purse, and willed Petruska to reappear.

The chatter drained away, and once more the room descended into silence.

"I can't believe she has the cheek to show her face," whispered a tall, dark woman in her fifties.

"Bloody Americans," muttered a shorter woman with curls. "They got no shame."

The voices rose as the patrons surged towards me. I was trapped. Within seconds the word "murderer" was being bandied about like a ball at Wimbledon, and I started to think my need for a second drink hadn't been my smartest idea. I felt an elbow in my back and I stumbled, landing smack bang in Bonnie Curry's lap.

I scrambled to my feet, but it was too late. Bonnie Curry, proudly modelling the damage inflicted to her second-best cardigan, was riled to full force.

"Standing over her, she was. Hands covered in blood. Murdering her own kin—it's indecent, that's what it is."

Bonnie Curry didn't look like it was indecent. Bonnie Curry looked like she was reveling in every gory detail.

The memory made my blood pressure drop. My knees started to

weaken and my pulse started to rise. I grabbed the bar to steady myself before being wheeled around to encounter the steely face of Magna Carter. Magna raised her finger like a mother chastising a toddler, but before she could add further insult a familiar voice rose above the hubbub.

"Leave. Her. Alone!"

The next thing I knew I was being muscled through the crowd by my rescuer, only stopping long enough to grab my belongings before herding me towards the exit.

There were several murmurs, a few pointed fingers, and Bonnie Curry yelled out something uncharitable but was immediately hushed.

Belle DeCorcy paused in the doorway and turned to face the masses. Raising her chin and narrowing her eyes, she surveyed the petulant crowd. "Really? You should all be ashamed of yourselves."

And then we were out in the street, but not before I caught a glimpse of the patron sequestered in the nook. It was the woman from the train station. The woman who was the spitting image of Finolla.

13

Belle hustled me down the steps and into the fading sunlight. I followed wordlessly as we tramped towards the duck pond.

Belle approached the bench and was about to sink onto an armrest when she stopped, bent over and reached out her hand. As I plunked onto the hard wooden slats I realized she had removed a tiny inchworm that was now slinking along her outstretched finger.

Belle finally took a seat and I found the words I'd been searching for.

"That was kind of weird. I mean, I've encountered bullies before. I'm a pianist, a music teacher in a public school, actually, so barely a day goes by when I don't witness something, but I have to say it's been a while since I've experienced it first-hand."

"You play the piano?" Belle held up the inchworm, as if to get a better view.

"Yes, and you?"

"Oh no," said Belle. "I can't distinguish a piano from a euphonium."

"The fact that you even know the word 'euphonium' is impressive. But thank you for...you know."

"It's best to ignore them," said Belle. "I do. It's just..."

"It's just this is the most interesting thing that's happened in

Milkwood since Christmas. Yes, I know, you told me." I paused. "Did Helen really make a pass at Adam?"

Belle nodded. "Winterbottom's not a bad sort, it's just she has the personality of a moist eel."

I smiled.

"Someone like DI Ward needs someone more interesting. Someone, perhaps, like you?"

"Me? But—"

"I heard you two were a bit of an item when you were younger."

Flippity flip flops, was nothing secret in this village? "It was nothing," I stammered. "A summer fling."

"One summer?" asked Belle, placing the inchworm on the back of the bench where it wouldn't get smushed.

"Okay, maybe two summers. Max three."

Belle nudged my arm, playfully. "Come on. Let's get you back to Plum Tree."

I contemplated my watch. "But it's not nine yet."

"Close enough. Besides, I have it on good authority they've removed the crime tape. Seems like an open invitation to me."

"There was crime tape?"

"You bet your Aunt Nelly there was."

Belle and I trundled along Unthank Road in companionable silence until we reached the turnoff to Brambley Lane.

I decided to ask a question that had been bothering me. "Belle, your father mentioned I was wearing 'dead woman's clothes.' What did he mean?"

Belle scrutinized her feet. When she met my eyes there was undeniable pain etched across her face and I wished I hadn't asked.

"Oh, Belle, I'm sorry."

"No, it's okay. Mummy died, gosh, ten years ago now but, you know, it's still hard."

I remembered Belle's mother from my summers in Milkwood. Hannah DeCorcy was a sweet, charming woman with hair as blonde as her daughter's and a smile that could stretch all the way to Amarillo. She had been kind and fun-loving and it was easy to see where Belle got both her looks and her quirky personality.

Belle changed the subject. "Do you want me to come with you?"

I glanced at the shadowy path that lay ahead. Heck yes, but pride shuttered the way. I had to pull myself together. "I'm good," I said, trying to stop my voice from quavering.

Belle cocked her head to one side, something I was fast realizing was a trademark move. "I'm sure you'll be fine, especially seeing that—"

However, before she had a chance to finish, the opening four notes of an iconic musical masterpiece pierced the air.

"Are you kidding?" I tried not to sound judgmental and failed. "The Village People?"

Belle scooped her mobile from her purse and gave an apologetic shrug. "What can I say? According to Daddy I have my mother's taste in music—in other words, harrowing." Belle raised the phone to her ear and listened. I watched as her entire demeanor changed. "What do you mean, out? Who let him out? Heavens to Betsy!" Belle hung up without so much as a goodbye.

"Josie, I'm so sorry. We have what you might call a family emergency."

"Your father?" I asked, trying not to think uncharitable thoughts as I remembered Lord DeCorcy leveling his shotgun at me.

"Good gracious, no. It's Claude. He's escaped. He can be dastardly feisty—has a habit of coming up behind people and head-butting them. For some reason he has a bit of a soft spot for me."

Belle took off towards the ford.

Good grief. What type of people did Belle employ at Barton Hall? Curiosity got the better of me. "Who's Claude?" I yelled. Games keeper, sommelier, personal trainer?

Belle turned. "Claude? He's our zedonk, of course."

At this point I stopped talking as, quite frankly, there's not much you can say to a statement like that. I had heard of zedonks, a mix of half zebra, half donkey, but never knew anyone who owned one. I watched Belle tear over the wobbly bridge, dash up the hill and disappear behind a rambunctious holly bush, wondering what she'd been about to tell me.

My attention turned to the bridge where Aunt Rose and I had spent hours playing games of Pooh Sticks. I turned onto Brambley

Lane, cognizant of the fact that twenty-four hours earlier I'd made the exact same turn, utterly unaware of what awaited me.

Yet again the lane was dark, with shadows from the hedgerow plunging across the rutted track. I had reached Rosewood and was passing a particularly menacing-looking gnome when I heard the same hissing sound I'd heard the night before. I paused, my heart quickening to a samba.

This time there was no Bonnie Curry peeking from behind the net curtains. Bonnie, and most of Milkwood, were happily ensconced in The Dirty Duck, no doubt raising a glass to my demise. I hurried on, accompanied by the early evening lullabies of swifts and swallows—thankfully no Puccini bellowing along Brambley Lane tonight.

Reaching the gate, I gave it a good shove, and heard it yawn in protest as I maneuvered myself and my measly possessions through and up the garden path. Plum Tree Cottage, normally brightly lit and welcoming, loomed dark and ominous.

I steeled myself. I was the woman who had taught beginner band to twelve-year-olds—I could do this. I reached for the door handle and met my first obstacle. It was locked.

Nobody ever locked their homes in Milkwood. Then again nobody normally got murdered in Milkwood. A locked door in such circumstances made sense. Plus, the legal owner was dead. The police wouldn't want to chance anything being stolen.

I cursed Detective Sergeant Winterbottom for not giving me a set of keys and wondered if they'd been left in the mailbox. But this was England. There was no convenient box situated by the side of the gate. Letters were delivered by forcing them through a tiny rectangular slot on the front of the door—not exactly conducive to the leaving of keys. Surely, Aunt Rose must have a spare key. Would she hide it? Leave it with a neighbor? Remembering the relationship between Aunt Rose and Bonnie Curry I considered this unlikely.

I checked under a potted plant, below the doormat and on top of the door jamb—no joy.

I decided to try the back door. Abandoning my bags, I ducked around the side of the faded brick cottage, coming face to face with the one-car garage standing squat and neglected. I gingerly stepped onto a higgledy-piggledy stream of pavers, following them to the back door. I paused as the aroma of honeysuckle greeted me like an old friend and breathed in the heady perfume. Honeysuckle, the fragrance I most associated with my childhood never failed to bring back memories of balmy summer nights.

Jostling the handle, I let out a sigh. Darn! It was then I recalled my covert exit strategy when sneaking from Plum Tree for my secret dates with a local teenager, who will remain nameless. Okay, so I think we've established it was Adam and, in retrospect, it seems like our surreptitious rendezvous were not as surreptitious as I'd once imagined.

I trudged around to the back and onto the patio. I gave the French windows a quick tug, but they were no help. Seconds later I found myself at the far north end of the cottage inspecting a gnarly sycamore. This had been my lifeline to adventure when I was a teenager. Plum Tree's wooden staircase was squeaky and unforgiving, but open my bedroom window and there lay a different type of wood—a veritable path to freedom.

Twenty years later, and it didn't look as easy as I remembered. I squinted upwards towards a first-floor window conveniently left ajar. This was my best bet unless I wanted to sleep in the hammock. I eyed the faded, mildewy fabric and decided to go for it.

I placed my foot on a limb and hoisted myself upwards. Easy. I only had another ten feet to go. How hard could it be? Okay, maybe a little less hard if I had better light, but I reminded myself that I'd climbed this tree a couple of hundred times. It would be like accessing muscle memory when relearning Chopin. It might be slow to begin with, but the notes, or in this case branches, would eventually spin into focus.

Raising my arms, I pulled myself onto the next branch, then the next. It wasn't quite like walking up stairs, but it was pretty close. The branches of the sycamore were wide, sturdy, and relatively close together. Finally, I grew level with the window, a bygone type kept open by a metal rod punched with holes at the base. I reached inside and dislodged the bar, causing the window to swing outward.

Placing my hands on the sill I hoisted my tummy upward and shimmied forward.

Surely, there had to be a tipping point? I kept inching ahead. The sill was now level with my hips. Abruptly, my upper torso plummeted and my legs pitched skyward, causing me to roly-poly into my childhood bedroom. It was not elegant and it was not graceful, but I was in, and currently that was all that mattered.

I was busy congratulating myself on my Everest-like climb when I heard a rustling behind me. I started to turn, when something hard and heavy straddled my back, digging its nails squarely into my neck.

14

I'd like to say I didn't scream, but I'm such a wimp—you do the math. I flattened myself onto the musty old rug and rolled. The nails undug themselves and the perpetrator let out a strangled meow.

I struggled to a sitting position and felt the warmth of the plump feline body wedge itself under my knees. This must be Elgar. Greyer, older and as dismayed to find himself locked out as I was. I'd never really been a cat person and I remembered Elgar as being cranky at best, downright mean-spirited at worst. I could almost guarantee that despite the friendly demeanor, if I reached to pet him I would be summarily scolded for my efforts. I did it anyway and a razor-sharp claw swiped towards my outstretched hand. Yep—that was Elgar.

The cantankerous tabby shot out from beneath my knees and disappeared under the counterpane. I took the opportunity to rise and take the first look in twenty years at the bedroom where I'd spent every summer of my childhood. I was delighted to see it was the same as my memories. Aunt Rose had never been one for change—something I'd once found annoying, but now thoroughly appreciated.

In front of me sprawled a queen-size wrought iron bed with a puffy mustard-colored eiderdown. The wallpaper was a William Morris pattern of faded pears, and on my far right lurked an antique wardrobe that for two uneventful summers I'd been convinced led to Narnia. To my left sat a chest of drawers and nestled between the two windows was a squat wooden dressing table with three movable mirrors. A spindly-legged stool reminded me of the hours I'd spent perched upon it, trying out new makeup and attempting, and failing, to French braid my hair.

Getting my breath back, I crossed to the wide oak door, eased it open and flicked on the landing light. It was ridiculous, but I felt like an intruder. I knew Plum Tree Cottage like I knew Beethoven's "Moonlight Sonata"—every sound, every nuance. Nevertheless, without Aunt Rose I felt like I was trespassing. Elgar bolted through the door and scampered out of sight. I followed, closing the door behind me. I passed the spare room and stopped. Aunt Rose's bedroom lay across the landing. I didn't feel up to poking my head around the door, so I padded down the stairs, which were as creaky as my teenage self recalled.

I was relieved to see the study door was shut. There was no need to enter and I had no intention of doing so. Instead, I took a right into the living room and groped along the wall until I found the light switch. The cottage seemed cold and, although light couldn't add warmth, it could at least lend a dash of cheeriness.

Aunt Rose had old-fashioned taste in furniture, and being incredibly frugal nothing was ever replaced unless broken or near disintegration. It wasn't the style I'd sought for my own modest two-bedroom apartment but, viewing the familiar mahogany furniture, it was surprisingly comforting.

The living room was the largest, with a bay window at the front and French windows leading onto the patio at the back. A fireplace rested along the outer wall with bookcases reaching out either side, filled with everything from Charles Dickens to Jilly Cooper. Aunt Rose was a voracious reader and her bookcases reflected this. No neatly stacked books for Aunt Rose, more of a muddled collection of well read friends. From a side table, I picked up a paperback with a bookmark sandwiched halfway through. The cover image consisted of a meringue with a dagger plunged into its side—a cozy mystery by D. Braith. Not the type of book I remembered Aunt Rose reading, but it had been twenty years. Her tastes had, no doubt, changed.

I headed towards the French windows and hooked a right into the kitchen. Flicking on the light, I surveyed the olive cabinets and oversized sink. A dark blue Aga huddled in a comfortable nook and copper pots dangled above a vase of yellow summer roses. The cottage looked like it was being staged for an open house—that American practice of letting strangers roam through your home on the offhand chance they might purchase it.

Then I remembered. Aunt Rose had been on holiday in the Peak District. Knowing my aunt, she would have tidied before she left and hadn't been home long enough to make a mess. For the first time I wondered if Aunt Rose had travelled alone or holidayed with friends. I hoped the latter. To be honest, I knew very little about my aunt's personal life. She had never married and, as far as I knew, was not romantically involved with anyone, preferring to throw her passion into her music. Now I came to think about it, friends never visited while I stayed and dinner parties were never hosted. As Finolla considered any day ending in "Y" a good day for a party, Aunt Rose's predilection towards solitude had been a welcome relief.

I made my way to the front of the cottage, past the downstairs loo, and along a corridor lined with framed images of Aunt Rose's favorite composers. As I strolled along the hallway, I tried to recall who was who. Aunt Rose preferred her music to be British and squarely rooted in the twentieth century. I easily picked out Benjamin Britten, Sir Edward Elgar, and Vaughan Williams, had a bit more difficulty with Gustav Holst and Frederick Delius, and drew a blank on the very last image of a man who could best be described as Alfred Hitchcock—on a good day.

Reaching the front door I spied a delicate antique table supporting a ceramic dish containing a spare set of keys—there was one problem solved. The ceramic dish was decorated with notes which I automatically sight read, revealing the opening bars to the *Coronation March, Crown Imperial*. I smiled as the last image's occupant was revealed to me—not Alfred Hitchcock, but Sir William Walton.

After unlocking the front door, I retrieved my bags and tossed them into the foyer. I contemplated the dangling keys, decided caution was the better part of valor and turned the latch. You know, to be on the safe side. It couldn't be ignored that Aunt Rose had been murdered in this very house and, it seemed, no one had the foggiest idea why. I had been informed by DS Winterbottom that there had been no forced entry and, as far as the police could make out, nothing had been stolen.

I tried the handle. Well and truly locked. If anyone attempted to infiltrate Plum Tree Cottage tonight, it would not be through the front door.

I glanced down to find the warm body of Elgar looping around my ankles. Like his namesake, he was proud and haughty and, right now, obviously hungry. Elgar let out a series of hisses before trotting down the hallway without a backward glance.

I entered the kitchen to find Elgar resting beside a Tupperware box. I grappled with the lid and noted Aunt Rose was running low on cat food. I scooped what I hoped was a sufficient amount into his bowl before refilling his water dish. It occurred to me that Elgar was going to have to find a new home—yet another issue to deal with before I could return to the US.

I waited for Elgar to finish, cleaned his dish and wished him goodnight. I made sure the French windows and back door were securely bolted before extinguishing the lights, grabbing my bag and heading upstairs. The creaks and groans of the staircase echoed my feelings of despair. Here I was, trapped in the village of Milkwood and unable to leave until the murderer was caught. I would have to put my trust in DS Winterbottom and the Surrey police. Unsurprisingly, the thought did not thrill me.

I checked my watch. A little after 9:30. Dusk had come to Milkwood and although it wasn't late I realized I was exhausted. I pulled off Belle's mother's dress, eased my feet out of my newly acquired sandals and upended the Waitrose carrier bag to review my worldly possessions:

- one pair of pink pajamas
- one pair of jeans

- one pair of shorts with slight tear
- three pairs of knickers, four pairs of socks, and one bra
  —hook slightly damaged
- two tee-shirts, one with the imprint of a tractor wheel
  imbedded on the sleeve
- a pair of damp sneakers
- and one sweatshirt declaring Keep Austin Weird

Everything was slightly worse for wear but immaculately ironed, with the faint smell of lavender. Mrs Crackenthorpe had obviously done her best and for that I was grateful. There was also a clean toothbrush, an unopened tube of Colgate and a selection of tiny toiletries that looked like they'd been pilfered from a luxury spa. Luckily my brush, makeup and trusty sleep mask had been in my handbag. It could definitely be worse.

I tugged on my favorite pajamas. They had the words "If You Can Read This Thank a Music Teacher" emblazoned on the front. Printed under the words was a particularly complex set of chords composed by the Six and a Half Foot Scowl or, as he was better known, Rachmaninov.

I grabbed my new toiletries and tootled across the hallway to the bathroom. Most middle-class homes in the US boast an en suite, but this was as far removed from the US as it was from Mars. There was one full bathroom upstairs plus a toilet, and what Americans would call a powder room downstairs. Finolla always insisted it was hard to keep secrets when one shared a bathroom—aggravatingly, my mother was about to be proved correct.

My ablutions finished, I found a clean, warm towel in the airing cupboard and dried my face. I draped the towel over the edge of the bath and that's when I spotted it. There, perched on the window sill, were three items that made me stop in my tracks: deodorant, hair gel and a bottle of something smelly. Nothing unusual, you might say—except they were all items used by a man—a young man.

15

Any worries I had in regards to falling asleep proved to be groundless, as I dove headlong into a pool so deep and dreamless that Brahms himself could not have done a better job.

This all ended five hours later when I bolted upright, alert and aware that something was not right. It took me roughly five seconds to recall where I was and then I heard it again. It was Puccini—*La Boheme,* to be precise—rising through the floorboards.

Puccini was the composer blasting from the stereo the night Aunt Rose had been murdered.

In fact, it was ricocheting off the walls at exactly the time Aunt Rose was losing her life, according to Detective Sergeant Winterbottom, time of death having been established as seconds before I found my aunt's warm, but lifeless, corpse.

Jumpin' Jehoshaphat! This was obviously a serial killer who terrorized their victims by playing Puccini at high volume while shoving them to their death. Okay, so this logic may have been a slight stretch. For one, *La Boheme* was not laying assault to my ears the way *Turandot* had the night before—but still, it couldn't be disputed that this *was* Puccini, a composer my aunt detested.

I pulled off my eye mask, planted my feet on the floor and did some deep breathing. I eyed the window and considered making a break for it, but that seemed like the coward's way out. I had never been known for my courage. Beat a hasty retreat and ask questions later had always been my motto—not exactly what you'd want emblazoned on your coat of arms. Of course, the Monroe family did not possess a coat of arms, although knowing Finolla, it was probably only a matter of time.

My eyes darted back towards the window and the trusty sycamore. No, if I was to meet my death at the hands of some strange Puccini-loving opera fanatic, then so be it.

I padded across the floor and eased open the door. I could hear it clearer now—Rodolfo declaring his undying love for Mimi as she lay on her deathbed in a Parisian garret. Great. The day before it was Liu pleading with the man she loved not to be complicit in his certain death. I had to admit it, the sycamore was looking more and more enticing.

Creeping along the landing, I squatted like a child at Christmas-time, peeking through the stair rails at the crack of light emanating from Aunt Rose's study. What the heck?

I inched my way down the stairs. Now don't get me wrong, I'm not stupid and I have the degree to prove it. If this was light seeping up from the basement there's no way I'd go investigate—especially if I was wearing a flowing white nighty. But Plum Tree cottage didn't possess a basement, plus this was no cellar, this was a study—a study where yesterday I'd found the body of my aunt, I reminded myself.

By now I'd reached the foyer with barely a betraying squeak. I tiptoed towards the study, pausing to pick up an old-fashioned umbrella from the hall stand. I'm not sure what I intended to do with said umbrella. Prod the intruder to death with the poky end? Regardless, it felt good to have something in my hands, even if it was more useful against precipitation than predators.

The music was louder now. Mimi was still dying and Rodolfo (the idiot) was about to figure this out. Noticing the door was ajar, I put my eye to the crack. Unfortunately, all I could see was the book-case and no axe-wielding murderer lurked there. I nudged the door slightly and it opened a couple more inches. I dared another inch and then another and then what I saw took my breath away. Lying in the exact same spot as Aunt Rose was another dead body.

Somebody started screaming. Apparently it was me. I started screaming a lot louder when the body sat up and waved.

16

The umbrella clattered to the floor with me close behind. Now, I would like to make it clear that I am not the fainting type. However, even I had to admit that, as of late, hitting the ground was taking over from playing the piano as my number one pastime.

My eyes flew open as a barrage of water cascaded over me. It seemed the dead body was now showering me with the watering can, most recently used for keeping alive Aunt Rose's aspidistra. I attempted to speak, but instead I inhaled a mouthful of stagnant water and started to splutter.

The watering can was lowered and I got my first good look at the previously assumed corpse. He was tall and slim with dark blond hair, piercing blue eyes and a scowl that would have given Rachmaninov a run for his money. A shirt that would not look out of place on an accountant was tucked tidily into jeans and his feet were bare, which struck me as unusual for a murderer. I put his age in the early forties. Finally he spoke.

"Who the heck are you?"

Now I am not a violent person and I am not, on the whole, an angry person, but what was with these people? Every time I woke from a faint someone seemed to be yelling.

"Who am *I*?" I responded.

"That *was,* er, the question."

"Who the heck are you?" I asked, rising to my feet and swiping a splotch of water from my face.

This seemed to startle him. "I'm, I'm Peter Lacey."

His response surprised me. I wasn't expecting him to give a name. Who gives his name when he's breaking into a house? Okay, not exactly breaking, more reclining, but you get the picture.

I recovered my composure. "And what are you doing in my aunt's study?"

"Your aunt?" Peter took a step back. "You're Josie?"

"No, I'm the freaking tooth fairy. Of course I'm Josie. But that doesn't tell me who you are."

"I told you. I'm Peter. Er, Rose didn't tell you about me?"

My thoughts flickered back to the bathroom and the men's toiletries. Good grief. Aunt Rose was having an affair with a man decades her junior and a good-looking man, too, if he ever stopped scowling. As if reading my mind his face relaxed and he held out his hand.

"I'm dreadfully sorry if I, er, scared you."

I surveyed his pale hand and noted his extremely long fingers. "Scare me? What the heck were you doing lying on the floor?"

He looked a little abashed. "I was listening to Puccini. I...I always listen to Puccini when Rose is gone. It's the only time she'll allow it."

By this time Rodolfo had come to terms with Mimi's death and we had moved onto "O mio babbino caro" from Puccini's comic opera, *Gianni Schicchi*.

"I didn't mean to wake you." Peter strolled to the CD player and lowered the sound on Lauretta's plea to have pity. "It's just I've...I've had a rough couple of days. I just got back from Prague and, well, things have been slightly difficult."

"Prague?"

"With the Philharmonic. I'm with the second violins. Not exactly overly impressive, is it?"

"First chair?" I asked.

"Second, but Montague, well to be blunt, he's about three hundred and sixty, give or take a month or two, so with luck he should pop off any day now."

"So you're telling me you've been in Prague?"

He smiled. "Landed at Gatwick a...a couple of hours ago. Dreadful pile up on the M25. Frankly, it's," he studied his watch, "it's taken me this long to get home."

"Home? This is your home?"

"Yes," said Peter. "Like I said. I...I find it difficult to believe Rose didn't mention me. I...I must have given you rather a shock."

That was the understatement of the evening.

"Rose can sleep through anything, but I keep it down when I get in late. Try not wake her."

The penny dropped and, along with it, my jaw. Peter hadn't heard about Aunt Rose, and now it would be up to me to tell him. Could this day get any worse? Okay, maybe Peter could have turned out to be a knife-wielding, Puccini-loving serial killer, that would have been worse—but at least he would already have known about Aunt Rose.

I took a deep breath and rallied my teacher's stance—appropriate for all manner of bad news.

"Peter, I have some bad news. Your girlfriend is dead."

Peter stared at me, incomprehension plastered across his face.

"And I'm sorry to tell you she was murdered," I continued.

There was silence. He was obviously in shock.

"Right here, actually. Where you were lying. You see, that's why I—"

"My girlfriend?"

"Yes," I explained, thinking this man really did have some comprehension issues. "Aunt Rose is dead."

Peter burst out laughing.

I placed my hands on my hips and gave him my best middle-grade teacher stare. He pulled himself together. They normally do.

"Rose isn't my girlfriend."

"Lover, then. Whatever you want to call her. Partner? Other half?"

"She's my landlady," said Peter, sinking onto the ottoman. "Wait! You're saying she's, er, dead?"

"Yeah. Slightly murdered. Very unfortunate." This was not going as well as I'd hoped.

"But that...that's impossible. She was here just..." Peter broke off. "I mean...I don't understand. Murdered? Do the police know who did it?"

"Right now I'm their number one suspect," I said, retrieving the umbrella.

Peter eyed the pointy end suspiciously. "You? But why? I...I mean, you didn't, did you?"

"Of course not," I replied, stomping the tip on the floor.

Peter shied back and I decided to forgo the umbrella, leaning it against the aspidistra for safekeeping.

"I just happened to find her. In fact, I practically fell over her. And then Mrs Curry appeared."

Peter rolled his eyes. Obviously he knew Aunt Rose's formidable neighbor—rolling of eyes being the default reaction from sane people whenever someone mentions Bonnie Curry's name.

"Anyhow, she found me covered in blood." My knees buckled at the memory and I reached towards the wall to steady myself. "And then she jumped to conclusions."

"Bonnie Curry, jump to conclusions? Now...now there, there's a first," said Peter, his voice tinged with sarcasm.

Peter was starting to grow on me both intellectually and physically. If you ignored the accountant outfit, he was magnificently easy on the eyes.

"You, you should have heard what she said when I first moved in. Vicious it was. As if anyone in their right mind would think I was having an..." Peter lost eye contact with me, shuffling his bare feet on the rug.

"Yeah, well. Moving on," I said, cognizant that if the situation was reversed with an older man and a younger woman the reality of them dating wouldn't raise so much as an eyelash. "How long have you lived here?"

"A year, maybe eighteen months. I...I was looking for somewhere quiet with an easy commute to London and someone recommended Milkwood. I bumped into Rose in The Dirty Duck. We got talking, as you do. She found out I was a musician and the next thing I knew I had somewhere to live. It's worked out rather wonderfully, actually," he added, with slightly too much emphasis. "Stupendous landlady. Charming, in fact."

"That sounds like Aunt Rose," I said, "always willing to help."

Peter's eyes flashed towards mine, but he said nothing.

"Well, now I know you're not an axe-wielding psychopath with a love of Puccini, I'm going back to bed."

"Excellent. I'll be right behind you. I mean. I'll...I'll be right up. Not *with* you obviously," said Peter, with a lopsided grin that was really quite adorable.

"I assume you're in the spare room?" I asked.

Peter nodded. He had turned very pale. The news was obviously sinking in. Not wanting to embarrass him, I headed out the door and up the stairs. Once in my room I strode over to the dressing table and fished around in the drawers. Finding a heavy shank key, I darted back to the door, placed the key in the lock and turned it. Peter might well be Aunt Rose's lodger and look like he belonged on the cover of *GQ*, but I didn't know him from the little old man in the pub.

I gave my hair a quick dry with a towel before cutting the overhead light. I padded back to bed and reattached my eye mask. I would learn more about Peter tomorrow and make sure he was who he said he was. In the meantime, my thoughts returned to the pub and the grey-haired woman sitting in the shadows. Tomorrow I would stop by The Dirty Duck and find out if Petruska could shed any light.

I removed my eye mask, letting light filter into my consciousness. What time was it? I found my watch, did the arithmetic and was still slightly confused. Could it possibly be 11:00am? Well, it couldn't be night. England enjoyed long summer days, but not long enough for it to be this bright at 11:00pm. With its north-facing windows, this was the gloomiest of the three bedrooms. I thought back to when I first visited Plum Tree and Aunt Rose had offered me the choice of the two spare rooms. One airy and light overlooking Brambley Lane, the other shaded by the boughs of the sycamore. Surprisingly, I had chosen the more shadowy of the two options, maybe because the darkness had felt like somewhere I could hide away and be safe.

Propelling my legs over the mustard counterpane, I stood and stretched. After my previous day's exploits I was happy to find I wasn't as sore as I should have been. Then the memories of the previous night came flooding back. Puccini and Peter, the secret lodger everyone conveniently forgot to mention.

I traipsed along the landing and down the stairs. No sign of Peter—which I considered a good thing. I didn't have the energy to be nice to someone this early (or late) in the morning. The door to the downstairs loo was ajar and I realized I was going to have to do something about Elgar's litter box. Not only was it starting to give off a pungent aroma, but there were also globs of escaped litter scattered across the bathroom floor. Reaching the kitchen, I located the kettle and filled it to the brim. This was going to be a five-or-six-cup-of-tea morning and that was without the thought of cleaning up after Elgar.

I flipped the kettle's switch and began the search for tea. Everything was tidily in place, with only the bare minimum covering the counter tops. A radio and toaster sat nestled together by the sink and a coffee maker lingered around the bread bin. It was then I saw the sticky note:

> *Josie. Gone to work. Be back late. Made coffee.*
> *Sorry for scaring you last night. Peter.*

Wow. Once again, another stranger had pottered around while I'd slept and I'd not heard a darn thing. I wondered how I could wake upon hearing Puccini, but the day-to-day mechanics of life could not stir me for Liszt or Mahler?

I poured a few drops of boiling water into the teapot, swirling it to warm the china before chucking it down the sink. I prized open Aunt Rose's Union Jack tea caddy and extracted one of Tetley's finest. Dropping the tea bag into the pot, I poured in the boiling water and stuffed a knitted tea cozy complete with pompom on top to keep everything warm.

Next on my agenda was food. I headed over to the mint green fridge and yanked open the door. The appliance reminded me of the retro refrigerator a friend had recently installed in her top-of-the-line Italian kitchen. However, this was not retro. This was the real deal, probably purchased in the 50s and still going strong—typical Aunt Rose.

The fridge contained all the usual condiments plus a pint of milk and a loaf of bread. Not quite as bare as DS Winterbottom's, but not exactly stocked for company. I reminded myself that Aunt Rose had been on holiday and Peter had been in Prague. I would have to go grocery shopping and hope my bank account didn't die of shock.

Thirty minutes later I'd consumed three pieces of marmalade-smothered toast and two cups of Tetley's decaf. I carried my dirty dishes to the sink and immersed them in a bowl of steaming hot water, squirting in enough Fairy Liquid to appease even the most conscientious of fairies.

I was in the process of pulling on a pair of daffodil colored gloves when the doorbell rang. Praying it wasn't Bonnie Curry, I abandoned my dishwashing and padded along the hallway. Taking a deep breath, I yanked open the door and almost got bowled over backwards as Belle DeCorcy strode through.

Belle wore a plain cotton dress with a wide leather belt and a pair of strappy sandals that enabled her to tower over me. Her wavy blonde hair was pulled into a low ponytail and her lips were coated with a pale gloss. She looked her normal self—that is, sickeningly stunning.

Wishing I wasn't wearing pink pajamas, I focused on the Lord of the Manor's daughter, and asked the only thing that came to mind. "How's Claude?"

Belle smiled. "All tip top. Some nincompoop left the gate open. He was halfway to Shere by the time we caught him. He has a horrible habit of treading on your feet if you get too close. Considering he weighs close to seven hundred pounds it can be a bit hairy."

Shere was a village no bigger than Milkwood a few miles up the road on the way to Dorking. Aunt Rose had taken me there as a child and I'd become fascinated by a parishioner named Christine Carpenter. The Anchoress of Shere, as she was known, was entombed into the wall of the church back in the fourteenth century in her attempt to become a living saint. As an impressionable eight-year-old, this story had given me nightmares well into my twenties. Heck, it still gave me the collywobbles.

"By the way," I said, traipsing back towards the kitchen. "Would it have hurt you to tell me about Peter?"

Belle flushed. "I was about to tell you when I received news of Claude. Besides, I thought Peter was away."

There was something odd in Belle's manner, but I couldn't put my finger on it. "He got back last night. Scared me to death."

"Oh, really?" said Belle, frowning. "Interesting."

I wondered what Belle was not telling me.

Belle slapped a smile back on her face. "But truly, Peter's a doll. Such a sweetheart and *so* good looking."

She had me there. I wondered—did Belle DeCorcy have a crush on Peter Lacey?

Belle thrust forward a smart wicker basket. "I decided you might need some provisions. You know, what with the cottage being empty. So I stopped and picked up a few necessities."

Ten minutes later we'd unpacked Belle's idea of necessities—something that was definitely at odds to mine. I was now the proud owner of two packages of *foie gras*, some exotic type of muesli and an array of seasonal vegetables, a couple of which I actually recognized. To top it off there was a delicious looking chocolate gateau and three bottles of wine. One white, one red and one bubbly. I hoped Belle wasn't expecting me to uncork one. There was no way I could start drinking before noon two days in a row. There was also a cluster of speckled eggs, a packet of sausages and some bacon bearing the vivid purple stamp that identified it as coming from a local farm. It looked like tomorrow I would finally get the great British breakfast I'd been unfairly deprived of.

"As a matter of fact, I need to go shopping," said Belle, pouring herself a cup of tea. "I thought you could come with me. You know, get out and all that. Have some fun. And then I thought we might have lunch. My treat, you know, for running you over."

"Belle, my aunt just—"

"Yes, she died, very sad, boo hoo. But you're alive and you deserve some fun. Believe me, I know about these things. Best not to wallow. Besides you hadn't seen her in what ten, fifteen...?"

"Twenty," I said.

"Twenty years!" said Belle. "You know, with the rate your skin sheds you've become a completely different person three times over. Really, your current self never knew Aunt Rose. Besides, what are you going to do all day? Sit around and wait for Frosty Knickers to arrive and ask more questions?"

I frowned. "Frosty Knickers?"

"DS Helen Winterbottom," said Belle, arranging the condiments in a straight line.

I hid my smile. There was no way I could argue with that logic, so I trudged upstairs and clambered into my remaining pair of jeans and the T-shirt without the tractor mark. I brushed my teeth, ran a comb through my hair and swiped on some mascara and lipstick before stuffing my feet into my still damp sneakers. There was no way I could compete with DeCorcy glamour and I wasn't even going to try.

18

Belle accelerated backwards along Brambley Lane at a speed that would have England's only astronaut peeing his pants. The hood was back, the Surrey sky was blue and Eva Cassidy sang softly about "Fields of Gold."

We zoomed through Abinger Hammer and under its whimsical clock, jutting into the road like an insistent pedestrian. I used to beg Aunt Rose to take me to see the clock with its miniature man dinging the bell when I was five or six, and I had named him Kevin —what can I say, I was young. Fifteen minutes later we approached Dorking City Center and Belle eased Roger into the only parking spot on the High Street that didn't have either a yellow line or a meter. I suspected things just fell into place for Belle DeCorcy and tried not to hate her for it.

Belle had parked so close to the curb I had to practically crawl from Roger's low slung chassis. Reaching the pavement, I scrambled to my feet and tried to look like this was the way everyone disembarked from sports cars. Belle had no such issues, exiting with ease and grace. Beaming with joy, she scooped her arm through mine and escorted me along Dorking High Street.

"Isn't it wonderful, Josie? Do you smell that?"

I sniffed. "Fish and chips?" I asked, inhaling a waft of vinegar.

Belle gave me a look.

"Diesel fuel?" I continued, watching a Waitrose truck chug through the one way system.

"I'm surprised at you, Josie Monroe, being so literal. What with you being a pianist and all, and your mother..."

So Belle knew who my mother was. No surprise there. You'd have to have been living under a rock or, failing that, Eastbourne, not to have heard of Finolla Monroe.

"...especially with your mother being so fabulously artistic," continued Belle, finally coming up with wording that did not include the adjectives "outrageous," "scandalous" or "brazen." Words normally associated with my mother, especially in the gutter press. "No, that's the smell of freedom. Imagine—we have the whole day ahead of us and I'm going to make sure you have fun if it kills me. Ah, here we are."

We stopped outside a hardware store where the window display featured a nifty black toilet with a sign stating, "Flush Your Cares Away." I will admit—this was not what I'd imagined Belle had in mind when she mentioned shopping, but then again, Belle DeCorcy was nothing if not full of surprises.

However, instead of heading towards plumbing nirvana, Belle cut a sharp right, descending a neatly hidden set of steps. I followed and quickly realized we were not entering a bargain basement—this was no Filene's—as I spotted an immaculately drawn sign announcing our arrival at René's. Dorking was not exactly known for its haute couture; however, I had a feeling Belle could sniff out designer clothes the same way terriers could sniff out a badger.

Belle pinged a discreet buzzer and we entered to the tinkling of bells, causing several angels to simultaneously receive their wings. A statuesque woman with onyx hair and prodigious eyes emerged from behind a burgundy velvet curtain. Gliding towards Belle on six inch stilettos, she opened her arms dramatically.

"Bella, darling."

The woman pronounced Belle with two syllables, making it closer to "Bella." She was impeccably dressed in a tight navy tunic hugging every angle. I would put her body weight index at around zero and the poundage of makeup around two. She exuded Frenchness, from her perfectly draped scarf to her perfectly placed beret.

Okay, maybe I'm lying about the beret, but the woman was distinctly Continental.

"René, let me introduce you to Josie Monroe."

René inspected me from my sneakers to my ponytail and did her best not to grimace.

She reluctantly put out her hand and I grasped it and gave it a good shake, hoping I wasn't meant to kiss it.

"Charmed, I'm sure," said René.

She turned her attention back to Belle, leaving me to wander aimlessly until I spotted a high-backed armchair nestled behind an overenthusiastic ficus.

My attention was diverted for a few minutes as I strained to hear the music playing quietly in the background. If I wasn't mistaken it was the sublime "Sanctus" from the *Requiem* by Fauré. An interesting choice for a dress shop. An obvious French link, but yet another piece centering on death. Would I ever hear music again without associating it with Aunt Rose's murder?

Belle and René had their heads together with the occasional sidelong glance in my direction. Could I be any more out of my depth? I suppressed a sigh and settled in for the long haul.

I had never been a girl who liked to shop. My idea of shopping was picking something from the aisles of Target, buying it a size bigger and hoping it would shrink. How Belle DeCorcy and I ended up on a shopping trip together was beyond me.

My memory jogged back to the pub the night before, where the locals had not only shunned me, but shoved me as well. With the exception of Petruska, Belle was the only villager to show me kindness. Okay, so she hadn't been exactly forthright in regards to the clothes she'd loaned me, and she had run me over—twice. But she had tried to help and, more importantly, she'd stood up to practically the entire village in my defense. Which led me to the question. Where was Adam? Okay, so yes, technically the man was leading a murder investigation of which I was the prime suspect, but could he not have called to find out if I was okay? Alive even? It dawned on me at that moment that I didn't have a phone and then something else dawned on me. Something far more relevant.

19

Forty minutes later, minutes made bearable only by the audio accompaniment of French composers Saint-Saën, Ravel, and Debussy, I had watched Belle try on, twirl and look gorgeous in roughly three million outfits—maybe four; after the first two it was hard to keep count.

Finally she was done. I hauled myself to my feet and suffered the indignity of being kissed on both cheeks before traipsing back up the steps to freedom. I had been in the US too long for double air kisses, which seemed way too European for this Texan transplant.

Belle hustled me down the High Street, stopping only briefly to play hopscotch with a young child, hug a stray dog and chat animatedly with a homeless woman before surreptitiously stuffing a twenty into her hands.

Ten minutes later we were seated in a restaurant, inhaling the aroma of garlic and freshly baked bread. My stomach danced a jig, all memories of the three rounds of toast I'd inhaled this morning conveniently forgotten.

We were shown to our seats by a handsome youth in his mid-twenties whose tongue all but unrolled when he set eyes on Belle. He quickly redeemed himself, but as Belle ordered two glasses of sparkling water, which I'd quickly amended to tap water, you could literally see him computing ways to slip Belle his number.

Belle waved away the proffered menus, ordering for both of us. She spoke so quickly and so competently that I didn't have a chance to interject. To be honest, I had such utter confidence in Belle's menu ordering skills that I decided to let it go.

"Did you get what you wanted at Rene's?" I asked, as the waiter sashayed towards the kitchen.

"For now," said Belle. "Plus I have a little something for you."

"What?"

"Mrs Crackenthorpe did her best. But there were some things that, let's just say, were irreparable. Honestly, I think that tractor did more damage than we gave it credit for." Belle reached into her capacious handbag and pulled out a bundle of orange tissue paper.

"Belle, I couldn't possibly."

"I insist on it. Besides, it's only a couple of dresses, it's not like I'm buying you a Porsche."

"Belle, I—"

"When's your birthday?"

"October," I said, sipping the iceless tap water placed before me.

"Then consider it an early birthday present for the Libran." Belle unwrapped the tissue paper and produced the cream dress she'd shown me the day before, plus another in a striking amber color. "And this time I have father's complete approval. Daddy felt quite awful about accusing you like that, you know."

It turned out that trying to win an argument with Belle DeCorcy brought back uncomfortable memories of teenage deliberations with Finolla. Discussions like whether I should have a pixie cut— Finolla decided I'd look more like a troll than an elf and that put paid to that. The question of whether I should learn Spanish or French. In the end Finolla convinced me to learn both and I hated to admit it, but being fluent in Spanish came in extremely handy while living in Texas. Finally, Finolla's *coup de grace*—whether I should marry Ryan, and we all know how that worked out.

I gave in, accepted the dresses, and folded them neatly into my handbag.

"Do you know a lot about astrology?" I asked, impressed that Belle had figured out my star sign.

"You bet your Aunt Nelly I do. My roommate at boardy, Squeaky

Simcox, was crackers about all that stuff. Wouldn't let me date Roofus Nash in year twelve because he was a Pisces."

I held up a hand. "You had a roommate named Squeaky? What kind of person has the name 'Squeaky?'"

"The kind of person I went to school with," said Belle, flapping out her napkin and arranging it neatly on her lap.

"Jumpin' Jehoshaphat, next you'll be telling me there was a Mufty, Tufty and Bunty."

"You know the Belleville girls?" asked Belle. "Such hoots. Of course, there was that unfortunate incident with the Turkish diplomat, but I believe that got hushed up rather nicely."

I stared Belle DeCorcy straight in the eyes and, for the life of me, I couldn't tell if she was feeding me a storyline from *Downton Abbey* or telling me the truth.

"So, Josie, what are your plans?" said Belle, tidying the condiments into a straight line.

"Plans?"

"Yes. Plans, Josie, plans."

"Well...er..."

Belle gave me a pitying look. "Ah, you see, here lies your problem. Currently you're supposed to be on a plane jetting back to Houston."

"Actually it's Aus—" I began.

"Instead you're stuck in Dorking about to partake in the finest food this side of Box Hill." Belle flipped her head to the side and gave this some thought. "Okay. So maybe this is not exactly as bad as one first imagined, but I assume you'd like to get back to your life in sunny Texas at some point."

I nodded. Right now I should have been cruising along at 40,000 feet, enjoying all the delights of first class travel.

"I hate to say it, but the long and the short of it is as follows: if Surrey's finest don't find out who killed poor Aunt Rose, you're not going home."

My glass of tap water slipped through my hands and landed with a thud. "You mean, you don't think they're going to find out who did it?"

"You've met Frosty Knickers, right?"

"I spent the night on her sofa after I found...well, you know."

I paused as our waiter placed several miniature plates on the table before backing away like he was serving the Queen. Belle tossed out a carefree smile and the waiter tripped over the adjoining table.

"Let me put it this way," said Belle, scooping up something crispy and delicious looking. "Do you think Frosty Knickers has an imagination? You know, someone who can think outside the box?"

I recalled DS Winterbottom's flat and its sparse, humorless environment. Sure, she seemed the type to be thorough, but thinking outside the box? Winterbottom was the type to find someone passed out by the side of their dead aunt, put two and two together, and recommend life without parole.

"I'm doomed!"

"Now you're getting the picture," said Belle, spearing a mushroom.

I plucked up a tomato-and-feta-covered triangular piece of toast with olive oil drizzled on top and popped it into my mouth. Oh my, that was good.

"So, as far as I can make out, we have only one course of action," said Belle.

"Mmmm," I said, as the flavors samba'd across my taste buds.

"I'm so glad you agree," said Belle.

"Agree? Erm...what have I agreed to?"

Belle leaned over and grabbed my hand. "It means *we* are going to have to find out who murdered Aunt Rose. You and me, together. We'll be like Bonnie and Clyde."

"Didn't they get shot?"

Belle took a second. "You might be right. Thelma and Louise, then."

"Went over the cliff in a convertible," I responded.

"Hmmm. That wouldn't be at *all* good for Roger. How about Lucy and Ethel?"

"That seems more likely," I said, remembering the skit in the chocolate factory.

"Then consider it a deal," said Belle.

"Wait! This is not a deal. I'm a piano teacher, not Miss freakin' Marple."

"But Josie, think about it. You know things the police don't."

"I do?"

"Of course you do. You must know your aunt better than anyone. All those summers you spent together."

"We've barely spoken in years."

"Details," said Belle, gathering up a cluster of bacon wrapped asparagus. "If we don't look into this, Rose's murder could be classified as an unsolved mystery. Or swept under the table as a break-in gone wrong. Then the suspicion of murder will always be there, looming over you. I might be wrong but I think they have rules about suspected murderers teaching in US schools?"

Flippity flip flops! I hadn't thought of that. These days you were lucky to be offered a teaching position if you had so much as an outstanding parking ticket. I could imagine the look on Principal Ratcliffe's face when she discovered I was suspected of murder.

"What do you tell your pupils when they want to figure something out?" Belle asked.

"Well, being a music teacher, I tell them to keep practicing and not give up at the first sign of a few demi-semi quavers or, as they're called in the US, thirty-second notes."

Belle stared at me like I was speaking Swahili.

"Fast notes," I explained.

"Righty ho. So let's start at the beginning. Tell me everything you know."

Belle produced a notebook and pen and ten minutes later she'd written down everything I could recall. From the phone call at the wedding, Aunt Rose's confusion when I spoke to her at the station, and finally the moment I approached the cottage with Montserrat Caballe on full blast.

"Do they know what time Rose was, erm, done in?" said Belle.

"Seeing I was speaking with her on the phone around 8:40 and I arrived at the cottage barely before nine, they can pretty much pinpoint it to the minute."

"Interesting. Very interesting," said Belle with a faraway look. "Did you hear anything else? I mean was there anyone else there?"

"I don't think so. I mean with all that Puccini it was hard to tell."

"So you didn't hear the murderer creep into the night?"

I shook my head.

"So, from what you're saying, Rose was killed minutes before you arrived."

I paused, a seared shrimp seconds from my lips. In the back of my mind I had known this, but having it spelled out unsettled me. What if I'd arrived earlier? Could I have saved Aunt Rose? Or the flip side. Would I have been murdered too?

Half an hour later we bumped to a standstill outside Plum Tree Cottage, where I crawled from Roger's clutches before meandering down the garden path with Belle in my wake. I disentangled the key from my pocket and jammed it in the lock.

Belle leaned against the doorframe and watched. "You locked up?"

"You mean you don't?"

"I don't think we feel the need. Daddy's a crack shot and so is Tillman. Come to think of it Mrs Crackenthorpe's not too bad either. After Mummy died Daddy was gone an awful lot, so we always keep a loaded weapon in the pantry. I think that probably puts off most blaggards."

I was stunned on so many levels I didn't know where to start, not least that Belle had inserted the word "blaggard" into a twenty-first-century conversation.

"Well, I figure it doesn't hurt to be careful. You know. Seeing a murder took place in the study."

"Right," said Belle. "It's rather like an Agatha Christie mystery. Instead of *Body in the Library* it's *Musician in the Study*."

"This is my aunt we're talking about, Belle," I reminded her, letting the door ease open.

"Yes, of course. Sorry about that. I keep forgetting you actually liked her."

I turned to Belle. "Did you know that Aunt Rose had been banned from The Dirty Duck?"

Belle looked suitably nonplussed.

"You mentioned before that she was horrible. What exactly did you mean?"

"Nothing. Nothing at all," said Belle, scooping up today's post and tidying it into one neat stack. "Pretend I didn't say anything."

I let it go.

"So, what are we searching for?" asked Belle.

"Two things, actually. First of all, I haven't come across Aunt Rose's schedule."

"A schedule?" asked Belle.

"Yeah, Aunt Rose always kept a detailed schedule."

"And the second?"

"A phone. I've been through practically the entire house and I've not seen any form of communication. If Aunt Rose doesn't have a landline then she must have been talking to me on her cell. And if she was—where is it?"

Belle punched me on the arm. "Look at you, going all Miss Marple on me."

"Well, it's just a thought. Plus, there are two rooms upstairs I still haven't been in and, of course," I nodded in the direction of the study, "I haven't been back in there."

"What are we waiting for?" said Belle. "You go hunt for telephones and I'll take a peek in the study, see if there's a schedule lying around."

"You okay going in there by yourself?" I asked. "You're not going to be weirded out?"

"Not in the slightest," said Belle. "I was raised on an estate that holds shooting parties practically every weekend. You can't swing a cat without falling over something fluffy and dead at our house."

"A dead body is a little different," I pointed out. "Some people might not want to be in close proximity to where someone died."

"All good, here," said Belle, flinging open the door. "Once more into the fray and all that."

Belle disappeared into the study and I plodded up the stairs and onto the landing. I automatically took a left towards my bedroom, deciding to leave Aunt Rose's room 'til last. There were three doors to the left: the bathroom, my room and the room occupied by Peter. I would start there. I approached the door and knocked.

Getting no response, I eased open the door and poked my head around. Empty. Phew.

Located at the front of the cottage, the room was prone to light and airiness and was exactly how I remembered. The bed was sturdy dark wood and positioned against the wall that divided Peter's room from mine. There was an oversized wardrobe on the left and two windows gazing over Brambley Lane along the front. On the far wall teetered a portly chest of drawers that always reminded me of a Dickens character.

At first glance there was no sign of a phone, but curiosity drew me in. There was little to distinguish the room. No photographs, no personal effects, other than a comb discarded on the chest of drawers and an overflowing suitcase from Peter's trip to Prague. The suitcase sat open and abandoned on the top was Peter's passport. Pure nosiness made me pick it up. I flicked it open and gaped at the blond foppish hair and startlingly blue eyes. Peter Lacey really was exceptionally good looking. Who looks like that in a passport picture? Not me, that's for sure, I thought, recalling the squinty-eyed images adorning both my passports.

I flipped through the pages. Peter was obviously a man who enjoyed collecting entry stamps. New York, Beijing, Istanbul, to name but three. I flicked to the back of the passport and found the stamp for Prague. There was the entry stamp dated two weeks ago, but no exit stamp. Nothing suspicious about that—maybe he forgot?

My eyes fell on a book sitting by Peter's bedside. I picked it up. *The Body in the Library.* Interesting choice. I flipped it open and a slip of paper fluttered to the floor. I scooched down to retrieve it before stuffing the would-be bookmark back inside. It was only then I noticed the rectangular paper was a boarding pass—a boarding pass dated June 12th—the date of Imogen's wedding. Now that was interesting.

I placed the passport back where I'd found it and closed the door behind me. Why would Peter lie regarding the date he flew back to London? Was he trying to hide something? Had he been here when Aunt Rose was murdered? I shook my head. There must be some simple explanation and, in my new role as Milkwood's Miss Marple, I must try to discover what it was.

I crossed the landing and lingered outside Aunt Rose's door. Taking a calming breath, I turned the handle and let the familiar aroma of *Anais Anais* waft over me. I'd loved playing with the squat white bottle when I was a child, with fond memories of Aunt Rose spritzing my wrists and showing me how to rub them behind my ears to diffuse the flowery scent.

I took a deep breath and stepped through the door. Aunt Rose's bedroom ran from one end of the cottage to the other, with windows at both ends. A beam of sunlight caught the pristine ivory covers and the memory of a childhood summer's day, when it was raining in the rear and sunny in the front, came flooding back. I remembered running from one end of the bedroom to the other, marveling that above the roof tiles was nature's divide.

However, that was practically all that remained the same. Gone was the four-poster bed and the flowery wallpaper so prevalent in the rest of the cottage. Also gone were the framed Holly Hobbie images, Laura Ashley curtains and shag pile rug. In their place was an ultra-modern low metal bed, pale grey painted walls, and drapes of sheer filmy lace.

I took another couple of steps and turned three-sixty to take in the strange new world. It was then that I spotted it. Not a telephone, but an antique writing desk, complete with carved legs and roll top.

In sleek mahogany it stood upright against the wall, as out of place as a soldier in a nursery. It had intrigued me as a child, and still fascinated me as an adult. I sank into the slatted chair and drew up the wooden top. It was exactly as I recalled: a green leather writing pad surrounded by tiny drawers with ivory pulls. It was not the most politically correct item of furniture, but it was beautiful with its inlaid wood and handsome swirls. I had spent hours playing with these drawers, carefully taking each one out and examining the contents before gently replacing them and pulling out the next. Each compartment had its own purpose. One held pens, another was home to rubber bands. One contained stamps and another paper clips, which I would string together to make daisy chains.

I reached around the side of the desk and found what I was searching for—a tiny hidden lever. I eased the lever back, causing the wood below the writing pad to spring forward. I cautiously inserted my fingers and eased the secret drawer towards me. It was by far the largest of the chambers, measuring a good sixteen inches wide and ten deep.

Lying on top was Aunt Rose's schedule. A strange place to keep it, but nevertheless, there it was. I pulled out the leather-bound book and flipped it open.

Aunt Rose's tidy, blue-inked handwriting stared back at me. At school we had been taught such a generic form of penmanship and I'd tried hard to emulate my aunt's beautiful, character-filled long-hand—and failed.

I was about to call for Belle when I glimpsed several other sheets of paper crammed against the base. Unlike the immaculate leather schedule, these papers had been scrunched up and smoothed back out before being placed face down. I pulled them out and flipped them right side up.

There were only a few words on the first, but my mouth fell open as I took in their meaning. I scanned the second and the third. They were all variations on a theme.

I know what you did last Thursday

I'm going to tell

Your sins will find you out

There was no getting away from it. Aunt Rose was the recipient of some mean-spirited poison pen letters.

The bedroom door opened and I instinctively thrust the papers back into the drawer and wedged it shut.

"I found nothing," said Belle, striding into the room and taking in the decor. "Gosh, this is a bit different."

"I did!" I waved the diary aloft.

"How come the police didn't find it?" asked Belle.

I shrugged. "It was under the mattress."

Belle cocked her head to one side and eyed me suspiciously. "What does it say?"

I opened the schedule to June and studied the contents. The diary was formatted with each week spread over two pages and going from Monday through Sunday. Aunt Rose couldn't stand schedules starting on a Sunday and ending on a Saturday. "Weekends are supposed to be kept together," she'd say, and it had amused me that she cared.

I handed the leather-bound book to Belle, who stepped over a suitcase lying unopened on the floor and perched on the edge of the neatly made bed. She flipped to the previous Sunday, where Aunt Rose had printed: *Dep for PD,* then back to the comments for this Sunday: *Josie arrives* followed by a little asterisk, as if to note something important.

I felt a lump rise in my throat and Belle, as if reading my thoughts, laid a hand on my shoulder and gave it a squeeze.

"Look here," Belle pointed at the day before. The Saturday evening. In pencil and far more hastily written were four letters: *QY PU.*

"Any idea what that stands for?" I asked.

Belle took her time before speaking. "No idea about PU, but I have a pretty good idea who QY is."

"It's a person?"

"Our resident maestro himself," said Belle. "Quentin Young."

21

I filled Belle in on the date of Peter's boarding card and, I must admit, was disappointed with her nonchalant reaction. To be honest, if I didn't know any better, I'd say she already knew.

"We are going to have to hand Aunt Rose's schedule over to the police," I said, filling the kettle.

Belle nodded, taking out her iPhone. "Absolutely, but not until after I've photographed every page. No reason why *they* should get the advantage."

"This isn't a competition, Belle."

"Technically no. But wouldn't it be super to beat Frosty Knickers at her own game?"

I had to agree the thought was tempting. I flicked the switch on the electric kettle and turned to face Belle. "Is there something you're not telling me about you and DS Winterbottom?"

Belle absentmindedly touched the scar notched on her eyebrow.

"Belle?"

"Okay, so maybe once, when I was very young, she threw me into the Tillingbourne."

"She did what?"

"I know, it's stupid, but I've never forgotten it and I seem to have held a bit of a grudge."

I stared at Belle, my mouth agape. Either Belle was confused or she had been extremely unlucky as a child when it came to water activities.

"It was late one summer and I was out for a stroll. Actually, it was at the back of Rose's property. Did you know there was a rope swing?" Belle didn't look up, but kept on snapping the pictures.

I knew it well.

"I was ambling along the bank, searching for wood pigeons if I remember correctly, and came across this wonderful rope swing. Frosty Knickers was lying on the bank with two boys. They were a few years older than me and obviously didn't want me there. They told me to go home, and when I didn't they grabbed me by the arms and legs and tossed me in the stream."

I couldn't stand it any longer.

"Belle?"

Belle lowered her iPhone. "Yes?"

"I'm not sure how to tell you this, but the girl who threw you in. That wasn't Winterbottom." I paused. "It was me."

Belle frowned, as if trying to recall some long-lost memory.

"I don't know what came over me. Trying to show off to Adam and Jimmy probably. But Belle, I can't let you go on thinking it was Helen. It wasn't. Besides, Helen would have been too young."

Belle paused mid-photo. I scrutinized her normally tanned and hearty-looking face—it was as pale as a snowman.

Belle staggered forward. "I have to get home." And seconds later I heard the door slam, the car start, and as quickly as Belle DeCorcy had entered my life, she had left.

Great, I'd had one friend in Milkwood and now I was officially back to zero. Brilliant, Josie. You had to go and blab. But I knew I had done the right thing. Belle DeCorcy might be many things, but she didn't deserve to be lied to. Okay, so maybe I hadn't told her about the poison pen letters, but that wasn't lying. That was withholding. I made myself a cup of tea and determined that I would give Belle a day or three to calm down and then I would find her and apologize.

Two cups of tea and a generous portion of chocolate gateau later, I decided to walk into the village and find someone who didn't hate me on sight. For some reason, the name Quentin Young rang a bell. However, for the life of me I couldn't recall which bell. I had no doubt that it would come back to me eventually. In the meantime I figured someone must know QY and if they knew him, maybe they also knew where he lived. I wanted to know if anything unusual had happened the day Aunt Rose died. Had Aunt Rose acted weirdly? Had she confided any concerns?

I decided to have another look through Aunt Rose's schedule—but it was gone.

22

I spooned out a dollop of kitty kibble and made sure Elgar had fresh water. This seemed to make him happy which, after Belle's hasty departure, made me feel slightly better. My track record on taking care of others could not be called exemplary. Back in Austin I owned one budgerigar, Horace, who was currently being cared for by my elderly neighbor, Mrs Ackerman. I'd never had children, I'd killed my cactus and I'd misplaced a husband—not the *best* credentials. Taking care of Elgar pleased me. A cat seemed like a step up from a budgie. I may not be able to retain a friend, a cactus or a husband, but at least I could remember to feed the cat.

After locking up, I strolled along Brambley Lane and into the village. The lace curtains at Rosewood's had twitched as I'd passed by, but other than that, Milkwood was deserted. I suddenly remembered that English schools did not break for summer until mid-July. Cedar Ridge Middle School in Austin had already been out for over two weeks, breaking up after Memorial Day. The six weeks' holiday at English schools paled in comparison to the long summer breaks American children enjoyed and I was not sure if this was a good thing or bad—I suppose it depended on who you asked, the children or the parents.

Trundling along Unthank Road, I turned left, crossed Peace-meal Street, and decided to visit the corner shop and test the waters. When I'd been a child the newsagents was run by an octogenarian Yorkshire woman named Mrs Waspit. She was tall, thin and nervous, never allowing more than two children into her store at a time. However, this was Milkwood—with the exception of Aunt Rose's bedroom things didn't change. For all I knew Mrs Waspit could be alive and well and living out her centenarian years terrifying local school children.

I jingled through the door and took in the familiar layout. There was a counter along the far right wall with four aisles stretching out horizontally. The whole setup was like a backwards American flag. Spying no one at the counter, I strolled to the far left corner and grabbed a local paper. I don't know why, but I was shocked to see Aunt Rose's face staring back at me. However, it made perfect sense. As Belle had pointed out, this was the most exciting thing to happen in Milkwood since Frosty Knickers' and Adam's Christmas kiss.

I headed towards the front of the store, got waylaid by the chocolate aisle and, five minutes later, staggered to the checkout with as much Cadbury's as a girl could decently cradle in her arms.

A woman in her late thirties with glossy brown hair, alert eyes, and ruddy cheeks appeared from a back room and took her place behind the counter. She wore a scarlet dress that looked more suited to the forties than the current decade and had a tattoo reminiscent of a Charles Rennie Mackintosh stylized rose trailing along her arm. However, what was most interesting was her smile. Obviously she had no idea who I was and I was hoping to keep it that way. Denying me breakfast was one thing; denying me chocolate might lead to something more drastic.

"You're Rose's niece, right?"

So much for my attempt at incognito.

I nodded.

"I'm Susan, Susan Ludlow." Susan stuck out her hand and I toppled the various chocolate bars onto the counter, followed by the newspaper, and took the proffered palm.

"Josie," I said, "Josie Monroe."

"My nan used to tell me tales about you," said Susan, raising her hand and patting one of her many pin curls.

"She did? I mean, really?"

"Yeah, laugh she would at all your exploits when you were young."

For a second I wondered if, like Belle, Susan was getting me confused with someone else. Suddenly it clicked. "Your nan is Mrs Waspit?"

"The very one," said Susan.

I realized I never knew Mrs Waspit had either children or grandchildren. How funny is it as adults to look back at childhood and realize how self-centered one was? Did it ever occur to me to inquire into Mrs Waspit's life outside of the corner shop? Of course not. I was too busy getting in trouble with Adam and Jimmy to wonder about the life of an elderly shopkeeper.

"Course, Ludlow's my married name. Divorced now, though. Thought about changing it back, but really the only good thing our Derek ever did was give me a half-decent surname."

There was a cough and a teenager wearing a black blazer and trousers, white shirt and crooked school tie materialized from a side entrance.

Susan's face lit up. "That and this scoundrel, of course."

The boy shuffled forwards in that round-shouldered adolescent way and wrapped an arm around his mum. This unselfconscious act of love warmed my heart, making me instantly like Susan Ludlow and her lanky teenager.

"This 'ere's Dan. In his last year at senior school, he is and right bang smack in the middle of his A Levels, poor sod."

Dan released his mum, nodded towards me and turned to leave. "All right if Gurminder comes over tonight, Mum? We're going to study."

Susan hesitated a minute too long. "If she's checked with Mrs Singh, Dan. But make sure she has. And don't forget ya deliveries. Mrs Curry's been complaining all day about needing some cough mixture. Just you make sure you run it over before you get settled."

Susan indicated a tray containing various yellow bags. Post-it notes stuck onto the front identified them as belonging to Milk-wood residents. Several of which, I was surprised to realize, I recognized.

Dan nodded before disappearing through the side door.

"Deliveries what keeps us afloat," said Susan, scanning a packet of Maltesers

I wanted to tell her the chocolate wasn't all for me, but that would be a blatant lie.

"The old dears love Dan. I fink half of them ask for delivery so they have someone to talk to. Can get lonely on your own, you know."

I nodded. Since my ratfink of a husband had left, loneliness was something I was all too familiar with.

"Must have been a shock, finding your aunt dead like that," said Susan, changing the subject completely. "Do you have a bag?"

I shook my head.

Susan produced a yellow plastic bag and cascaded the chocolate into its cavernous mouth. "That'll be twelve pound thirty-four pence, and that includes the bag."

Dang, that was a lot of money to waste on chocolate. I opened my purse and tried to distinguish the dimes from the five pences and the quarters from the tens. After several false starts, I sorted the correct change and toppled it into Susan's outstretched palm. I grasped the bag and was turning for the door, when I recalled my initial reason for coming in—information.

"Susan, do you know someone named Quentin Young?"

"Who, the angel?" Susan tapped an 8 x 11 flyer Sellotaped to the counter. "Delivered this last Friday, he did. Insisted I put it in a *prime* location."

I glanced down and read aloud.

Maestro Quentin Young
Presents the World Premiere of
Enchanted Summer
by Quentin Young
St Ethelred's
June 20th at 7:00pm
Donations Accepted towards St Ethelred's Roof Fund

"Impressive," I said, a nagging memory tugging at my brow.

"It's something," said Susan, rolling her eyes.

"Do you happen to know where I can find him?"

"Whatcha need him for?"

"Oh...it's just my aunt, er, had something of his and I wanted to return it."

I don't know why I lied, it just seemed easier and I was amazed the way the fabrication rolled off my forked tongue.

"He lives on the DeCorcy Estate. Rents one of their cottages down by the Tillingbourne, he does. Actually, it'll be easier to go along to The Dirty Duck around eight tonight. No doubt the maestro himself will be propping up the bar."

Susan gave me a brief description of Quentin and I immediately understood the "angel" reference. Thanking her, I headed out the door. Susan seemed a nice person, but nowhere in that conversation had she said what most people say when someone dies—that they were sorry. Nor had Bonnie, Irene or Magna, although, in their defense, considering they thought I murdered her, offering condolences wasn't particularly likely.

Lost in thought, I turned the corner and was immediately bowled over by a substantial woman wearing jodhpurs and other equestrian paraphernalia. The bag containing my purchases flew from my grasp and chocolate toppled into the gutter. Fearing the appearance of another tractor, I dropped to my knees and stuffed the candy bars back into the handleless bag.

"Some people should look where they're going," said an imperious voice.

I was thinking I could have said the same, when a waft of perfume drifted up my nostrils—and not in a good way. I knew that smell—mothballs with a hint of sore throat syrup thrown in for good measure. I also knew that voice. It might be older and deeper, but there was only one person in Milkwood who could be guaranteed to blame anybody for anything.

I stuffed a wayward *Aero* back into the shopping bag, clambered to my feet and stared my assailant in the face. "Wendy Williams?"

The woman had dishwater blonde hair and a wholesome face, which would have been attractive if it hadn't been for the pinched lips and accusing eyes. Wendy surveyed me from my tattered sneakers to my ponytailed hair, producing a sneer I would have known anywhere.

"It is, isn't it?" I continued.

The words came out like she was loathe to part with them. "Wendy Fitzpatrick, now. And you are?"

"Oh, come on, Wendy. You must recognize me. The first time we met you tried to stick a conker up my nose. The last time we met you were snogging Jimmy Gilmore behind the bicycle shed."

Wendy's face assumed the posture of one who has stepped in something brown and gooey. "Oh heavens, it's Josephine Conrow."

"Monroe," I corrected. "Josie."

"Good Lord! You look like you've been dragged through a hedge backwards," said Wendy, her eyebrows rising precipitously.

"And it's lovely to see you too," I said, grinning.

"Never married I take it?" Wendy gawked blatantly at my left hand.

I perused my ringless fourth finger. "I married," I said, defensively.

Wendy sniffed. "Divorced then, I take it. Of course, it was obvious even when you were a child that you'd never be able to keep a husband."

I remembered back to the summers spent in Milkwood when Jimmy, Adam and I tore around the village like a pack of wild animals. I then recalled the stuck-up do-gooder Wendy Williams, who wanted to be part of our gang so badly she would have wet her pants if Jimmy so much as glanced her way.

I don't know what made me say it, but I blurted out. "Actually, my husband, Ryan, he died...in a train wreck. Body parts every-where. Had to identify him by a mole on his upper thigh."

Wendy looked like someone had shoved a poker up her bottom, but she pulled herself together and gave one of her customary sniffs. "Sounds like the type of thing that would happen to someone like you. Couldn't lose a husband to cancer or something respectable. Of course my husband would never be so reckless as to die in such an unconventional way. Duncan will die in a traditional, respectful way. A heart attack, stroke. You know, like normal people."

This was so like Wendy. The fact that she thought she could dictate the way her husband would die. Who does that? Wendy Williams, that's who.

"Who's having a stroke?" said a broad Scottish voice behind me.

"No one is having a stroke," said Wendy, rolling her eyes like you would in response to an ill-informed child. "Don't be so ridiculous, Duncan."

"Glad to hear it," said Duncan. "And who do we have here?"

I turned, interested to see who would marry such a woman. The answer almost knocked me off my feet. He was no longer wearing a kilt, nor slurring his words, but I would recognize that half-shaven face anywhere. I couldn't resist a smirk as I stared into the terrified face of Don Hamish, the drunken Scotsman.

23

Duncan was a large man, but as his memory of our encounter on Saturday night slowly surfaced, he seemed to shrink.

"Did you get the oatmeal, Duncan?"

"I dunnae ken," replied Duncan, which I believed was Scottish for either "I don't know" or "shoot me now." Judging from his expression it was fifty-fifty either way.

Wendy eyed the bag in Duncan's hands and prodded what I suspected to be a bumper tub of oatmeal. Her entire demeanor seemed to scream "stupid man." Truth be told, I was starting to feel rather sorry for Duncan.

Bulldozering me out of the way, Wendy issued another command. "Come *on*, Duncan."

Duncan wrenched his eyes from me with a pleading look and hotfooted after his wife.

It was too early for Quentin to be downing pints at his local, so I decided to give Adam a quick call and let him know about the missing phone. I would have to use the public phone box until I bought myself a cheap mobile, so I trotted along the High Street until I was nose to glass with the iconic red phone box.

I fished out Adam's business card and dialed the number. The phone rang once, twice before voicemail clicked on and I heard Adam's professional voice float through the line.

This is Adam Ward, I cannot take your call right now (well, duh), *please leave your details and I will get back to you.*

This was not a message I wanted to leave on an answer machine. Or was it that I wanted an excuse to talk to Snookums, as Belle had called him? I ejected this thought from my mind and hung up. I exited the phone box and was deciding what to do next when the phone trilled to life. Is it just me or is there something that reeks of Russian spy novels when an empty phone box starts ringing? Tentatively, I opened the door, stepped inside and grasped the receiver.

"Josie, is that you?"

I almost dropped the phone. "Crispy pancakes!"

"Yep, that's you," said the voice.

"Adam?"

"Who else is it going to be?"

"But—"

"I traced the number to the phone box opposite The Dirty Duck. Considering you're the only person in the entire British Isles over the age of eight who doesn't own a phone, I took a wild guess."

I was silent as I took in this information.

Adam continued. "You don't make DI without having at least a tiny amount of detective skills, you know."

"Yeah, sorry. Of course."

"Josie, are you hungry?"

"Am I what?"

"It's just I'm heading your way and I've not eaten all day. I wondered if you fancied getting a bite to eat?"

I studied my watch. It was almost 5:00pm. Time for The Dirty Duck to start serving.

"Should you be fraternizing with a murder suspect?" I said flippantly.

"Come on, Josie. We both know you didn't do it. Don't give me that rubbish."

"Well, I wish you'd tell that to the residents of Milkwood," I countered. "I'm public enemy number one down here."

"So, is that a yes or a no?"

"Sure. Want to meet in The Dirty Duck?"

"I'll be there in ten." And the line went dead.

I replaced the phone and strolled across to the squat, sixteenth-century, timbered building that lurched into the street at a drunken angle. I assumed it had once been known as The King's Head or The Red Lion; however, the name "Dirty Duck" seemed to suit it perfectly.

Pushing open the door, I noticed the same old man from the day before slumped in his usual chair but, alas, Finolla's doppelganger was nowhere to be seen.

I strolled over to the bar and Petruska popped up like a jack-in-the-box from behind the counter.

"Cluck a duck!" I exclaimed, as I jumped backwards, my heart pounding.

"I scared you?" said Petruska.

"Just a tad," I replied.

Petruska smiled. "I scared zee killer."

I sighed. I had foolishly believed Petruska was one of the two residents of this village who didn't think I'd killed my aunt.

"I joke," said Petruska, as if reading my mind. "I am sorry about zee other night. After you left I gave zem zee good talking to. Zis Magna Carter. She is zee nightmare, no? Can you believe it, when I marry Carl she told me to go back to Poland."

I gasped with shock.

Petruska did an expressive gesture with shoulders, hands and mouth that I took to be the Eastern European equivalent of the French shrug.

"I would not mind, but I am telling her I am Bulgarian."

"You are?"

"No!" said Petruska. "I am Polish. But no one in zis village can tell zee difference."

I was getting a newfound respect for Petruska.

"I told zee beesh I'd ban her, and she keeps her forehead down ever since. Zee rest of zem are not so bad. Zay are like zee bunch of chickens. Wherever she goes, zee rest of zem will waddle."

"It's okay. I assume they're mad their friend is dead," I said.

Petruska shrugged. "We can go with zis, if you like. What can I get you?"

"Actually I'm waiting for a friend, but before he gets here I wanted to ask you about an older lady sitting in that nook the other night."

Petruska obviously didn't have a clue.

"She's quite Bohemian looking. Longish grey hair, older, but not ancient?"

Petruska raised a heavily bejeweled finger. "I know who you talk about. She is not from here. She stays at zee Magna Carter bed and breakfast. She has been here...four, five days? She has zee weird accent. I am thinking she is Australian."

This surprised me. I don't know if you can tell someone's nationality by looking at them, but my mystery woman had not struck me as Australian. She looked as English as I did—for what *that* was worth. What also surprised me was the news that Magna Carter ran a bed and breakfast. I couldn't imagine the immaculate Mrs Carter donning a flowery pinny, (an apron to my American friends) each morning and frying up the requisite full English. What can I say? Life is full of surprises.

"Do you happen to know her name?"

Petruska's brow furrowed once more. "Maisy, Daisy, Paisley? Zeese English names all sound zee same to me." Petruska turned and yelled behind her. "Carl, what is zee name of zat woman who visits from Australia?"

An amply sized, bald man appeared in the doorway, a blue and white striped apron secured around his waist. When he spoke it was with a sing-songy accent, which I instantly recognized as Welsh from my many years in Shropshire.

"Right you are. That'll be Daisy Pond. But she's not Australian. She's a Kiwi."

24

I ordered my favorite soft drink, pineapple juice and lemonade, and wandered over to a booth. I had only taken a couple of sips before the door creaked open and Adam stepped inside. He waved at me and made the universal sign for "I'm getting a drink."

There was no getting away from it, Adam had grown into a handsome man. Back in the day he had been a short kid with not much brawn. Jimmy had been the looker of the two. It occurred to me that I really must ask what Jimmy was up to.

I watched as Adam pulled out his wallet. He was wearing a traditional policeman's suit, shirt and tie, but somehow he managed to make it less ill-fitting and more sexy than your average TV detective. Petruska leaned across the bar and laughed and I realized that Adam had that effect on women. He was easy to get on with. Men liked him and women felt safe with him. It had been that way since we were kids.

Adam headed towards me and I made a concerted effort to study the old horse brasses suspended from the uneven wall. Not the most original pub decor but, for The Dirty Duck, it worked.

Adam dragged out the opposite chair and sank into it. He raised his pint glass and we clinked.

"Cheers."

"Your health," I replied.

Adam grabbed the menu and gave it a once over. "You going to eat?"

I thought back to my delicious lunch in Dorking and compared it to The Dirty Duck's pub grub. About as different as Mendelssohn to Mahler; however, I knew which option I'd choose if my death row meal ever came into play.

"Fish and chips for me," I said.

Adam shook his head. "The food here is robust, but if you want fish and chips, try Andy's on the High Street. Carl does his best, but you just can't get the amount of grease that's truly necessary for a decent fish and chips."

I debated whether I should be annoyed that Adam was criticizing my dinner choice, but let it go.

"Does shepherd's pie meet with your approval?"

"Perfect," said Adam, my sarcastic tone lost on him. I had obviously been in the US, a country big on comedy and low on sarcasm, for too long.

"It's not cottage pie masquerading as shepherd's, is it?" I checked the ingredients. There had been several times in the States when I'd ordered shepherd's pie, only for it to turn up with beef instead of lamb. No amount of explaining had made any difference and I'd stopped ordering the British "delicacy" in favor of something Texans did well, the three "B's"—burgers, brisket and BBQ.

"Who would put beef in shepherd's pie?" Adam grabbed my menu. "That's just wrong."

Five minutes later, Adam had placed our orders and joined me back at the table, another pineapple and lemonade in his hand.

"Well remembered," I said, as he placed the glass in front of me.

"I have a good memory," said Adam. "Take your drink choices, for example. Tea, not coffee, black not white, always decaffeinated, and never in a Styrofoam cup."

"That's impressive," I said, racking my brain for any info I had on Adam's choice of beverage and, with the exception of beer, came up blank.

"So," said Adam. "What have you been doing since I saw you last?"

I couldn't help but smile. The way Adam said it made it sound like I'd last seen him over a chilled bottle of Chablis, rather than across the scarred wooden table loitering in the custody suite of Dorking Police Station.

"Oh, you know," I said. "Not too much. Especially since your DS banned me from leaving. Milkwood is many things, but I wouldn't exactly call it cosmopolitan."

Adam smiled. "Yeah, Helen does like to go by the book. She's young. She'll soften up as she gets older."

Quite frankly I couldn't imagine Frosty Knickers softening even if she outlived Irving Berlin—one of music's better known centenarians.

"But what I meant was, what have you been doing since, you know, that summer?"

I practically choked.

"Just the highlights?" said Adam. "You know, married, kids, prison sentences?"

"Very funny," I replied. "You first. Married? Kids? I will assume no prison sentences considering your profession."

"It was a near thing."

I gave him my "yeah right" look, but realized he wasn't joking. "You're being serious?"

Adam nodded. "Remember Jimmy? Regrettably, our James became way more reckless as time went by. Petty theft and hotwiring cars until he graduated on to theft with a deadly weapon."

My jaw fell open.

"Yeah. It was all fun and games to begin with, scrumping apples, swiping the odd bottle of milk. Once we even snatched a pair of Bonnie Curry's unmentionables."

"You didn't?" I said, suppressing a laugh.

"Only the once," said Adam, shuddering at the memory. "They were so large we could have gone camping in them." Adam got serious. "But then Jimmy started hanging out with the Ayles boys."

The Ayles boys were a couple of years younger than us, but even as ten-year-olds they were terrifying. Their mother worked as a part-time charwoman at the manor house. She was the first woman I'd ever seen with peroxide blonde hair. An encounter that went a long way to explaining why I'd never dyed my naturally dark brown locks.

The Ayles family had not been a happy one, and it was common knowledge that their father sold drugs to anyone able to hand over the readies.

"Unfortunately, they were a prime example of the apple not falling far from the tree," said Adam. "Their dad was a perpetual offender and their poor mum couldn't say no to him."

This was true in more than one way. Mrs Ayles had gone on to have four girls after Griff and Terry. Goodness knew what kind of life they'd endured with such a father.

"Anyhow, Jimmy got mixed up with them, and then ten years ago they decided to break into the manor house." Adam paused to take a long sip of his beer. "Let's just say, it all went terribly wrong."

There was something in Adam's demeanor that I couldn't put my finger on. Anger? Disappointment? Relief that he'd not been that stupid? My thoughts turned to Belle and I hoped she'd not been in residence when the break-in occurred.

"Anyhow, they all went down. Luckily I saw the way the wind was blowing and got out well before."

I smiled, trying to lighten the mood. "So your criminal record consists of scrumping apples, stealing knickers, and swiping the occasional bottle of milk?"

"More or less," said Adam. "And then I left school and became a copper. Thought my dad was going to have a stroke when I told him."

Adam's family had been the absolute antithesis of Jimmy's. His mum was what they would now call a stay-at-home mum, complete with pinny and perpetually baking vanilla biscuits. His dad was a bricklayer by trade, but could turn his hand to anything. They were upstanding citizens who worked hard and enjoyed a drink down The Pig & Whistle every Friday night. I wondered if they were still alive.

It was as if Adam read my mind. "Both doing great. Dad's retired and they've got a holiday home in Lanzarote. Mum's over the moon. Dad pretends to hate it, but once he discovered Factor 50 and found a pub that served a decent pint you couldn't stop him."

"I'm sorry to hear about Jimmy. He was such a..." I paused. *What had Jimmy been? Crazy, charming, confident? A true rebel.* "Well, he was a lot of fun. And you? Are you married? Children?"

"Nope," Adam stared me straight in the eye. "Never found the right girl." Adam took a swig of beer. "Your turn. What have you been doing since that fateful summer?"

I gulped. "Actually, I met an American at one of Finolla's grand openings. Got married. Didn't work out. You know, the usual thing."

"I was sorry to hear about his passing," said Adam.

"What?" I choked on my pineapple juice. "Ryan died? But—"

Adam grinned. "According to Darcy Blythe he was blown up—by a train."

"Oh criminy," I said, reminded of my offhand comment to Wendy Williams. "Is nothing secret in this village?"

"Not a darn thing," said Adam. "So I take it that might have been blown out proportion slightly?"

I groaned at the pun. "Slightly."

"And how is that mother of yours?"

"I can reliably say that age has not mellowed her."

Adam nodded. No surprise there. "Kids?"

"Around thirty of them."

Adam looked like he was in danger of dropping his beer.

"Per class," I added. "I lead a boring, respectable life as a music teacher at Cedar Ridge Middle School, Austin, Texas."

Seeing the confusion on Adam's face, I added. "It's a school for eleven-to fourteen-year-olds. You know—the joyous troubled tween phase. But I enjoy it. They're good kids on the whole. Come from an affluent district, lots of money for private lessons, and they learn fast."

"I thought you were going to—"

I broke in. "We don't always follow our pipedreams, Adam."

Adam shrugged. "I didn't think it was a pipedream, Josie. And nor did Rose. You were a talented pianist. Very talented. Who was that guy you used to play? Something to do with knives?"

I peered at Adam, blankly.

"Eastern European? Russian, Scandinavian?"

The pub was starting to get busy and I raised my voice as I listed some of my favorite composers. "Grieg? Liszt? Chopin?"

"That's the one," said Adam, grinning. "Told you it was something to do with knives."

I groaned.

Carl appeared, carrying two plates. "A shepherd's pie for the lady," he said, placing an overflowing plate in front of me. "And bangers and mash for the gentleman."

"That'll do nicely, Carl," said Adam, unwrapping his cutlery and stuffing the serviette down his shirt.

There wasn't much talking, as Adam grabbed his fork with his right hand and his knife with his left and dug in. I enjoyed my food, but Adam devoured his. He had always eaten like he may never see food again. I'd been amazed to find out he was an only child, as this behavior, in my experience, was far more common in extensive families where you ate with gusto, or not at all.

There was no use trying to talk to Adam while he ate, so I plunged into piles of fluffy mashed potato to find perfectly seasoned lamb, tender carrots, and peas all nestled together in a thick gravy—perfection itself.

Ten minutes later Adam abandoned his knife and fork and removed the crumpled napkin from his shirt. "It's good to see you again, Josie."

I smiled, trying to ignore the disapproving stares from several patrons standing at the bar, pretending not to listen. "You too."

"In fact, if it wasn't under such circumstances I might—" Adam stopped in mid-sentence as his phone did a little jig. Adam sighed, flipped the phone over, and inspected the display. "Sorry, Josie, I should—" He grasped the phone and held it to his ear. "Ward," he said curtly.

I could hear muffled sounds and Adam's face lost its post-bangers and mash softness, to be replaced by his policeman's scowl. His brows furrowed and I assumed he was not getting good news. Adam barked a few commands into the phone before dropping it back onto the table.

"I'm going to have to go."

"Sure," I said. "Trouble in Milkwood?"

"You wouldn't believe me if I told you. Let's leave it at 'petty theft.'" Adam bent towards me as if to say one last thing, thought better of it, turned and left.

As the pub door slammed I realized I'd forgotten to tell him about the phone, the schedule, *and* the poison pen letters.

25

W ith nothing else to do, I decided to stay and read the local paper. I turned my back on the plethora of hostile stares emanating from the bar and dug in. Half of the front page was devoted to the murder, the other half outlined the spate of petty thefts in Milkwood. The section dedicated to Aunt Rose gave no details other than what I already knew. DI Ward described Aunt Rose as a stalwart member of the Milkwood community and the article ended with the usual, *The Police are asking the public to come forward if they have any information pertaining to this case and are asking for calm*—i.e. please help us as we're as baffled as you, but don't worry, we don't think there's a mass murderer on the loose.

I continued flipping through the paper, noticing another advert for Quentin Young's upcoming concert. I aced a four-star Sudoku and started the crossword puzzle, but I'd been in the US too long to be able to complete English crosswords anymore. There were way too many questions that required residency in the UK for the past ten years to answer proficiently. I could tell you what river runs through Shrewsbury, and name all six wives of Henry VIIII and in chronological order, but I could *not* tell you who won "The X Factor" or identify anyone new to British telly since circa 2000. Mind you, I couldn't tell you who won "American Idol" either.

The paper contained the traditional pictures of locals holding marrows and Girl Guides collecting bottle tops. On the back page was a picture of the local cricket team and, to my astonishment, I recognized several faces. In the top row stood Petruska's husband, Carl, and Wendy's husband, Duncan. Seated upright in the middle was the man who'd accused me of stealing his dead wife's clothes. However, most surprising was the man seated on the far right. To be honest, I'd have pegged Adam as more of a Crystal Palace supporter than a cricket fan.

The volume in The Dirty Duck was rising as fast as a Wagnerian opera, so I put away the paper and scanned the bar. Magna, Bonnie and Irene were clustered together in a formation reminiscent of the opening of *Macbeth*. I also recognized several patrons from my previous visit. Thankfully, they were not clutching pitchforks or baying for my blood. Maybe Belle had been right assuming the villagers would soon forget.

Suddenly the door burst open and a striking-looking man with shoulder-length white hair strode into the fray. Whereas the rest of the pub contained people in shorts or summer dresses, this man was dressed in a way that was best described with one word: theatrical. He wore an immaculate pair of white trousers, a matching waistcoat and a pale pink shirt with extremely floppy sleeves. The ensemble was finished off with white lace-up shoes and a Frank Sinatra fedora. I was under no illusion as to who it was, as well as becoming blindingly aware of why he was nicknamed "the angel."

I abandoned the paper and set off to make contact, giving the Witches of Milkwood as wide a berth as possible. Reaching the bar, I wedged myself in next to Quentin and tried to figure out how to start a conversation.

Petruska came to my rescue. "Josie, how is being zee shepherd's pie?"

"Please tell Carl it was delicious. Best one I've had in years."

"Zis is, in all likelihood, zee *only* one you have in years, but do not worry. Carl will not let zat stop him from feeling most superior."

I cut my eyes right and saw Quentin giving me the once over. I smiled and stuck out my hand. "Hi, I'm Josie Monroe. Rose Braith-waite's niece."

Quentin hesitated and I saw a flicker of something pass through his eyes. Straightening up, Milkwood's maestro grasped my hand and, as if we were in a 1940s musical, unexpectedly drew it to his lips.

"The pleasure is all mine," said Quentin, in a voice that used to be de rigueur on the BBC back in the 1960s. I would have bet my 1955 copy of the *Goldberg Variations* that the man had attended Oxford, Cambridge, Eton or Harrow—or maybe all four. Definitely not Dorking Comprehensive, that was for sure.

I removed my hand from Quentin's grasp and signaled Petruska for another drink.

"Same again?" she asked. I was becoming a regular, who knew.

"I think I might have something a bit stronger. How's your chardonnay?"

"Like gnats' piss," said Petruska. "Try zee pinot, it won't rot your gut."

"Pinot it is." I pulled out a tenner, and dropped it next to a beer-soaked bar towel. I was really going to have to figure out my finances, but right now I needed all the Italian courage I could muster.

Petruska reappeared with a glass filled to the brim with pale amber liquid. She placed it on the bar, grasped the tenner and tossed it towards me. "Your boyfriend opened a tab—we add zis to it."

"Actually, he's not my—" But Petruska had moved on to the next patron. I jammed the tenner back in my purse and focused on Quentin.

I took a gulp and smiled. "Did you know my aunt?"

Quentin took a sip of his pint. "I'd see her round and about. Mind you, everyone knows everyone in a village this size, you know."

Okay, this questioning was harder than it looked. DS Winter-bottom made it look easy. Maybe it was more about confidence. Darn, I was sunk. Luckily Quentin took up the conversation and, to his credit, never let go.

"Very sorry to hear about her death, though. Must have been a shock, finding her like that."

"I wouldn't want to repeat the experience."

"And you have no idea who perpetrated this abomination?"

What was with these people? Quentin was the third, or was it fourth, member of the public to ask me this. Did they not think if I knew who did it I'd have told the police and be jetting my way back to sunny Texas? I shook my head. "I didn't see a thing."

"Tragic," said Quentin, leaving me in some doubt as to whether he meant me finding my aunt's body or that I couldn't identify the killer.

"So when was the last time you saw my aunt?" I asked, in my most nonchalant voice.

Quentin took a long sip of beer. I'd been a teacher long enough to know that when you ask a child a question and they hesitate, it's because they're trying to conjure a lie. I waited to see what piece of fiction Quentin was doing his best to summon.

He replaced his pint on the bar and smiled. "Not for days. Possibly weeks."

Gotcha. Unless there was anyone else in the village with the initials QY, Quentin Young was telling a whopper. Now all I had to do was find out why.

26

Thirty minutes later I'd heard all about Quentin, his compositions and how everyone who was anyone would be at his concert next Saturday. Yeah—right. Call me skeptical, but I doubted a classical music concert in the middle of nowhere was going to pull a substantial crowd. I'd also encountered a boob brush and barely avoided a pinched bottom. Quentin was obviously not the angel his name might suggest.

After bidding goodnight to the effusive maestro, giving Petruska a wave goodbye and avoiding eye contact with the Witches of Milkwood, I headed out the door and ran bang smack into Daisy, Maisy, or was it Paisley, from New Zealand.

It was getting dark, but I was certain this was the lady I'd seen previously at the train station. Up close she bore an even more remarkable resemblance to Finolla. The likeness took my breath away.

"Hey," I said, sticking out my hand. "I'm Josie." Her name came back to me. "And you're...Daisy?"

Daisy didn't even make eye contact as she scooted past me into The Dirty Duck. I thought about following her, but confrontation was the last thing I needed. The woman was obviously either a) having a bad day, b) didn't want to talk to me or c) a complete cow. It was up to me to figure out which.

I puttered along Unthank Road and was about to swing a left

when something caught my attention. Knee deep in water and slurping from the middle of the ford was a substantial horse. What on earth was a horse doing out alone at this time of night? I took a step closer and then another. As the moonlight illuminated its coat I realized this was no horse. With a brown face and body and striped legs and undercarriage, this must be Belle's zedonk. I racked my brain for his name and then it came to me.

"Claude!" I exclaimed.

Claude glanced up from his evening libation, took one look at me, and charged. I should mention that when I say "charge," I don't mean in the opposite direction. I believe we've established that I am to bravery what Woody Allen is to cage fighting. That said, I dived into the bushes and reappeared only when the clip-clopping of zedonk hooves subsided into the distance.

I picked myself up and plucked off some leaves, several twigs and two hardy acorns and hoped against hope I'd not landed in a patch of nettles.

I continued down Brambley Lane, but this time I was more used to ominous rustlings from the hedgerow and did not become alarmed. Pausing, I called out and within seconds a plump grey tabby entwined himself around my ankles and omitted a hungry hiss. That was more like it.

"Come on boy, let's go home. I'll get you dinner." That must have sounded like a good idea to Elgar, as he trotted along beside me, more dog-like than feline.

As I approached the gate, I realized that Plum Tree was not empty. Lights were on and Puccini's arguably most famous aria, "Nessun dorma," was playing softly from Aunt Rose's study. Regardless of the sound level, my recent association with Puccini and death meant that my heart gave a lurch. As the aria predicted, not much sleep for *me* tonight while *Turandot* drifted from the windows.

Reaching the front door I tried the handle—unlocked—great. I stuck my head around the door and called out a hello. No answer. Was it Peter? Or was it the murderer come back to kill me to a tune forever associated with Italy's favorite tenor? I decided that if a killer lay in wait he was probably not going to be playing one of

England's most beloved tunes. With that crazy logic I knocked on Aunt Rose's study door and entered.

Peter paused like a child caught with his hand in the candy jar. His sapphire eyes darted back and forth, like he was watching some imaginary tennis tournament—I'm gonna go with Wimbledon, if I had to choose.

"Hi," I said. "Everything okay?"

Peter was one twitch away from developing a full-blown seizure. "Okay? Yes, yes, of course."

The man looked like he was about to develop a nervous tic.

"Why wouldn't I, er, be?"

"No reason, it's just you look a little..." I tried to figure out which word fitted here... Dislodged? Terror-struck? Apoplectic? All seemed appropriate in my head. None of them seemed kind if said out loud. I elected for "...unsettled?"

Peter grabbed a nearby stack of music and started to tidy. "Nope, all good here. In fact, I'm rather tired. I think I'm going to go to—"

His sentence was interrupted by a loud rat-a-tat-tat at the front door. I recognized the knock as easily as I recognized the perfume wafting from behind the study door.

I shelved that thought as the rapping became more forceful. Ah, that famous rat-a-tat-boom. I wondered if the perpetrator knew they were emulating the opening notes of Beethoven's Fifth? Probably not.

I strolled towards the front door and flung it open. Silhouetted against the porch light was a terrifying figure wreathed in black, their face hidden by a heavy lace veil—the kind not often seen unless visiting the pope or attending an Edwardian funeral.

I instinctively took a step back and inhaled a steadying breath. "Hello Mum."

Finolla Monroe was playing the grieving sister with gay abandon. From her oversized veiled hat and black gloves to her stylish knee high boots, the woman reeked of grief, glamour, and Galliano.

"Josie! Darling!" exclaimed Finolla, flinging her arms wide.

I cringed through several rounds of air kisses, finally giving way to Finolla as she swanned into the foyer, leaving three weeks of luggage on the doorstep. I decided we could deal with the suitcases later and slammed the door on Louis Vuitton and ten of his square brown friends.

"What are you doing here, Mum?"

"Doing? What do you mean, what am I doing? I have come to witness the burial of my beloved sister. That's what I'm doing."

"Mum, they haven't released the body yet. It's a murder inquiry. It could take weeks."

"Maybe we could have a wake?" said Finolla, pursing her lips.

I gave Finolla a look.

"Sit shiva?"

"Mum, we're Church of England. We just turn up on time and look sad."

"How about an open casket?" Finolla lifted her veil to reveal kohl rimmed eyes and scarlet stained lips.

It was then I remembered Peter.

Peter stood in the study doorway, looking even more flummoxed.

"Peter, I'd like to introduce you to my mother, Finolla Monroe."

Finolla spun like a ballerina at Sadler's Wells. "Darling, you didn't tell me we had company." Finolla studied Peter like she was about to sketch DaVinci's David, taking in every nook and crevice.

"Peter lives here," I explained.

"Oh, he does, does he? In what capacity?"

I'm not sure who spoke first, Peter or me, but the combined effect was the word "lodger" coming across loud and clear.

"Excellent. I've often thought of getting a lodger of my own," said Finolla, removing her glove finger by finger like she was Gipsy Freaking Rose Lee. I don't know who was more mortified, me or Peter, but I'd put odds on favorite it was me.

The glove removed, Finolla put her hand out to be shook, kissed—who knew? Peter bounded forward, grasped my mother's immaculately manicured hand and raised it to his lips. Truly, nothing ceases to amaze me anymore.

"And you might as well bring Wendy out," I said to Peter. "You can smell her from three counties away, and besides I can see her through the hinges."

"I...I don't know what..." Peter began, but luckily Wendy had more dignity. She stepped from behind the door, eyes full of loathing, until she spied Finolla. My mother has many personality defects: she can't cook, she has the patience of a gnat, and is always at least half an hour late for any and every event. However the woman has one enviable talent—being able to leave strangers utterly star struck, whether by her looks, her presence, or a combination of both. I've never figured it out, but my mother could bring Khachaturian's "Sabre Dance" to a halt in mid twirl. Wendy didn't stand a chance. Her whole face softened as she took in the vision in black and any spiteful words disintegrated like snowflakes in Texas.

"Oh hello, Wendy. Fancy seeing you here?" I said, trying not to smirk. If Wendy Williams hadn't hidden behind the door then I may not have given any thought to her presence. It was an active village, people must become friends. But the fact that she'd concealed herself, mixed with the pale pink lipstick staining the top of Peter's rumpled shirt, made the evidence conclusive.

"Wendy is it? Not the Wendy Williams Josie used to speak so highly of?"

"That's the one, Mum." I tried desperately not to roll my eyes.

I knew my mum. I could not be blinded by her beauty, her charm or her wiles—apparently, the only one this side of the continental divide who was immune. However, even I had to admit that Finolla was a connoisseur when it came to charm. She could have sold not only the ice to Eskimos, but the vodka and tonic that went with it. Wendy was putty in her hands.

Wendy staggered forwards, grasped the proffered hand and gave it a good sportsman-like shake. "I've heard so much about you. Read articles in the paper. *The Times*, no less. Is it true you once dated—"

Wendy was cut off, as Finolla raised a crimson tipped finger to her lips. "As I'm sure you understand—a lady never tells. Now, Josie. Why don't we leave these two fine people and you can put on the kettle and show me to my room. Peter, darling, would you be a love?" Finolla motioned towards the front door and Peter practically fell over his bedroom slippers in his attempt to do Finolla's bidding.

Finolla strolled along the passageway and I, like so often in life, followed. I grabbed the kettle, blasted it with water from the cold tap and set it on its cradle. This was the last thing I needed.

"Are you okay sleeping in Rose's room?" I asked, as a laden-down Peter staggered towards the kitchen door.

"Whatever's easiest, darling. I'd hate to put anyone out."

"Could you, Peter?" Considering Peter would have flown to the moon to purchase cheese if my mother had asked him, I figured it was a safe bet he would take my mother's luggage upstairs and deposit it in his deceased landlady's bedroom.

I decided to ignore the "put anyone out" comment. Did Finolla think arriving unannounced was not going to inconvenience anyone? It was then I remembered how hard I was to reach and decided to cut my unscrupulous mother a break.

I made the tea, set two cups on the counter and pulled out a chair.

"Mum?" Okay, I couldn't keep up the "mum" thing. It had been fine over the phone, but face to face it wasn't working. "Finolla, really, what are you doing here?"

Finolla removed her hat, a good idea for someone about to slurp down some tea. "Darling, I felt I needed to be here."

"But you hated Aunt Rose."

"Hate? Hate is a very harsh word, Josephina."

I hated it when my mother called me Josephina, but this did not seem the time to tell her.

"Okay, so let's just say you had a severe dislike and you'd barely spoken to each other in ten, fifteen—"

"Twenty," said Finolla, airily waving a hand.

"Exactly. I'm thinking if you wanted to get emotional you may have missed the boat."

"Bluntness is not an attractive quality, Josie. Remember that."

"But really, Finolla, I don't know when Aunt Rose's funeral is going to be. It could be days, weeks—months."

My mother reached out and touched my hand. "Then we'll face it together."

Oh, joy.

Per her instructions, an hour later I had changed Aunt Rose's bed linen, run Finolla an extremely bubbly bath, and boiled the kettle for a hot water bottle. The fact that it was summer was obviously lost on my mother. I also put together a plate of Belle's gourmet food, vetoed the idea of disappearing down the pub, and packed my mother off to bed with a cheery wave. Having a mother like Finolla was never easy. Her new role as grieving sister was going to be near impossible.

After feeding Elgar and doing the dishes I finally slipped into bed and pulled the covers high. Time to take stock:

1. Most of the villagers thought I was a murderer.
2. I had offended my only friend.
3. Peter was lying about when he returned from Prague.
4. Quentin was lying about when he last saw Aunt Rose.
5. How was I going to figure out why?
6. Why was Daisy from New Zealand ignoring me?
7. Who had written the poison pen letters to Aunt Rose?
8. How was I going to live in the same house as Finolla without another murder being committed?

Not knowing whether to be happy about Finolla's presence or appalled, I decided to settle on happy and learn to live with disappointment.

27

The door to my bedroom was flung open, the curtains tossed to one side, and my eye mask peeled back and let go with a snap. Finolla had always possessed the most dreadful habit of waking early. I'd reiterated over the years that artists were supposed to rise at noon and party till dawn. Finolla had the partying part down; unfortunately she hadn't mastered the sleeping part.

"Mum, you do know I'm on a different time zone, right?"

"Rubbish! When I fly to America I rise with the cock."

I decided it was not worth explaining that she could wake with the rooster because England was six hours ahead. Six o'clock in the morning in Texas was lunch time in England.

I knew from experience that it was easier to get out of bed, face the music and pray the aforementioned music was neither country nor rap.

"I thought we could tootle up to London and visit some friends, darling."

I wanted to meet my mother's friends about as much as I wanted to attempt Rachmaninov's third piano concerto before breakfast.

"See you in the kitchen," said Finolla, drifting back into the hallway.

I briefly thought about burrowing back under the sheets, but figured Finolla would only return. I was going to have to face the idea that I was up for the day. I ambled along the hallway, used the bathroom and creaked down the stairs.

Finolla had abandoned her mourning attire and donned a flowered pinny over a pair of jeans and plunging maroon top.

"Omelets, darling," said Finolla, flourishing a pan.

"Er, no thanks, Mum." I had not eaten egg whites since an unfortunate incident involving Wendy Williams' twelfth birthday party and an undercooked meringue. Nothing egg-like, be it benedict, Florentine, or deviled had passed my lips since – only the yolk, something that had caused me to be nicknamed "the egg lady" at my favorite local breakfast haunt in Austin.

I searched through the larder hoping for cereal. Damn, Aunt Rose ate way too healthy for me. Porridge, oats or granola seemed to be my only choices. But what was that nestling on the back shelf? Kellogg's Frosties. Bingo.

I grabbed a bowl, poured myself an obscenely large portion and was trudging towards the fridge for milk when the doorbell rang.

"I'll get that," called Peter.

Thirty seconds later Belle strolled into the kitchen carrying a purring Elgar. "I found him curled in a pothole," she said, by way of explanation.

I had never heard Elgar purr before. Belle must have the magic touch. I decided if Elgar was a peace offering I was happy to accept. I glanced towards Belle and mouthed the words "sorry" which made the corners of Belle's mouth twitch upwards. I wasn't sure why Belle had forgiven me, but I'd take it.

"Belle, this is my mother. Finolla, this is Belle DeCorcy."

Belle released Elgar, and crossed the room to shake my mother's hand.

"So nice to meet you." As always Belle was beautifully but simply dressed in a bias-cut emerald green dress and tight fitting pink cardigan. She reminded me of an English Lilly Pulitzer. Her hair was tied in a low ponytail and she smelled faintly of something floral.

I prayed that Belle was not going to be as star-struck as Peter and Wendy and, to give Belle credit, she didn't swoon or go all googly eyed. However, she did ask my mother about her latest show, which went on for forty minutes—approximately thirty-nine minutes too long, in my opinion. However the good news was it was long enough for me to eat my Frosties, pour myself a cup of tea, dunk in several Hobnobs, go upstairs, clean my teeth and get dressed.

I was coming out of the bathroom the same time Peter was emerging from his room. Other than our first inauspicious meeting and last night's debacle, I hadn't had a chance to actually chat with Aunt Rose's good-looking lodger.

Peter was dressed in his "accountant's" uniform of pressed trousers, button-down shirt and inoffensive tie. I swear, if I didn't know he was a musician I'd think he worked at a Fortune 500 company—one of the stuffier ones.

I had several things I wanted to ask, not least why he was lying about the date he arrived home from Prague, but not knowing how to insert that into the conversation I settled for my second most pressing question.

Peter had reached the top of the stairs and had one severely laced foot hovering over the precipice. It was now or never.

"Peter, Aunt Rose, she wasn't..." How to put this. "Erm, was she, you know?" Good grief, I was officially the worst interrogator in history. "What I'm trying to say is. When I first got to Milkwood I called Aunt Rose and she seemed to have forgotten I was coming. I'd only spoken with her the day before, so it seemed a little odd."

Peter gave the question some thought. "Rose was sharp. You know, she was, er, getting on a bit, but she was definitely compos mentis if that's what you're referring to."

I nodded. "Thanks."

I was happy to know Aunt Rose had been fully functioning, but it still didn't explain her reaction when I called.

By the time I returned to the kitchen Belle and Finolla had covered Gainsborough and Van Gogh and were galloping through Western Europe towards Gaudi.

Belle turned to look at me and smiled. "Are we still on for today?"

I stared blankly at my friend. "Today?"

"Yes, Finolla told me she was taking you up to town, but I told her I was afraid we'd made plans."

My eyes widened. "Oh, *those* plans."

Finolla replaced her cup on the counter. "Such a shame, darling. But do not fear, we will squeeze in some yummy mother-daughter time later."

"Absolutely." I gave Finolla a quick kiss on the cheek, grabbed my bag and practically waltzed out the door.

Roger was parked at a jaunty angle behind a sporty Lexus boasting the personalized license plate "FM001," which I assumed referred to Finolla's initials and not some low-on-the-dial radio station.

I sank into Roger's luxurious leather seat and Belle reversed along Brambley Lane at a speed that made me happy Elgar was tucked safely away in the kitchen.

"Where are we off to?" I asked. Although, to be frank, I didn't care. Any day not spent traipsing around London galleries with Finolla was a good day.

"It's a surprise," said Belle.

"Like the surprise shopping trip yesterday?" I asked, my heart sinking.

"Like that, but better," said Belle. "Trust me, you're going to love it. In the meantime tell me what's been happening since I last saw you."

I filled Belle in on the conversation with Quentin and Peter's ticket, but for some reason I still couldn't bring myself to tell her about the hate mail.

"Is there anybody else that has the initials QY? What about PU?"

Belle shook her head, or at least I think it was a shake, it was hard to tell as she bobbed and weaved along to Bobby McFerrin, who was insisting we not worry and be happy.

Roger sped west along the A25 before veering left into a car park. Belle slid into a space overlooking the expansive countryside spreading gloriously below and applied the handbrake.

"You must be wondering why we're here," said Belle, shifting to face me.

"You fancied a walk?" I suggested, spotting a windswept woman in muddy wellies and a sturdy Barbour plunging up the hill.

"I thought we could get inspiration," said Belle. "This is Newlands Corner."

I racked my brain, trying to recall what was special about Newlands Corner. I came up blank.

"December 1926? An abandoned car?" said Belle, unhelpfully.

Confused was the only expression I could muster. "I give up."

"The Queen of Crime herself." Belle added, mysteriously. "You must have heard of the disappearance of Agatha Christie. Dame Agatha went missing for almost two weeks."

"They found her in Harrogate, didn't they?"

Belle nodded, enthusiastically. "Newlands Corner is where the police found her abandoned vehicle."

My jaw dropped. "What are we waiting for?" I said, practically falling out of Roger in my haste. "Lead the way."

Half an hour later we'd legged it down the hill, past a brick structure that Belle identified as a Second World War pill box, and arrived at the old chalk pit to view the infamous spot. It was incredibly underwhelming, but regardless, I loved it.

As we turned and meandered back to Roger, I decided to grasp the moment. "Belle, I'm sorry about—"

Belle raised a hand. "Josie. I gave it some thought and realized that it was a long time ago. Truth be told, you're the first person in this village I actually like. I'm not going to let an event that happened so long ago get in the way."

"Well, I'm sorry all the same," I said. "It was a mean thing to do."

"Forget about it. It's water under the bridge." Belle paused. "Forgive the pun."

"And now, I guess, you can forget your grudge with Frosty Knickers?"

Belle stopped mid stride. "Never in a million years."

28

Belle cruised back towards Milkwood and into the village of Gomshall. Seeing there was a good chance Finolla was still at Plum Tree I decided to join Belle for lunch. I checked my watch and added six hours—just gone noon and my breakfast of Frosties seemed a long time ago.

Belle swung Roger into the carpark of Gomshall Mill. The seventeenth-century riverside restaurant had always been one of my favorites, due in part to its indoor view of the rustic waterwheel.

It had turned into a resplendent azure-skied day, but not warm enough by my Texan standards for outdoor seating. Our decision to sit indoors was strengthened by the presence of Bonnie Curry, Magna Carter and Irene Blogget huddled around a picnic table, looking suspiciously witch-like over their tomato soup and buttered rolls.

Unsurprisingly, it was Bonnie who hurled the initial insult. "If it's not the 'murderer' with her loony friend, Crazy Corcy" she said in a whisper so loud my friends back in Travis County could have heard.

A young couple with a cocker spaniel at their shoes and an elderly man, wearing coke bottle glasses, stared openly in our direction, while a middle-aged mother drew her toddler towards her knees.

I was getting sick of this and was about to tell the Witches of Milkwood what they could do with their unsubstantiated accusations when Belle grabbed me by the arm and hustled me bodily towards the entrance.

"Ignore them."

She must have felt some resistance because she continued. "Truly, Josie, they're not worth it. Believe me, I've had years of practice."

Inside we found a table close to the waterwheel and my indignation faded as Belle ordered the quiche and I ordered the cheapest thing on the menu—a ploughman's.

Belle reached into her bag and brought out Aunt Rose's schedule and a carefully folded piece of paper. "Now, don't get mad, Josie, but I went through it and noticed something odd." Belle opened the schedule to the second week in January and pushed the leather book across the table towards me. "Normally Rose writes what she's doing in full. If she's going into Dorking she'll write 'Dorking 11:00am' or if she's going to The Dirty Duck she'll write 'Dinner at *DD* 7:00pm' and always in a blue pen. But look at what she wrote on the 20th."

I examined the entry. In bold red letters were the initials *FG*.

"Now flip to February 20th."

I flipped forward and saw the initials *DL*. March had the initials *GS*, April *BC*, and May *WWF*, all in the same thick red pen.

"Initials again?"

"As a matter of fact, I think they are," said Belle.

"Well, I can guess April and May."

"Bonnie Curry and Wendy Williams Fitzpatrick," said Belle, nodding. "And I think I can take a stab at Florence Greene and Dan Ludlow for January and February."

"Who's Florence?"

"The vicar's wife," explained Belle, while taking great interest in the salt and pepper. She looked back up, her face slightly flushed.

"Your vicar is called Reverend Greene?" I suppressed a smile. "As in Reverend Greene in the ballroom with the candlestick, Reverend Greene?" I said, recalling the British game of Cluedo.

"The very one," said Belle, straightening the condiments. "And believe me, he's heard all the jokes—lead piping in the conservatory—all done to death." Belle smiled. "Forgive the pun."

"I love Milkwood," I said. "It's so darn quaint."

"Quite," said Belle, "but help me figure out who *GS* is."

I discarded my initial thought, seeing that William Gilbert and Arthur Sullivan were probably not residing in Milkwood, especially as they'd been dead over a hundred years. I thought back to everyone I'd met while in Milkwood and couldn't recall anyone whose name began with a "G." I glanced across the room and saw another flyer promoting Quentin Young's *Enchanted Summer* like the one I'd seen at Waspit's while chatting with Susan. "Gurminder Singh," I said, snapping my fingers.

"The Singhs own the Indian takeaway," said Belle. "But I don't believe either of them have the name Gurminder."

"It's their daughter," I said. "Ben Ludlow mentioned her when I was at the corner shop. He asked if Gurminder could come around and Susan said he had to ask Mrs Singh."

"Do you know, I think you might be spot on," said Belle. "Look at you, Miss Marple."

Our meals arrived and we both tucked in.

"Was there anything else in the schedule worth noting?" I asked, watching Belle cut her quiche into bite-sized portions.

Belle shook her head. "Not that I could work out. Just your regular kind of life things. Nothing that seemed relevant, but you might want to take a look before you hand it over to Snookums."

I decided to ignore the "Snookums" comment. "Will do," I said, balancing a wedge of Wensleydale onto a slither of crusty bread. Oh my, how I missed English food.

Belle hastily added more names to her rapidly growing list of "suspects" and launched her notebook towards me. I ran my eyes over the list and smiled, especially at the penultimate name and Belle's subsequent comment.

Suspect	Status	Reason
Bonnie Curry	Neighbor	Neighborly dispute?
Petruska and Carl Llewellyn	Pub Owners	Banned from DD – why?
Peter	Lodger	Lying about returning to UK
Quentin Young	Composer	Lying about when he last saw Rose.
Florence Greene	Vicar's wife	No earthly idea?
Dan Ludlow	Mother runs village shop	No idea?
Wendy Fitzpatrick	Runs local riding school	No idea?
Josie Monroe	Niece	Found body—obviously not guilty
Gurminder Singh	Parents own Indian takeaway	In cahoots with Dan?

There were far too many question marks for my liking, but at least it gave us a place to start. If I was going to be stuck in Milkwood I might as well keep busy.

"Of course, what we're forgetting is the murderer doesn't have to come from Milkwood," I said, stabbing a pickled onion.

"You're right, of course," said Belle. "But I have a feeling they do."

We finished our meals in companionable silence and I signaled for the bill. The waitress placed a saucer between us containing the bill and both Belle and I reached for it.

"Belle, you paid for lunch the other day. It's my turn."

Belle gave the plate a sharp tug in her direction. "That was to apologize for running you over."

I pulled the plate back in my direction. "And this is to apologize for chucking you in the river."

Belle raised her orange juice. "Resulting in my lifelong fear of water."

My eyes widened. "Really?"

"Don't be so silly. I overcame my water phobia the following summer. Holidaying in the Seychelles will do that."

I reached into my purse, pulled out my debit card and tossed it onto the plate. It bounced once and I prayed that would be the only bouncing it did. Our waitress approached the table, pulled out the rectangular credit card machine and swiped my card. I'm pretty sure I held my breath until the machine buzzed to life and spat out a receipt. I signed the paper, realizing that if the murder of Aunt Rose wasn't solved soon I would also have to find myself a job.

29

Belle and I stopped at a local stationer's and made two copies of Aunt Rose's schedule. We had decided to hand over the leather-bound book to whomever was on duty at Dorking Police Station. It seemed the easiest way to get the item into the hands of the police, with the added benefit of not having any explaining to do. That would, no doubt, come later. It would also give me time to figure out what to do with the poison pen letters. I had come to the inevitable conclusion that I'd have to hand them over, but this was something that needed to be done face to face. I would call Adam and fess up to finding them. Alternatively, I could wait for him to come to me, which probably wouldn't be long once he'd got his hands on the schedule.

After reintroducing myself to the desk clerk, Fitz, I relieved myself of the diary and walked as quickly as decency permitted towards the exit. Belle jettisoned out the car park and, before I knew it, we were careening down the A25 speeding back to Milkwood.

During our drive, Belle and I decided the best way to start our foray into detection was to start eliminating names off our suspect list—the easiest way of doing this being to work on establishing alibis. Whoever was left wouldn't necessarily *be* the murderer but, then again, you never knew. What can I say? We were novices, with absolutely no idea what we were doing but, in true British fashion, we were doing it anyway.

There had not been a single clown, ballerina or strongman adorning the police station, but as we passed an open field I saw a colossal yellow and white striped tent nestling in the shadow of the Denbies Hills. Ten minutes later Belle dropped me off on the south side of Milkwood and promised to see me later.

"I hope you understand, Josie, but I promised Daddy I'd help with a shooting party."

"Don't your brothers help with that kind of stuff?" I asked, hoping I'd remembered correctly about Belle having brothers.

"Jasper's in New Zealand, doing something with whales and Bay works in the City."

"Doing something with sharks?" I joshed, as Belle pulled away. That reminded me, I must try and corner Milkwood's own Kiwi, Daisy Pond.

I watched Belle accelerate around an unsuspecting weeping willow before disappearing in a flash of red and a puff of petrol.

I turned and strolled towards an opening in the hedgerow with a sign proclaiming Williams Riding Ranch. I smiled, unkindly, hoping the person whose job it was to answer the phone didn't have a lisp.

The air was redolent with that country smell that would normally be cow manure, but in this case was horse dung. I had many memories from my teens when Wendy's family had started a joint American/British style riding center and not all of them were bad.

I entered the courtyard and was greeted by a waggy-tailed border collie and two tabby cats. It was obvious the venture had proved profitable. The stables had been extended and upgraded since I last visited, but the picturesque cottage, nestled amongst a riot of honeysuckle, seemed to be unchanged, as were the surrounding paddocks with their wooden fences and faded jumps.

I scooched down and patted the puppy dog before heading towards the cottage's Hunter green front door. I checked my watch and did the calculation—almost 3:00pm. The local children would soon be out of school, but currently the stables were deserted. I hoped Wendy would be in residence and not off running errands before afternoon lessons.

A lot of city people think the countryside is peaceful. Nothing could be further from the truth. Okay, so we didn't have police sirens wailing into the night, or the emptying of clubs at 3:00 in the morning. Instead the air was filled with the clanking of combine harvesters, the rumbling of tractors, and the mooing, bleating or neighing of nearby livestock. However, through the cacophony of barnyard sounds I could hear music. Cluck a duck—it was Puccini and it was coming from the cottage.

My heartbeat started to samba. I rushed towards the front door, peeped through the square window and saw no sign of life—not a particularly good omen, in my opinion. I knocked—still no answer. Slowly, I turned the handle and let myself into, aptly named, Bridleway cottage.

I now recognized the music. One of the most famous arias of all time, "Un bel dì vedremo," better known as "One Fine Day," which, if I knew anything about sopranos—and I was pretty sure I did— was being perfectly executed by the remarkable Renée Fleming.

Okay, so it wasn't a death scene, but it was arguably the saddest aria ever written as Butterfly pines for her lover, the rascal Pinkerton. The music emanated from behind the door on my left. I moved closer and put my ear to the wood. Nothing but Renée declaring her love. There seemed nothing for it but to enter. My hand shook slightly as I turned the handle and eased open the door. I found myself in a sitting room with two high-backed armchairs facing an unlit fireplace. Sprawled, with one arm flung over the side, head back and eyes closed, was Wendy Williams Fitzpatrick.

This was going to go down a treat with Frosty Knickers. For some reason Oscar Wilde came to mind as I misquoted *The Importance of Being Earnest*: "To find one dead body may be regarded as misfortune. To find two looks like carelessness."

I moved closer to the lifeless body and bent forward to listen for breathing. I couldn't help but notice that her face was puffy and her eyes red. Had she been strangled? It was at that precise moment that Wendy Williams opened her eyes and walloped me around the head.

30

What in cluck's name do you think you're doing?" I asked, from my face down position on a well-worn rug.

"I could ask you the same question," said Wendy, rising to her feet.

"I thought you were...well, I thought you might have been sick or, you know, dead." I struggled to a sitting position and thought for one minuscule second that Wendy might offer me a hand. Good job I didn't waste a second more on that thought.

"Why on earth would I be dead, you stupid girl? I was taking a power nap."

I decided to ignore the "stupid girl" comment.

"Oh, I don't know. Maybe it has something to do with the fact that you didn't seem to be breathing, and the fact that you were blasting Pu..." I petered out. It did seem a little ridiculous. People napped in the day. Not teachers, perhaps, but I'd heard of others in less structured professions who indulged in such pleasurable pursuits. It was then I noticed a sea of tissues around the base of Wendy's chair. Had the hard-as-nails Wendy Williams been crying, and if so, why?

"What are you doing here?" Wendy lunged towards the stereo, lowering the volume on "The Humming Chorus"—the only aria my ex bragged he knew all the words to—to pianissimo.

I rose to my feet. What *was* I doing here? The shock of discovering what I'd presumed to be a dead Wendy Williams, plus the whack around my temple, left me temporarily confused—at least I hoped it was temporary. My purpose came back to me with a jolt—find out where Wendy Williams was on Sunday night. But how? This detecting lark was harder than fictional sleuths made out.

"I wanted to, erm, you know, see how you were doing?"

Wendy stared at me with utter incomprehension. I might as well have told her I was about to scale Kilimanjaro, Steinway and all.

"Well, you know. We didn't exactly have much of a chance to talk the other day. I thought we could, you know, catch up." Even as the words exited my mouth I could hear their hollowness. She was never going to fall for this.

"Do you know what time it is?" asked Wendy.

"Er..." This was not the response I was expecting.

Wendy pointed towards an empty spot on the mantelpiece. "Darn carriage clock went missing last week. I keep asking Duncan to buy a new one, but you know what men are like—bloody useless."

"It's getting on for 3:15," I said glancing at my watch.

"Good Lord!" said Wendy. "Then you can make yourself useful. Help me get the ponies ready for this afternoon's lesson."

"Great," I said, forcing a smile. I hadn't saddled a horse since my late teens. Surely it was like riding a bicycle? There was a bridle, a bit and a saddle. As long as I remembered which part went in the mouth and which went on the back I should be home and dry.

I followed Wendy into the courtyard and over to the stables. Wendy had never been what you'd call a "people person," but, as was so often the case when someone was socially inept, they excelled when it came to animals. Wendy was no exception. As she strolled past the boxes, the horses nuzzled towards her outstretched palm as she patted the occasional nose or mane.

"Here, we'll start with Ace and Tinkerbell." Wendy indicated two stalls next to each other. "I'll take Ace, you can saddle Tink, but be careful, she nips."

Of course she does, I thought, unlatching the stable door.

"Nice Tinkerbell. Good Tinkerbell," I whispered, approaching the mare. Tinkerbell lowered her muzzle and I swear she gave me a look.

I grabbed Tink's bridle and edged my way towards the nippy end. I decided to avoid the whole issue of Wendy and Peter and stay closer to home. "So, Duncan seems nice," I said, trying to encourage Tinkerbell to open her mouth.

There was no answer.

"Seems, you know, dependable."

There still was no answer. It seemed I was going to have to forget trying to be sneaky and go for forthright. "Did you like Aunt Rose?" I yelled through the wooden partition.

Wendy appeared at the gate leading Ace by the reins. Damn she was quick. I stuffed Tinkerbell's bit into her mouth and tossed the reins over her ears.

"Like your aunt? What a strange question."

"It's just I heard she could be..." What was the correct terminology? Belle had called her "horrid." I decided on "difficult."

A plump teenager with Scandinavian blonde hair and pink cheeks strolled over to the side of the box and gave Ace's mane a stroke.

"Ah, Lucy," said Wendy, with a sniff that spoke volumes. "About time. How about you saddle Giselle and Kipper and meet us in the paddock."

Lucy gave a curt nod, turned and disappeared into the next box where I could hear her softly humming "I Vow to Thee My Country" from Holst's "Jupiter." I loved it when teenagers liked classical music.

The bridle secured, I grasped Tinkerbell's saddle and aimed it towards her ample flank. "So, do you have any idea who may have killed Aunt Rose?" I continued.

"No, I most certainly do not," said Wendy, as she adjusted a stirrup. "I don't waste my time on such matters. Rumors around the village insinuated that the woman was an utter nuisance."

"Interesting," I said, trying to keep my voice calm. "I have to say, that's not the Aunt Rose I knew. Back when I was a kid she was a lot of fun."

"Times change. If you have to know, Rose Braithwaite was a manipulative, evil witch," and with that, Wendy Williams led Ace out of the stable and our conversation was over.

Don't hold back, tell me what you really think, were the words I was thinking, but by the time I got around to saying them Wendy was gone. Timing had never been my forté.

I was tightening the saddle when Lucy materialized. "Ignore her. She's pissed because Duncan came home late from some wedding he'd been to up north."

"Oh, really?"

"Apparently he got absolutely plastered and missed his train. Had to catch a ride back Sunday evening."

"Wendy told you this?" I asked, unable to believe Wendy would share such information with her stable girl.

"I read between the lines," said Lucy, tucking a stray blonde hair behind her ear.

"Why didn't Wendy go with him? You know, out of curiosity."

"We had a gymkhana. It was bad timing. Besides, who wants to go to the wedding of some trumped-up deb?"

I decided this was *not* the moment to mention the trumped-up deb was my half-sister. I thought back to Wendy's puffy eyes and the discarded tissues. "So Wendy was upset about Duncan coming home late? It's just she seemed a bit, erm, sad earlier."

"Cripes, no. She's pissed at Duncan for missing his train, but honestly, she couldn't give two hoots." Lucy leaned back to make sure Wendy was out of earshot. "If you ask me, the reason she's so miserable is because her boyfriend dumped her."

31

I left Tinkerbell in the paddock and waved my goodbyes. It would take fifteen minutes to reach Milkwood and was a stroll I'd always enjoyed, ambling through the lanes in the shade of the towering hedges.

I thought about what I'd achieved in the past hour—not much, unless you consider being whacked in the head and called "stupid" an achievement. Obviously, Wendy and Duncan's marriage was not as strong as she pretended, but this did not come as a surprise. I had also already surmised Wendy was having an affair. Why else hide behind the door in Aunt Rose's study?

However, hearing about Peter and Wendy's breakup was news to me and it seemed it was Peter who had initiated the breaking. I wondered if the reason for their split had anything to do with Aunt Rose's death? Probably not, but you never knew.

I'd been on the road about five minutes when a mud-splattered Land Rover meandered around the corner. The rule when traversing narrow country lanes is to stick to the side of oncoming traffic. Roads, like those surrounding Milkwood, date back as far as Cromwell, if not before. The roads are narrow and the hedgerows vast. To counteract this conundrum, dotted at various intervals are slender laybys for traffic to pass safely. It wasn't going to help if you met a lorry or a combine harvester, but for most eventualities the cutouts sufficed.

I was approaching such a layby and hustled into the mud-rutted grooves to wait for the Land Rover to pass. It didn't. Instead it lurched alongside me and the passenger window powered down. It was Duncan and he looked worried.

"Hi, erm..." he began.

I waited for Duncan to recall my name. For heaven's sake, the man had proposed marriage to me five days ago.

"Jackie?"

I shook my head.

"Jenny? Jamie? Saints be with me."

Okay, so he had the initial letter and the number of syllables correct. I'd cut the guy a break.

"It's Josie."

"That's right, Josie. Sorry. I..." Duncan eyed the two teenagers in the back. They were wearing earbuds and were engrossed in their phones. Satisfied they weren't paying attention, he continued. "I wanted to apologize for, you know."

"It's okay. You're forgiven."

"It's just if Wendy found out." Duncan lowered his voice. "I'm under no illusions. The woman would kill me."

I smiled. Obviously Duncan didn't know about Wendy's philandering, and I was *not* going to be the person to tell him.

Duncan misread the look on my face as one of disbelief. "No truly, she would. Once the gardener dug up her petunias mistaking them for some type of weed. The woman went after him with a pitchfork."

I stored this away under useful information, as well as a reminder to never hire Wendy's gardener.

"We don't have the best marriage but, you know, we have the wee bairns," said Duncan with a quick glance at the two teenagers, made oblivious by technology.

"Don't worry," I said, "I haven't said a thing and I won't."

The relief on Duncan's face was palpable. "That's grand. Actually, I don't know what came over me. I did my best to find you on Sunday. I wanted to apologize, but your mum said you'd already left."

"Yeah. Spending time with my extended family is not my forté."

Duncan smiled. "Not mine either, but your mum was, actually... well, she was a delight. Told me all about her exhibitions and her time in France and..."

The list of Finolla's accomplishments and adventures rolled on —the escapades in Rome, the art auctions in Paris, the jail time in Barcelona. Sounded like Finolla had held nothing back. This was so typical. Duncan had gone in search of me and instead found himself subject to the Finolla Monroe episode of *This Is Your Life*.

"Actually, chatting with your mum was the best part of my weekend. Or at least the only part I can remember with any sort of clarity. I have to say, it was awfully kind of her to give me the lift back to Milkwood."

My jaw dropped. "Wait a second. Finolla took you home?"

"Aye. Said she was heading down this way. I was stupid enough to miss my train. Had a bit of a hangover, if you can believe it." Duncan rubbed his temple as he relived the memory.

"What time did you get back?"

"Och, it was around seven. Luckily Wendy was out when I arrived. Thought I might be able to fudge it, but she stormed in an hour or so later nigh on furious."

I couldn't believe it. This meant Finolla had been in Milkwood an hour before Aunt Rose was murdered. I'd assumed she was still in Shropshire and she'd given me no reason to think otherwise. Suspicious or merely Finolla-like? Either way it meant that the person who disliked Rose Braithwaite more than anybody in the entire universe had been in the vicinity at the time she died.

I felt like the worst daughter in the world, but as soon as I got home I was going to get out Belle's list of suspects and add Finolla Monroe.

32

I encountered three more cars on my stroll from the riding center, a Lycra-clad cyclist, and a dozen of Farmer Dale's prized and, I may add, incredibly slow Herefordshires. I averted my eyes as I strolled past both Crumbs and Irene's Milk Jug and waved hello to Petruska as she exited the corner shop carrying two yellow shopping bags.

The lukewarm sun had produced a flurry of young mums fussing around their trailing offspring. I paused to watch Milkwood's youngest residents toddle around the duck pond. The duck pond was deeper than it looked. I knew this due to a regrettable, but memorable, pond submersion aged six, and the reason my father made sure I could swim like a fish by seven.

I smiled at the memory, only to realize that every mother had shepherded their child behind their knees and were staring at me with open hostility. Deciding this was probably not the time to proclaim my innocence, I gave them a little wave and hurried along Unthank Road. In fact, I was hurrying so hard that I didn't see the gate to Wisteria Villa swing open and a young boy emerge. My reaction was quick, and the only thing to hit the deck, this time, was the shopping bag he carried.

The teenager bent to scoop up the familiar yellow bag and when he straightened I stared into the steadfast eyes of Dan

Ludlow, great grandson of the formidable Mrs Waspit, son of corner shop owner Susan Ludlow.

"Sorry," Dan mumbled, before scuttling across the road and up the path of Clandon House.

Susan had mentioned that deliveries kept the corner shop in business and I assumed this was what Dan was doing.

I continued towards Brambley Lane and ten minutes later found myself at the familiar iron gate. Finolla's silver Lexus was parked at an impudent angle and, as it was best to do when it came to all things Finolla, I steeled myself for all eventualities.

I entered Plum Tree Cottage, not to the sound of Puccini, but to the sound of laughter—male laughter. I darted towards the kitchen. Which unsuspecting man had Finolla sunk her claws in today? I almost put my ear to the door, but to quote Finolla, "one should never listen at doors, especially if there's a chance one's going to get caught."

Instead, I inched open the door and found Finolla in Adam's arms and, if I wasn't mistaken, they were doing the tango. I'll be honest, I was speechless. Not so Finolla.

"Josie, darling, you're back and just in time."

"Just in time for what?" I could hear the petulance creep into my voice and, gosh darn it, I couldn't do a blessed thing to stop it.

"To be my partner. Adam here is hopeless. Here, let's show him how it's done. I'll lead, shall I?"

Before I had a chance to protest, Finolla pressed a switch on the CD player and Astor Piazzolla's *Libertango* blasted across the toaster. Next thing I knew, Finolla had me in a vise grip, arms locked, toes pointed and was leading me across the floor towards the dustbin. Our faces were cheek to cheek and I took advantage of this.

"What the heck do you think you're doing?"

"Oh darling, don't tell me all those dance lessons were wasted?"

I heard a snigger. I was going to slap Adam Ward when I got out of this.

"Argentinian tango, darling. That summer in Buenos Aires with Tomás. *Bueno!*"

"It was Joaquín," I corrected, instinctively kicking my leg backward from the knee. "And I got hives from my polyester hot pants."

Finolla dipped me and I hung on for dear life. "I'd forgotten that part. All that calamine lotion. The Pink Panther had nothing on you."

"Yeah, it was hysterical," I hissed.

Finolla broke away, letting me tumble to the floor. "Oh, Josie, was it really that bad? Remember the empanadas, the chimichurri, the Malbec?"

"Mum, I was thirteen." Although, as a matter of fact, I did recall the Malbec—it had been superb.

"Oh, that's right—dreadfully awkward age."

"Can you tell me what you're doing?" I held up a hand as I staggered to my feet. "No, wait, I don't even want to know." It was amazing how quickly Finolla had dropped the grieving sister routine.

Finolla wafted towards the kitchen counter, grasped a half-empty wine glass, and raised it to her cherry-red lips. "Actually, it's rather a funny story. I was lunching at some fabulous trattoria on the South Bank, which is quite lovely these days, you know. When, of all the people in the world, I bumped into Steven."

My stare was blank.

"You must remember Steven, darling?"

A list of famous Stevens ran through my mind. Spielberg, Fry, King, Martin? In all honesty it could be any one of them.

"You know, Steven—the Marquess."

I drew a blank. There had been a stream of Earls, Barons and Dukes flowing in and out of my childhood. Frankly, I'd lost track.

"Oh, that Steven," I replied.

Finolla did not look convinced. "Anyhow, the darling boy has invited me to his country estate for the weekend and I've accepted. There will be a spot of polo, and apparently he's invited a couple of Argentinians."

"And this brought on the tango?" I asked, incredulously.

"One can never be too prepared," said Finolla. "Anyhow, you don't mind, do you, darling? I thought it might help, you know, with my grief."

I shook my head mutely. There really was no arguing.

"Besides, Alan, here—"

"It's Adam," said Adam and I together.

"Oh, silly me, yes of course, Adam here explained it could be quite the time until Rose is released."

She made it sound like Rose was coming out of rehab, rather than her body being set free for burial.

Before I had a chance to respond, Finolla's phone trilled to life. She studied the screen and her entire face lit up. "Steven —sweetie..."

33

A dam grabbed my hand and pulled me into the hallway. "Thank God you showed up. She'd started mentioning the mambo. I don't even know what a mambo is. I thought it was some kind of snake."

Adam and I were crammed in the hallway wedged sideways between the disapproving Edwardian stares of Holst and Delius.

"I can barely waltz," continued Adam.

"You can *waltz*?"

Adam rolled his eyes. "My mum taught me by making me stand on her feet when I was young."

I could imagine Adam's mum doing this. Dora was a sweetheart and would consider teaching her son to dance a mother's duty.

"You were laughing," I said, accusingly.

"Was I?" Adam swept a stray hair from my cheek. "I can only put it down to nerves. Dancing has never been my strong suit. But what about you? You kept those dancing lessons a secret."

"Not a highlight of my adolescence. I was always more comfortable playing instruments than dancing to them."

"Oh, I don't know," said Adam, inching closer. "You looked pretty good in there. If you hadn't been dancing with Finolla, it could even have been sexy."

I gave him a look. I was many things. Sexy was not one of them.

Adam swiped his pointy finger across his chest. My heart fluttered at the cuteness.

"Were you here to see Finolla?" I asked.

Adam's eyebrows rose incredulously. "No, I was here to ask you about this." Adam reached into his jacket and pulled out the familiar leather schedule. In an instant he was back to being professional.

"Oh!"

"Yes, Oh. My team searched the entire house, so the question is, where did you find this?"

I motioned Adam to follow me as I clambered up the stairs. I had no idea what to tell him and decided feigning ignorance was my best option.

I took a right and flung open the door to Aunt Rose's bedroom. The order and neatness had evaporated with clothes hanging from every surface imaginable. Shoes littered the floor and Aunt Rose's pristine desk was now being used as a makeup station. The bed was unmade and a filmy nightdress dangled from the bedpost.

Hopscotching over to the desk, I located the tiny switch. The drawer clicked open and I pulled it towards me.

"Ah," said Adam. "And you found this when?"

I hated lying, but I did it anyway. I turned my back and picked a path through the jumble of Louis Vuitton cases. "Last night."

"Josie, I am going to take this opportunity to remind you that there is a murderer out there. This is not some kind of game. Not to scare you, but someone who can kill once can kill again."

I gulped. When I turned Adam was feeling in the drawer.

"And what about these?" said Adam, eyebrows raised.

"What about what?" I asked, feeling my cheeks flush.

Adam reached into his pocket and removed a pair of latex gloves. Talk about being prepared. He snapped them on before pulling out the letters.

"What are *they*?" I said, with an indecent amount of innocence.

Adam held up a piece of paper so I could read it. I managed to grab it. My fingerprints were going to be all over them, I might as well endure the wrath of Adam now than suffer the accusations later. Adam looked at me bemused. I obviously wasn't fooling him for a moment.

"Flippity flip flops," I said, genuinely surprised. Before I realized what I was doing I grabbed another, then another.

The notes were the same, but this time I spied something I'd previously overlooked—a tiny red mark in the bottom right hand corner, a corresponding set of familiar initials.

34

Adam bagged the poison pen letters and returned to Dorking. He had immediately seen the connection between the initials on the letters and the initials in Aunt Rose's schedule. I had to come to terms with the sad fact that Aunt Rose had not been the recipient of the poison pen letters, but more likely the originator. I had also mentioned the missing phone—something else Adam was fully aware of.

I retired to my room and sprawled on top of the mustard-colored eiderdown. How could this be? How could my aunt be the kind of person who wrote mean letters to people? Some of the recipients were practically children. It made no sense and what was worse, it meant I had to reassess the horrifying fact that Finolla may have been right. She'd always insisted that her sister was mean-spirited and petty, and I always thought she was being typically Finolla—i.e. someone with no judge of character.

There was a knock on my door and Finolla swanned in.

"Darling, I'm ravenous. Do they have food in this hole of hell or should I order from Fortnum's?"

I wanted to continue to lie on my bed with a pillow over my head, but my stomach was betraying me.

Finolla eyed my wrinkled tee and jeans.

I raised my hand. "Don't say a word."

Fifteen minutes later I had run a comb through my hair, swiped on some lipstick, and was ready to go. I tossed some kitty kibble into Elgar's bowl and gave water to the yellow roses of Texas that were busy dying on the kitchen table.

"Do you think we could go somewhere local? Somewhere within walking distance?" I asked, as Finolla pulled out her car keys.

"Absolutely. Let's rough it, darling." Finolla linked her arm through mine as we promenaded along Brambley Lane.

"Mum, I need to ask you something."

"Of course, darling, anything, but if it's to do with that little incident regarding the Balfour ruby I'm going to plead the fifth. Besides it was a present and my solicitors have stated I'm under no legal obligation to give it back."

I frowned. "You can't plead the fifth. This is not the States. Besides...wait a second! *What* Balfour ruby?"

Finolla waved an airy hand and I gave up.

"It's got nothing to do with jewelry," I continued. "This is about Sunday."

There was silence.

"I was talking to Wendy Williams' husband, Duncan, and he said you gave him a lift back to Milkwood."

"Did I?"

"Yes. Which leads me to the question. Did you visit Aunt Rose?"

More silence.

"Mum, I know you did."

"Oh, darling, don't be so silly, you couldn't possibly know."

"The roses in the kitchen. They're the same as the roses at Imogen's wedding."

"Ah! You noticed that, did you?"

"Well, duh! Mum, what were you doing there?"

Finolla ran a hand through her perfectly coiffed hair. "Thought I'd stop by and, you know, say hello."

"What?"

"It had been an absolute age since I'd seen Rose. I thought it was time to—what's that saying? Bury the hatchet."

I decided to ignore the unfortunate metaphor.

"Really, Mum? You've not spoken to Aunt Rose in..." I petered out. I was hardly one to judge on this front.

"Anyway, it's all utterly irrelevant because Rose, in her usual slapdash fashion, was not there to greet me," said Finolla.

The fact that Finolla's arrival, the first in two decades, had been totally unexpected was lost on my mother. I let it go.

"What time did you arrive?"

"I don't know, Josie. You know me, timekeeping is not my strong point. Anyway, as I said, Rose wasn't there, so I let myself in, dropped off the flowers, and left."

I decided to not even ask how she'd gained access. I doubted it was via the sycamore tree. "Did you see anyone?"

"Like who, darling?"

"Like the murderer, Mum."

"Oh, I don't think so."

"You don't think so? Think, Finolla. It's kind of important. Aunt Rose was dead within an hour of your visit. If this was planned the murderer could have been there already, or at least hanging around."

"Oh, I'm sure that wasn't the case."

How could Finolla be so sure? Of course, the obvious solution was that she'd been the one who'd thrust Aunt Rose to her untimely death. I decided to shelve this thought under highly unlikely. Okay, maybe not *highly* unlikely, but hopefully untrue.

Finolla took a right towards The Dirty Duck, and I put out a hand to stop her.

"Would you mind if we ate at The Pig & Whistle? I really can't bear another evening of angry looks and insinuations."

Finolla looked like she was about to comment on my lack of self-confidence, but to my surprise she settled for, "Anything you want, darling."

"Then The Pig & Whistle, it is." Steering Finolla left, we passed the corner shop and Frosty Knickers' flat. We had barely reached the salmon pink building housing Milkwood's second public house when the door opened and Daisy Pond came bustling out. She took one look at Finolla and the blood drained from her face.

Finolla barely raised an eyebrow. "Oh hello, Daisy. Fancy seeing you here."

"You know this woman?" I asked, wondering if there was truly anyone in this world Finolla did not know.

Finolla gave me a look halfway between incredulity and pity. "Of course I know her, Josephina. She's my twin."

35

I had to take my hat off to Finolla. If one was judged by their ability to deal with the unexpected, Finolla would be valedictorian of the entire British Isles and a healthy portion of Western Europe. Her cool demeanor was one of a long list of characteristics I had not inherited, like her confidence, her success and her ability to ensnare men.

Daisy recovered her composure next and was the one who guided me into The Pig & Whistle for a cozy little talk—sister to sister.

The pub was not how I remembered. Gone were the dark-wooded booths and cozy nooks, replaced by shining steel and glass-topped tables. Two gaming machines pinged and whizzed from a far corner, and a band I couldn't recall the name of wailed from a loudspeaker so shrilly that I was beginning to wish we had gone to The Dirty Duck.

Regardless of the decor, it was a night I would never forget. I had lost one aunt and gained another—but how? How could I have lived my entire life and not known about a third sister?

"It's complicated," said Daisy, her New Zealand twang making it even more surreal, as I dumped a round of drinks on the table with an unceremonious clunk.

Up close it became obvious that Finolla and Daisy were not identical twins. But the likeness was palpable. Finolla's money and success had afforded her the best in skin care, personal trainers and chefs. Her hair was blonde and her waist was tight. Daisy was two shades darker from time spent in the Kiwi sun, plus her hair was coarser, greyer and styled with far more practicality in mind. However, with the same intelligent blue eyes, snub noses and high cheekbones there was no doubt they were sisters.

"But why has no one ever mentioned you?" I turned accusingly to Finolla. "Does Dad know about this?"

"I may have mentioned it once or twice. Let's just say I had some explaining to do when he unearthed one of my baby pictures and there were two of me."

I was instantly aware that I had never seen baby or childhood pictures of my mother. It occurred to me that this was probably not normal.

"It's really not a big deal," said Finolla. "Daisy left home when she was eighteen and we all kind of forgot about her."

"Forgot about her? That's awful," I said.

"In Finolla's defense, it was my decision to head out for a bit of a wander," said Daisy, raising her pint.

"And if memory serves correctly, it was also your decision to drop all contact with the family and ban us from writing to you," said Finolla, taking a sip of The Pig & Whistle's finest merlot and wincing.

"She's got a point," said Daisy, nodding.

"But why?" I asked, truly puzzled.

"Did she ever meet Mum?" Daisy asked.

"Once," replied Finolla. "Luckily she was too young for Mum to inflict any permanent damage."

This was getting curiouser and curiouser. "Nanny Braithwaite died when I was a toddler, right?"

"Yeah, let's go with that," said Daisy, downing another gulp.

"You mean she's not dead?"

Both sisters were silent. I was totally confused. As far as I knew both Nan and Grandad had gone to meet their maker many years ago, and if Finolla had ever been invited to get together with aunts, uncles or cousins, it had most certainly not been with me.

"Let's just say me and Mum didn't get on," said Daisy, neatly changing the subject.

"There's the understatement of the year," said Finolla, risking another sip of merlot.

"Yeah, there were a few humdingers," said Daisy. "So I left home, took the first boat to New Zealand and started over. Met a good bloke, Teddy Pond, and settled me self down. Seemed like it was for the best, at the time."

"I can understand that," I said, giving Finolla a sideways glance.

"Oh, darling," said Finolla, "compared to Daisy and Lillian, you and I were like..." Finolla paused to think. "Let's just say we never had the neighbors call the police...or MI5, for that matter."

MI5? Wow! "And you guys have not spoken since?" I asked, incredulously.

"Not a word," said Finolla. "Mind you I *have* been rather busy."

"Me too," countered Daisy.

"Really, doing what?" asked Finolla.

"I could ask the same question," said Daisy.

I could see this was going nowhere. "But *why* are you in Milkwood? Were you here to see Rose?"

"I came on business," said Daisy. "Thought I'd stop by and see Rosie. Nothing wrong with going to see my older, *sweeter* sister. Perfectly acceptable as far as I can tell."

"But she was on vacation," I said. "And you waited for her to get back? Sounds more than just a spur of the moment visit to me."

And that was where it had ended. Daisy had clammed up and Finolla had upended her questionable merlot, declaring she was no longer hungry. Both women had, to coin a phrase best associated with Elvis, "left the building," and I sat there shell-shocked, wondering what else my mother had not mentioned over the course of my life.

36

By the time I'd paid the tab, both Finolla and Daisy were nowhere to be seen. I imagined Daisy had returned to her bed and breakfast and Finolla—who knew? One could assume she was retreating to Plum Tree Cottage, but she could just as easily be heading to The Dirty Duck, the West End, or Magaluf.

I strolled along Peacemeal Street until the intoxicating smell of chicken korma brought me to a stop. Finolla had given me her debit card to pay for our drinks. Seemed like it would still be within the spirit of "having dinner with my mother" if I used the card to actually buy us dinner, and I could think of no better place to splurge than Naan's Takeaway.

I grappled with the door and stepped inside. Naan's was empty, other than a young girl slouched behind a utilitarian counter, engrossed in her phone.

"We're out of lamb," the girl said, without looking up. "Something to do with a balls up at the local farm."

"You source your ingredients locally?" I asked.

"Da no. We're just out of lamb, all right?"

I approached the counter, retrieved a slender menu, and flipped it open. It had been a long time since I'd experienced exceptional Indian food. The Indian food in Austin wasn't bad, but in my memory even the lousiest Indian takeaway in England compared favorably to Indian food in the States.

My salivary glands went into overdrive as I perused the menu. I skipped over the lamb section and placed my order, three appetizers and three main dishes (medium spice) with rice and several plain naans, figuring there was nothing better than leftovers. I replaced the menu next to a cute statue of a multi-armed elephant and retired to one of the padded chairs located underneath a silenced TV.

As soon as the order was placed the girl went back to her phone. She was a pretty girl, around seventeen, with dark hair pulled into a thick ponytail and wearing the same familiar tie and blazer as Dan Ludlow.

I flashed back to Dan's reference to Gurminder Singh. Unless Gurminder had a sister I assumed this must be the girl in question and, if so, was she also the girl whose initials appeared in Aunt Rose's schedule and on one of the poison pen letters? There were not too many teenagers in the village. There was also not a lot of diversity. Until entering Naan's the only other Asian I'd encountered since arriving in Milkwood was Helen Winterbottom, and Petruska being the one token Eastern European. Of course, you only had to take a train ride forty minutes north and you'd be in London's cosmopolitan heart. But here, in a small, rural village, it was like stepping back to the 1940s.

The young girl's cell phone rang and she swiped right. She listened intently before checking over her shoulder to make sure she couldn't be overheard. Obviously, I was no one she had to worry about so, when she spoke in a hushed murmur, I heard every word.

"Just keep your head and we'll be fine," she whispered, peering back to look at me. I feigned interest in the circus flyer hanging on the wall and she hunched in the opposite direction before continuing. "I think we've got away with it. All you have to remember is the cow is dead and d'you know what the wonderful thing is about the dead? They can't talk."

37

I awoke to silence. At some point during the night I had snuggled beneath the candlewick bedspread and fallen into an uneasy sleep. I decided today I was going to get serious. No more long lunches or energetic walks, I was going to sit down and figure this whole thing out.

I tumbled out of bed and arrived in the kitchen to find a Post-it note stuck to the kettle.

> *Gone to Norfolk. Be good or be naughty—your choice. Back soon.*
> *Love F xx*

Perfect. At least that was one less thing to worry about. I was all too familiar with Finolla's definition of the word "soon." This could mean anything from a few days to an entire semester and I found myself hoping that Finolla could enjoy the delights of Norfolk at least until Aunt Rose's funeral—something else I was going to have to figure out.

I made a pot of decaf and rifled through the fridge for chocolate. After tearing off a few chunks of Galaxy, I pulled Belle's list of suspects from my purse, turned it over and made some adjustments and additions. Ten minutes later I sat back and studied my handiwork.

March had the initials *GS*, April *BC,* and May *WWF*, all in the same thick red pen.

Suspect	Date	Status	Notes
Florence Greene	Jan	Vicar's wife	Must meet.
Dan Ludlow	Feb	Son of Susan	Does deliveries for his mother.
Gurminder Singh	Mar	Works at Naan's	Says "they got away with it and dead people can't talk", but could Aunt Rose's death really be the work of a teenager?
Bonnie Curry	Apr	Neighbor	Neighborly dispute?
Wendy Fitzpatrick	May	Runs riding school	Having affair with Peter at time of Aunt Rose's death. Unhappy marriage.
Petruska and Carl Llewellyn		Pub Owners	Banned Aunt Rose.
Peter Lacey		Lodger	Lying about when he returned to UK.
Quentin Young		Composer	Lying about when he last saw Rose.
Finolla Monroe		Sister	Was there close to time of murder.

Argh! The list was getting longer and more complicated by the second. I took a sip of tea and a handful of Maltesers and settled down. One step at a time. Right now I had to prioritize. Surely the police were interviewing all the people whose initials appeared on the poison pen letters? And then, to hear Gurminder talk, it sounded like a full-fledged confession. But surely that couldn't be? I thought back to the night before. Maybe instead of focusing on the poison pen recipients I would be better off talking to three of the people who did *not* appear on that list.

My decision made, I tidied the kitchen, made sure Elgar was fed and watered, and headed upstairs. The day had dawned sunny and warm and I meant to take advantage of it. I decided to be brave and wear my one remaining pair of shorts combined with my light-weight sweatshirt as a way of hedging my bets. I had been lured by way too many periwinkle-skied mornings in England, believing the day would be sunny and warm, only to find myself suffering from near frostbite by teatime. That was a mistake you didn't repeat often.

Exiting my bedroom I ran straight into Peter, clothed in crinkle-free striped pajamas and a nifty pair of tartan slippers. I decided to ignore the dubious fashion statement, remembering that Peter was top of my list of people to talk to.

"I thought you'd already left."

Peter slinked towards the stairs. "Day off."

I trailed him step by step. "So, I bumped into Wendy yesterday." It was unbelievable how subtle I was.

Reaching the foyer, Peter didn't break stride. If anything he sped up, as he hooked a left and hightailed into the kitchen.

"She was...well, she was a little upset."

Peter loitered around the coffee pot, doing something technical with filters.

I kept going. "I was wondering, you know, if she was okay?"

Peter swung around. I tried to read his face. Guilt, anger, trapped wind? I was so not good at this.

"To tell the truth, we broke up." He pushed a floppy lock off his forehead. "Although, frankly, there wasn't much to break up from." Peter gazed at his tartan slippers. "I'm n...not proud of it, but there it is."

"So you and she were...?" I left the question suspended, in the hope Peter would fill in the blank. Lovers, good friends, swing dance partners?

Peter swept a hand through his tousled hair. "Would you believe me if I told you we were just friends?"

I gave him a look of disbelief.

"Friends who, it seems, became a little carried away over the past few weeks. But...but nothing happened, I swear."

I remembered the lipstick on Peter's collar the night Finolla arrived, but I let it go. I would assume he meant nothing in a horizontal position happened.

"I'd been trying to break it off almost as soon as it started, but there was never a good time." Peter lost interest in his slippers and chanced a look my way.

I adopted what I hoped was a sympathetic face and he continued.

"It was stupid. She's married, with children, and I should never have let it get as far as it did."

Knowing Wendy Williams I doubted Peter had done much of the chasing. Wendy was like a rat terrier—tenacious and bossy with scarily large ears.

"It's no excuse. Actually it was all a bit one-sided. I should have been...been less of a cad and more of a man and said no."

I nodded. "I won't say a word. I'm good at keeping secrets."

"Unfortunately, it's...it's not quite that simple," said Peter, reaching for a mug. He stopped and stared at me, as if debating what to say next. I continued with my most sympathetic and nonjudgmental face, which must have worked.

"Rose found out. She...she threatened to tell Duncan and asked me to leave. Said she didn't want someone," Peter did the universal symbol for air quotes, "with questionable morals living under her roof."

I didn't know what to say, but that didn't stop me. "Peter, I'm sorry. I'm finding out some things about my aunt. Let's just say she'd changed a lot since I last saw her."

"Yes, unfortunately it got pretty nasty and then...then Wendy received this note from Rose saying she was going to tell Duncan."

"What?"

All the color drained from Peter's face. He sank against the counter and raised his hands to his head. "We met on Sunday evening to try and decide what to do. To try and figure how we could talk her out of it."

"This Sunday evening?"

Peter nodded.

"What did you decide?" I asked, omitting the fact that Peter was supposed to be in Prague on Sunday.

"I...I was going to potter along and find somewhere else to live and Wendy was going to beg Rose to not tell Duncan."

"And where did this meeting take place?" I asked in my most Miss Marple-like tone.

" We were...were..."

"You were where?" I asked, my hands on both hips.

"Josie. We were here the night Rose was killed."

38

I was stunned. At least this explained why Peter had lied about which day he had returned from Prague.

"So you were here when I arrived at the cottage?"

Peter resembled a teenage boy whose cell phone had been confiscated by the teacher. "I...I know this doesn't look good."

"And when Aunt Rose was murdered?" I continued.

"I'd gone upstairs to pack. After finding us, Rose threw Wendy out and insisted I leave, well, straight away, actually. The first thing I knew about it was when I...when I looked out the window and saw Bonnie Curry tearing down the path."

"Bonnie Curry?"

"She must have been heading back to Rosewood to call the police. I rushed downstairs and you and Rose were..."

I thought back to our conversation when I'd first met Peter, when he'd feigned complete ignorance of Aunt Rose's death. I made a mental note to add "competent liar" to Peter's list of attributes. "And you left me?" My blood pressure started to rise.

"Josie, you have to understand, I...I had no idea who you were. I couldn't even see your face."

"Details! You made a run for it?"

"I...I panicked. I had no idea what had happened. There was blood everywhere and it looked like there were two dead bodies lying in the study."

I gave Peter a look.

"Josie, I'm...I'm not proud of what I did."

I felt like telling Peter this was the second time in five minutes he'd told me he wasn't proud. "How did you get out without Bonnie Curry seeing you?"

"I...I went out the French windows and through Bonnie's back garden. There's a path at the bottom that leads to The Dirty Duck."

"And you didn't see anyone?"

Peter hesitated. "No. No one."

Why didn't I believe him?

"You... you have to understand. We weren't expecting this. I...I wasn't expecting Rose back for another few days." His eyes met mine. "It's not what you think. Wendy and I were here to talk things through. Somewhere we'd not be seen or overheard. You know what it's like."

I did indeed. It seemed anything I did or said was top of the local gossip mill in a matter of minutes.

As if to prove the point, the kitchen door flew open and Belle burst into the room.

"Josie, is it true Daisy Pond is your mother's twin?" Belle paused as she noticed Peter. "Oh, hello Peter. Nice slippers."

Peter eyed his footgear and visibly winced. It was all right dressing like a sixty-year-old man in front of me, but no one in their right mind wanted to be caught in their Ovaltine outfit in front of Belle DeCorcy. I almost felt sorry for him—almost.

I nodded. "Yes, I seem to have lost one aunt and gained another."

Peter went to say something, but thought better of it.

Belle sank onto a stool. "So very strange. Did she say what she's doing here?"

I shrugged. "She wouldn't say."

"Very suspicious. Anyhow, the good news is you are no longer prime suspect in the Rose Braithwaite case. According to Darcy Blythe's cook, who mentioned it to Petra Ainsworth-Browne's groom, whose hairdresser—"

"Oh for goodness' sake, Belle—what?"

"Sorry. To be brief, I have it on excellent authority that Adam was parked outside Magna Carter's guest house early this morning and took Daisy away for questioning."

My heart lurched. "Probably standard procedure. I mean, it *is* kind of weird that Rose's long-lost sister arrives unannounced a few days before she's murdered. It makes sense they'd want to talk to her."

Peter was busy making his coffee and obviously trying his best to get the heck out of Dodge. I watched him add two teaspoons of sugar and give the coffee a quick stir before making for the door.

"We'll talk later," I said, not wanting him to think he was getting away with this.

Peter stopped midstride, gave me a curt nod and, for an infinitesimal second, locked eyes with Belle before disappearing down the hallway.

Belle's perfectly arched eyebrows rose. "What was *that* all about? It was all anguish and intrigue in here."

I filled Belle in, first on Finolla: explaining about her not giving me a lift to the station, but finding the time to bring Duncan all the way to Milkwood, putting her squarely in the vicinity at the time of the murder. Belle didn't look too interested.

I followed with the news about Peter and Wendy *also* being at Plum Tree Cottage, deciding at the last minute to omit the reason why. That was Peter's secret to tell, not mine. I half expected Belle to ask what they were doing here, but Belle went quiet, staring off into the distance as if in another place. Damn! The girl was hard to impress.

"Belle? Are you okay?"

Belle turned away. "Absolutely. Spot on."

I decided to leave it. Obviously she didn't want to talk. "I was about to go down the pub and talk to Petruska. Do you want to come?"

Belle brightened. "You bet your Aunt Nelly, I do."

Belle and I strolled down Brambley Lane and along Unthank Road. The day was beginning to feel like summer and I was starting to regret wearing long sleeves. Belle, once again, looked charming in a lemon cotton dress and espadrilles. Her long tresses flowed over her shoulders and there was a silk flower nestled over her left ear. I had never been interested in fashion, but Belle made it look effortless. I made a mental note to wear one of my three new dresses someday soon, although I would give the flower a miss.

We chucked a right at the duck pond, stopping briefly so Belle could feed said ducks, before trudging up the steps and into the low-beamed expanse that was The Dirty Duck. Petruska wore a silver lamé top and blood red lipstick reminiscent of a Dracula poster I'd once seen. She was busy polishing glasses and smiled as we made our way towards her.

Belle ordered sparkly water with half a lime and a miniature umbrella and I ordered a pineapple juice with lemonade. Petruska plonked our drinks on the bar and I handed over a fistful of pound coins.

"Petruska, I need to ask you a question."

"I am good with questions," said Petruska, pursing her scarlet lips.

"It's a little delicate," I continued.

"I can be very delicate."

"Well..."

"She wants to know why you banned Rose from the pub," said Belle, twirling her umbrella.

Petruska raised a perfectly sculpted eyebrow. "Are you sure you are wanting to know?"

Jeepers! What had my aunt done? Got drunk? Caused a fist fight? Stuck gum under the table?

Petruska leaned over and whispered in my ear. I turned and contemplated the offending object—the ancient and dilapidated piano sitting so innocuously in the corner. Seconds later I started to laugh.

39

I was easily talked into staying for a cheese and pickle sandwich while Belle regaled me with stories about the bankers from London who had helicoptered in from the City the day before.

I pushed my empty plate away. "Belle, I know very little about country life but I thought the shooting season didn't start until later."

"Absolutely," said Belle. "Grouse season starts mid-August, pheasants in October."

"Then what were they shooting?"

"Themselves," said Belle, demolishing the last bite of Branston.

I gave her a disbelieving look.

"Paintball," said Belle, clarifying. "Daddy put in a paintball course a few years ago. It's proving very popular with the suits."

"Of course he did," I said, trying to ignore the banoffee pie that was calling my name.

"They were dreadful shots, though. I could have done better blindfolded."

This made sense. Belle was a country girl of a certain class. She would have been raised to ride, shoot, and fish with an ounce of polo thrown in for good measure.

"Of course, I don't really shoot any more. How about you?"

I shook my head. A lot of my friends owned guns in Texas, but it was something I'd never felt comfortable with.

"I could teach you archery if you're not afraid of fast-moving string."

I dreaded to think what type of damage I could inflict with either of these pursuits and decided to shelve that idea in the "not in my lifetime" compartment, along with attending Formula One racing, listening to country music, or attending an Andre Rieu concert—a girl has her limits.

Belle glanced at the piano and smiled. "I can't believe the reason Rose was banned."

My shoulders started to heave. Petruska's story had been priceless. In so many ways Aunt Rose may not have been the woman from my childhood, but her sense of humor had been very much how I remembered her.

Aunt Rose had not been banned for rowdiness, drinking too much or any of the other notions that had filtered through my mind. It was simply for playing inappropriate themes on the piano whenever Magna, Irene or Bonnie entered the bar. It seemed I was not the only one who thought of the trio as witches. Aunt Rose had started innocuously enough, belting out the better known parts of *The Sorcerer's Apprentice* and Saint-Saëns' *Danse Macabre*, but had soon progressed to music they recognized, and that was when the problems started. Not even Bonnie Curry could fail to recognize "You Put a Spell on Me" and the theme from *Bewitched*. By the time Aunt Rose got around to "Devil Woman," made famous by England's answer to Elvis, Cliff Richard, and "Ding Dong the Witch Is Dead," Carl had been summoned from the kitchen and asked Rose to stop. After she refused, an amused Carl had escorted Aunt Rose off the premises. Oh, how I wish I'd been a fly on the dartboard that night.

I suddenly remembered I needed to tell Belle about the poison pen letters. I don't know why I'd kept their existence a secret, but now I was certain they were *from* Aunt Rose and not *to* Aunt Rose, I needed to confide in my erstwhile partner in crime.

In a village like Milkwood I guess I thought Belle would already know about their existence. I was wrong.

"Poison pen letters?" said Belle, lining up the salt, pepper and vinegar for the nine-hundredth time. "That's unexpected."

I nodded.

"And you say Adam found them when you showed him the secret drawer?"

"Kind of," I said, lowering my head. "I may have accidentally found them when I discovered Aunt Rose's schedule."

"Oh!" Belle nodded like this made perfect sense.

"I didn't say anything because I didn't want what you'd said about Aunt Rose to be true and if she'd been the recipient of poison pen letters it would seem you were probably right."

"So now you know she wrote them, that makes it *better*?" asked Belle, cocking her head to one side.

I looked suitably chastised. "Not exactly."

"I'm astounded the whole village didn't know," said Belle, idly swirling the mustard around the HP sauce. "I mean, I know what Petra Ainsworth-Browne had for dinner last night."

"You do?" I asked.

"Roast pheasant," said Belle. "Rumor has it the poor bird was acquired not completely legally, either. But I digress. What I'm trying to articulate is, I find it very hard to imagine a village like Milkwood being able to keep something like this quiet."

I had to agree. I would assume that most people didn't talk about it out of embarrassment, but had one person kept quiet because they knew they were going to commit murder?

Our cheese sarnies finished, we wandered back to Plum Tree and collected Roger. After hearing Petruska's explanation, I felt I could wipe her and Carl from my inquiry, plus I now had an explanation for why Aunt Rose sent a letter to Wendy. It didn't mean she and Peter hadn't killed her. Peter had admitted to being in the house, but somehow my gut said no.

I hoped I would have as good luck with the third person we were about to visit. Belle backed Roger along Brambley Lane in her usual haphazard, terrifying way, before spinning the sports car around to face the ford. Belle really was the worst driver in the history of the universe. This was all the more impressive, considering how low the bar had been set during my teenage years, with

Finolla ricocheting us through several unsuspecting parts of South America.

Belle crunched Roger into gear and we ploughed through the ford like an Olympic ski jumper. It was a ten-minute drive to our destination and Belle made it in under five. As she hung a left through the familiar iron gates I wondered how I'd ever managed to climb them. Athleticism had never been my forté. I was lucky I was still not impaled on the top, flashing my undercarriage to half of Surrey.

"By the way," said Belle, scrunching to a stop. "If you ever need to get out in a hurry there's a box on the wall right there with a buzzer."

I turned and there, nestled amongst the foliage, was a bright blue box. How could I have missed it?

"Of course, if you want to launch yourself over the gate like a pole vaulter then you're more than—"

"Hey!" I said, punching Belle on the arm. "I used to like you."

Belle smiled, put her foot to the metal, and soared along the wide driveway before careening Roger onto a dirt track. I remembered our destination with fondness. Secluded and remote, it had been the natural choice for my and Adam's liaisons. So, as we rounded the bend, it was with surprise that I viewed the structure before me. Gone was the ramshackle hut, and in its place sat a charming country cottage that would not have looked out of place in *Home and Gardens*.

"Voila!" said Belle. "Chez Young."

I heaved myself out of Roger and strolled towards the antique horse door painted in duck egg blue. I'd barely raised my hand to knock when the top half flew open, revealing the torso of Quentin Young. Quentin wore a cream shirt, the kind associated with shepherds wandering through a Constable painting, paired with a floppy purple beret. It was an interesting combination, but somehow Quentin pulled it off.

"Ladies, to what do I owe the honor?"

He had me there. *Quentin, where were you when Aunt Rose was killed?* Or *Quentin, I want to know why you were lying about when you last saw Rose?* Both seemed slightly confrontational, if not downright rude. I didn't know for sure he was lying; it was purely a feeling. Kind of like that feeling when you know you have to pee—a feeling that should be ignored at your peril.

Belle came to my rescue. "Showing Josie around the estate, Quentin."

Quentin's eyebrows disappeared under his beret. "I recognize you. You're Adam Ward's bit of fluff."

"Actually—" I began, flushing with indignation.

"Splendiferous day for it," said Quentin, with vigor. "Come in, why don't you and I'll pop the kettle on."

I decided to let the "bit of fluff" comment go, and hoped Adam wasn't hearing the same remarks. The thought that he might assume I was the instigator of these baseless comments made my heart turn cold.

Quentin unlatched the bottom half of the door and we traipsed inside. If the outside looked different from my teenage years, then the inside was unrecognizable. Gone was the 1970s Formica kitchen and paisley wallpaper, and in their place resided chic furnishings combined with a hint of wacky professor thrown in for artistic measure. A grand piano dominated the living room, with a desk and computer to its right, and a cozy sitting area to its left. The kitchen stretched along the back wall with two doors that I knew led to a bedroom and a tiny bathroom. Everything was immaculate, other than some scratches on the bottom of the piano legs.

I grasped a gilt frame and gazed at a photo of Quentin with a dopey-looking Dalmatian sitting by his feet. "Yours?" I asked.

"A friend's," said Quentin, dismissively. "I'm not exactly a dog lover."

I replaced the frame and took a seat.

"Shall I be mother?" said Quentin, carrying over a tray laden with cups, two teapots, milk and a doily overflowing with Bournville creams.

"I did a pot of decaf too," said Quentin. "Rose did like her decaf, so I've got in the habit."

Belle refused sugar, but took a healthy dash of milk before Quentin removed the tea cosy and upended the teapot. I refused both milk and sugar and opted for the decaf—yay for Aunt Rose.

This was the kind of ritual I missed and it made me smile to see a man in his sixties partaking in such an English tradition.

I scooped up a Bournville, gave it a healthy dunk and let it melt in my mouth. How was I supposed to proceed here? Again, Belle stepped in.

"Quentin, Josie would really like to know more about her aunt. She's trying to get closure and it's really hard. We've been asking different people in the village for their memories, but let's just say people are being a tad reluctant. You're a musician, Rose was a musician, surely your paths must have overlapped? Besides, I know she was such a huge fan."

We had no evidence at all in regard to this last sentence, but it had the desired effect.

Quentin relaxed into his chair, a bone china cup balanced on his tummy. "Ah, what can I say about Rose? Such a doll."

This was new. Every person we'd spoken to so far couldn't stand my aunt and most, it seemed, had good reason. Was Quentin trying to spare my feelings? Given his personality it seemed unlikely. Or was he the only person in Milkwood who actually felt some affection for my aunt?

Quentin continued to talk highly about Rose as a musician before turning the subject back to himself and his upcoming concert. To condense the next fifteen minutes: Quentin assured us that he and Rose were not close, but had a mutual appreciation of each other's talents.

"So, how was my aunt the day she died?" I asked. "Did she say anything that might help me understand what type of mood she was in?"

Quentin paused, his teacup halfway to his lips. "I think I told you, dear girl, I hadn't seen your aunt in quite a while."

"Oh! For some reason I thought you'd spoken to her the day she died. It's just I—"

"Sadly, no," interrupted Quentin, not sounding sad at all. "You will be coming," he continued.

This was more of a statement than a question.

I stared at him blankly.

"To the concert," said Quentin.

Belle did her best to sound non-committal as I stood and approached the CD player. There was a CD case lying open and I picked it up.

The entire time we'd been having tea I'd been aware of a music playing softly in the background. It sounded vaguely familiar and I was intrigued to find out its origin. I was normally good at identifying composers—okay, I was more than good—I was excellent, but this piece was eluding me. Definitely contemporary, definitely English, but that was where my guesswork ended.

I grasped the CD and my heart quickened.

"We'll be there," I said. "We'll definitely be there."

40

I refused Belle's offer of a lift home, preferring to cut through the forest past the cluster of silver birches from which Milkwood derived its name. I found myself humming the tune that had been playing on Quentin's CD player. It was catchy and familiar and I racked my brain as to where I'd heard it before. Soon I was on the bank of the Tillingbourne searching for the secret way across. I hadn't gone far before I spied the stones that made a natural crossing.

If I had continued north I would have reached the location of the infamous rope swing debacle. Surely after all these years it was no longer part of the landscape? I decided this was not the time to find out, instead turning my attention to the softly flowing Tillingbourne and the slick-as-mustard stones.

I took a deep breath. I could do this. I had done it a hundred times before. Okay, a couple of decades had passed since I'd last crossed the river, but it had never been difficult. I tottered down the bank, steeled myself and took a flying leap, landing perfectly on the nearest stone. I recovered my balance and prepared to take a second.

I swear I would have made it if it hadn't been for someone calling my name, me looking up and my ankle turning, plummeting my body into the ice-cold water.

"Cluck a duck!" I spluttered, sinking to my knees.

I heard a sound and looked up. Adam stood on the far bank, doing a really bad job of trying not to laugh. Jeepers, I hated men. I made the mistake of trying to get back onto the rock, slipped and went belly first in the stream. You had to be freaking kidding me. Now I was wet from the waist down.

"Do you need help?"

I'm not proud of it, but I think I growled. I pulled myself to a standing position and decided to abandon the dry route. I was already as wet as a whale, I might as well wade across the river bed rather than risk another plunge. It was harder than it sounded. My sneakers were waterlogged and squidgy, and a sudden cool breeze caused me to break into goosebumps.

Finally, I reached the bank. I ignored the outstretched hand and hauled myself to shore. I made it as far as the grass before collapsing. I was wet, I was cold and I was humiliated. Could life get any worse?

"If you say a word, I'm going to hit you," I said, not looking up. "I don't care if I get done for assaulting a policeman. It'll be worth it."

Adam leaned over and put something warm around my shoulders. "Not a word."

I peered up to see him jacketless. I hadn't banked on kindness. The stress from the past few days washed over me the same way as the Tillingbourne. I didn't want Adam to see me cry, but it was too late. Adam settled beside me and ran his arm around my shoulder.

"Don't be kind. You'll make it worse."

"Okay," said Adam, easing me closer.

"Don't laugh at me either," I added, looking up.

Adam wasn't laughing any more. He seemed so very earnest.

"Hey, I'm the one that fell in the river, not you."

This produced a wry smile.

I leaned my head against Adam's shoulder. "I've just been to the old shack."

"Fun times," said Adam, his breath warm on the back of my neck.

"It's changed," I said.

"We've all changed, Josie. That's what time does."

"Not me. I'm the same, just with more wrinkles."

Adam lifted my chin and stroked my cheek. "Rubbish. You don't have wrinkles. But you've definitely got fewer zits."

"Hey!" I said. "I was a teenager, we all had zits. Besides, you weren't such an oil painting yourself back then, Adam Ward."

It felt good to joke with my old friend. We sat in companionable silence, listening to the rippling of the Tillingbourne and the twittering of the birds. For the first time in a week I felt happy. Like I belonged.

Here, with Adam's arm around me, I felt safe, something I hadn't felt since finding Aunt Rose's body. I hated to admit it, but there was a definite air of menace around. Maybe that's what murder does to the community of a close-knit village, everyone looking at everyone else, wondering, gossiping, suspecting.

Adam was the first to break the silence. "Don't you want to know what I'm doing here?"

I hadn't thought of that. This was the third time Adam had arrived in time to witness me making a fool of myself. I was starting to suspect he'd dropped a tagging device in my bag. I made a mental note to check as soon as I got back to Plum Tree.

"Sure," I said. "Surprise me."

Adam told me and I scrambled to my sneakers and took off running.

41

I tramped up the sloping lawn towards the gaping French windows. Squinting against the sun, I could see the outline of Frosty Knickers crossing the patio, plus two figures huddled beneath the sycamore. I recognized the one facing me as Peter and was the other one who I thought it was? Strange.

I plodded farther up the garden, past the swing and hoisted myself up the steps onto the patio. I took a quick peek into the living room and found Helen perusing the bookshelves. I gave Helen a look designed to strike terror into fourteen-year-olds who had forgotten their instruments. After a moment, I gave up. This might work on teenagers, not so much on DS Winterbottom.

I turned to face Peter. His companion was gone and he was lounging in one of those antiquated deckchairs. The kind that are easy to get into and impossible to escape.

"Hey, Josie."

Before I had a chance to answer, another policeman came around the corner and a third emerged through the kitchen door holding a rubbish bag.

My hands were on my sodden hips. "You let the police in?"

Peter had the decency to look sheepish. "It...it seemed the best thing to do. They could always get a search warrant and *I* don't have anything to hide." Peter colored at the roots. "Other than a rather embarrassingly large collection of Beanos."

I had nothing to hide either, but it still didn't mean I relished the thought of Frosty Knickers pawing through my unmentionables.

"And was that Belle you were talking to?"

"Belle? I've...er, not seen Belle in days."

I frowned. Okay, so the sun had been in my eyes and I was a little disoriented from falling in the Tillingbourne, but I could have sworn Belle DeCorcy had been chatting to Peter only seconds before. Why would he deny it?

"Josie...you're, erm, wet."

I glanced down. My shorts were sticking to my legs and my sweatshirt had gone from baggy to soppy. I perched on the side of the ornamental wall, pulled off my sneakers, and peeled off my socks. A trickle of water dribbled onto the stone patio as I gave the socks a squeeze.

"Tillingbourne," I said, as a one-word explanation of my predicament.

Peter nodded. "A bit cold for a swim, but I...I guess it takes all sorts."

The idea that Peter thought I would go swimming fully clothed amused me. I shrugged. Better he imagine I did this voluntarily than through clumsiness.

I heard footsteps climbing the stone steps and stiffened. Adam could rot in hell. I knew it wasn't his fault and was probably even out of his control, but this second search of Aunt Rose's home seemed personal.

"Found anything?" asked Adam.

Frosty Knickers emerged through the French windows and glanced my way with a look one iota above pure hatred. "Only this." DS Winterbottom held out some foolscap paper.

Nothing to do with me, I thought. And then I rethought. Dang, those were the copies Belle and I had made of Aunt Rose's schedule, plus the list of our suspects.

"Found them in a drawer in Miss Monroe's bedroom," said DS Winterbottom, with an emphasis on the "Miss."

Adam took the pages and studied them before looking over at me.

I shrugged. Photocopying Aunt Rose's schedule wasn't a crime. At least I didn't think it was.

"That's fine," said Adam. "I think we can leave this with Miss Monroe. Anything else?"

Frosty Knickers shook her head and I gave some consideration as to whether I should be worried about DS Winterbottom. It was obvious she disliked me, but the look she had given me earlier made me wonder if she could keep things professional. Was she the kind of copper who if irked would plant evidence? I hoped not.

Adam placed the pages in my hand. "Josie, a word?"

I squelched to my bare feet and followed Adam towards the swing.

"I'm sorry to invade your aunt's home, but after missing Rose's schedule we wanted to make sure we hadn't missed anything else."

"Whatever." I sounded like a petulant teenager.

Adam turned me to face him. "Listen, Josie, two things. First, I want you to be careful. This is a murder enquiry, not petty theft. This could be dangerous. Second, if there's anything you're not telling me, this is the time to spill."

I said nothing.

"Josie, I understand that you want to find out who murdered your aunt. Remember, I knew Rose too. But, at the risk of repeating myself, if there's something you're holding back, this is the time to tell me."

Gosh darn it. I hated it when he made sense.

I thought back over all I knew. That Peter had been here when Aunt Rose was murdered. That Wendy and he had been having an affair. I gazed at Peter wearing his absurd slippers, sitting in a deckchair made for a sixty-year-old man and decided not to drag him into this. Instead I decided to share with Adam the one piece of information I did think might be valid.

"You're right, I do want to find out who murdered my aunt. To be honest, I know less than you think, but I do know this. I'd look at Quentin Young."

"And why's that?" asked Adam.

"Because I was just listening to a CD of his music."

"Sorry about that," said Adam.

"Actually, it was exceptional."

"Didn't see that coming," said Adam.

"The CD's called *Rosetta's Throne*."

"Nice play on words."

I waited for the penny to drop.

Finally it fell. "And Rosetta is Rose's full name."

42

Frosty Knickers and her band of merry men finally departed and I headed upstairs, still humming the familiar tune, and took a warm shower. I wasn't sure if Quentin Young naming his CD *Rosetta's Throne* was a coincidence or if there was something more to it, but in my mind it definitely needed to be looked into.

I wrapped myself in a bath towel and slinked along the landing to my room. It seemed Peter was home for the day and I didn't want to meet him face-to-face encased only in an oversized piece of fluffy cotton. I reached the bedroom and locked the door behind me. Turning, I spied an intruder on my bedspread. Like the enigmatic Sphinx, Elgar was stretched out, looking as haughty as a teenage cheerleader. He eyed me with disdain and let out his signature hiss. This reminded me to add "call local animal shelter" to my growing list of things to do. I didn't like rehousing animals. For me an animal was for life, which was why my commitment to fluffy companions stretched only as far as Horace, my budgerigar. Maybe I could ask Peter if he'd like Elgar as a pet? Or maybe Wendy would have room for another feline at the stables? Elgar didn't look much of a mouser, more of a "scratcher" if some of the legs on the downstairs furniture were anything to go by, but you never knew. He could certainly climb trees, which was no doubt how he had once again gained access to my bedroom.

I pulled open a drawer and surveyed my pathetic pile of clothes with dismay. It was too hot for jeans and my only pair of shorts lay in a soppy wet pile on the floor. It was time to break out one of Belle's gifts. Deciding on the cream dress with the flower border, I slipped the soft cotton over my head and wedged my feet into the borrowed sandals. I ran a comb through my hair, slapped on some moisturizer and was contemplating a lick of mascara when the doorbell rang.

Crispy cringles, who could it be now? I checked my watch. It was 5:00pm. Not exactly an unsocial hour, but I really wasn't up to talking with anybody likely to call me a murderer—i.e., the majority of Milkwood. The bell rang again and, seeing that Peter didn't seem to be within hearing range, I toddled downstairs and inched open the door to find a nervous looking teenager on the doorstep.

The girl wore a serviceable grey skirt and jacket with a navy and gold striped tie. She had on sensible shoes and clutched a soft leather briefcase. Her hair was dark blonde and fell either side of her ruddy cheeks. I put her age around fifteen.

The girl gave me a nervous smile and eased past me into the foyer.

"I'm Georgina." Georgina placed the battered briefcase on the floor and rummaged in a pocket. "Here." She handed me a crumpled piece of paper, reminiscent of those found in Aunt Rose's secret drawer.

I smoothed out the paper and read the tidy print within.

Ms Monroe—Georgina needs help before taking her Grade Five. I have it on good authority that you are the best. Hoping you can fit her in at your earliest convenience. An hour lesson should suffice. Sincerely, Ivy Lewis

"Oh, and there's this too." Georgina produced an envelope, this time in pristine condition.

I tore open the envelope and peered inside. A crisp fifty-pound note was nestled within.

"I'm assuming my earliest convenience would be now?"

Georgina nodded. "I need help."

I dropped the envelope and letter onto the hall table and

nudged open the door to Aunt Rose's study. Holding it ajar, I saw Georgina hesitate. I gave her an encouraging smile. There was nothing left to see. The police had cleaned up the blood and taken away the rug. Only memories remained. "Nothing to worry about, unless you don't know your E flat minor scale, and then we'll have to have words."

It had been a long time since I'd taught Grade Five piano. I'd been around eleven when I took the exam myself, which was considered extremely young. I was worried that I wouldn't remember all that Grade Five entailed, but it seemed Georgina was prepared. Before plonking herself on the piano stool she handed me a third piece of paper, then brought out her sheet music and placed it on the piano shelf. Listed were all the arpeggios and scales needed to pass Grade Five, plus the three pieces Georgina was expected to perform.

Georgina was about to start playing when she turned and gawked towards the fireplace. I was sure she knew all about Aunt Rose and I could only imagine how much bribery it had taken to get her here. However, the study was cozy, with a lived-in feel that bordered on chaotic. So chaotic that I couldn't even find the metronome, and with Georgina having forgotten her iPhone there wasn't even the possibility of downloading an app.

An hour later I had listened to Georgina play a very commendable Chopin, a passing Purcell and an extremely heartfelt Gershwin. I had no doubt the girl would pass with distinction although, even without a metronome, I could tell her E flat Minor scale could definitely do with speeding up.

It was only after I'd said goodbye that I wondered who had suggested me as a piano teacher. There could only be one person presumptuous enough, and when I next saw Belle, I would be sure to thank her.

Shutting the door on Georgina I returned to Aunt Rose's study and was surprised to find Peter sitting at the piano.

"I miss hearing it played. You know, properly," he said, not looking up, his long pale fingers bridging a lower octave.

I knew what he meant. Georgina was a superior pianist, but she wasn't anywhere close to Aunt Rose's talent—few were. Aunt Rose had played the piano like Ella Fitzgerald sang jazz. There was a confidence, a subtlety, a lightness of touch that commanded the room and drew you in. I would bet money that she could even make the rundown piano at The Dirty Duck sound like it belonged at Carnegie Hall.

I sat next to Peter. Our thighs brushed together on the narrow stool and I was surprised that he did not scoot up. I laid my hands on the keys and started playing a duet that Rose and I had enjoyed when I was young—the sweetly melodic *Berceuse* from Faure's *Dolly Suite*. To my surprise Peter reached forward and filled in the bass. He was no Aunt Rose, but he was more than passable. The piece rose and fell and our hands mingled back and forth and by the end I was smiling, joyous in the performance.

I turned to look at my slightly dubious lodger. I knew so little about him, yet here we were sleeping under the same roof, drinking from the same teacups. He seemed harmless, but as I'd learnt earlier Peter Lacey was a first rate liar. These thoughts and more were churning through my head when Peter leaned forward and drew me towards him.

I was so surprised that to begin with I didn't pull away—at least that's what I told myself. Maybe the second reason I didn't pull away was that Peter's hands, now enveloping mine, were tender and he smelled like fresh laundry. I had involuntarily closed my eyes and when I opened them Peter's blue irises stared back, his lips inches from mine. Self-consciousness flooded through me and I pulled back. The last thing I needed was to start a relationship with my deceased aunt's lodger.

43

Friday dawned with bruised grey skies. Ah, you had to love summertime in England. Elgar had spent the night curled at the bottom of my bed, a hissing, furry hot water bottle snuggled against the crook of my legs. As long as he didn't bite, I found I was actually okay sharing my bed with the cantankerous feline, and it was with a sense of newfound cordiality that we descended the stairs for breakfast the next morning.

The neatly stacked dishes by the sink informed me that Peter had already left for work, and I found myself wondering about the unexpected "moment" from the previous afternoon.

This was a complication I didn't need. Yes, Peter was good-looking—ridiculously so. He was of above-average intelligence, an excellent violinist and a pretty decent piano player. He left the toilet seat down, cleaned and stacked his dishes and, as far as I could tell through the adjoining wall, did not snore like an albatross. All ticks in the "for" column. I pulled myself together; this was no time for pros and cons. I had a murder to solve, not a love life to start. What I needed was to find out who murdered Aunt Rose so I could make like a tree and leaf!

My traitorous mind flashed backed to the previous afternoon. Peter, like me, had most likely been caught in the moment. Music could do that—forge unexpected intimacy—it wasn't like we'd be the first. I thought back to Peter's reaction as I had pulled away, blushing like a fourteen-year-old schoolgirl.

"Tea?" he had asked, releasing his grip on my fingers, and I had slowly nodded. Half wondering that if instead of the words "tea," he had said "bed," would I still be nodding? However, instead of bed we had spent a convivial evening sharing memories of Aunt Rose over a dish of marinara pasta that Peter had whipped up with a competency that was both impressive and beguiling. The evening had ended at the top of the stairs when Peter had drawn me into a hug and wished me sweet dreams. I would be lying if I didn't admit to a twinge of regret as I entered my room—for the first time, not locking my door.

I pulled myself together. I had nothing to feel guilty about. Peter was not in a relationship with Wendy and I certainly wasn't in a relationship with Adam. Instead, I turned my thoughts to how I would spend the day. I made tea and toast and disposed of several chocolate Hobnobs before extracting my list of suspects. I added what I knew about Quentin before returning to the beginning.

I had now met with the three people whom I originally thought wouldn't be on the police's radar. The fourth, of course, was Finolla, but who knew when I'd see my mother again. Time to get serious. Time to tackle the people who had been sent poison pen letters. I would start with the one I thought was easiest. Also, the one I had a different question for.

Half an hour later I was dressed in jeans and a tee, both of which looked relatively clean if you kept your distance. I made a mental note to purchase more clothes as well as groceries. I should also talk to Peter about his financial arrangement with Aunt Rose. I assume he paid rent? Did he pay for his own groceries or was it more of a communal relationship?

Once again I found myself strolling along Brambley Lane. The kindergarten club were nowhere to be seen, but the ducks were out in force. I cruised past the pond, hung a left, and headed up the steps of the corner shop.

Susan Ludlow was behind the counter. Her hair was neatly encased by a red-polka-dot kerchief with matching cotton blouse and adorable wide legged trousers. She embodied the look of the

1940s housewife as she glanced my way and smiled. "Hey, Josie. Back for more chocolate?"

I remembered the fifty nestling in my purse and gave it some serious thought. "Why not?"

I snagged a shopping basket and delved into the chocolate aisle. There were many things I'd adapted to while living in the US—American chocolate was *not* one of them. I picked out Rolos, Maltesers and Flakes, plus a replacement pack of Hobnobs, before approaching the counter. I emptied the contents and routed around in my bag for my purse while Susan totaled my purchases.

"I'm surprised to see you still here," said Susan. "Bag?"

I nodded. I must remember to bring bags out with me in future.

"That'll be another 5p," said Susan, shaking out the familiar yellow bag.

"I'm not really meant to leave the area. You know. Until they sort out who killed my aunt."

"You a suspect, are you? I'd have thought what with you and DC Ward being sweethearts..."

I almost choked. This was getting out of control.

"Sweethearts? I don't think so," I said, dropping the fifty onto the counter.

"That's not what I've heard," said Susan, adding my purchases to the bag.

I decided to change the subject. "You don't happen to know anyone in Milkwood with the initials *PU*, do you?"

Susan shook her head. "Sorry. There's Petruska, but her married name's Llewellyn." Susan handed me the bag. "Ben said he saw you the other day."

"Yes, he was coming out of Wisteria Villa."

Susan's face lit up. "That would be delivering to Mrs Drinkwater. She's a regular."

"Did he ever deliver to Aunt Rose?"

Susan gave my question some thought. "No, Rose used to get most of her groceries from Dorking. If she did pop in, it was for a paper, or the odd pint of milk."

"It's just the day I arrived we had fresh milk and bread."

"Oh, that!" said Susan. "Yes, that day she did. Dan was running the store and I'd popped down to get some flour when Rose came in to get some bread and milk. She'd just returned from holiday. But she got distracted and left without them."

"What?"

Susan frowned at the memory. "Actually, it was rather weird. She was telling me about her holiday and she got out her purse. She was almost out of money and had to shake the coins onto the counter."

"She didn't pay by card?" I asked.

"Never did. Old fashioned, was your aunt. Preferred cash. A bit frugal, if you want to know the truth. Then she took off. Left the bread and milk, she did. Plum forgot about it."

"Strange. Was she normally forgetful?"

"No. Not at all. Your aunt may have been many things, but she was on the ball. Anyway, as soon as Dan closed up shop I sent him over with her purchases."

I dropped my change into my purse, grabbed my bag and made my goodbyes. My suspicion was confirmed—the young teenager I'd seen on my first day had been Dan. This meant that along with Finolla, Peter and Wendy, Dan Ludlow had also been at the scene of the crime. Now I just had to find out why Aunt Rose had sent him a poison pen letter, and if it was bad enough for him to kill her.

44

I strolled back to Plum Tree Cottage and dined on pâté and Maltesers. I sighed at the thought of interviewing Dan Ludlow. If I was truthful, I couldn't imagine such a caring, diligent boy being a murderer, but stranger things had happened.

I tried to recall what each of the letters had said and regretted not having taken copies. They had all been much of a muchness. Things like: *I know what you did, I'm going to tell on you,* etc. Wendy's note had implied that Rose was going to tell Duncan about Peter. Dan's had said something about telling on him—probably to his mother. But telling his mother what, and was it related to the letter his friend Gurminder Singh had received the month before? In all likelihood yes, but in reality it could be totally unrelated.

I pulled out my list of suspects and decided I'd have to wait until I saw Belle before proceeding. We had made no plans to see each other and I was beginning to find not having a phone problematic. Knowing Belle, she would arrive unannounced. I would give her twenty-four hours before hunting her down. In the meantime, I decided to go shopping.

I locked the cottage and trudged across the front garden to the stand-alone garage. Aunt Rose's key chain contained four keys. One for the front door, one for the back, one for the garage and one for what hopefully resided within. I placed the key in the lock and pulled the doors wide open. Nestled in the gloom was a red Citroën

2CV, the French equivalent of a VW Beetle, but skinnier and slightly cooler—of course it was French, what would you expect?

Belle was not the only one in Milkwood to christen their mode of transportation. Aunt Rose had named her car Jenny, short for Genevieve, after the 1950s movie about the old crocks race from London to Brighton. Jenny also had the added advantage of a manual crank, which would often have to be deployed as an alternative way of starting the querulous beast.

I thought back to my utilitarian Toyota in Texas. Reliable, beige and boring—much like me. I would no more think of giving it a name as I would my teapot. I edged down the side of the garage, opened Jenny's door and slid behind the wheel. The car was built in the 1980s and had been originally designed for French farmers transporting eggs over bumpy fields. I struggled, in the dimly lit garage, to find the ignition, but eventually the key found purchase and I gently turned. The engine spluttered a death knoll before quitting. I tried again and again. On the fifth try I was lucky. This was why you named cars like this. It was to prevent you driving them over a cliff in frustration.

However, the frustration didn't stop there. I had been a passenger in this car hundreds of times. Why, oh why, had I not paid more attention? Contrary to most cars, the gears on Jenny poked out of the dashboard in a gung-ho type of fashion. Ten minutes later I had finally found first, enabling me to kangaroo hop my way out of the garage. I kept the car running as I opened the gates and attempted to drive through. Never have I been happier with Plum Tree's remote location than I was today. The fewer people who saw my attempt to locate second gear the better. By the time I'd reached Unthank Road I was cruising at a respectable fifteen miles an hour. At this rate I'd reach Dorking by Thanksgiving.

Third proved easier, and by the time I reached the A25 I had made it all the way to fourth. I was golden, as long as I didn't have to change gear or stop. A very stressful thirty minutes later I reached the city center and found a meter in front of the police station. I had enough coins for an hour and ten minutes' parking. I studied my watch, added on six hours and set off. I was a woman on a mission and I had an hour and ten minutes to accomplish it.

One hour and twelve minutes later I returned to the car and did a little happy dance to see no ticket on the windshield. I piled my purchases onto the backseat and decided to be brave. The weather had improved and it was now almost a balmy twenty-three degrees centigrade. Positively tropical. I clambered inside Jenny, raised my arms, and dislodged the struts that held the roof in place before rolling the canvas back, like a tin of sardines. Voila—a convertible.

My shopping trip had been a success. I had found a clothes shop with a going-out-of-business sale and purchased four more outfits, several pairs of knickers, three more bras and a pair of snazzy sandals. I had more than doubled my wardrobe and felt quite heady in the anticipation of wearing something not featuring tractor stains.

The roof rolled back, I turned the ignition. Nothing. I tried again. Nada. Ten minutes later I was still sitting there. There was only one thing for it. I reached onto the back seat and located the long metal rod. Hurrying to the front, I crouched low, inserted the crank-start and gave it a sharp clockwise turn. Still nothing. I'd seen Aunt Rose do this a thousand times, so I knew it worked. I merely needed patience—never my strong suit. Four turns of the manual crank and two grazed knuckles later I found myself sitting criss cross applesauce in front of Jenny banging my forehead against the metal grill.

"Hey, Puke."

Crispy pancakes, no.

"Need any help?"

I removed my forehead from the grill and stared up into the familiar eyes of Adam Ward.

"I'm fine," I said haughtily, adding a better-late-than-never "Thank you," to be polite.

I gave the manual start one more almighty heave and, miracles of miracles, Jenny spluttered into life. I could have kissed her.

I rose to my feet, dusted off my bottom and headed for the door.

"It's this side," said Adam, holding open the driver's door.

Phoey! "I know that," I said, backtracking.

"And we drive on the left here."

"I know that as well," I said testily.

Please let Adam go far far away, I entreated the universe. I may have got Jenny started, but I still had to get her into first. Something I did not need witnesses to.

"I'm glad I bumped into you."

I ignored Adam, pulling my seatbelt over my shoulder. I felt a hand on my arm.

"I thought you'd like to know we've released Rose's body."

The third movement of Chopin's Piano Sonata No. 2, better known as the *Funeral March*, ran through my head. I was so sick of being an adult. I didn't know how to organize a funeral. Darn, I could barely organize a sandwich.

"And one more thing. DS Winterbottom contacted Rose's solicitor. Turns out your aunt was a very wealthy woman and had one beneficiary."

Flippity flip flops! I hadn't thought about that. Where was I going to go if I got turfed out of Plum Tree?

Adam turned me to face him and slipped a piece of paper into my hand. "Josie, the beneficiary is you."

My drive back to Milkwood was a bit of a blur. I think I was in shock. Turned out Aunt Rose had left everything to me. Her money. Her house. Even Jenny.

I bumped along Brambley Lane, wedged Jenny into the garage and reattached her roof. It was only then that I saw a gaggle of children huddled outside Aunt Rose's, or should I now say *my,* front door?

I retrieved my purchases and started towards them. "Can I help you?"

There were four children in all, attired in various school uniforms. The oldest was about twelve, the youngest roughly seven. The twelve-year-old stepped forward.

"Piano lessons, Miss."

"Oh, right."

"I've got my Grade Four next week, Miss."

Various grades were mumbled by the other three.

"I see. And you all want lessons?"

"Yes, Miss," they all chorused together.

"Okay then." Honestly, I was surprised students were willing to come to Plum Tree after a murder had been committed within its walls. However, I was not going turn the aspiring pianists away.

I approached the door and found a hastily scribbled note

wedged into the handle. I recognized the large loopy handwriting immediately. Belle's.

Be ready by 6:45. We're going out. B xx

Well, that was the rest of my day settled. Earlier, in a moment of madness, I'd inquired of Adam if he had plans this evening. He had informed me that he was working, and I'd immediately wished I hadn't asked.

I swung open the front door and the four children jostled inside. "All right, who's first?"

Two hours later I had completed four half-hour lessons. I had also received four more crisp fifty-pound notes. Two of the students, Charlotte and Timothy, were pre-teens and incredibly proficient; however twins Alfie and Ralph were just starting out, and I had a lot of fun teaching them "Twinkle, Twinkle, Little Star"—the first tune Aunt Rose had taught me to play on the piano. Aunt Rose and I had enjoyed making up lyrics and setting them to nursery rhymes, and I promised the twins I would see if my aunt had kept the book of tunes we had collaborated on when I was their age. All had promised to return the following Friday. I wasn't sure what the going rate was for piano lessons, but I was pretty sure I was being overpaid. I could live with that.

I scrambled a couple of egg yolks, toasted some bread and vowed to go shopping for groceries tomorrow. Dinner sorted, I traipsed upstairs. I cleaned my teeth, ran a comb through my hair and unpacked my latest purchases. I had *no* idea what we were doing tonight. Knowing Belle, it could be anything from dinner to tobogganing. I decided to remain in my jeans and tee shirt, adding a splash of deodorant for good measure.

I was descending the staircase when I heard the familiar roar of Roger bravely traversing the potholes of Brambley Lane. I threw open the door and watched as Belle exited the little red sports car and strolled along the garden path. She too was wearing jeans, but trendy, cute ones that ended three inches above her ankles. With a boat neck, three-quarter length tee and her hair tied in a low ponytail she reminded me of a blonde version of Audrey Hepburn. Did the woman ever have a bad fashion moment?

I grabbed my bag, locked the door and strolled along the path to meet her.

"Where are we going?"

"I rather thought I'd keep it as a surprise. By the way, did you break down earlier today? It's only Petra Ainsworth-Browne was getting a pedicure at This Little Piggy Nail Salon and—"

"I was having car problems," I said. "Nothing I couldn't take care of. By the way, did you stop by Plum Tree yesterday, after we'd been to Quentin's?"

Belle gripped the steering wheel a little more firmly before she answered. "Why the dickens would I do that? Besides, I'd just seen you."

She had a point. I decided to let it go and blame it on a trick of the light.

Five minutes later we were on the A25 speeding towards Dorking. Belle chucked a left and I started to laugh. Looming on the landscape was the yellow and white striped tent we'd seen when returning from Dorking on Tuesday.

"Are we going to the circus?"

Belle beamed. "Yes! But don't worry, it's not one of those ghastly shows that makes animals do tricks. This is a human circus."

I thought back to Monday and the motley crew assembled at the Dorking police station—humanity in all its various forms.

Two young men in sunny yellow shirts waved us onwards and five minutes later we had a primo parking spot ten strides from the ticket booth. Honestly, this girl bounded from one piece of luck to the next.

Belle and I retrieved our tickets from the ramshackle booth and hurried into the tent. There was barely a spare spot, but Belle managed to snag what seemed to be the best seats in the house. The minute we were seated the lights extinguished and a spotlight burst to life. It was as if they'd been waiting for us.

I hadn't been to a circus since I was a child. Ryan and I had once purchased tickets to Cirque du Soleil, but he'd feigned vertigo ten minutes into the opening act and we'd had to leave. This was everything I'd imagined Cirque du Soleil would be, and more. I spotted both the ballerina and the strongman from the police station and thought I recognized one of the acrobats twirling high above. By the time we reached intermission I was in love with all of them.

"Let's get popcorn," said Belle, rising. "Or, you're American, maybe you'd like a hot dog?"

Belle was almost giddy with the food options. There was something so very endearing about her excitement. Some may have labeled it childish. I found it charming.

Belle joined the queue for popcorn and I decided to take the opportunity to use the bathroom—praying it wouldn't be a porta potty from hell. Turned out, it was the upmarket kind of porta potty, not the type that you couldn't look into the bowl without risk of puking. I passed the line of men who seemed to be moving at a satisfactory clip and headed to the women's, situated a good fifty meters further away. This line was neither clipping nor clopping, just a dead standstill, reminiscent of the M25 on a Monday morning.

I strolled to the back of the line and took in my surroundings. For someone who had only been in the area a week, it was amazing how many people I recognized. Several of my pupils said hello as they scurried by and Grade Five Georgina tapped me on the shoulder and introduced her older sister, the teenage stablehand, Lucy. I ignored the distant death stare from a hotdog-eating Bonnie Curry and, instead, chatted with an amicable teenager about gnomes, on which she had an animated opinion.

I'd been standing in line for roughly five minutes and moved exactly two inches when I saw two more people I knew: Dan Ludlow and the girl from Naan's, whom I assumed was Dan's study partner, Gurminder. Both wore jeans and matching tee-shirts emblazoned with the name of a band that I assumed was popular, despite the fact that I'd never heard of them They seemed far older out of their school uniforms, and far more furtive, glancing over their shoulders as they took a sharp left around the back of the now-empty ticket booth.

Recalling Gurminder's phone conversation, and the fact that I now knew Dan was at Plum Tree the evening Aunt Rose was killed, I made a split-second decision, abandoning my need to pee.

Strolling as nonchalantly as I could towards the open field, I was wondering where I could hide when I spied Roger's glistening hubcaps. I sauntered towards the sports car and, reaching the driver's side, began to fumble in my purse as if searching for keys.

I could see the outline of my two "suspects" roughly ten feet away, against the aging wooden kiosk. I could see them, but I couldn't hear them. There was only one thing for it, I'd have to get closer. Alternatively, I could abandon my current course of action, which seemed a far more sensible thing to do, and head back to the tent and have popcorn. I decided to throw caution to the proverbial, and tiptoed across the grass towards the kiosk. Why I tiptoed I could not say, but it seemed in keeping at the time.

It was around then, as I stood with my back to the kiosk and inched towards the corner, that I realized I was not cut out for spying. My heart rate was approaching *allegrissimo* and I was a demi-semi quaver away from *presto*. If I didn't have a heart condition after tonight it would be an early Christmas miracle.

However, at this distance I could, if the beating of my heart piped down, finally hear their conversation. Gurminder was talking and she sounded exactly as she had the other night—in other words, annoyed.

"Stop worrying," said Gurminder. "No one knows and no one's gonna know. You just gotta keep your mouth shut."

"They'll kill us," said Dan, his voice faltering. "Or at least put me in prison."

"No one's going to prison, do you hear me? And nobody can kill us if they don't know," replied Gurminder.

Crispy pancakes! Was this a confession? I took one more step towards the corner and would no doubt have caught the very next words if I hadn't fallen over the gnome-like creature sitting hunched at the base of the kiosk.

It's hard to go "splat" when you fall on grass, but I seemed to manage it nicely. I scrambled to my knees before peering into the disapproving faces of two surly teenagers.

"You spying on us?" asked Gurminder, taking a step forward and missing my hand by an inch.

Dan put an arm on her shoulder and dragged her backwards. "Come on, Gee. Of course Ms Monroe wasn't spying."

"Spying? Why would you think that?" I said, citing my old childhood mantra: deny, deny, feign no knowledge, deny. It never worked with Finolla, but one can never give up hope.

"What else would the old cow be doing?"

I would like to think she was referring to the heifers in the adjoining field, but I was pretty sure Gurminder was referring to me. Frankly, the girl had some serious anger issues. Serious enough that she would kill Aunt Rose?

Gurminder turned and huffed off towards the car park. Turning, she spat out one more insult, but her words were extinguished by the resounding tones of music associated with circuses worldwide. In my opinion, the score was one of the most inaptly named pieces of all times, with Julius Fucik's "Entrance of the Gladiators" more commonly associated with the entrance of clowns than Roman swordsmen.

I hurried back to the tent and found my seat. I wanted to tell Belle my news, but the music grew louder and the lights dimmer. It would have to wait. The second half of the show was equally marvelous, but all too quickly the evening drew to a close and the house lights resumed with a flicker.

Belle and I joined the throng and shuffled our way towards the exit. Two rows in front sat Gurminder Singh slumped next to a stern-looking woman in her forties, whom I took to be her mother. On the opposite side of the aisle sat Dan with his mother. Susan was wearing one of her signature 1940s dresses and gave me a hearty wave as I descended the steps. With Dan and Gurminder being on such excellent terms I would have assumed they'd come together. Obviously not.

"Don't look left," said Belle. "but there's Frosty Knickers."

I looked left.

"You don't exactly take direction well, do you?"

"I'm hoping she's running away with the circus," I said, watching Helen Winterbottom loiter by the porta potties.

"I'm surprised she's here, truth be told. I wouldn't have thought the circus was her thing."

"Oh, I don't know," I said. "I think she'd make a rather admirable clown."

"Maybe she's on a date," said Belle, nudging me. "Takes all sorts."

I felt a lump in my throat as Frosty Knickers' "sort" emerged from behind a rotund elderly gentleman and disappeared with his DS into the crowd.

I awoke to a sunny summer's day—which did nothing to reflect my mood. Seeing Adam and Frosty Knickers together sat like a lead balloon in my chest. But it didn't make any sense to be upset. I had no hold on Adam, and he definitely had no hold on me. It had been years since we'd been an item. So why was I bothered?

I fixed myself a balanced, nutritious breakfast consisting of a four-fingered Kit Kat and three cups of decaf, and tried to ease myself out of my funk. I had no plans for the day other than to get groceries and start organizing Aunt Rose's funeral. Neither of which filled me with joy.

Elgar wound his furry tail around my ankle and I made a mental note to add cat food to my shopping list. There had been an insignificant amount of kitty kibble in a Tupperware bowl on the counter and two tins of wet cat food, which I had blown through with ease. I wondered how Horace, my budgerigar, was doing back in Austin. Mrs Ackerman was a conscientious animal lover and Horace was no doubt being spoiled. In reality he might never wish to return. I had given my neighbor a sack containing more millet than you could launch a raccoon at, plus a month's supply of paper for the bottom of Horace's cage. This led me to a question—who had Aunt Rose entrusted to watch Elgar while away?

I was about to head upstairs when I heard a commotion. I

yanked open the front door and there stood two young girls, both wearing Disney tees and jeans.

"May I help you?"

Both lunged forward and started speaking at once. I watched with interest as they punctuated their conversation with elbow digs. If either had pigtails I had the feeling they'd be pulling them.

I held up a hand. "Are you here for piano lessons?"

They both nodded.

"But I was here first," said the brunette.

"Fibber," said the blonde. "I got here first."

"Only because I held the gate open for you," said the brunette, literally stamping her foot in frustration.

I had never encountered such enthusiastic pupils. It was rather touching. I gazed at my watch. "Shouldn't you both be at school?"

They looked at me as if I was slightly deranged. "It's Saturday," said the brunette.

Good grief, I'd completely lost track. "What grades are you?" I asked, as they simultaneously muscled their way through the door.

"Three," they both said together.

"And you both want to go first?" I asked, trying not to smile.

Brunette and blonde both nodded.

"Then I'll give you a pop quiz. How does that sound? Whoever gets the correct answer goes first."

The blonde seemed unsure, but nodded anyway. I plucked a piece of paper off the hall table, ripped it in half and handed it to each girl. "While I get dressed I want you to jot down the difference between a concerto and a symphony." I tossed them each a pencil and headed up the stairs.

By the time I returned the brunette was perched on the bottom step, while the blonde lay sprawled against the door stroking a non-hissing Elgar. Both seemed to have calmed down.

"Okay, what you got?" I asked the brunette. "And by the way, what's your name?"

"I'm Elsie and I'm nine. She's Poppy and she's eight."

"And three quarters," added Poppy.

Elsie stood and read from her paper. "A symphony is longer than a concerto."

"Good job," I said. "And you, Poppy?"

Poppy handed me her paper and I smiled. On it she had written,

A symphony has four movements. A concerto has three and a solo instrument. Let Elsie go first. She did hold open the gate and I like cats.

"Okay, Elsie. In you go." I said, indicating Aunt Rose's study.

Elsie rose to her feet and strutted in, head held high.

I glanced at Poppy and she winked. I had a feeling I was going to like Poppy.

Four more children showed up that morning, and it was 1:00pm before I'd finished lessons. Like I had done with the previous children, I had written out a receipt, a note to their parents thanking them for their patronage, and my pricing for half-hour and hour-long lessons, promising the extra money could be put to the next lesson if they continued.

As it was, each student promised to return. I had no idea how word of my piano teaching prowess was spreading, but I was not about to put a stop to it. I may be the sole benefactor of Aunt Rose's estate, but it could be weeks until the will went through probate.

I finished off the last of the pâté and added Poppy and Elsie to my list of pupils. So far eleven children in three days. Pretty impressive.

I did the washing up and decided to call Aunt Rose's solicitor. I found the scrunched-up piece of paper Adam had thrust into my hand, and once again realized how inconvenient it was to not own a phone. The sun was dappled and the sky blue as I sauntered along to the village phone box and dialed the number. Were English solicitors open on Saturday? The phone rang twice before a young man's voice announced Padfoot & Strong. My gosh, it sounded like something out of *Harry Potter*.

I explained who I was and was put on hold. Nice to know some things were the same both sides of the Atlantic. Thirty seconds later the phone sprang to life and a very nice man named Douglas explained I would have to come into the office, but the generalities were as follows: I was, indeed, the sole beneficiary and, even better,

Aunt Rose had a comprehensive funeral plan in place—all I would have to do was follow the instructions. I said a silent prayer of thanks to Aunt Rose and hung up, promising to visit their premises on Monday.

Now all I had to do was head to the grocery store and stock up on provisions. I decided to motor into Dorking and try my luck at the Waitrose I'd spotted on the High Street.

I trekked back to Plum Tree Cottage and eyed the garage with trepidation. Miraculously, Jenny started on my first try. Feeling feisty, I decided to roll down the top and damn the consequences.

Once in Waitrose I practically gallivanted along the aisles, tossing in fresh fruit and vegetables with gay abandon. Who am I kidding? I purchased packaged dinners, two frozen pepperoni pizzas, and a slab of Cadbury's milk chocolate immense enough to feed a minor African nation. A plethora of extremely unhealthy desserts completed my shopping expedition, and I loaded my groceries onto Jenny's passenger seat with a smile on my face and a spring in my falsely acquired sandals.

The gods must have also been in a particularly favorable mood, as Jenny burst into life on the first try. It wasn't until I was passing the turnoff to the circus that I felt a decrease in speed. I checked my mirror. There was nobody behind me, which was fortuitous as Jenny was fading fast. I indicated and pulled over to the side of the road. I had no phone and I was roughly halfway between Dorking and Milkwood, so not ideal.

I stared at my groceries and wondered what on earth possessed me to purchase today's special—a bumper tub of raspberry ripple. There was no way ice cream was going to make it home without melting. I reached into the bag, pulled out the tub and decided to make the best of it. Getting out of Jenny, I squatted on the verge and prized off the lid. I seriously considered digging in with my hands, until I remembered a plastic spoon I'd snagged off the plane and rummaged around in my handbag until I found it. I may have broken down and I may have been sitting on the side of the road but I had ice cream. Things could be worse.

I was daydreaming about chocolate toppings and sprinkles

when I realized a car was chugging down the track leading from the big top. I stood and shielded my eyes against the afternoon sun. The car drew to a halt and I moved towards it. I had taken three more steps when the sun lurched behind a cloud and I got my first good look at the white Volvo and its driver.

47

Adam Ward stepped out, leaned against the driver's side door, and crossed his arms. "Need any help?"

I swear my dentist could hear me grinding my teeth all the way in central Texas. I so wanted to say no, but it was pretty obvious I hadn't pulled Jenny onto the side of the A25 to have a picnic, even if I did have a tub of ice cream in my grubby little mitts.

"She stopped," I said.

"You don't say," said Adam, strolling towards me.

"I know you don't know anything about cars, Adam Ward, so don't pretend you do."

Adam leaned through Jenny's open window, turned the key and inspected her dashboard. "You're right, I don't, but I *can* tell when a car has run out of petrol."

I shut my eyes. Out of petrol? Oh, good grief. I'd like to have blamed this on jetlag, but I'd been in the UK for almost two weeks. Even to my ears that excuse sounded lame.

"Don't worry," said Adam, strolling back to his car. "I am your man."

He remoted the boot open and hauled out a can of petrol. At that exact moment the sun reappeared from behind a mottled cloud, bringing out the highlights in Adam's hair, illuminating his chiseled cheekbones and basically making the guy resemble a still from a James Dean movie. I swallowed hard and made a mental note to get real. The guy was in a relationship and I was heading back to Texas as soon as Aunt Rose's killer had been caught. My feelings had disaster written all over them.

"Who goes around with petrol in their boot?" I said, pulling myself together.

"Your friendly law enforcement officer," said Adam, unscrewing the top, "that's who."

Adam sploshed petrol into Jenny's tank and rescrewed the cap.

"Were you seeing a matinee?" I asked, nodding towards the big top.

"No, business. But I caught a few acts last night. It was amazing. You should go."

I wanted to say that I'd been there last night, that I knew he'd been lying about having to work, and that I'd seen him with his girlfriend, but I couldn't find the words.

"I was back again today because there's been another theft."

"Isn't that a bit beneath you?"

"You'd think, right?"

"How are you getting on with the murder?"

Adam's eyes met mine. "We're making progress."

"Can't you give me more details? This is my aunt we're talking about, or am I still prime suspect?"

I thought briefly about Gurminder and Dan and teetered on the edge of telling Adam what I'd overheard. I had no proof that Dan was the murderer, only a few jumbled words. Would I look stupid? Would I be getting them in trouble for no reason? I thought of Susan Ludlow and her pride in her only son and decided to keep mum until I had actual proof.

Adam reached forward and linked his fingers between mine. "Josie, you know I've never considered you a suspect."

"Oh, really? It certainly doesn't feel that way when you have your subordinates rummaging through my drawers."

Adam sighed. "Believe me, no one wants to solve this mystery more than me."

"Really? Why's that then?"

"Because I can tell you're unhappy. Once the murder's solved you can return to your life in America and put this whole episode behind you."

Adam was right, but for some reason going home suddenly wasn't as urgent as it had once been.

48

It was 6:30. Time to head to St Ethelred's and the world premiere of Quentin Young's *Enchanted Summer*. I changed out of my shorts and tee and decided to don the last of Belle's hand-me-down dresses—this one in striking tangerine. I had made one more stop while in Dorking, where I had purchased the most adorable strawberry-red sandals. Finolla lived by the motto that every girl should have a pair of red shoes. I was about to see if she was right. I removed the tags, slipped them on and was feeling slightly spiffy. I hated to admit it, but maybe Finolla was right? I wasn't sure what the dress code was for a local premiere, but figured I could at least make an effort.

I tossed some kitty kibble into Elgar's dish and refilled his water bowl before locking the front door and heading to the church. I had never seen Unthank Road so busy. The residents of Milkwood were dressed in their proverbial Sunday best and, like migrating birds, all heading in one direction. I loved this show of community spirit but, if I was honest, I was slightly surprised.

By the time I got to the duck pond I was starting to wish I'd not worn my new sandals. By the time I was halfway around the village green I was wondering if anyone would notice if I slipped off my shoes and entered St Ethelred's barefoot.

I decided to suck it up and hobbled my way towards the squat, stone tower. If I remembered correctly St Ethelred's was a Norman church originating in the twelfth century. I had never been able to tell my Norman from my Saxon and would have to have a flying buttress shoved in my face before I could identify a structure as being remotely Gothic. However, it was an attractive church, nestled amongst a plethora of higgledy-piggledy gravestones—no Arlington Cemetery precision here. To say the graveyard was over-subscribed would be like saying Chopin enjoyed the piano, and I couldn't help wonder where Aunt Rose would be laid to rest. Surely not here? There wasn't the room.

I joined the throng as a flow of music lovers streamed through the arched doors. I read the sign displayed by Lucy Lewis saying "Save Our Roof" and dropped a twenty into the bucket held by her sister, Georgina.

It was 6:50pm, and already there was barely a seat left. I spotted the Witches of Milkwood wedged firmly into the back row and Wendy Williams and family loitering near the baptismal font. I was tootling down the aisle searching for an empty spot when I heard someone call my name.

Belle waved me over. She sat in the third row from the front and I hurried towards her. She wore a stunning red silk dress with matching fascinator and her hair was rolled into a chignon. Do I have to say it? She looked stunning.

Belle held onto a smart silk clutch and stood to let me pass. I took a seat between Belle and a sweet-looking elderly lady in a pea green dress and carrying a large wicker basket. With me in the middle, the three of us resembled a human traffic light.

"I thought you disliked classical music," I whispered.

"Hate it," said Belle, glancing backwards.

I reached down and released my feet from the torture device my newly purchased sandals were turning out to be. "So, why are you here?"

"Heavens to Betsy, no one in their right mind would miss this. The last time Quentin held a premiere the principal viola player's teeth fell out and Holly Drinkwater's cocker spaniel trotted up the aisle and had a wee on the double bass."

"You're joking?" I was stunned. I had encountered disasters during middle school concerts: stands collapsing, clarinets squeaking, but nothing that came close to this type of calamity. No wonder Quentin had spoken of his dislike for dogs.

"It gets better," said Belle, her eyes searching the crowd. "The time before, two of the violinists' chairs gave way and let's just say the tenor had spent an hour too long in The Pig & Whistle. During a bit of a lull, he decided to launch himself into the audience for some crowd surfing."

My jaw plummeted.

"Plus, Quentin throws a massive party afterwards at The Dirty Duck," said Belle, still gazing over my shoulder. "You have to come to the concert to get the free drinks afterwards. It's just good manners."

Turning, I tried to figure out who Belle was looking for. I got a "howdy" from Daisy Pond and a wave from Susan Ludlow, but not much else for my trouble. I surveyed the crowd. Could one of the people here tonight be Aunt Rose's murderer? A tingle of apprehension sprinted down my spine as I scrutinized each of the Witches of Milkwood, moved onto Wendy Williams and ended with Wendy's long-suffering husband, Duncan, pale and glistening under the unforgiving glow of a well-aimed spotlight. The vast numbers of people present was still shocking to me and I wondered if the vicar pulled such a crowd on Sunday. Somehow, I doubted it.

I was about to press Belle for more details on the tenor when I saw a figure emerge from a side door, nonchalantly stroll through the north transept and lean against a pillar. He shifted position and a shaft of light illuminated a face not easily forgotten. I say not easily forgotten because the man was simply beautiful. There are no other words for it.

I felt Belle shift in her seat and turned to ask if she knew who Mr Perfection was, but stopped. Belle was looking determinedly in the opposite direction and I was left in no doubt as to whom Belle had been searching for.

The numerous questions I had were put on hold, as the musicians started to take their places. I was surprised to see Peter amongst their number, as last time we'd spoken he'd mentioned spending the weekend with his folks. Dressed in a tuxedo and bowtie, he waggled his bow in my direction and I took in a breath.

My lodger was undoubtedly handsome, but take away the M&S slippers and accountant's outfit and add one dapper tuxedo—and the words "George Clooney" sprang to mind. I realized I had not mentioned the "almost" kiss to Belle and made a mental note to keep it that way.

Ten minutes later there was the sound of single clapping and Quentin Young emerged from the vestry. The clapping spread and soon the entire church was whooping and wailing for the Maestro of Milkwood. I peered at the program Belle had given me. *Enchanted Summer* was a choral work divided into eight movements and had the typical soloists—soprano, alto, tenor and bass. I sought out the tenor, normally the slighter of the two male singers, and wondered if it was he of the crowd surfing fame. One could only hope.

The cheering faded and the lights dimmed. There was an anticipatory silence before a single cello pierced the air. Within seconds I was transported by lush melodies and soaring crescendos. It was magical, and had the bonus of not a single musician losing their teeth or being peed on.

Forty-five minutes later, the cello wept its dying notes as *Enchanted Summer* came full circle. I lunged to my feet and applauded the man who truly deserved a wider audience than the backwaters of Milkwood. Quentin Young was in the ascendant, and one day I would be able to say I'd been there when he took off.

The elderly woman sitting to my left struggled to her feet and joined in the heartfelt applause. This was a surprise, as the woman had been asleep by the time the trumpets had joined the party. No mean feat on benches as hard as granite or trumpets as enthusiastic as Quentin's. Maybe she was just happy for it to be over and get to The Dirty Duck. However, one by one people lumbered to their feet and soon Quentin Young was enjoying a thoroughly deserved standing ovation.

"What did you think?" I asked Belle, sinking back onto the pew and gingerly reattaching my sandals.

"You're the expert, what did you think?"

I winced.

"That bad?" asked Belle.

"No. It was incredible. It's just...well, I'm having a bit of bother with my feet."

"Here you are, lovely." My formerly dormant neighbor reached into her basket and pressed a box of plasters into my palm.

I sighed with relief and hoisted my ankle onto my knee, intent on patching my self-imposed injuries.

"Keep the box," said the elderly lady, inching her way along the pew. Reaching the end she turned and observed my progress. Smiling broadly, she added, "Anything for DI Ward's girlfriend."

I was speechless. I turned to voice my complaint but my concert companion had vacated her seat and was scuttling towards the north transept. I squinted into the darkness in time to see Belle and Mr Perfection slip silently into the night.

49

I hobbled out of St Ethelred's and tottered across the village green towards The Dirty Duck. I scanned the surroundings, but Belle and her mystery man were nowhere in sight.

By now I was among the dregs of the exodus, and found myself limping alongside two women not much older than me whom I recognized as the pair who had jostled me during my first night at The Dirty Duck. The taller woman wore a plain beige dress approximately one sneeze away from being ripped in two, while the shorter woman with curls wore a dress so voluminous it could have doubled as a circus tent. The Jack Spratt and his wife of the fashion world, I thought uncharitably.

"Wasn't too bad, I suppose," said the woman in the way-too-tight frock.

"Would have been better if someone lost their teeth, though," replied the other.

"Or if Holly Drinkwater's dog had come in and had a poo," said the first, reaching for her friend's arm to steady herself.

Tent Lady roared with laughter as the two stumbled towards The Dirty Duck.

I paused. Such dedicated music connoisseurs. Truly, it brought a lump to my throat.

There was already an overflow of excited concertgoers on the cobbled pavements outside the pub and, as I eased my way through the door, it was obvious that the citizens of Milkwood were in vibrant spirits. A second later a cheer erupted and I turned to see the maestro himself emerge with a theatrical flourish. He was wearing an ivory tuxedo with flowing tails paired with a cream turtleneck. His snowy white locks invoked a TRESemmé commercial, and his matching shoes were so polished you could practically see your reflection waving back. A pathway materialized and Quentin swanned towards the bar, clasping outstretched hands and receiving claps on the back.

I took the opportunity to follow him through the Moses-like opening and watched as Quentin was engulfed by his adoring public. Adoring as long as there was an open bar.

Snagging a glass of pinot and a mini sausage roll, I was resuming my pursuit of Quentin when I felt an arm envelop my waist. I spun around and found myself inches from the bright blue eyes of Peter Lacey.

"What...what did you think?" asked Peter, flush with post-performance energy.

"It was, erm, amazing," I said, searching for an appropriate adjective and failing.

"Wasn't it," said Peter, inching closer.

My mind flashed back to our previous encounter. Surely Peter was not going to kiss me in the middle of The Dirty Duck with the entire population of Milkwood looking on?

I turned my head sharp left to avoid such an attempt and instead of the piercing blue of Peter's eyes I met the steely brown of Adam's.

Before I had a chance to extricate myself Peter whispered something about public transport and petunias, planted a kiss on my forehead and disappeared into the crowd.

I gave a halfhearted grin at Adam, who pointedly turned his back. Great, not exactly the response I would have liked. Not knowing what to do next, and with no Belle in sight, I sidled towards a familiar face.

I smiled as I approached and, to Daisy's credit, she didn't make a run for it. It wasn't that our conversation at The Pig & Whistle had gone badly; it's just that the conversation had ended with a lot of unresolved issues. Not knowing how long Daisy planned to stay in Milkwood, this seemed like an excellent time to tackle her.

Daisy bore a striking resemblance to Finolla, but, I suspected, that's where the similarities ended. Daisy clutched a pint in her left hand and wore wide legged trousers and a floppy shirt with an eye-popping floral design. Her hair was tied back with a wide orange scarf and her earrings were of the hooped and large variety. She was not the height of fashion, but I thought she looked chic.

"No Finolla?" asked Daisy.

"There was a marquess," I explained. "Plus a stable of Argentinian polo players, which led to something to do with the tango. Anyhow the upshot is Mum's gone away for a few days."

Daisy's expression barely registered, and I had the impression none of the aforementioned came as a shock.

I wasn't sure how to continue. I settled for the mundane. "I like your earrings."

Daisy reached up, felt her earlobe and smiled. "My friend Mila made these. She's very talented."

I nodded, not knowing what to say next. I really sucked at this interrogation stuff. "Aunt Daisy?"

Daisy raised a heavily ringed hand. "Don't you think you're a little old for the whole 'aunt' thing? Why don't we stick with 'Daisy?' Besides, you calling me 'aunt' makes me feel like a bit of a fossil."

Daisy neither sounded like her twin nor dressed like her, but here was something the two had in common—a resounding wish not to appear old.

"Listen, Josie. I didn't want to talk about what I was doing here in front of your mum. But it's no big deal and knowing what this village is like, you're probably going to find out anyway."

I could relate. Trying to keep anything private in Milkwood was like trying to play the opening bars of Jeremiah Clarke's *Trumpet Voluntary* quietly—it couldn't be done.

"You see, it's just that Finolla has made such a success of her life, and I...well, I'm not quite so successful and the thought of your mum—"

"Judging you," I suggested.

Daisy looked me in the eye. "Bingo! Got it in one. I married a sheep farmer, and Edward Pond, God rest his fleecy little soul, was a good man, but let's just say he wasn't exactly one for airs and graces —not the kind of bloke your mum would have approved of."

"If it makes you feel any better, I'm a school teacher. You can imagine how that went down. Actually, I think Finolla tells her friends I'm in prison—either that or I'm gay—anything to make me sound more adventurous."

Daisy draped an arm around my shoulder and gave it a squeeze. "Ah, ya poor thing."

I laughed. "It's not that bad. Of course, moving to a different continent helped. Amazing how 5,000 miles can make such an improvement to a mother-daughter relationship."

"I think we may have more in common than I thought," said Daisy, raising her pint. "The truth of it is, I'm a novelist. Now don't get too excited. I've written several semi-successful mysteries and then Mila suggested I try my hand at English cozies and I thought why the heck not?"

The revelation that the third Braithwaite sister had artistic leanings did not come as a huge surprise. Now, if Daisy had said she was a mathematician or nuclear physicist, I'd have been floored.

"So, where's the best place to write a cozy mystery?" said Daisy.

"You were here doing research for your book?"

"Spot on. I'd written to Rosie several times over the years and Milkwood sounded like the perfect place to set a murder mystery. I thought I'd surprise her, but it was bad timing. She'd just up and left for the Peak District."

"You didn't let her know you were coming?" I asked.

"I'm not exactly known for my pre-planning skills," said Daisy, taking another swig of beer.

Our conversation was interrupted by the clink of silverware on glass, as Quentin Young prepared to give a speech. I surveyed the scene. Everyone who was anyone was here, including Frosty Knickers, wedged into a corner with Adam. Helen Winterbottom whispered something in Adam's ear which produced a smile and I felt my *joie de vivre* plummet.

"You spoke to Rosie, right? Was she in good spirits?" whispered

Daisy, as Quentin launched into a heartfelt speech of gratitude—although the gratitude was mainly for himself.

I thought back to our phone conversation. "She said she had something exciting to tell me."

"Any idea what it was? You don't think that's why she was killed, do you?"

I hadn't up to now, but maybe that was *exactly* the reason.

"I missed her by one day, you know. One lousy day. She was a great sister. She'd always stick up for me when I was a kid—nothing like Finolla, thank goodness. I wanted to know how life had treated her?"

I didn't want to shatter Daisy's memories, but it was bound to come out. I took a deep breath. "Actually, it looks like Rose was writing nasty letters to some of the residents of Milkwood."

Daisy paused, her beer halfway to her lips. "That don't seem right."

"I thought the same, but I've seen the letters. Plus everyone I've spoken to didn't like her. Well, with the exception of Quentin Young," I said, watching the maestro waft through the crowd, absorbing his well-earned glory.

"Whatcha think happened?"

It was the question I'd been asking myself since Belle DeCorcy let slip that Aunt Rose was, in her words, "horrid." What had happened to my aunt to make her into Milkwood's most hated resident—and was her exciting news the reason she was killed?

50

Daisy and I spent the rest of the evening getting to know each other. Turned out my mysterious aunt and I had a lot in common. We enjoyed the same books, thought body waxing totally overrated and, being expats, had a love of England found only in those who no longer have to live without air conditioning or suffer the indignities of the M25 on a daily basis.

We talked about Daisy's life in New Zealand, then she described being taken in for questioning, which was all going swimmingly until IT opened her laptop.

"Had some explaining to do when they discovered the past ten hits were variations on how to kill someone using a sock," said Daisy.

My eyes widened.

"All in the name of research, of course. You can't be a mystery author and not have a seriously messed up browser history."

Daisy reminded me of a thinner, jollier Aunt Rose, with a more outlandish sense of fashion. Already I was starting to dread the thought of her returning to New Zealand. I had just lost one aunt; I didn't want to lose another. She was easy to talk to and I found myself telling Daisy all about finding Aunt Rose while *Turandot* blared from the CD player. I then moved on to how I'd thought Wendy Williams had copped it while listening to *Madame Butterfly*, explaining that I may never be able to listen to Puccini again, such was the association. I also confided my goal of finding out who killed Aunt Rose and my complete ineptitude at getting information.

"Let's just say I won't be relinquishing my day job to become a detective any time soon."

"Josie, you're an utter delight. I would bet you could do anything you wanted if you set your mind to it."

I grinned. This was possibly the nicest thing anyone had ever said to me.

"So you have no idea who killed Rosie or why?" asked Daisy.

"None," I replied, frowning.

"What is it, girl? Spit it out."

"I know there was someone at Plum Tree that night, but I can't believe they would murder Rose; it's not in their nature."

"You gotta go with what your conscience tells you," said Daisy. "Trust your gut, is what I say."

I nodded. But was my gut right? The list of people at Plum Tree Cottage was expanding daily, but I couldn't believe any of them had actually killed my aunt.

The evening passed quickly and by the time I left the beer was flowing freely and the piano was in full force. I said my farewells and reluctantly exited into the warm summer night. The toads were croaking and the crickets were singing, as were the remaining patrons in The Dirty Duck.

I chucked a left and passed the wildfowl clustered on the bank for the night. I was not looking forward to the trek home, my feet only recently having stopped hurting, and I'd barely gone ten paces when I heard someone call my name.

Turning, I saw a plump figure plunging down the pub steps.

"Just you wait a minute, young lady!"

Great, this was all I needed.

Bonnie Curry swayed towards me wearing a sturdy summer dress and a scowl.

"I gotta have a word with you. Someone's gotta put you right."

The ducks scattered and I awaited my fate. How to deal with a tipsy Bonnie Curry? This was definitely not covered in my teacher's manual. Heartbroken teenage girls—got it. Annoyed parents—expert. Belligerent old age pensioners—not a clue.

Of course, at that exact moment, every patron of The Dirty Duck also decided to head home, therefore witnessing the altercation, as Bonnie Curry hiccupped towards me. I steeled myself, but what she said next was not what I was expecting.

"You think you're so clever swanning around with that DeCorcy girl." Bonnie jabbed my arm with her stubby finger. "You don't know the half of it. The things I could tell you about her'd make your hair curl. She's not right, she's not." Bonnie placed her finger by the side of her unruly curls and started twirling. "Unhinged, she is."

This was rich coming from the woman who'd accused me of murder. I turned to face her. "I'm not going to listen to a bad word about my friend. Belle DeCorcy is the nicest, kindest person I've ever met." She was also the worst driver, but I felt this was not the time to mention such trivialities.

Bonnie turned to her audience, smirking like a Cheshire cat before turning back to me and getting way too close for comfort. "Crazy Corcy's a loon and won't no one here deny it. She's as nutty as a bag of almonds. Ask anyone. She's dangerous, she is, and I wouldn't be surprised for one moment if she was the murderer."

And then before I realized it, Bonnie Curry lunged towards me. I dodged to the left, which had the advantage of not getting hit, but the disadvantage of leaving Bonnie floundering dangerously close to the duck pond.

Flinging myself after her, I wrapped my arms around Bonnie's substantial midriff, instantly turning us into that famous scene from *Titanic* with Bonnie teetering on the edge of the duck pond; her an aged Kate Winslet, me the female version of Leonardo DiCaprio but with more hair and considerably less charm. One inch more and she'd take us both down. Memories of my seven-year-old duck pond incident came flooding back. I gave one almighty tug and Bonnie Curry and I toppled backwards onto a grass full of duck poo.

"Crispy pancakes!" I murmured, as Bonnie thrashed around on top of me like an upended beetle.

Distant cackles rang out as I tried, unsuccessfully, to heave the considerable bulk of my neighbor off me before she collapsed my lung.

"And what do we have here?"

I shut my eyes and tried to take a deep breath—but failed. "Don't just stand there," I muttered, through gritted teeth.

"Are you sure?" Adam asked.

Jiminy Cricket, I could tell he was smirking. "Get her off!" I gasped.

Adam reached down and grabbed a flapping arm. She didn't budge an inch. DS Winterbottom grabbed the other arm, and Bonnie Curry was winched upwards, allowing me to inhale some desperately needed air. Obviously those weights in Frosty Knickers' bedroom were not just for show.

I glanced up and saw the impenetrable almond eyes of Frosty Knickers glaring at me. Now there was someone I would not want to meet down a dark country lane—which basically incorporated the whole of Milkwood.

DS Winterbottom held out a hand and before I had a chance to demur she grasped my palm and hauled me to my feet, crushing several fingers and almost dislocating my arm in the process. I decided to forgo the thanks as I rubbed the assaulted arm, simultaneously ignoring the duck poo damage inflicted on my once-beautiful dress.

"Did you see that?" said Bonnie Curry, glaring at Adam. "She tried to throw me in the duck pond."

I was speechless, and not only due to having the oxygen squeezed from my lungs.

"Really?" said Adam, patiently. "Because that's not what I saw."

"I've got witnesses," said Bonnie, jabbing a finger towards the burgeoning crowd.

"Mrs Curry," said Adam, in his best policeman's voice, "I saw you rush Ms Monroe and, if it hadn't been for her, you'd be up to your neck in frogspawn."

"Give it up, Bonnie," said Susan Ludlow, passing by. "Give a thank you to the lass. She saved ya from getting a soaking."

Bonnie Curry sniffed, turned on her heels and began her unsteady journey home.

"I'd better go after her," I said. "She's not in any fit state to navigate the potholes on Brambley Lane in the dark."

"I'll come with you," said Adam.

"There's no need." But Adam had already fallen into step beside me.

"I can take Miss Monroe home," said DS Winterbottom.

"We'll be fine, Helen. You get back to your flat."

I turned in time to see Helen Winterbottom give me the look of death and for the first time I wondered about her quick arrival on the scene after Aunt Rose's murder. How close to Plum Tree had she been when she received the call from Bonnie Curry? As far as I knew there was no reason for Helen to kill Aunt Rose, but she *had* referred to her as being "a nasty piece of work." Was that a reason to kill her?

Adam and I trailed Bonnie Curry along Unthank Road and onto Brambley Lane. The night was warm and the clouds were low, blocking out the silver moonlight and making the inky night as dark as pitch—whatever pitch was.

Bonnie continued to mumble her discontent all the way to her front door. Owning neither a torch nor a cell phone, I was glad of Adam's presence, as he shone the light from his mobile phone towards Bonnie's sturdy brogues. This, at least, gave her a better chance of making it home without twisting an ankle or breaking her neck. Either of which I was sure I'd be blamed for.

Once I saw her safely inside her cottage, I happily let Bonnie Curry slam the door in my face and prayed the woman found her bed and not another bottle of chardonnay.

Adam checked his messages while he waited for me at the garden gate. "She didn't try and get in a last punch, did she?"

"It was a near thing, but luckily there was a policeman nearby, so I believe she thought better of it."

"I do have my uses," said Adam, slipping his phone into his pocket.

"Well, goodnight," I said.

"Wait a second. I'm not going to let you walk alone!"

"I'm a grown woman, Adam. I believe I can find my way home from here."

Adam smiled.

"What?"

"You referred to Plum Tree as 'home.'"

"You know what I meant. Anyhow I'm good." I turned and was about to limp into the distance when I froze.

Adam laid a hand on my shoulder. "Josie, what's wrong?"

I took a step backwards. "It's Puccini."

51

A dam pulled out his phone and flipped the torch back on. I was hurrying now as the nearer we got to the cottage the louder the music became.

We reached the garden gate and Adam put out his arm. "Stay here."

I shoved the proffered arm away. "Are you nuts? I'm not staying out here by myself. There's some Puccini-loving, crazy psychopath out there armed with a deadly metronome. I'm coming with you."

Adam leaned forward and kissed my forehead. "Come on then. But stay behind me."

I figured this was an excellent compromise and hobbled along the garden path behind him. Puccini was practically bleeding through the windowpanes at this point—not a comforting thought.

"This couldn't be Peter, could it?" Adam asked, as we reached the front door.

"Peter caught the last train out of Milkwood to visit his parents in Cambridge. He left muttering something about his father's sweet peas, a jam roly-poly and an award-winning sausage roll recipe. I'm hoping it's something to do with a village fete, else he has some explaining to do."

"And you've not invited anyone to stay?"

"Adam, with the exception of you and Belle, the entire village hates me. Who the heck do you think I'm going to invite for a sleepover, Magna and the Witches of Milkwood?"

I saw a smile cross Adam's face at the "witches" comment. "And I'm assuming you locked up?" Adam poked the front door with his finger, causing it to swing open.

"What? Do I *look* stupid?"

Kicking off the offending sandals, I followed Adam into the entryway. The door to Aunt Rose's study was shut.

"I mean it, Josie. Stay here."

I didn't need much persuading. I had many fine qualities. Alas, bravery was not one of them.

Adam strode across the foyer and placed his hand on the door handle. My heart thumped louder than *Tosca's* "Vissi d'arte" currently blasting from behind the door.

The door inched open and Adam stepped inside, disappearing behind the aspidistra. I counted to five. I counted to ten, then I could stand it no more. I edged towards the opening and stuck my head around the door.

Adam looked up. He was crouching beside the CD player. "For God's sake, Josie, show me how to turn the darn thing off."

I dashed over and pulled out the plug—it was just easier.

"Looks like it was set to repeat," said Adam, straightening up. "There's no one here, but we'd better search the rest of the house. Make sure there's no one hiding in the cupboards."

Five minutes later we had completed searching the downstairs. Let's face it, unless there was someone lurking inside the tumble dryer there weren't too many places to conceal yourself. Upstairs was going to be an entirely different matter. Inside wardrobes, behind shower curtains, under beds—I'd seen enough scary movies to know there were a multitude of places available to your run-of-the-mill psychopath.

First we checked Aunt Rose's room, followed by the bathroom, Peter's room and lastly mine. Eventually I had to admit that unless the intruder was skulking around the attic I was good to go. Adam checked all doors and windows until I was as secure as the gold inside Fort Knox. So why was my heart still pounding like a jackhammer?

I sank onto the puffy eiderdown. "That CD player didn't start by itself, Adam. Someone was here."

"Have you told anyone about the Puccini connection?"

I thought back. Had I mentioned it to Wendy when I found her listening to *Madame Butterfly*? I couldn't remember. Then I recalled my earlier conversation with Daisy.

"I was telling my aunt earlier tonight, but she wouldn't have done this. Besides she was still in The Dirty Duck when I left."

"I agree it doesn't seem something your aunt would do. This was designed to scare you, nothing else. Unfortunately, when you were discussing the link with Puccini, half of Milkwood was most likely standing within earshot."

Adam was right. The pub had been heaving. At any given time we could have been overheard by practically anyone present. I could have kicked myself for my stupidity.

"Come on," said Adam. "See me out, and I want to hear you bolt the door as I leave."

I felt sick. I did not want to stay alone at Plum Tree. I was scared, but I didn't want to admit it.

I stood and headed for the door. Adam caught my hand. "Or I could stay?"

I felt so overwhelmed with gratitude that my legs buckled. Adam reached out and caught me, drawing me into an embrace.

I felt his chest expand as he drew me closer. Smelled the musk of his cologne.

"Come on Monroe, don't go all soft on me now."

"I am not soft," I whispered.

Adam ruffled my hair and I thought my legs might betray me once more. "You're right. You're not soft. You're perfect."

52

I awoke to dappled sunlight streaming through the window—I had obviously forgotten to put my sleep mask on. I rolled over and felt something warm beside me. Something warm and hissing. I opened my eye to see Elgar poised to bat me on the nose.

Elgar would have to wait for his food—it was way too early. But wait, how had Elgar entered my bedroom? He most definitely wasn't there when I'd removed my clothes and fallen into bed.

Elgar lurched off the bed towards my dressing table and started clawing the legs.

"Hey, stop that," I said, launching a pillow at him.

Sufficiently rebuked, Elgar slunk over to the door, giving it a not-so-surreptitious scratch. I was about to chastise him, but my attention was derailed by the steaming cup of tea, pile of Hobnobs, and note resting on the bedside table.

Didn't want to wake you. Adam.

I sat with a jerk. Oh my stars, Adam. I thought back to the night before and flushed with the memory. Phooey! This was going to be another complication I didn't need in my life.

Elgar and I traipsed downstairs for breakfast. Rooting through the cupboards, I located a fresh box of Frosties and, wonder of wonders, an ample stash of kitty kibble hidden away at the back. I poured myself out a bowl of Kellogg's finest and added a splash of milk before scooping an extra-large portion of kitty kibble into Elgar's bowl. I decided to put the whole Adam scenario on hold and concentrate on Aunt Rose. My conversation with Daisy had been illuminating. All I needed to do was find out what Aunt Rose was so excited about.

I was musing over this when the doorbell rang. Criminy, the list of people I did not want to see was rapidly rising. I thought about ignoring it, but a second, more urgent press got me heading down the hallway. I inched the door open and sighed with relief.

"Oh, thank heavens, I thought you might have been someone else."

"No such luck. Only me," said Belle, swanning into the foyer.

"I looked for you at The Dirty Duck last night."

"Did you?" said Belle.

"Yes, you disappeared so quickly. I was worried. Another escaped zedonk?"

"Yes! Yes, it was Claude. Dreadfully hard to catch, don't you know. Hates having his name called. Will charge you if you so much as whisper it."

This explained a lot, and I decided not to tell Belle about my embarrassing incident with Claude and the hedgerow a few nights previously.

"Come on, we're going to be late if you don't get a move on." Belle wore the simplest shift in pale pink, a filmy cream scarf caressing her neck. Tiny pearls dotted her earlobes, flat espadrilles covered her toes and from her arm hung a handbag reminding me of something I'd seen Queen Elizabeth clutching circa 1970s. On anyone else it might have seemed old fashioned. On Belle it was charming.

I stared at my watch. It was 3:45am in Texas. 9:45am in Milkwood. What could we possibly be late for?

"Chip chop," said Belle, ushering me towards the stairs.

I realized what day it was and reality dawned. "No? Really?"

"Absolutely," said Belle, "and hurry, else all the primo seats will be gone."

Five minutes later I'd dressed in my one remaining new outfit, a summery A-Line skirt and sunny cotton blouse with a V-neck I hoped wasn't too low. My hair was brushed, my teeth were clean and I had run a damp flannel over all the important bits. I prized my poor, abused feet back into Belle's mum's sandals and hoped for the best.

Belle was already in Roger and my feet were in no state to argue. With practiced ease, Belle reversed down Brambley Lane and did a handbrake turn onto Unthank Road. Two minutes later we made our way around the village green and found a primo parking spot. There's a shocker.

I eased myself out of Roger and ambled through the kissing gate. Obviously the village was far more traditional than I gave it credit for, as I watched the citizens of Milkwood saunter towards St Ethelred's for their weekly commune with the almighty.

Belle grabbed my arm. She hustled me along the uneven path and past the beckoning graveyard with a sign stating NO DOGS. A sign added after Quentin Young's previous concert, I wondered?

We entered the church and, like the previous night, the place was packed. I had never seen a church this busy unless it was high holidays, weddings or funerals. That reminded me—I must talk to the vicar about Aunt Rose's funeral and set a date.

Belle marched down the aisle, veered around the brass rubbings and found us two spots in the front row. I took a pew and tried to remember the last time I'd attended church on Sunday. I had never been particularly religious, but did have vague memories of attending St Ethelred's with Aunt Rose during the summer. What I didn't recall was it being so popular. I glanced around the congregation and noticed something odd. Whereas last night the audience had been divided evenly between men and women, today the church was filled primarily with God's fairer sex.

Belle leaned towards me. "By the way, I heard what happened last night."

"Of course you did. Let me just say—I did *not* beat up Bonnie Curry."

"I should hope not," said Belle. "But I heard you stood up for me." Belle took my hand and gave it a squeeze. "Thank you, Josie."

My attention was diverted as the organist pounded out the first three notes of Bach's Toccata and Fugue in D Minor, the following chords stacking like a New York BLT. A murmur of anticipation ran through the congregation and I felt the air electrify. Maybe Milkwood's residents were more religious than I'd given them credit for? The vestry door eased open and out stepped the Adonis from last night. Okay, so the Adonis was wearing a long white dress accented with an emerald silk scarf, but nevertheless, I knew an Adonis when I saw one. It was as if the entire congregation had been holding its breath waiting for this moment. The only person who didn't seem particularly interested was Belle, sitting as cool as a cucumber sandwich, eyes downcast as if in prayer.

Surely this couldn't be the vicar? My suspicion was confirmed as the blue-eyed blond was followed by an elderly man outfitted in similar garb. The Adonis must be the curate, but no socks with sandals or stereotypical bad breath, here.

Once again, the organ burst into life and Milkwood's faithful sprang to their feet as my piano student, Poppy, paraded the cross down the aisle. I must admit I was slightly blindsided by Belle's atrocious singing voice, but you had to hand it to her, she was loud and she was enthusiastic. The fact that she seemed to be singing an entirely different tune was beside the point. Edging slightly away from Belle, I joined in the words to "All Things Bright and Beautiful," skimming through the hymn book to see what the morning had in store. I smiled, seeing "Love Divine, All Loves Excelling," and "Praise My Soul the King of Heaven" were next. No artsy-fartsy happy-clappy songs at St Ethelred's and for that I did a silent prayer of thanks.

An hour later the service was over and I had to say, for a man who could appear on the cover of *GQ*, the curate was surprisingly erudite. His heartfelt sermon had touched on forgiveness and love, and had been full of hope with a dash of history thrown in for good measure. Gosh darn it, Milkwood's curate was quite something, leaving me briefly ashamed at my earlier assumption that the parishioners were there purely for the man's looks.

Belle and I waited in line to exit the church and have the obligatory chat to either the reverend or his adorable curate. There were two queues blocking the aisle, one considerably longer than the other. As I needed to have a word with the vicar I chose the shorter one.

I reached the front of the line and stuck out my hand. "Hi, I'm Josie Monroe."

Reverend Greene had watery blue eyes, shiny alabaster hair and a pair of half-moon spectacles perched haphazardly across his bulbous nose. His cheeks were ruddy, his eyebrows unruly and his gut a little wider than he probably would have liked. The reverend clasped my hand in both of his and shook them warmly. He must have been over seventy, but his grip was firm and his eyes were shrewd.

"Ms Monroe. You must forgive me for not visiting since the untimely death of your aunt. I have had a rather severe summer cold and my curate has spent the entire week on a training course in Bristol. I'm afraid this has not been our finest hour in parishioner care. My wife did drop by, but alas there was no one home."

His voice was deep and resonant. Just the sound of it made me feel like everything was going to be okay.

"Think nothing of it," I said, as I narrowly missed being side-swiped by three giggling teenagers.

The reverend reached out a hand to steady me. "Ah, yes. Philip is a wonderful curate and does tend to pack a crowd when he preaches. I could so easily be jealous, but that would be rather churlish, don't you think?"

I shrugged. "I guess, but it would be understandable."

"Bums on seats, Ms Monroe. Bums on seats. Our Mr Upton brings in the youngsters, and I like to think I still have the power to bring in the more devout of our congregation." He shrugged. "Enough about us. You must be wanting to make arrangements for Ms Braithwaite's funeral. Why don't you pop along this afternoon, say around four, and we can have a nice cup of tea and discuss the details?"

I thanked him and was about to head across the uneven path when I felt a hand on my shoulder.

"Ms Monroe, may I add my condolences to those of the rector?"

I gazed into the face of the Adonis. His smile was wide and

welcoming, his eyes compassionate, and I mentioned the sapphirine quality, right?

He grasped my hands in his. "Rose was..."

He paused. No doubt trying to find the words to describe Milkwood's most hated resident.

"...so kind to me when I first arrived. She was quite a lady and I will miss her quiet wit and her excellent taste in music."

By "quiet wit," was he referencing The Dirty Duck debacle? Regardless, his words were not what I was expecting. Letting go of my hand, the curate bobbed his head in my direction before returning to his queue of restless parishioners.

Wow, the guy was not only good-looking, he was sincere, kind and eminently likable.

No wonder half of Milkwood was swooning over him.

I loitered outside St Ethelred's waiting for Belle and entertained myself by reading the church history, displayed on a board next to a giant thermometer where red lines had been inked across in a shaky hand, as the roof fund rose tile by tile. It looked like last night's concert had contributed several more lines and for that I was glad. St Ethelred's was a splendid church and it deserved a new roof. I had moved onto a small wooden sign, where information on the vicar and times of service were beautifully etched in gold, when Belle came hurtling along the path.

"Lunch?" said Belle, grabbing me by the arm and spinning me towards Roger.

I nodded. "I'm starving." But I was not a fool. I had immediately seen what Belle had obviously attempted to hide: the names of The Reverend Charles Greene and his curate, Mr Philip Upton.

Belle careened Roger towards a pub tucked away on a twisty turny road that I would never have found even with a GPS and second sight. We ordered two roast lamb dinners at the bar, grabbed a couple of glasses of red and found a seat.

Settling in, I said. "Belle, I have to thank you for sending me so many piano clients."

Belle stared at me wide-eyed.

"Belle, I know it was you."

"If you insist," said Belle, turning the salt and pepper so they faced the same way.

"But you can stop now, really."

"Josie, your inheritance is all good and dandy, but Rose's estate could be wrapped up in probate for months. You're going to need something to live on."

I lowered my glass. "How do *you* know about my inheritance?"

Belle waved an airy hand. "Mrs Crackenthorpe heard it from Petra Ainsworth-Browne who overheard it at her butcher's who—"

"Okay, I get it. The village grapevine."

"But, honest to goodness, Josie, you shouldn't be thanking me. I only sent you Georgie. Her mother, Ivy Lewis, did the rest. Georgie told her mum that she hasn't had a piano teacher explain so much in so little time. Plus she liked you, and Georgie likes no one. For some unexplained reason they all think you're fabulous."

"Well, duh!" I said, smiling.

Our lunch arrived and I spent the next half hour telling Belle about Bonnie Curry's pond-side attack, my chat with Daisy and the Puccini emanating from Aunt Rose's study.

"Aren't you forgetting the most important thing?" asked Belle, who I couldn't help but notice had separated all the food groups on her plate into non-touching piles.

"I thought the Puccini was pretty important," I said, frowning.

"Oh yes, very," said Belle. "But I'm talking about Adam."

"What about him?" I said, coloring.

Belle tilted her head. "According to Darcy—"

It was my turn to give Belle a look.

"The long and the short of it is, Adam was seen emerging from Brambley Lane early this morning," said Belle.

"And the whole village now knows this?" I asked.

"One would assume so, although probably not Susan Ludlow, she doesn't go in much for gossip."

My knife and fork clattered to the plate. "Belle, I made a huge mistake."

Belle drove us back to Milkwood—and I use the word "drove" loosely—the experience being best described as "catapulted." When we drew alongside an imposing two-story brick house I tumbled out—literally. I had not got the hang of getting in and out of Roger and probably never would.

I waved goodbye to Belle and toddled up a garden path fringed with fragrant lavender and enough honeybees to strike fear into all but the most intrepid pedestrian.

I rapped on the door, admiring its beautiful glass work and shiny brass knocker. Getting no answer, I knocked again. Still nothing. I checked my watch. Two minutes past four—surely Reverend Greene hadn't forgotten?

Putting my ear to the door, I listened. I could hear the faint sound of music. Satie, if I was not mistaken, *Gnossienne No. 1*—music intended to transport you to the Dordogne on a languid summer's day. I was just happy it wasn't Puccini.

I tried the handle and the door swung inward. Tentatively, I stepped into a cool, dimly lit passageway. After shouting hello a few times I decided my best bet was to follow the music. The vicarage smelled of cake and strawberries and, propelled by the thoughts of afternoon tea, I found myself in the kitchen. Still no one to be seen, although I had found the origin of the music—an old transistor wireless, turned to face an open window.

Descending into the tranquil garden I discovered signs of life. Lounging in an old-fashioned striped deckchair was the lady I had sat next to at Quentin's performance. Her eyes were shut, her hands beating time. As if realizing she was being watched her eyes opened and, on seeing me, she smiled and waved me forward.

"Welcome, welcome. If it isn't Adam Ward's girlfriend."

Not again. I gritted my teeth as I navigated past a water feature, a perennial border and a rather splendid gnome wrestling a fishing rod.

"I'm Florence. Florence Greene. I've been expecting you."

I bent forward and offered my palm. Like her husband Florence grasped it in both liver-spotted hands and gave it a hearty squeeze. She too was stronger than she appeared.

"Please forgive me for not getting up. However, once you get into these contraptions it's so very inconvenient to get out."

I knew exactly what she meant. As a child you never gave a thought to getting in and out of England's famously impossible-to-put-together, low-slung deckchairs. As an adult it seemed the only escape was to launch yourself sideways and pray no one was watching.

Florence was in her mid-seventies. Her hair was a soft grey, her smile was bright and her dull sapphire eyes twinkled with mischief. She wore a faded pair of cotton trousers combined with an over-sized tangerine striped shirt. From the mud stains on her knees I assumed Florence had been gardening or, alternatively, practicing getting in and out of said deckchair. I instantly liked her, making it even more confusing as to why she would be the recipient of January's poison pen letter.

"I'm afraid Charles was called out to a parishioner, but he should be back shortly. In the meantime I've made tea and home-made scones." Florence observed me with a trace of doubt. "I hope you like scones. These have raisins. Not everyone likes the humble raisin, I'm afraid." She shook her head. "I've always felt they were a very misunderstood fruit."

"No, I love raisins. Well, that's not exactly true, but I love them in scones," I assured my host.

Florence's face lit up. "Would you be mother?" Florence

motioned to a table laden with teapot, cups, milk, sugar, and a plate of scones with jam and clotted cream. It was as if I had died and gone to culinary heaven.

"I'd love to," I said, happily pouring the steaming beverage.

I passed Florence a cup before sitting in the spare deckchair, luckily an upright plastic affair that, although far less attractive, was not going to cause me any embarrassing issues when it was time to leave.

"I was so sorry to hear about Miss Braithwaite." Florence scooped up a broad floppy hat that had previously been abandoned to the daisies and positioned it on her head.

"Really?" I stopped and regrouped. "Wait, that came out wrong. It's just I've not had a lot of condolences. I don't mean to be blunt, but I get the impression my aunt wasn't very liked."

"That may well be," said Florence. "But I am still sorry. Nobody should meet their maker through the hands of violence."

"Did you know Aunt Rose well?"

"Oh yes, dear. She was our church organist for going on fifteen years."

"Cool," I said, enjoying learning something about my aunt that seemed more in keeping with my childhood memories.

"Yes," said Florence, giving my offhand remark some thought. "Of course, she handed in her notice last year."

"Really?" I replied.

"Called dear Charles' sermons, now let me think, oh yes, 'sinfully boring.'"

"She did what?" I asked, my chin dropping, my eyes widening.

"Oh yes, quite comical it was, although come to think of it Charles wasn't too pleased."

"I'm sure he wasn't," I said. "Maybe it was a misunderstanding?"

"Oh, I don't think so, dear. Rose made it abundantly clear in her three-page—oh no, wait, make that four-page—resignation letter."

"I'm so sorry," I said.

"Water under the proverbial," said Florence, flapping away a lazy dragonfly. "There was a time when we were the best of friends. But in the last two or three years she had become extremely...*distant* is the best way to put it. The letter did not come as a surprise. At first I was sad and then I came to the conclusion that all friendships run their course and this was just our time."

"That's very philosophical," I said, slathering raspberry jam onto my scone.

"When you get to my age, dear, you learn that pragmatism is often best."

Florence and I chatted while we waited for the reverend. She peppered me with questions about my job and enthused over Aunt Rose's talent as a pianist, admitting that neither she nor Charles had a musical bone in their bodies.

It turned out that we had both been to the circus, and our favorite act had been the flying trapeze. I learned that she had once been a midwife, that she loved the US television series *The Big Bang Theory*, and that she spent most of her days baking and sharing her culinary skills with the residents of Milkwood.

"I run a baking class every Monday night from six to eight. You should come."

"Oh, I don't know," I said. "Nobody in this village seems to like me very much."

"They won't like you any better if they don't get to know you. Will they?"

I hated being baffled by logic.

"Besides it's normally just me, Mrs Ludlow, and Mrs Llewellyn. Petruska," she added after seeing my blank stare. "Last week we had to change it to Sunday because Susan had something at Ben's school Monday evening."

I nodded, unconvinced.

"I always find it such fun to visit other people's kitchens. You know, take a gander at all their little gadgets and whatnot. Last week we gathered at Mrs Ludlow's flat. She lives above the shop, you know. We made some splendid roly-polys and fruit tarts. They turned out rather well, even if I do say so myself."

"Sounds wonderful," I said.

"Oh yes, it's so much fun. You get to know everyone's prefer-ences. Mrs Ludlow is a sucker for ginger scones, whereas Mrs Llewellyn has a soft spot for cheese and herb tarts—says it reminds her of something her Grandmother Ulanowski made back in

Poland. I often share our little treats with the villagers. I leave them on the kitchen counter if people are out. I always think it must be so nice to come home to something tasty after a long day at work."

As I was trying to figure out how to indicate my willingness to leave every door and window in Plum Tree Cottage unlocked if there was any hope of a classic Victoria sponge showing up unannounced, the back door opened and Reverend Greene came stumbling down the steps. And when I say stumble I mean "stumble" — the man went splat like an overenthusiastic pancake. I rushed over to help, rolling him gently onto his back. All color had drained from his face and he was obviously in pain.

Florence finally made it out of her deckchair and joined me. "Oh, Charles. You really need to get some new glasses."

Charles winced. "Yes, dear."

"Josie, will you be a dear and pop inside and get some brandy?" asked Florence.

"Florence, no," said the reverend, but his wife was too busy fussing over him for me to take much notice of his protestations.

I bolted into the kitchen and searched several cupboards but came up emptyhanded. Maybe the brandy was in the living room? Hurrying back along the hallway, I opened a closed door. The curtains were drawn, so I flipped on the light. Bingo! In front of me sat a rustic dining table and nestled in the corner loomed a well-stocked drinks cabinet. It was a room that obviously got little use. The chairs were piled with books and the dining room table was weighted down with various objects ranging from an antique clock to a garden gnome dressed as a clown.

I paused and gave a particularly fine metronome the once over before continuing to the drinks cabinet. Locating the brandy glasses and a half-full bottle of Hennessy, I sploshed a snifter full into the glass before racing back to the garden.

Reverend Greene was on his feet being supported by Florence to my empty deckchair. Some color was beginning to flush his face, but that may have been embarrassment. He snatched the glass from my outstretched hand and took a sip.

"Are you going to be okay?" I asked.

The reverend stared coldly into my eyes. "That will depend."

54

Monday morning dawned and I awoke once again with a hissing cat wedged into the crook of my knees. Elgar was becoming practically friendly—you know, other than the hissing. Maybe he was missing his owner? Guilt flooded through me. Maybe I should be missing Aunt Rose a little more, too?

After a quick shower and an even quicker breakfast, I parted the garage doors and eyeballed Jenny. *Please let her start*, were my only thoughts as I approached the cantankerous vehicle. Someone must have been listening, as ten minutes later Jenny and I were cruising along the back lanes to Godalming. I passed a particularly pretty church and I thought back to my meeting the day before with Reverend Greene. He had finally recovered his composure and we had discussed possible dates for Aunt Rose's funeral, but his earlier bonhomie had vanished like a Christmas tree in January. In fact, I got the impression the reverend couldn't wait to get rid of me.

As I motored across a bridge barely wide enough for a Sainsbury's trolley, I reveled in the glory of the English countryside. Clusters of Tudor cottages, duck ponds and picturesque pubs dotted the landscape, all reminding me how much I missed this green and pleasant land.

I found a car park on a side street and paid and displayed, assuming three hours would be more than sufficient. Godalming was a historic market town, where the Russian Tsar, Peter the Great, once spent a night. The main High Street rose on a modest incline until you reached Godalming's former town hall—a picturesque octagonal building in ballet slipper pink—who could possibly say the English lack whimsy?

I located a one-hour dry cleaners and dropped off my three grass-stained, duck-pooped dresses before returning to the High Street in search of my destination. I had just spent five minutes gazing in the window at the strangely named clothing store, Fat Face, when I spotted Dan Ludlow and Gurminder Singh loitering outside WHSmith. They were back in school uniform, sharing a bag of cheese and onion crisps and actually smiling.

Could these two teenage schoolchildren really be behind Aunt Rose's death? Surely not. I suspected that beneath Gurminder's fierce demeanor lurked a young lady who was more a misunderstood teen than a murderer. I watched Gurminder screw up the crisp bag and launch it at a nearby rubbish bin. It missed, and Dan scooped to pick it up, much like he had done the day I'd seen him delivering groceries.

The crisp packet now safely disposed, they turned and strolled up the High Street, bumping shoulders in that teasing way friends sometimes do.

I consulted my watch and turned my attention to finding my destination. Two minutes later I found myself gazing at a discreet gold plaque mounted on the side of a three-story Edwardian building, the sole identifier of the premises of solicitors Padfoot & Strong. I pulled open the door and was surprised to find the architecture was decidedly modern, and I applauded the designer who'd managed to combine two different styles so effortlessly.

A young man in a yellow bow tie sat behind a glass desk talking into a headphone. He acknowledged my presence with a warm wave and indicated a slim leather sofa on which to sit. Two seconds later he pressed a button and removed the headphones.

"Ms Monroe?" He stood and came out from behind the desk to shake my hand. "I'm Douglas Stapleton. Ms Padfoot is expecting you." His voice was polished, his demeanor friendly. Padfoot & Strong had got themselves a real gem in Douglas Stapleton.

"Can I get you tea? Coffee?"

I shook my head. "I'm fine, thanks." I hadn't realized before, but I was nervous. Dealing with my aunt's solicitor seemed so grown up. I was a professional. I paid taxes, I rented property, I owned a sizable budgerigar: however, this seemed like a whole new level of that millennial term "adulting."

Minutes later I was sitting opposite the smartly dressed Ms Padfoot, who turned out to be much younger than I'd imagined. Considering how old-fashioned Aunt Rose was, Ms Padfoot seemed a strange choice, but then I recalled my aunt's curiously modern bedroom. Maybe Aunt Rose had finally started to embrace the twenty-first century?

As it happened the meeting with Edwina Padfoot was pretty uneventful. The only thing that was shocking was the amount of money Aunt Rose had in her bank account. After informing me of the sum, Ms Padfoot had discreetly rung a bell and Douglas had appeared with neither tea nor coffee but a snifter of brandy that put to shame the one I had recently offered Reverend Greene.

Fifteen minutes later, I left Padfoot & Strong and ambled along Godalming High Street in a daze. I had worked all my life and it had not been easy. Since Ryan's unexpected departure I had struggled on my meager teacher's salary, renting my cramped apartment and forgoing the luxuries that so many of my peers took for granted. Those days were over. I was rich—or I would be rich, as soon as Aunt Rose's estate passed through probate.

To say I was stunned was an understatement. Aunt Rose had left me Plum Tree and that alone was overwhelming. However, the cottage, combined with stocks, bonds and a sizable savings account, meant my work days were over. Obviously, I would have to give this some serious thought. In celebration I found a music store and bought several sheets of piano music, a biography of Sir Edward Elgar and a traditional triangular metronome. My purchases completed, I strolled into Fat Face and bundled everything I fancied, and more, into the changing room. Life was looking up, with the added bonus that I might never have to do washing again.

55

I arrived back in Milkwood and admired my purchases. I was now the proud owner of two pairs of jeans, some shorts, three skirts, several tops, new bras and knickers, a dressing gown, and a pair of pink fluffy slippers. Truly, what more could a girl want?

I fixed myself a late lunch and tried to figure out what to do next. I was stacking the final dish when the door opened and in strolled Belle.

"I wanted to let you know. Quentin is having a modest get-together this evening and you're invited."

"Really? What's the occasion?"

Belle shrugged. "No idea. Birthday? Bar mitzvah? Could be anything, really. Anyhow, it's a party and one must admit that Quentin Young really *does* know how to throw a party."

Belle pulled out a bar stool and perched on the edge. She was wearing a pair of wide-cut cotton trousers in snow white and a matching navy and white boat neck tee with espadrilles. She looked like she was part of a very chic French Naval Academy.

I decided to ask Belle something I'd been wondering for days. "Belle, what exactly do you do?"

"Define 'do.'" said Belle, reaching for the condiments and placing them in a neat little row.

"I mean for work? It's just you seem to have a lot of spare time."

Belle went silent. Great! I'd offended her again.

"Belle, I'm sorry, it's none of my business."

"It's not that, it's just..."

"No, really, Belle, you don't owe me any explanations."

Belle looked so sad I could have kicked myself.

"You see, after Mummy died...unfortunately, it was all rather traumatic. I'm ashamed to say I didn't handle it with particular aplomb. I'm okay now, but for a few years, well, let's just say it was pretty lousy."

"Oh, Belle." I felt dreadful. I had a mother *and* a father and as annoying as they both were I couldn't imagine life without them.

"See, the truth is I had a bit of a turn, and I went away for a while, Anglesey actually, a beautiful part of the world. Anyway, when I got back...I didn't seem to excel at anything."

Bonnie Curry's vile words at the duck pond came back to me, and I wondered if Belle going away was what she'd been alluding to. What an old trout. Belle had needed help while she grieved for her mother and all Bonnie Curry could do was mock her. I vowed next time I'd let Bonnie Curry fall in the bloody duck pond.

"I find that hard to believe. I'm sure you're, erm, competent at many things."

"Oh no, it's true. Daddy put me in a cordon bleu school and I blew it up—"

"The oven?" I exclaimed.

"No," said Belle, studying her feet. "The school. After that I tried motor mechanics, and a psychology course. Daddy says the lecturer is feeling much better now. Unfortunately, I'm not allowed within twenty, or is it forty, feet of him? But that's okay, I barely ever find myself in Cambridge and if he comes to Surrey he normally gives Daddy a heads up and I stay inside."

I gazed at Belle open mouthed. *Was she joking?* I dared not ask.

"However, I'm an excellent rider and I'm rather lucky at salmon fishing, and I used to be able to outshoot practically anyone in three counties. But it's not the stuff you mean when you say 'work,' is it? Of course, I also help Daddy around the estate. And Quentin's talked me into giving him a lesson tomorrow evening. I shouldn't really but—"

"A lesson in what?"

"Shooting, of course. Quentin is dying to attend one of our weekend shooting parties, but he doesn't know his stock from his barrel."

I tried to look like I knew what Belle was referring to and failed.

"The pointy end from the, er, not pointy end," explained Belle. "Maybe you should come with us?"

My eyebrows rose. Guns were not my thing.

Belle cocked her head to one side. "Anyhow, I wanted to find out how you were getting on with the investigation. Do tell all."

I was happy to change the conversation. I recapped my afternoon with Florence, told Belle all about Reverend Greene's coldness and finished with my meeting with Ms Padfoot.

I had known people throughout my life that detested other people's good fortune. Belle DeCorcy was *not* one of those people and her pleasure was palpable.

"Heavens to Betsy, Josie, that's wonderful."

I shrugged. "It's something. But I've still got to figure out who killed Aunt Rose if I ever want to get back to Texas."

"Oh!" said Belle. "I thought maybe now you might...you know...stay."

"Belle, I have a home in the US. My work is in the US. I can't just up and leave."

"Really?" said Belle. "Why on earth not?"

It was an excellent question, and one that had been on the back-burner of my brain for several days.

"Well, for one, I can never see Adam again. I'm so embarrassed."

"Josie, you have nothing to be ashamed of. You did the honorable thing."

"I made the man sleep on the sofa," I said, dropping my head in my hands, not bearing to remember. "Who does that? Who makes a man sleep on the sofa when he's offered to stay over?"

"Someone who thinks he has a girlfriend, that's who," said Belle.

"Thinks? Belle, I saw him and Frosty Knickers together at the circus."

"You also told me Adam said there'd been a theft. Maybe they were there on police business."

"Yeah, right," I said.

"Anyhow, girlfriend or not—you did what you thought was best. Besides, he brought you tea and biscuits the next day. He can't be *that* mad."

I hoped Belle was right. I also hoped Adam would be transferred to Colchester or the Outer Hebrides. I wasn't fussy—either would do.

Belle and I adjourned to the patio and spent the rest of the afternoon going over our suspects.

"Unfortunately, I think we can rule out Bonnie," I said. "They may have had their differences, but I don't think having someone play "Devil Woman" every time you walk in the pub is probable cause for murder."

"My, how I would have paid good money to have seen that," said Belle.

"Plus, she was at home—I saw the curtains twitch. I'm pretty sure she couldn't have got from Aunt Rose's to her cottage in time."

"Good point," said Belle. "Who else has an alibi?"

"Peter says he was upstairs packing when it happened and Wendy was hurrying home with her tail between her legs."

"Yes, Darcy Blythe says she spotted her hurtling through the village around 7:45pm."

I had no idea who this Darcy Blythe was, but by the sounds of it she spent a lot of her time with her nose pressed against her window.

"Can Darcy be relied on?" I asked.

"She's the local magistrate's wife, so it's questionable," said Belle.

"I think we can rule out Finolla?" I said. "She may have been in the vicinity, but it does seem somewhat out of character, even for her. Of course it doesn't explain why she was here."

"Oh, that's easy," said Belle.

I gave Belle the "this might be easy to you, but I have absolutely no idea" look.

"You mentioned earlier you were fed up waiting for your mum

to give you a lift to the station and took a taxi."

"So?"

"Josie, Finolla barely ever sees you and you left without a farewell. I'd bet my second-best mare that your mother came to say goodbye."

My eyes widened as I thought about this possibility. Could Finolla *really* be developing a sense of motherhood this late in life?

"You're sweet for thinking that," I said, "but I seriously doubt it."

I pulled the conversation back to our suspects. "Belle, I've asked half of Milkwood if anyone knows what the initials *PU* stand for, but no one knows. Or if they do, they aren't telling me."

Belle glanced away. "How about Quentin?"

I had learned lots of interesting facts about Belle DeCorcy over the past week, but this latest interaction confirmed she wasn't as competent a liar as she thought. I let it drop and shook my head. "I have no idea why Quentin's lying about the last time he saw Aunt Rose or why he named his CD *Rosetta's Throne*."

"Maybe they were having a torrid affair," said Belle.

I stared at Belle in disbelief. "Did you ever meet my aunt? There are many words to describe her, but 'torrid' is not one of them."

Belle shrugged. "You may be correct. But fact is often stranger than fiction."

"Oh, I almost forgot. Florence Greene has a baking circle that was together until after 8:00pm Sunday night. Susan and Petruska were both there. So we can rule those three out."

"Unless they were in it together," said Belle.

"That's ridiculous," I said. "Besides, Florence Greene is too nice to hurt anyone, although I wouldn't put it past Susan, especially if you crossed her boy."

I had almost forgotten about the conversation I had overheard at the circus. Seeing Adam together with Frosty Knickers had thrown me for a loop. I clued Belle in, also adding what I'd heard at Naan's.

Belle's perfect brow furrowed. "Did we ever find out why Dan was on Aunt Rose's list?"

I shook my head. "Maybe it's about time we did."

The afternoon passed quickly, and before I knew it the doorbell rang and two more children stood on the doorstep, piano books in one hand, pristine envelopes in the other.

"Really, you have to stop doing this, Belle."

"I told you. Nothing to do with me. Purely Ivy Lewis and Milkwood's grapevine. Come to think of it, you must be tiptop at this piano malarkey."

I gave Belle a look. "Well, duh!"

"Anyhow, I have to be going. I promised Daddy I'd pick up Claude from the equine hospital. He got a bit of a nasty gash on his leg the other day and they had to do some minor surgery."

Claude was feisty when he was in robust health. I hated to think how he would be after sustaining a wound. Good luck to whoever came across Claude in the next few days.

Belle waved farewell, promising to see me later while I ascertained the names of my two newest pupils, eight-year-old twins named Owen and Ophelia Hadleigh.

They handed me a note that I glanced at before ushering them into the study. I located my list of students and added their names to my growing roster. By the time I entered the room they had disappeared. "Erm, Owen? Ophelia?"

Ophelia emerged from behind the piano. "We're over here. Playing with your kitty cat."

I was about to explain that Elgar was not my cat, but for all intents and purposes, right now he was. I'd give them a couple of minutes to settle down and in the meantime pulled out the note I assumed was written by their mum.

The handwriting was prim and to the point. I wondered how much you could glean of someone's personality from their cursive. From this note I would assume Mrs Hadleigh was around 5' 2" and extremely uptight. Her words did nothing to dissuade me of this impression.

Needs work on their Grade Two. Nanny will retrieve at 5:00 sharp.

I moved towards the back of the piano to shoo out Elgar and that's when I saw it, all around the base of the piano legs, and suddenly I knew exactly what *PU* stood for.

I chose the cream dress with the flowered border and Belle's mum's sandals, knowing my own traitorous sandals could not be trusted not to rip my feet to shreds. As I swished back and forth, I marveled at the change in my appearance from one week ago, when my wardrobe staples had been shorts, tees and jeans. Now I owned more dresses and skirts than trousers, plus several nice blouses. I was flabbergasted at my new sense of fashion, although maybe this was what people did when they had money to spare?

I fed Elgar, checked the cottage was locked and hurried towards the garage. I eased open the doors and eyeballed Jenny. She had been starting beautifully the past few days and I gave a silent prayer that she continued with her winning streak.

I obviously need to get my hearing checked, because I did not hear anyone approach, only becoming aware of their presence when they placed a hand on my shoulder.

I sprang into the air like a pogo stick and my heart started to samba. I spun around and came face to nose with Peter, his hands flying skyward like a bandit.

"Criminy, Peter. You scared the life out of me."

"Josie, I'm...I'm most dreadfully sorry."

"What do you want?" This came out harsher than I'd intended, so I added a halfhearted smile to the mix. I'd not seen Peter since he'd left for his parents' sausage roll event on Saturday night, and even *I* had to admit this wasn't the warmest of welcome homes.

"I...I heard Quentin was throwing one if his shindigs. Was wondering if, er maybe, I could catch a ride?"

I noticed Peter's suitcase by his feet and realized he must have come from the station.

"Sure, of course," I said, embarrassed at my jumpiness.

"Give me five to get rid of this and have a quick wash and I'll be back in a jiffy."

Five stretched to ten, but eventually Peter emerged wearing a clean shirt and pressed trousers, carrying a bottle of wine.

I had pulled Jenny forward and was idling alongside the front gate. I had learned from experience that once started Jenny did not like to be stopped. I avoided thinking of my carbon footprint, and instead thought of my dress and what it would look like if we had to hike across the Tillingbourne.

Peter strolled around to the passenger side and climbed in. "You do know how to drive this thing, right?"

I gave him a look. "You can always walk."

Peter raised his hands once more. "No, I mean, I tried to drive it once. I...I couldn't get out of first gear. Actually, I couldn't even get it *in* first gear."

"It's easy," I replied, conveniently forgetting the times I'd had to coast around bends unable to find second.

It was as if Jenny was out to prove how cooperative she could be —sailing along Brambley Lane, bouncing gaily through potholes. I adeptly navigated the ford and soared up Honeycroft Hill, slowing as we reached the turn for Barton Hall. I motored through the imposing gates and followed the road until we reached the turnoff to Quentin's lodge.

"Josie, I've been meaning to ask you. News on the grapevine is that you inherited Plum Tree Cottage."

I nodded.

"I was wondering if you wanted me to, you know, move out?"

I gave this some thought. I had lived by myself ever since Ryan left and I had become used to the solitude. On the other hand Peter was neat and quiet and at night it was comforting to know there was someone on the other side of the wardrobe, even if that other person was wearing plaid pajamas and M&S slippers.

"Peter, I'm not sure what I'm going to do with the cottage. Sell it? Rent it? Not the foggiest. So, why don't we keep going like we are. I assume you paid Aunt Rose rent. Just keep paying and we'll figure it out when things are a little clearer."

Peter's smile was charming. "I'd...I'd like that. Thank you, Josie."

"You're welcome, but it does mean you're going to have to start taking out the trash."

Peter laughed. "You have yourself a deal. I'll take out both the American trash and the British rubbish."

"And don't forget Elgar's litter box," I added.

"Done," said Peter.

"By the way, do you know who Aunt Rose asked to watch Elgar while you were both gone?"

Peter scratched his head, thinking about this. "No idea. I...I think this was the first time we were both away at the same time. Rose didn't tend to get out that much—bit of a homebody."

I nodded. That was the Aunt Rose I remembered.

"But she must have left him with someone," said Peter. "He couldn't have survived the week by himself."

I nodded. "Peter, before we get to Quentin's, I have a question about Belle that is a bit delicate."

"Yes, I believe it's true Belle is officially the worst driver in the whole of Surrey," said Peter, laughing. "I...I think there was a poll. A kindergartner named Chris came in second."

I smiled. "No, not that, it's just she mentioned about her mum dying and having a bit of a breakdown."

Peter was silent for several seconds before he spoke. "Look, Josie, Belle's a great gal. One of the best and if... if that kind of thing bothers you..."

"No, not in the slightest," I said, veering to avoid a bounding rabbit. "It's just the ever-delightful Bonnie Curry brought it up, and I've always found it's best to know the facts when going into battle, and yes, I believe Bonnie Curry and I are at war."

Peter smiled.

"I don't care about Belle's past, I'd only want to be able to defend her if anybody else says something mean and, to be frank, it's hard to do that when you don't have all the facts."

Peter nodded. "Truth is that when Lady DeCorcy died Belle had a breakdown. She was young, she did several...well, she was a bit odd. One...one day she just disappeared. Disappeared from Milkwood altogether, so I believe. Rumors, as you can imagine, ran riot, but it finally came out that her father had sent her to a psychiatric facility near Snowdon. You...you can imagine how that went down."

I could imagine all too well.

"Of course this was way before my time," said Peter. "I'm...I'm only repeating what Rose told me."

"Thanks, Peter, I appreciate you telling me." At first glance it seemed Belle DeCorcy had it all—the looks, the money, the car—but it was the same with everyone I'd ever met. Below the surface there was always something hidden, something that made even the most privileged of us merely human.

I turned onto the dirt track and bumped along the rutted lane. There were several cars parked along the side of the track and I pulled in behind a mud-splattered Land Rover. Peter and I climbed out and trekked along the rutted path in companionable silence.

As we approached the thatched cottage I couldn't help but smile. The trees were drenched in twinkle lights and a long trestle table groaned under the weight of several tons of food. Laughter could also be heard as Quentin's guests enjoyed the sweet summer sun.

I realized, with some surprise, that I knew practically all the guests. Peter wandered off to mingle with Rex DeCorcy, Reverend Greene and Quentin, while the Witches of Milkwood huddled together by the chocolate eclairs. Florence Greene was rooting around in her wicker basket, while Wendy Williams clinked glasses with the two women whose conversation I had overheard when leaving Quentin's concert. I heard the names Petra and Darcy, and realized these were Milkwood's two infamous gossips. Duncan was loitering by an overstocked wine table with a couple of men I assumed to be the husbands of the aforementioned. I finger waved at him as I passed, causing him to flush like a bottle of strawberry wine.

A hand shot up and I saw Belle beckon me towards her. I was happy to see that Daisy had been invited and the two of them were chatting with a woman with rich red hair and a wide, inviting smile.

"Josie, let me introduce you to Ivy Lewis. I believe you've already met her daughters Lucy and Georgina."

I shook Mrs Lewis' outstretched hand.

"Georgina raved about you," said Ivy. "Said you're the best piano teacher she's ever had. And believe me, she's had a few."

"She's a sweet girl," I said. "And a talented musician. Her Grade Five will be a doddle."

"We're so happy you're staying in Milkwood and we all adore Adam. It's about time he found a bit of happiness."

"Wait! What? No that's—"

Ivy laid a hand on my arm. "No need to deny it, love. If I wasn't happily married I might think about dating him, too. He's so...rugged."

Apparently the entire population of Milkwood thought Adam and I were an item. As a well known Queen was wont to say, I was not amused; however, the more I denied it the more Mrs Lewis was convinced of my duplicity.

"I see Petra Ainsworth-Browne and Darcy Blythe, but where's Holly Drinkwater?" asked Ivy.

"Quentin stopped inviting her after Mr Kibbles peed on his leg during the maiden voyage of *Rosetta's Throne* a couple of years ago," said Belle. "He's never forgiven her."

"He's too proud for his own good," said Ivy, glancing over at Quentin, who was dressed, predictably, all in white.

I smiled. "You finally write a masterpiece and a dog pees on you at your very first performance? I have to say I'd be pissed off too."

We continued to chat. Daisy waxed lyrical on the research for her murder mystery, Ivy spoke about a watercolor class she was taking and I filled them in on my work in the US. It was refreshing to be in the company of women who did not feel the need to talk constantly about their children, as so many of my friends in the US were wont to do.

I couldn't help but notice that Belle was barely talking. Like at Quentin's concert, she was gazing around in search for someone.

This time I knew who it was and smiled as the blond Adonis strolled along the lane, causing Belle's body to tense.

I watched the curate greet his host and shake Rex DeCorcy by the hand, before whispering something in his boss's ear. A wave of relief seemed to wash over Reverend Greene as he mouthed "thank you."

Conversation had dwindled as Philip joined the gathering. The women were too busy enjoying the view. The men? Who knew what the men were thinking, but I was pretty sure it wasn't too charitable.

"You must excuse me," said Belle, gliding towards our new arrival.

"Me too," I added. "Must find the loo."

I circumnavigated the various groups until I reached the picturesque cottage. *Rosetta's Throne* was wafting gently through the open windows and once again I admired its simple beauty. I had found myself humming the uncomplicated tune several times over the past day and marveled at what you could do with merely a violin, viola, cello and double bass.

I slipped through the door and paused at the piano to quickly examine the scratch marks—identical to the ones on Aunt Rose's Steinway. I had one more stop to make before I was going to be certain of my hunch. I headed towards the bathroom—not to pee, but to search.

I slipped inside and locked the door behind me. Luckily for me, on a scale from one to ten Quentin's bathroom cleanliness level was hovering around an eleven. With the exception of a pair of muddy shoes, obviously awaiting cleaning, the bathroom was immaculate. Regardless, I quickly realized I was wearing the wrong clothes, as I crouched by the toilet and examined the floor. At first I thought I might have been mistaken, but after several unpleasant seconds I found what I was searching for—the most minute remnants of kitty litter.

57

I exited the bathroom and was about to head outside when the cottage door jettisoned open and Belle practically tumbled into the living room, followed by an anxious-looking Philip.

Belle's face was flushed. I had never seen her so perturbed.

"Belle, what's wrong?"

Belle grabbed my hand. "Josie, Philip and I have something to tell you."

"Belle, it's okay. I know you and Philip are an item."

"Excuse me?" said Philip and Belle, simultaneously springing away from each other.

"We are not an item," said Belle. "What on earth gave you that idea?"

Why did I have that idea? I had no discernable answer, purely a gut feeling.

"Belle is delightful, but I'm afraid she is not my girlfriend. Partner in crime, maybe, but alas, that is all." Philip shot Belle a look and Belle blushed.

I was utterly confused.

Belle dragged me to a seat by the open window and pushed me onto the plump pillows. "Josie, I'm so sorry, but I have to tell you something. Something I should have told you when we first met."

Philip perched on the arm of the sofa and put his arm on Belle's shoulder. For two people not dating they were doing an admirable impression.

"The night you arrived. The night Rose died..." said Belle.

"Yes?"

"We. Philip and I. We were...I mean, what I'm trying to say is..."

"We were at Plum Tree," said Philip, finishing what Belle could not.

I must have looked confused because Philip repeated it.

"Let me get this right," I said. "You and Belle were at the cottage the night Aunt Rose died? The night I was accused of murder by Bonnie Curry?"

"Correct," said Philip.

"Okay, and you didn't tell me because?"

"Because it's a secret," said Belle, her voice tiny.

"What's a secret?" I asked, rising to my feet.

"I'm afraid it's not our secret to share," said Philip. "We made a promise."

"A promise?" My voice was filled with sarcasm. "Do you know, right now it seems easier to ask who *wasn't* at Plum Tree the night Aunt Rose died. Finolla, Dan, Bonnie Curry, Peter, Wendy and now you two."

Belle hung her head in shame.

"Did you see me on the floor lying in my aunt's blood as well?"

"Of course not," said Belle.

"So you didn't see Aunt Rose dead?"

Belle shook her head.

I could feel my blood pressure starting to rise. "But that doesn't make any sense. Nobody saw you. I didn't see you and Bonnie Curry obviously didn't see you, else you know she would have told Frosty Knickers."

"We came in the back way across the Tillingbourne," explained Philip.

"Except we didn't fall in like you did," added Belle.

Flippity flip flops, were there no secrets in this village?

"We didn't expect anyone to be home. As soon as we realized something was going on we left," said Belle.

This was sounding more and more like the clandestine meeting they were refuting. Why else go to someone's house knowing they weren't there if not to meet in private?

"And you didn't see anyone?" I asked.

Belle and Philip were silent. Finally Philip spoke. "We did see someone, but we're pretty sure he had nothing to do with it."

"Honestly, we feel dreadful," added Belle.

"Belle has hated keeping this secret from you and unfortunately I've been on retreat all week, so she had no one to ask for advice. I didn't even know about your aunt's death until I saw Belle on Saturday night."

I thought back to when I first met Belle. That fateful day when she'd run me over with Roger.

"You didn't run me over on purpose, did you?"

"What? No! Why would I do that?"

"So you could befriend me and ask questions about the night of the murder."

Belle reached for my hand and I snatched it away. "Josie, I would never..." Belle flushed. "Well, maybe a little, but I didn't run you over on purpose. I'm *really* that bad a driver, I thought you'd know that by now."

"So basically, you pretended to be my friend to find out what I knew."

"That's absolutely not true," said Belle, sounding stunned.

"Well, it sounds true to me." And with that I rose and stormed out of the lodge and out of Belle DeCorcy's life.

58

I awoke sad and lonely. Even Elgar had deserted me, having abandoned his usual nighttime position.

I was pretty sure I'd discovered the reason why Quentin Young was penciled into Aunt Rose's schedule, although it didn't explain why he had lied about it. I also needed to talk to Adam. I had a niggling suspicion I had stumbled upon something important. If I could ask him one tiny question.

I stuffed my feet into my fluffy new slippers and drew on my dressing gown, snapping off the tags as I did so. I then remembered the bag of piano music sitting in the kitchen and vowed to give Aunt Rose's study a bit of a tidy before my students arrived. I smiled as I recalled my buying bonanza. Nothing I couldn't have lived without, although the metronome would be a blessing, as until now I'd been relying on an app on my students' phones.

I was halfway down the stairs when I realized I could smell bacon. Hurrying into the kitchen I found Peter wearing a flowery pinny and dishing up bacon, sausage, egg, and mushrooms. Two pieces of toast popped from the toaster and Peter adroitly caught them with a plate before smothering them with Kerrygold.

"Wow!" I said. "Impressive."

Peter grinned. "I...I thought after last night you could do with a hearty breakfast."

My memory ran through the previous evening's events, when I

had stormed from the lodge, almost bowling Quentin over in the process. I had stomped along the rutted driveway and, due to Philip's battered old Vauxhall blocking me in, proceeded to execute a fifty-two point turn. Finally, with Jenny facing the correct direction, I had chugged down the track with as much dignity as a girl who had just executed a fifty-two point turn can muster. It hadn't been the most seamless exit, but it had served its purpose. I'd needed to get away from Belle DeCorcy and that's exactly what I had done—even if it had taken me roughly ten minutes longer than I would have liked.

Peter slid a cup of tea in my direction and I sank onto one of the bar stools. I took a sip. The tea was black, decaffeinated and not too strong—exactly how I liked it. I was awful at remembering how my friends took their tea or coffee and an unexpected warmth ran through me as I realized Peter must have made an effort to notice my preferred beverage and how I liked it to be prepared.

I speared a piece of bacon and chowed down. English bacon was not streaky like in the States and therefore had more meat to it. I realized I was ravenous, having driven straight home last night and gone to bed without eating a morsel.

It was then I had a realization. "Oh my stars, Peter. I'm so sorry. I was your ride last night."

Peter shrugged. "Not a problem. I squeezed in with Darcy and Neville Blythe. They were giving George and Petra Ainsworth-Browne a lift, so it...it was no trouble."

Ah, the infamous Darcy Blythe and Petra Ainsworth-Browne, they of the lace curtain brigade—i.e. the reputable snoops.

"Was everything...? Well, I'm assuming my departure last night received some comments."

Peter shrugged. "Actually, nobody said a word. They...they were too busy dealing with Belle."

I couldn't help myself. "What about Belle?"

"To be honest she was pretty distraught. You know, since her mum...well, sometimes she doesn't do too brilliantly under stress. Anyhow, nothing to worry about. Philip took her home and I'm sure she'll be fine."

I didn't want to think about that now. Belle had deceived me and she could deal with her issues any way she saw fit.

I forked another mouthful of bacon into my mouth, savoring the flavor. "Peter, this is delicious."

"Excellent," said Peter, smiling like he'd won a school prize. "Now you're going to be my landlady, I thought I should start things off on the right foot."

"Absolutely," I said, grinding pepper onto my sausages. "Although maybe not a full fry up every morning. I'll settle for the odd bagel with lox."

"I...I quite enjoy cooking," said Peter. "The boys at prep used to tease me, but it...it relaxes me."

These were words you would never hear me utter. Cooking to me was purely a means to an end—the end being to not starve.

"How about a curry tonight?" said Peter. "I could stop off at Waspit's on the way home and pick up a few bits and bobs."

Seeing I had finished off the leftovers from Naan's several days ago, this seemed like an excellent idea.

I smiled. "Sounds like a plan."

"Great." Peter scooped up the empty dishes. "It's a date."

I dashed upstairs after Peter refused help doing the dishes and picked out a new outfit to wear—a pair of pink shorts and a stripy tee. I added a French-looking scarf, tying it self-consciously around my neck in an attempt at sophistication. I was in the bathroom when I heard the front door slam and watched as Peter strolled down the path, his violin case slung over his back. Reaching the garden gate he turned and, seeing me in the bathroom window, waved. Peter's last words had been preying on my mind. I was hoping when he said the word "date" he had meant more of an actual time and not the other meaning. Would it be it be so bad if he had? He was good looking, employed and the man could cook. Let's face it, I could do a lot worse.

59

I decided to visit the village shop and purchase more tea. Peter had mentioned that he'd used the last of the decaf, and there was no way I was driving all the way to Dorking for one item. The day was warm and overcast and I'd worked up quite a sweat by the time I reached Unthank Road.

Other than a rider on a dappled bay clip-clopping towards me the road was deserted. Equestrians were not an uncommon sight in a village like Milkwood and it was only as I drew closer that I recognized the rider as the tall dark woman from Quentin's party. Belle had mentioned either Darcy or Petra having a groom and I tried desperately to recall which one.

"Oh hello," said either Petra or Darcy, bringing her bay to a stop.

"Hi, erm..."

"It's Petra. Petra Ainsworth-Browne," said the woman, coming to my rescue.

I nodded. "Nice to meet you." I reached up and patted the mare's nose.

"One couldn't help but notice you left in a bit of a hurry last night."

I shrugged. What was I going to say? I'd been duped into a friendship based on lies. I was about to wish Petra *adieu* when she continued.

"Of course, you probably know all about Belle's little episode."

"Episode?"

Petra didn't even try to hide her smugness. "It's barely ever mentioned now but, of course, with a murder in the village, you can't help but wonder."

"Wonder what?" I blurted out.

"About Belle DeCorcy."

I frowned. "What about Belle? If you're talking about the breakdown after her mother's death..." I was starting to dislike Petra Ainsworth-Browne. I might have fallen out with Belle, but it didn't mean I was going to listen to mean-spirited gossip.

Petra waved an airy hand. "Oh, is *that* what we're calling it now? A 'breakdown?' Attempted murder is more like it. Perk of being the Lord of the Manor's daughter, I suppose."

"What are you talking about?" I asked, unable to stop myself.

Petra was one smirk away from being slapped, but I'd been sucked in and there was nothing for it now than to listen.

"Of course they blamed it all on her mother's death, and never let it be said that it wasn't absolutely awful. A break-in gone wrong is what they called it."

I held up a hand. "Wait...what?"

"Lady DeCorcy. She was shot. Didn't you know?" Petra resembled the cat who had inhaled the cream.

I took a step back. I had assumed Lady DeCorcy died of cancer, the horrific disease that takes life indiscriminately, old or young.

"I had no idea," I said, covering my mouth.

"Oh, that's a surprise. I would have thought your copper would have told you all about your old friend, Jimmy."

My eyes could not have opened any more if I'd used toothpicks. "Jimmy? What's Jimmy got to do with this?"

"My, oh my," said Petra. "Lover boy *has* kept you in the dark."

I clamped my jaw shut. Nothing good was going to come out, but I swear, the next person who called Adam Ward my boyfriend was going to get a mouthful.

"Jimmy Gilroy and those awful Ayles boys broke into the manor house not knowing anyone was home and Lady DeCorcy disturbed them. Shot her, right through the chest. She didn't stand a chance.

Course it was unfortunate, but Belle was home from school and saw the whole thing."

I thought back to Adam and our conversation in The Dirty Duck. Adam had mentioned that Jimmy had gone down for breaking into the manor house. He hadn't said anything about killing Lady Hannah DeCorcy in the process.

"Quite appalling for a young impressionable girl and, of course, we were all most sympathetic...at first."

I swallowed a lump in my throat. I had a feeling I was not going to like what was coming next. I was right.

etra Ainsworth-Browne clip-clopped along Unthank Road
and I stood motionless, stunned by what she had told me.
How could Adam have failed to mention this? Did he think
I wouldn't find out? As much as I hated to admit it, Petra's
comments had put Bonnie Curry's accusations in perspective. No
wonder Bonnie thought Belle was crazy.

Pulling myself together, I continued towards the duck pond. I
was about to cross Peacemeal Street when Frosty Knickers came
barreling around the corner and charged up the steps into Waspit's.

Great! The last thing I wanted was to see Helen Winterbottom. I
would loiter by the duck pond and wait until she exited. Was this a
grown-up response? Probably not. Did I care? Not so much.

I plonked myself on the bench and watched the ducks bob up
and down, reflecting how I wished I'd let Bonnie Curry take a nose-
dive. Next time.

I stared at my watch. It had been over five minutes and DS
Winterbottom had not emerged. I was starting to wonder if I could
go without decaf for a day or two when a squad car drew up across
the road. I watched as the two police officers—the same two who'd
combed through Plum Tree—hurried from the car and hastened
inside.

Curiosity got the better of me and I crossed the road and
pressed my nose against the glass. The window must have had

really excellent soundproofing, because Susan Ludlow was obviously screaming and I couldn't hear a word. Frosty Knickers was gesticulating, the two police officers looked embarrassed and Dan Ludlow stood in the middle, head downcast.

I felt a tap on my shoulder. "Didn't your mother ever tell you not to eavesdrop?"

I narrowed my eyes as I turned to face Adam. "Finolla told me not to run with scissors, drink too much tequila, or get pregnant on a first date, but eavesdropping—not so much."

Adam took a step back as he took in the look on my face. I was so furious at his duplicity regarding Jimmy; even worse was not telling me about Belle. But right now I had other things on my mind.

"What's going on in there?" I asked.

"We've caught our thief. Turns out Dan has been sneaking off with trinkets every time he makes a delivery."

I was beyond stunned. "I don't believe it."

Adam shrugged. "I know, but he was caught with an item of the Singhs'."

"Only one item? Nothing else?"

Adam did a slight eye roll. "DS Winterbottom thinks he may have hidden the rest."

"So what item did he *not* have the sense to hide?" I asked, my blood pressure rising.

"An elephant," said Adam.

"Are you freaking kidding me? Does that shop look big enough to hold an elephant?"

Adam resisted the urge to smile and failed. "Not a real elephant. A statue."

"Are you sure you're not getting mixed up with the item stolen from the circus?" I asked.

Adam shook his head "Nope, that item was their good luck talisman."

"It wasn't by any chance a particular type of garden ornament, was it?"

Adam stared at me. "Josie, is there something you need to tell me?"

The tinkling of the shop bell prevented me from answering as Frosty Knickers hastened down the steps, thrusting a sorry-looking Dan in front of her. The car door opened and DS Winterbottom dropped a hand on the top of Dan's head as she maneuvered him into the car.

"Adam, you've got to stop her. Helen has this all wrong." I had to yell this last sentence as Susan emerged on the top step screaming words that Finolla had *definitely* told me not to use—at least not in public.

"Tell me what you know," said Adam. "And quick."

I filled him in as fast as I could. The car pulled off and Adam stepped in front. It was a near miss, and if Belle had been driving Adam would have been salami.

The car door opened and DS Winterbottom emerged. "Sir?"

Adam nodded towards the store. "Helen, let's take the boy back in. Ms Monroe has a few things she'd like to share."

61

We traipsed inside the corner shop and Adam flipped the sign to "Closed." Susan Ludlow was flushed so red she looked fit to pop. DS Winterbottom didn't look much happier, whereas Dan just seemed defeated.

"What's going on, sir?"

"It's harassment, that's what it is," said Susan. "Coming in here accusing my boy of theft. Complete bollocks."

Adam raised a hand and Susan stopped. I think she was finally running out of puff.

"Josie, tell Winterbottom what you told me."

I took a deep breath. "I don't believe Dan is the thief."

"He was caught with an item reported stolen by the Singhs," said DS Winterbottom, flashing me a look.

I tried to catch Dan's eye, but he continued to scrutinize the linoleum.

"It was a statue of an elephant, right? The one with all the arms?"

"Correct. Apparently it's some kind of Hindu god," said DS Winterbottom.

"Ganesha," I explained. "He's the Lord of Good Fortune. One who provides prosperity and removes obstacles from your path. That's why Gurminder gave it to you, right, Dan? You guys were trying to figure out a way to get her parents' approval."

Dan remained silent.

"Is this true, Dan?" asked Susan.

Dan shuffled his feet, nodding imperceptibly.

"Then why didn't you say so, you daft apeth?" asked Susan, who seemed ready to shake some sense into her son.

"I think it's because he didn't want to get his girlfriend into trouble," I replied.

"Gurminder?" said Susan. "Gurminder's not his girlfriend."

"I think you'll find she is," I said, "but they've kept it a secret because Gurminder's parents wouldn't approve. Am I right, Dan?"

Once again, Dan nodded assent.

"And that's why Rose sent you both poison pen letters. She'd seen you together and she knew your secret. She was threatening to tell your mum and then Gurminder's parents."

"Poison pen letters?" said Susan. "What poison pen letters?"

"Later, Mum," said Dan. "But I didn't kill her. And nor did Gee. We hated the old bat, but we didn't do her in."

"Dan!" said Susan, shocked. "You do not call Miss Braithwaite 'an old bat.' Especially in front of her niece," she added as an aside.

"That's okay," I said. "Believe me, I'm starting to think she may deserve that and worse."

Dan muttered a half-hearted apology.

"But you were there Sunday night?" I continued.

"Just delivering the milk and bread she'd forgotten. The house was unlocked, so I went in and put the stuff in the kitchen. I called out, but there was no one there." Dan's eyes flickered back and forth between Adam and his mum. "You've gotta believe me."

"So if Rose didn't go home after leaving here, where did she go?" asked DS Winterbottom.

'That's easy," I said. "She went to pick up Elgar."

DS Winterbottom viewed me like I'd gone insane.

"I believe Josie is referencing Ms Braithwaite's cat," said Adam.

"Well of course I am," I said. "Who else would it be?"

Susan held up a hand. "Back to this nonsense with the elephant. If Dan isn't the thief, and I never thought he was, mind," said Susan, "who is?"

I glanced over at Adam. "Yeah, well, that's a bit more complicated."

62

Adam insisted we all head to Dorking Police Station to make statements, which was bad enough. However, by the time Susan, Dan and I exited the store a crowd, not normally seen in such multitudes outside of royal weddings, had gathered outside Waspit's. Of course, the Witches of Milkwood had been front and center, all but rubbing their hands with glee at the sight of me being hauled off in a police car. Photos had been snapped, names had been called and I was pretty sure we'd been videoed and were now well on our way to becoming a local YouTube sensation.

By the time I returned home I was hot, I was tired and I was sick of being asked questions by an increasingly irate DS Winterbottom. Adam, whom I was still mad at, had been called out on an emergency and Frosty Knickers had taken full advantage of his absence to make my life as miserable as possible.

It was only when Gurminder and her parents were ushered into the interview room, and Gurminder admitted that the sacred image had been given to Dan as a gift, that DS Winterbottom let it drop. The Singhs had marched their stricken daughter home and the Ludlows and I had forgone the offer of a police ride and taken the bus—where I had paid double. I had felt sorry for Dan and Gurminder, but then again true love was notoriously known for its lack of straight paths.

I fixed myself a late lunch and decided to spend what was left of the afternoon sorting through Aunt Rose's study. Whereas the rest of the cottage had been neatness itself, the study was the one place Aunt Rose enjoyed an organization system best defined as coordinated chaos.

Entering the study, I pulled out the piano stool and perched on the edge. Hard to believe that this beautiful instrument was now mine. I rummaged through the bag of music I'd purchased until I found the piece I was searching for—the "Melodie" from Orfeo ed Euridice by Gluck—and ran through a few opening bars. Utter perfection. Back home in Austin I played the piano daily and I vowed from this moment on to play every day for as long as I was in Milkwood.

I retrieved the triangular-shaped metronome that I'd bought in Godalming, unwrapped it, and placed it on top of the piano. Aunt Rose had always said there should only ever be two things on top of a piano—piano music and a metronome. Would you put a vase of flowers or a cup of tea on top of a violin, she'd ask—no? Then neither should you put them on top of a piano. I couldn't argue with that.

I snatched up the book on Sir Edward Elgar and decided to find a spot for it on the bookshelf. I had peeked at it the night before and determined I needed something a little less Edwardian for my light reading pleasure. There were plenty of other biographies already crammed on Aunt Rose's shelves and I decided the perfect place for Elgar would be wedged between Malcolm Arnold and Gerald Finzi—not exactly chronologically correct, but at least alphabetically pleasing. I nudged Finzi to the right and a flutter of score papers cascaded onto the floor.

I gathered them together and was about to squeeze them back onto the shelf when something caught my eye. This was an original piece, written in Aunt Rose's immaculately printed hand. I knew Aunt Rose had dabbled in composing when she was younger, but they had been nursery rhymes on the piano, for which we would make up silly words. This was for four instruments: cello, viola, violin and double bass. I sight read the first few bars and stopped. I recognized this piece. I darted over to the

Steinway and played the main theme. Six bars in I stopped. There was no doubt in my mind.

I was about to turn to the next sheet when I was distracted by a hammering at the front door. The door flew open and Adam burst, into the foyer. I say "burst," but really it was more of a limp.

All my earlier annoyance with Adam evaporated as I saw the look on his face. "Adam, what's wrong?"

"Phil has been attacked."

"No, I mean your leg. You're limping."

Adam studied his foot as if he had no idea what I was talking about. "It was that blasted zedonk. We found it halfway to Godalming and there was a bit of a disagreement whether it should keep going or go back home."

"Yeah, Claude doesn't like having his name called," I said. "It's common knowledge."

"Not that common," said Adam, wincing.

"Who won?" I asked.

Adam rolled his eyes. "I did, eventually, but not without some casualties—namely me."

"Who's this Phil you're talking about?"

Adam became serious again. "The curate."

I gave Adam a death stare. "Cluck a freakin' duck! Really? And you're checking to see if I have an alibi? You've wrongly arrested one person today, are you really going to make it two? And while we're on the sub—"

"Don't be stupid, Josie. I'm checking to make sure you're safe."

"Oh." All my indignation evaporated. "What happened? Is he okay?"

"He was found behind the church. He's being rushed by ambulance to The Royal Surrey. We'll know more once the doctors see him, but he's lost a lot of blood."

My head woozed purely at the mention of blood and I sank onto the piano bench. "Like Aunt Rose?"

"Exactly like Aunt Rose," said Adam. "A shove to the back and another unfortunate landing."

"That's dreadful. I was speaking with him and Belle only yesterday." I flushed as I remembered the way we'd parted, ignoring Belle's insistence that I had it all wrong.

"Actually, Josie, it's Belle I'm looking for."

The speed with which Adam Ward hurtled down Brambley Lane made Belle's driving seem practically saint-like.

At the end of the lane, Adam jammed the car into first and ploughed through the ford. We roared up Honeycroft Hill until we reached the gates of Barton Hall, where Adam slammed on the brakes and let out an expletive. The gates stretched before us, towering and impenetrable. I launched myself out of the car and dashed towards them to see if I could force them apart, but they were well and truly locked. I lunged towards the metal box containing the intercom and frantically rammed the button inward. I tried again—no answer.

"You're sure she's home this afternoon?" Adam asked, leaning over the top of the car. "DS Winterbottom phoned ten minutes ago and Tillman said she was out."

"Yeah, I'm sure. Unless she's had a change of plans, she's supposed to be giving Quentin shooting lessons."

Adam and I locked eyes. This was getting desperate.

"Here, give me a boost." I stuck my foot out.

Adam gave me the "you've got to be joking" look.

"There's a switch on the other side of the gate," I explained.

Adam surveyed the ten-foot structure, realized his zedonk injury was going to get the better of him and reluctantly linked his fingers, creating a makeshift step. I will draw a veil over the next two minutes, but let's just say I was glad I was wearing shorts, and Adam assured me the gaping tear in my blouse was barely noticeable as long as you didn't take a gander in the direction of my left boob.

I filled Adam in on my deductions as we continued at breakneck speed up the driveway. All we had to do now was find Belle. However, that was easier said than done. Both Adam and I knew from our unauthorized visits as children that the estate was vast. As the shooting range was a relatively new addition, there was no way to know where it was located.

"Adam, tell me about what happened when Belle's mum died."

Adam didn't take his eyes off the road.

"She was sent away."

"But before that. After her mother's death." I decided to leave out the part about Jimmy—we could discuss that another day.

"Belle got a little confused," said Adam. "She was upset. Distraught, really."

I turned to look at my old friend. "Adam, did Belle try and kill Bonnie Curry with a shotgun?"

Adam took a deep breath. "There have been many people in this village who have thought about a world without Bonnie Curry, but yes. Bonnie was in The Pig & Whistle one day and Belle entered with a shotgun. There were words, a scuffle ensued, and the gun went off. Luckily no one was hurt, but yes, Belle was sent away after that. Said she couldn't remember a thing. How she got there, why she had the shotgun, or why she and Bonnie Curry came to blows."

I could think of lots of reasons as to why someone would come to blows with Bonnie Curry, but this didn't seem the time to list them.

"I still find it hard to believe," I said.

"My mum and dad happened to be at the bar for their weekly pint. Scared the heck out of Mum. Then Lord DeCorcy sent her to a place in Wales."

"Anglesey," I interjected.

"That's the place," said Adam. "Belle came back a year or two later and she's been a model citizen ever since."

"You've seen her driving, right?" I asked.

"A model citizen, bar her driving," said Adam, breaking a smile.

"Until now."

"Yeah," said Adam. "Until now. And you're sure she's giving Quentin a shooting lesson, today?"

I nodded.

Adam roared past the turnoff for Quentin's, sweeping past the manor house and ignoring the gravel spitting skyward. The road stretched up a slight incline before splitting at a T-junction.

"I figure the shooting range is going to be fair distance from the main house and so this seems like a good bet," said Adam, explaining his reasoning.

"I thought with you being a policeman you might have been to the shooting range yourself."

Adam gave me a look. "Do I seem the type to interact with the blue bloods, Josie?"

He had a point. Adam was far from the ragamuffin child of his youth, but he was never going to be mistaken for a toff.

Adam reached the T-junction, jerked the car to a halt and powered down his window. He leaned out and listened. I followed suit. At first there was nothing, but then in the distance there was the definite sound of a pop. I knew gunshots could echo, giving you the wrong sense of direction, so I yielded to Adam's hopefully greater knowledge of firearms.

"This way." Adam rammed the car into gear and careened to the right.

The road ahead was sheltered by a canopy of trees, which aided in blocking out the meagre sunlight. It had been an overcast day to begin with. Whereas the branches would normally let through dappled sunlight, today they gave a more ominous feel.

The road rose steadily until, in the distance, a clearing came into view. Belle was sharply outlined against the horizon as she hoisted her shotgun and took aim. Quentin Young stood about twenty feet to her left, both with their backs to us. Suddenly, Belle swung towards Quentin, her shotgun raised. The next few seconds seemed to happen in slow motion, as Quentin Young lifted his firearm, aimed in Belle's direction, and shot.

Adam rammed his zedonk-damaged foot to the metal and we veered off road, bouncing across the rutted earth. The Volvo was not built for such terrain and Adam begrudgingly brought the vehicle to a juddering stop. Both doors flew open as we hurtled towards our suspect. With an unimpeded ankle, I reached Belle first. I dropped to my knees and felt for a pulse. She was face down, lying spread eagle like the outline you so often see of a dead body.

I felt rather than heard Adam's presence beside me, as he too dropped and felt for a pulse.

Quentin lumbered up beside us. "Did you see that? Crazy Corcy tried to kill me!"

Quentin rattled on about self-defense and I continued to ignore him as I tried in vain to find signs of life.

Adam stood and put out his hand. "I'll be taking that, Mr Young, if you don't mind."

Quentin took a step back, his hand clasped around the gun's non-pointy end.

"Mr Young," said Adam, more forcefully.

"But you saw what happened, right?"

Adam nodded, his arm still outstretched.

"I'm not going to get into any trouble?" Quentin continued. "I mean everyone in the entire village knows she's insane."

I'd heard enough. I spun around and faced the man who had shot the one woman in Milkwood I called a friend.

"You're a big fat liar. Belle would never shoot you. You must have yelled something awful for her to turn like that. You were looking for an excuse."

"Josie!" said Adam, a note of warning in his voice.

I ignored him. "And now you've killed her and Aunt Rose and who knows, maybe Philip too."

Quentin's mouth tightened. "You better shut your girlfriend up, Ward."

"I know you did it," I said, my temper rising. "You killed Aunt Rose just as clear as I'm standing here and I have the proof. And I am *not* his girlfriend."

Quentin Young once again raised his shotgun. "That's good, because you won't care so much when I shoot copper boy."

Adam wrestled me behind him.

"Will you stop that," I said, pushing Adam away. "I am sick and tired of being rescued by you."

Adam spun to face me. "Really? This is the time you're going to go all feminist on me?"

"Feminist? I'll give you feminist." I dragged Adam by the shirt and propelled him behind me.

"You do realize I have a gun here, right?" said Quentin. "I've shot one of you. I've got nothing to lose. I might as well shoot all three of you. I'll say it was the crazy blonde here. That she went nuts. They'll believe me; it's not like it didn't happen before."

I gave Quentin a look of utter contempt. "How dare you talk about my friend like that. Belle DeCorcy was worth ten of you. You're just a washed-up composer. Belle was sweet and kind and, okay, she was a really bad driver, but she was generous and beautiful and—"

A cracked voice pierced the air. "Excuse me, I heard that remark about the driving."

I peered down, Belle had rolled to a sitting position and was nursing a shoulder dripping with blood. My blood pressure dropped and my legs buckled, but this time I was determined not to faint. I sank to my knees, removing my scarf and wrapping it around Belle's blood-sodden shoulder.

"I thought you were dead," I said, fighting back tears.

"'Course not. Takes more than a scratch to kill a DeCorcy," Belle frowned. "Actually, I think that might be our family motto."

"Have you all forgotten I'm still here?" said an increasingly belligerent Quentin.

I turned and my eyes widened in surprise. Inadvertently my arm rose as I pointed behind Quentin and screamed one word at the top of my lungs.

"You think I'm going to fall for that old trick?" yelled Quentin, his face pulsing with rage. He raised the shotgun, did something technical with the trigger and aimed in my direction. "Say hi to your aunt for me—"

I shut my eyes, but instead of gunfire there was a scream of pain. I opened my eyes to see Claude the zedonk galloping into the distance and Quentin sailing through the air, like the angel he so definitely was not.

64

I've always had a sneaking suspicion that hospital waiting room chairs are there for one reason—to make you leave. After several hours of being wedged into the unmalleable plastic, I woke from a dreamless sleep to see Adam standing in front of me. I uncrooked my neck and unkinked my back before noticing that his arm was outstretched in my direction, reminiscent of earlier in the day, when trying to coax the shotgun from Quentin's reluctant hands. This time, however, his hands contained a cup with rising steam.

"Sorry, I know you like decaf, but this was all they had. Please notice I asked for an actual cup—I know how much you hate Styrofoam."

I straightened and took the proffered mug. My tongue felt like it had been trekking through the Sahara and the hot liquid resembled nectar from the gods.

The tea was not strong enough to take away the hospital smell, and glancing down at my hands I could still see traces of Belle's blood under my nails.

"How is she?" I asked, unsuccessfully trying to rearrange the hole in my blouse, relieved I'd worn a new bra and not the ratty one, recently run over by a tractor.

I had refused to go home and change, insisting I go in the ambulance with Belle. Regardless of Belle's family motto, this

DeCorcy had lasted roughly thirty seconds after her valiant speech before she passed out, most likely from a combination of blood loss and shock.

"Belle just came out of surgery," said Adam. "They say she'll be fine, although they did have to give her a blood transfusion."

Merely the mention of the word "blood" was enough to make my legs go limp.

"And Philip?"

"Nasty concussion and a few stitches. He'll have to stay in for a day or two for observation." Adam smiled. "Personally I think the nurses on Ward Ten don't want to let him go."

Adam dropped into the seat beside me, leaned forward, and placed his head in his hands. "You know, Josie. Next time someone has a gun—"

"I know. I'm not sure what happened. Belle was on the floor and Quentin was saying such horrible things." I reached for Adam's hand. "Adam, I'm so sorry. I put both you and Belle at risk. Please forgive me."

Adam raised my hand to his lips and was about to either blow a raspberry or kiss it, when Frosty Knickers materialized from behind a stack of bedpans.

Adam dropped my hand and rose to his feet. "Yes, Detective Sergeant?"

Was I mistaken or did I detect a note of coolness in Adam's tone? Had the love birds fallen out?

"Miss DeCorcy is awake and she's asking for Miss Monroe."

I leapt to my feet and dashed along the corridor.

Belle had been placed in a private room and had already accumulated four vases of flowers, two bowls of fruit and an overstuffed donkey. Milkwood's grapevine had obviously been working overtime.

Lord DeCorcy sat slumped in a chair in the corner. He was a shadow of the man he'd been when I last saw him.

The last thing I needed was more confrontation, but I needn't have worried. Lord DeCorcy stood and paced across the linoleum in our direction. He extended his hand towards Adam, shook it warmly, then did the same to me.

"I hear I have the pair of you to thank for saving my girl from that monster."

If I was honest, it had been Claude who saved the day, but right now I was willing to take the credit.

"You're welcome, sir," said Adam.

Lord DeCorcy produced an ample handkerchief and dabbed his brow. "I'll leave you to it, shall I? Not too long though. Arabelle's been through enough."

Belle was so pale she practically blended with the sheets. I wasn't sure if blood transfusions took time to restore color, or whether it was the after-effects of the operation. Either way I wished Belle would hurry up and regain her rosy complexion. This ghost-like look was freaking me out.

Belle opened her eyes and managed a weak smile. "Hello, Josie."

I sank beside the bed and grasped her hand. Before I could speak I spied the drip protruding from her vein and my legs went from beneath me. I attempted to pull myself together and failed. I settled for a very high pitch. "Hey, Trouble," as I pulled myself off the floor and into a sitting position.

"I want to know how you found out about Quentin," Belle said, in barely a whisper. But before I could say a word Belle's eyes flickered shut, her breathing deepened and Belle DeCorcy fell into a deep, restorative sleep that she would not awake from for hours.

65

I t was only on the way to the car that I realized Adam had gone from limping to hobbling.

I glanced down to see a very unattractive NHS boot on his left foot.

He shrugged. "The nurses made me get it x-rayed. Two cracked bones and a torn ligament."

"That Claude is really something," I said.

"You can say that again. Mind you, I got off easy. Quentin's laid up with six broken ribs, a broken arm, and his hair full of cow poop."

"I know I shouldn't be happy, but I can't be sad. He *was* going to kill us."

Adam remoted the car door open and I slipped into the warm leather interior.

"Plum Tree Cottage?" asked Adam.

I nodded. The words brought back the night Adam helped me search for the intruder who had blasted Plum Tree with Puccini. My cheeks reddened at the subsequent memory when he offered to stay and I'd slipped him a fluffy blanket and asked him to sleep on the couch. However, the events of the day seemed to have eclipsed any previous awkwardness. I guess having a gun pointed at you and seeing your new best friend shot in cold blood will do that.

We bumped to a stop outside Plum Tree and I stumbled out of the car, more from sheer tiredness than clumsiness.

The lights were blazing but no Puccini blasted through the airwaves, which I took as a good sign. I felt Adam slip his arm around my waist and together we strolled up the garden path.

"Do you want to come in?" I asked, loitering under the porch light like a teenager.

Adam leant forward and drew me into a hug that squished all the air from my lungs. Kind of like when Bonnie Curry landed on top of me, but far more enjoyable.

"I thought I was going to lose you today, Puke."

I inhaled Adam's cologne and lay my cheek on his shoulder. My heart was doing a great impression of a jackhammer and I hoped Adam couldn't feel it through my ripped blouse.

I broke away and gazed into Adam's face: so earnest.

"You were brave today."

"I was stupid," I replied. "I almost got us killed."

"That too, but you defended your friend and that took guts. Proud of you, Puke."

Adam leaned forward and kissed me on the forehead. Then he kissed me on the nose and I believe he was about to head a smidgen farther south when the door flew open, flooding us with light.

Adam and I pulled apart like we'd been caught by our parents. Peter didn't seem to notice.

"Josie, I've been worried. Where were you?"

I stared at Peter with incomprehension. When did I start having to tell Peter Lacey my whereabouts? Then I caught a whiff of curry and I remembered.

"Did you forget about our date?" Peter continued.

I felt Adam stiffen beside me.

"No. I mean yes. I mean."

It was at this point Peter finally took a good look at me. I was muddy and bloody and my clothes weren't fairing too fabulously either.

"Josie! Poor girl. What...what happened?" Peter reached for my hand, pulled me inside, enveloping me in a bear hug.

It took me three seconds to disentangle myself, which was exactly the time it took for Adam to hobble down the path and disappear into the night.

66

I showered and changed while Peter reheated the curry. We dined late into the night, me filling him in on the extraordinary details of the afternoon, and he suitably stunned—as one might be after hearing Milkwood's maestro had been taken out by a zedonk named Claude.

The next day Peter received a text from Adam asking me to appear at Dorking Police Station to give a statement. I had duly reported and had the pleasure of DS Winterbottom's undivided attention for what seemed like more time than it takes to write an entire symphony.

Adam had been conspicuous by his absence and I was too stubborn to ask if he was around.

If he was going to get upset because another man hugged me, then so be it. I had no obligation to Adam and he had none to me. Let's face it, he was supposed to be dating Frosty Knickers.

I arrived home from Dorking to find a kitchen full of gifts. The Milkwood grapevine had gone into overload as the news of Belle DeCorcy and her near-death experience spread like measles in a kindergarten. There was a basket overflowing with chocolate from Susan Ludlow, and a steak and mushroom pudding from Petruska and Carl. Florence Greene had baked me not only a Victoria sponge, but also a plethora of fairy cakes, each as light and fluffy as Tchaikovsky's Sugar Plum Fairy.

It seemed I had also found favor with the Witches of Milkwood. Bonnie Curry had presented me with a rather splendid gnome and Irene had gifted me a certificate for a free breakfast of my choice at The Milk Jug. A woman with more pride might have scoffed at such gifts. Luckily my pride was obliterated by my love of a good English fry up and the cuteness factor of the gnome involved. No, truly, the gnome was adorable.

Whereas before my presence in the village was met with undisguised dislike, now I could do no wrong. Walking from one end of Unthank Road to the other could take upward of thirty minutes, as grateful villagers swarmed from their abodes to thank the conquering hero for saving Belle. I assumed the fuss would die down in time, but currently it was easier not to leave Plum Tree, which was inconvenient, as there was one thing I had to do and I needed a phone to do it. I finally borrowed Peter's mobile and made a long-distance call to Mrs Ackerman who, after some queries on her part, unlocked my apartment and found what I was asking for —proof.

Two days had passed and Peter, who had taken time off work to be with me, had been cooking all afternoon. I had volunteered to be his sous chef, but somewhere between crying over the onions and squishing the mushrooms I had been confined to setting out the silverware and turning on the twinkle lights. I had also visited Rose's study and chosen a combination of Debussy and Faure for tonight's listening pleasure. I could only wonder how long it would take for me to be able to listen to Puccini again without imagining dead bodies.

Belle and Philip had both been released from hospital and were due to arrive at Plum Tree for a celebratory dinner with Peter, Daisy and me at six.

There was a hearty knock at the door, and I was delighted to hear the familiar voice of Daisy Pond. My aunt had visited me twice in the last week, and her common sense, mixed with a dry sense of humor, had been great solace. Plus, I had learned more about her— she had been a widow for five years and had a daughter and two sons in their early twenties—all longing to visit the Motherland. Frankly, they sounded like the family I'd always dreamed of.

Daisy and I were in the process of upending a bottle of Waspit's finest when we heard the door open for a second time and Philip and Belle arrived, looking considerably less dead than the last time I'd seen them. Color bloomed on Belle's cheeks and Philip looked dashing with a jagged scar above his right eyebrow. I couldn't help but notice that the scar was a mirror image of the one Belle had sustained during her unfortunate submersion into the Tilling-bourne, all those years ago.

Philip and Belle may have insisted they weren't a couple, but you wouldn't know it from either their demeanors or their color-coordinated outfits. Philip wore a beige pair of trousers and a soft purple shirt, while Belle wore a lilac summer dress with a beige cardigan draped around her shoulders. Other than the fact that Belle's shoulder and left arm were immobilized in a sturdy sling, you'd hardly know she'd been shot.

I ushered Philip and Belle onto the patio and poured them both a drink—cranberry juice with a signature umbrella for Belle and a tonic water for the curate, minus the baby umbrella. Philip tiptoed around Belle like she was made of glass. Deny it all you might, but I'd set fire to my 1945 copy of *Liebesträume* if they weren't dating by the end of summer.

As we tucked into dinner I realized how much I enjoyed having Peter as a housemate. His risotto was sublime and his sticky toffee pudding was the best dessert I'd ever inhaled. I was about to scoop another portion of pudding into my empty bowl when the French doors opened and out limped Adam.

Peter was the first one to speak. "Adam, please...join us. Josie and I are hosting a celebratory dinner."

If this was supposed to appease Adam it didn't work. Adam froze in the doorway, his jaw set, his fists clenched.

"I need a quick word with Josie."

I paused mid-scoop, scraped back my chair and followed Adam into the living room. I felt like a school child being summoned by the headmaster—a headmaster in a highly unattractive NHS boot.

"What is it, Adam?"

Adam suddenly seemed inordinately interested in Aunt Rose's Japanese rug.

"Josie…"

This was so weird. Adam was never at a loss for words. What on earth could have happened to make him act so strange? I started to get worried. Had Finolla been imprisoned? Dad suffered a stroke?

I was about to speak when Adam found his voice.

"Josie, I'm sure you must have realized over the past couple of weeks that I, well, that I still have feelings for you."

I sank onto the couch. Okay, so my mother wasn't indisposed At Her Majesty's pleasure, but this was equally stunning, if not more so. Sure, there had been moments when I felt a connection, but the fact that he was dating Frosty Knickers seemed to be a good reason not to let those feelings get the better of me. In fact, why was he saying these things at all, when he was dating Helen?

"Josie. Obviously I don't know how much longer you're going to be staying in Milkwood. But I'd like to see you while you here."

Again, all I had was silence. Not a regular occurrence for me.

Adam stopped shuffling his feet and looked me in the eyes. "I know it's stupid, with you going back to the US and all. But anyway, I thought I'd ask, but if you're dating Peter…now's the time to tell me and I'll back off."

I folded my arms across my chest and gaped at him in amazement. "Me? Dating Peter? What about you dating Frosty Knickers?"

Adam seemed confused. "Who the heck is Frosty Knickers?"

"Winterbottom. You know, your DS."

"Ah!"

My temper started to rise. "And you have the cheek to ask me if I'm dating Peter."

"Josie. I am not dating Helen, and I'm sorry if she gave you that impression. I have spoken with DS Winterbottom and you need to know that we are not and have never been an item. I'm her boss, for pity's sake."

"That's not the impression I got," I continued.

"Then your impression is misinformed," said Adam. "It's as simple as that."

"What about the kiss at the Christmas do last year?" I asked, coloring as the words more suited to a high schooler fell from my lips.

Adam absorbed my gaze and I felt as if all the wind had been knocked from my proverbial sails.

"Josie, DS Winterbottom had drunk way too much. It was the Christmas party, it was late and Helen got caught up in the moment. It was a one off thing and one I subsequently informed her must never happen again."

"Oh," I said, rather pathetically.

"Josie, keeping our relationship professional during this investigation has been harder than you could imagine. But now the case is closed. You are officially no longer a suspect, so I have one question for you—do you or do you not have feelings for Peter?"

I gave the question some thought. There was no doubt that Peter was attractive. Plus he was easy to live with, he was an extraordinarily competent cook, and we both had a love of classical music, where as I was pretty sure Adam, if questioned, would identify Puccini as a type of pasta.

"I like Peter very much," I said, pausing. "But he'll never be you."

Adam's whole body relaxed. "Thank goodness for that. I'd hate to have to lock him up and throw away the key."

I rose and wrapped my arms around him. This time we kissed and it was definitely worth the wait.

67

"So tell me again from the beginning what happened," said Daisy. "I believe I've heard roughly thirty versions to date. Each more elaborate than the last."

"My favorite is where Adam gallops up on a zedonk and saves the day," said Belle. "As if Claude would let anyone ride him."

"I heard from Darcy Blythe that Josie clobbered Quentin around the head with his *Enchanted Summer* manuscript until he begged for mercy," said Daisy. "Gotta say, that gave me quite a chuckle."

After ten minutes, Adam and I returned to the garden and, much to their credit, nobody mentioned either my flushed cheeks or Adam's mussed up hair. If Peter noted that Adam had his arm around my shoulder he hadn't commented, other than to pour himself an extravagant glass of red and down approximately half of it.

"So come on, Josie, spill the beans," said Philip, as I poured Adam a generous glass of merlot.

"Well, I wouldn't have got involved, but seeing the entire village suspected me of murdering my aunt it seemed the smart thing to do —you know, to clear my name."

Adam raised his hands. "Josie, you know I never thought you'd murdered your aunt. But considering you were found at the scene with blood on your hands—"

"Literally," interrupted Peter.

"We had to at least keep you in the picture until we could rule you out," said Adam.

"Actually, it was Belle who started the whole thing, really," I explained.

"Was it?" said Belle. "How fun!"

"Belle suggested we investigate. She'd be Lucy and I'd be Ethel, or was it the other way around? Anyhow, Belle convinced me that we needed to do something, and seeing I didn't have anything better to do, it seemed like a good idea, at the time. To be honest, I think wine was involved."

"Sounds, er, about right," said Peter, raising his half-empty glass in my direction.

"Anyhow, the first thing I did was find Aunt Rose's schedule."

"How come the police didn't find it?" asked Daisy, looking at Adam.

"In Adam's defense it was hidden in a secret drawer that only Aunt Rose and I knew existed. In it were certain initials all on the same day of different months. Belle recognized who the initials belonged to and so we decided these people would be our top priority."

"Oh my gosh. I...I had no idea," said Peter, leaning back.

"It turns out that interrogating people is a lot harder than it looks. Sadly, I stink at it. Everything that happened was more to luck. One by one all the suspects seemed to fall away or have alibis. There was only one person where things didn't seem to add up and that was Quentin. Aunt Rose had him in her schedule for the night she returned from the Peak District, yet he said he hadn't seen her in weeks. So I asked myself, why was he lying?"

"Because he'd killed her," said Daisy, "that's why."

"Well yes, but there really *was* a good reason for Aunt Rose to have him in her schedule if only he'd admitted it."

There was silence.

"I give up," said Belle. "What was the reason?"

"Elgar!"

"Like the *Enigma Variations*, Elgar?" asked Philip.

"No, like the cat Elgar," I replied. "Aunt Rose had been on vacation."

"Holiday," corrected Peter, reaching for a refill. "You're in the UK now."

"She'd been touring the Peak District and Peter was in Prague. She had to have someone watch Elgar and that someone was Quentin."

"How d'ya figure that out?" asked Daisy.

"Four things," I explained. "First of all, when I first arrived there was a medium-sized Tupperware box containing a few scoops of kitty kibble on the counter. Most people keep their pet's food in a much larger container and only transfer it to smaller containers if their pet's not staying in the house. At least that's how I do it with Horace."

"Who on earth is Horace?" asked Adam.

"It's her budgerigar," said Belle.

"You have a budgerigar named Horace?" asked Adam, seemingly unable to let this piece of information go.

"Believe me, when you have a zedonk named Claude it's easy to not pass judgement on other people's pet's names," said Belle.

I smiled. "Second, the piano legs at both Aunt Rose's and Quentin's were scratched," I turned to Peter. "You know how the litter in the litterbox gets everywhere. We can never seem to sweep all of it up. Well, I found tiny traces of litter in Quentin's bathroom. That was the third thing."

"Oh, she's smart," said Daisy. "Watch out copper, there's a new sheriff in town."

"What was the fourth?" asked Belle, pouring herself some more cranberry juice.

I glanced towards the curate. "Actually it has to do with Philip."

"Oh yes," said Philip. "Do tell."

"Written in Aunt Rose's schedule on the Sunday night were two sets of initials. *PU* and *QY*."

Everyone turned to look at Philip, who shrugged, nonplussed.

"I found out pretty fast who *QY* was, but no one knew who *PU* was, seeing everyone refers to you as Philip or Curate, and those who did know refused to tell," I said, glancing at Belle, remembering how she'd tried to shield me from reading the church message board where the name Philip Upton was engraved in gold.

Belle looked like butter wouldn't melt as she sipped her cranberry juice.

"But as it turned out the initials *PU* were not the initials of a person. They stood for 'pick up.' Pick up from Quentin Young's."

"See," said Belle, triumphantly. "I knew Philip had nothing to do with it."

"But if Quentin and Rose were friends why did he murder her?" asked Philip.

"I don't know for sure," I replied, "but I have a feeling Quentin and Aunt Rose were more than friends."

"Eww!" said Daisy, lowering her glass. "There's a visual I don't need."

"So you never suspected anything between them?" asked Adam, looking at Peter.

Peter shook his head. "Mind you, I'm gone all day and I...I travel a lot."

"That's good," said Adam, putting a proprietary hand on top of mine.

Peter continued. "Frankly, Rose could have belonged to a secret cult and I...I doubt I'd have known diddly squat."

"But what makes you think they were more than friends?" asked Belle.

"Several insignificant things that when put together add up. First, Quentin was the only person in the village who admitted to liking Aunt Rose."

"He could have lied," said Daisy.

"That would have been the sensible thing to do, but I think he still had feelings for her and couldn't bear to say anything bad. Second, he knew exactly how Aunt Rose took her tea. That's the type of info you only retain when you've been around someone often."

"That's a bit of a leap, isn't it?" asked Philip.

"Na, she's got a point," said Daisy, upending the red.

"But surely someone would have seen him coming and going to

the cottage?" said Philip. "This village is many wonderful things, but it's rife with gossip."

"He didn't have to use the main roads. He could cut across the Tillingbourne," said Belle.

"Exactly, and that's how he came the night he murdered Aunt Rose. What he didn't know was that half of freaking Milkwood was at Plum Tree that night."

"Really?" said Adam. "Who else was here?"

Peter flushed and Belle and Philip feigned interest in a butterfly fluttering past.

"My mother—"

"Your mother?" exclaimed Adam.

"And Dan Ludlow," I added, quickly changing the subject.

"Ah yes," said Daisy. "Half the village is talking about Dan's wrongful arrest. Should've heard what Magna has to say about it."

"And the other half is talking about Claude the zedonk," said Philip, tactfully redirecting Adam's attention.

"But it was finding out that Dan delivered groceries that got me wondering. Why did Aunt Rose forget her groceries? It was such an out-of-character thing to do."

"But that's exactly what you've been saying about your aunt. That she'd changed so much," said Belle.

"Ah yes, I'm going to get to that. But first I had to figure out why she'd left her groceries. When I'd spoken to Aunt Rose the night before, she was really excited about something and couldn't wait to share her good news. At first I thought maybe she had a new cat, but over time I realized it was something much bigger. So what happened at Susan Ludlow's store that made her leave without even getting her change?"

"Don't keep us guessing, girl," said Daisy. "What was it?"

"She looked down," I said.

Not surprisingly, there was silence. I continued.

"She spotted the flyer for Quentin's upcoming concert," I replied. "It was there on the counter."

"But why would that make her leave her groceries behind?" asked Philip.

"Because of what was written on it. Or, more precisely, what was *not* written on it—Aunt Rose's name."

There was silence.

"I don't get it," said Daisy. "Why would Rose's name be on Quentin's poster?"

"Because," I said. "Quentin Young did not write either *Enchanted Summer* or *Rosetta's Throne*. Aunt Rose did."

68

Peter went inside to fetch more wine as the assembled guests took in this surprising information.

"Are you sure, Josie?" asked Daisy. "I mean, I know Rosie was talented, she was an amazing pianist, but composing? She never mentioned anything about that."

"I think at first she helped him and eventually became more involved. Remember, Quentin was nobody until he released *Rosetta's Throne* a couple of years ago."

"She has a point," said Peter. "*Rosetta's Throne* was Quentin's breakout piece. His masterpiece, you might say."

"And he named it after our Rosie," said Daisy.

"He did. I think as a kind of peace offering because I know Aunt Rose wrote that piece of music."

There was silence.

"Wow," said Peter. "I...I didn't see that coming."

"I don't think Aunt Rose minded at first. Maybe Quentin took the piece to another level—who knows? At that time she loved Quentin, and was happy for him to take the credit."

"Okay, am I the only one who thought the man batted for the other side?" asked Peter.

There was general nodding.

"He was flamboyant, I'll give you that. But gay—no. I could tell the night I met him at The Dirty Duck," I said, recalling the pinch to my bum and the numerous boob grazes.

"Again, ew," said Daisy, uncorking the large bottle of red Peter had plonked on the table.

"But it was different with the second piece. I think over the past couple of years he'd stopped loving her. After *Rosetta's Throne*—he was jealous. He knew she was the talent and he started to resent her. I would bet money that Aunt Rose expected to see her name on that flyer."

"Wow!" said Peter.

"I think that's what he promised her before she left. That's what she was excited about. When she returned and didn't see herself credited, she went storming around to his cottage to confront him. She most likely picked up Elgar when she was there. I think she told him she was going to come clean."

"He wouldn't like that very much," said Peter. "It...it would destroy his career."

"I can't prove it, but I think Quentin cut across the Tillingbourne so he'd be back here when Aunt Rose returned. I don't know whether he wanted to make her see his side, or whether he planned on murder, but that was what Aunt Rose was talking about on the phone when I called. She wasn't saying she'd just seen *me*, or asking *me* why I was here. She was talking to someone else and the only other people she'd seen that day were Susan Ludlow and Quentin Young."

"So how do you know it wasn't Susan?" asked Peter. "I...I mean it seems unlikely, but it also seems equally unlikely that it was Quentin."

"Because Susan was having a cooking lesson with Florence and Petruska," I replied.

"How could she be having cooking lessons and be selling Rose provisions at the same time?" asked Daisy.

"Because Dan was manning the shop. Susan happened to come down for more flour and got talking to Rose about her holiday."

"That seems to rule her out," said Daisy. "Good. I like Susan Ludlow. She's a gooden."

"But then the *coup de grace* was finding the original theme of

Rosetta's Throne, laid out in Aunt Rose's neat handwriting. And then it came back to me. The tune had been refined, it had gone from a simple piano piece to a quartet. But the main theme was something Aunt Rose made up when I was five. She would write a tune and we would set it to silly words. The theme seemed so familiar and eventually I figured out why."

"I think I will be suggesting my entire team goes on a refresher course on how to search a house effectively," said Adam, shaking his head.

"Actually, I doubt they would have made a connection. It was scraps of music to them," I said, not believing I was defending Frosty Knickers. "I think these were the rough drafts Aunt Rose used before Quentin put them into some type of computer software, the type composers use these days to write music."

"You mean composers don't sit hunched over a desk armed with only a candle, quill, and those pages with the five lines on them?" said Daisy, laughing. "Times *are* changing."

"Well, for Aunt Rose that was almost exactly what she did, except she used a pencil and worked by the glow of the electric light. I'm sure Quentin had no idea they even existed, else he would have taken them."

Adam scraped back his chair and stood. "Josie Monroe, your deductions are..."

I held my breath while Adam decided on which adjective to use —disastrous, preposterous, earth shatteringly spot on?

He decided on the word "correct" which was not quite as extravagant as I would have liked, but this was *Adam* we were talking about.

Adam put on his copper voice. "Once down the station Quentin confessed to the entire thing. He admitted that Rose had been the one to write *Rosetta's Throne* and that at first she hadn't minded him taking the credit. But when she found out he hadn't included her on *Enchanted Summer*, she went ballistic. Threatened to tell everyone."

"And, of course, Quentin couldn't have that," said Peter. "It would have ruined him."

"Not to mention the embarrassment," said Daisy. "He couldn't stand for that."

"Exactly," said Adam. "As soon as Rose left with Elgar, Quentin hopped across the Tillingbourne and entered the cottage seconds after she'd arrived. He had no idea Peter was here, thinking he was in Prague, and somehow he missed Wendy leaving."

"Wait, Wendy was here?" asked Belle. "But we only saw Peter." Too late Belle realized what she had said. "But, it's okay because Peter couldn't have done it. Besides, I asked him and he categorically denied it."

"Oh, so that's what you were doing here after we visited Quentin."

Belle gave a shrug. "I needed to check. We agreed we both couldn't possibly have done it and to mention it would only confuse the inquiry."

"It, erm, seemed like a good idea at the time," said Peter.

"Are you sure you want to be sharing this in front of a police officer?" said Adam.

There was a general shuffling of feet before Adam cleared his throat and continued. "Anyhow, as far as Quentin knew Rose was at Plum Tree by herself. He says he wanted to talk sense to her, but she mocked him. The one thing a man like him could not stand. So when she turned her back he lunged at her. She fell, landed badly, and the rest we know."

"But what about the Puccini?" asked Belle. "Josie said it was blaring."

"Ah, I might be able to throw some light on that" said Peter, coloring. "That was me. After Rose asked me to leave—"

"Rose asked you to leave?" said Belle, looking more and more confused.

"I'll explain later," I said.

"I'm embarrassed to say, but I was so mad that the minute she went upstairs I cranked up the Puccini full knowing it would annoy her. She must have come down to turn it off when she encountered Quentin."

"What about the Puccini the night you saved Bonnie Curry from landing face down in the duck pond?" asked Daisy, smiling at the memory.

"I'm pretty sure that was Quentin," I said.

"Why Quentin?" asked Philip.

"I don't have proof, but mainly because of a muddy pair of shoes. I think Quentin slipped out of The Dirty Duck while all the brouhaha was going on and came the back way through Bonnie Curry's garden. As for why? I've no idea."

"Josie's right," said Adam. "Quentin overheard you talking with Daisy at The Dirty Duck about trying to solve the murder and decided it might be a way to try and scare you into leaving."

"But I wasn't allowed to leave."

"I know that, and you know that, but by that time he'd imbibed his sixth beer he wasn't exactly thinking clearly," said Adam. "He cut through the path that leads from The Dirty Duck through Bonnie Curry's back garden and came in that way."

"But why on earth did Quentin attack Philip and Belle?" asked Peter. "What did *they* have to do with it?"

"Ah, I think I can shed some light on that," said Philip, inadvertently raising a hand to feel the neat line of stitches along his brow. "He must have overheard us at his party. We were explaining to Josie that we'd been at Plum Tree the night Ms Braithwaite died." Philip cut his eyes to Adam. "I'm sorry Adam, but we were sworn to secrecy. We said we saw someone and we did—Peter. Quentin must have jumped to the wrong conclusion and thought we meant him."

"You guys were all so busy protecting each other, nobody could tell *what* was going on," I said.

Adam blew out a sigh. "So, that's all come out of the woodwork. The Reverend Greene visited the station yesterday and explained the whole thing."

"Charles?" said Daisy. "Don't tell me he's mixed up in all this."

"Not the murders," said Adam. "The thefts."

"Choice," said Daisy, nodding. "Reverend arrested in crime spree, I can see the headlines now."

"Nobody's been arrested," explained Adam, retaking his seat.

"You arrested Dan Ludlow," interjected Daisy.

"And we let him go pretty sharpish after Josie put forward an alternative suggestion," said Adam, shrugging. "Philip, would you like to explain?"

Philip focused on Belle and took a deep breath. "It turns out Florence has a touch of dementia. She's charming and sweet, but in the last six months she's stolen several items out of parishioners' homes when she visits."

"Actually, I think it's when she delivers cakes," I said.

"Anyhow, when Reverend Greene found out what Florence was doing he was desperate for it not to get out. Not because he was worried about his reputation, let me make that clear, but because he didn't want to embarrass Florence."

"So he asked Philip to take all the things back," said Belle. "I happened to overhear and offered to help."

"And that's what we were doing the night Ms Braithwaite was killed. We thought Plum Tree was empty and so we were trying to return her metronome," said Philip.

"Nothing she stole was really worth anything. She wasn't stealing for money," said Belle. "It was only the odd trinket. A picture frame here, or an ornament there. Basically, anything small enough to put into her basket."

"And then, of course, she stole the gnome from the circus," I said.

"How on earth did you know that?" asked Belle.

"When I went to talk about Aunt Rose's funeral, Reverend Greene fell down the back steps. I went to search for brandy and found myself in the dining room. On the table were all the things Florence had taken over the past few months, including a metronome, Wendy Williams' carriage clock, and a gnome dressed like a circus clown. Florence had already admitted that neither she nor her husband had a musical bone in their body, so it seemed odd that they owned a metronome, especially one of such excellent quality. Plus, I'd always wondered what had happened to the one Aunt Rose owned. You can't be a piano teacher and not own a metronome."

"I'll take your word for that," said Daisy.

"The gnome was the circus's lucky mascot," said Adam.

"So that's what the circus performers were doing at the police station," I said.

"Apparently they felt very strongly about Alf."

"Who's Alf?" asked Daisy.

"It's their gnome," said Adam, shaking his head. "It's best not to ask."

"At least this explains why Reverend Greene was so cold to me after I fetched his brandy. He must have been worried I would put two and two together."

"Which you did," said Adam, "eventually."

"Philip and I spent the evening of Quentin's concert trying to return as much as possible," said Belle. "But what with all the thefts, people were far less trusting and so many doors were locked. We didn't feel we should actually break in—"

"Glad to hear that," said Adam.

Belle shrugged, noncommittally. "So we had to bring everything back to the vicarage and try some other time."

"I guess that's why all the objects were piled onto the dining room table," I said.

"Is this all going to have to come out about Florence?" asked Philip. "She really is a spectacularly nice lady."

"We're going to do our best to keep it quiet," said Adam, "and Belle here has kindly offered to accompany Mrs Greene when she delivers her cakes in future."

"And thoroughly check the basket before we leave," added Belle. "It will be super fun."

"Did you ever find Aunt Rose's phone?" I asked, turning to Adam.

"Funny you should mention that," said Adam. "Frosty...I mean DS Winterbottom called about an hour ago to let me know that Police Constable Davis fished a cell phone out the Tillingbourne early this morning. It's currently sitting in a bed of rice and once it's dried out we'll hand it over to IT and see what they can do."

"Will you be able to get anything off it after all this time?" asked Daisy.

Adam shrugged. "It's immaterial, really. The minute we told Mr Young that Ms Braithwaite's phone had been found he seemed to lose all hope. It's one thing for him to have confessed, but it's another to have hard evidence. Let's put it this way. The finding of Rose's phone was the nail in the coffin."

69

Bells are portentous instruments. During the war they slept silently, only to be used at the onset of invasion. Nowadays they peal to announce the marriage of the young or toll to mark the passing of the old. Today it was the latter, as we laid Rose Braithwaite, sister, aunt, friend, pianist and, most recently, composer, to rest in Milkwood.

Considering that before her death Aunt Rose would have had trouble mustering up a doubles partner for tennis, it had been an extremely well-attended service. In fact, the entire village had turned out, wreathed in funereal black, stark like magpies against a glittering, blue-skied day to pay their respects to the woman they had once loathed.

Reverend Greene had done Aunt Rose proud, and the funeral had been full of music that Aunt Rose would have approved of—English, classical and pre-1950, along with one rather unusual addition: "Devil Woman"—specifically listed in Aunt Rose's funeral requests as the exit music.

To be honest, I shouldn't have been surprised at the turnout. The story of Quentin's musical deception had spread like wildfire. A dearth of interesting news stories meant that Aunt Rose, her death, and her musical genius had made for some serious column inches. With the press's discovery that Rose Braithwaite was the older sister of famous painter, acclaimed socialite, and artistic superstar Finolla

Monroe, a few column inches had rocketed from a minor local-interest story onto the front page of the Nationals and Milkwood had been crawling with reporters ever since.

Everyone from Petruska Llewellyn to Susan Ludlow had been interviewed. Even Bonnie Curry had been quoted as describing her sadly departed neighbor as "a good friend who would be sorely missed." It was amazing what a splattering of fame could do to redeem a sullied reputation.

I had avoided the press, the cameras and the general hullabaloo by staying firmly put at Plum Tree. Belle, Adam and Daisy had visited, not by driving down the now Piccadilly Circus-like Brambley Lane, but via the Barton Hall estate and across the softly flowing Tillingbourne.

"You know, Josie," said Belle, as we wandered towards The Dirty Duck. "I still can't help wonder why Rose sent those letters in the first place."

I nodded. "I've been giving a lot of thought to why she become so bitter and I have a theory."

Belle stared at me expectantly.

"What is the one thing the recipients of the letters had in common?" I asked.

"They all live in Milkwood?" Belle replied.

"Now who's being overly literal. True, but something deeper."

"Josie, I'm on enough painkillers to fell three of Daddy's best stallions. You're going to have to spill the beans."

"They were all in love. Arguably Wendy was more in lust, but she wanted a relationship with Peter and Dan wanted to be together with Gurminder."

"What about Florence?"

"Well yes, that one does break my rule, but the Greenes are so in love. This would have destroyed them."

"And Bonnie?"

"That was pure dislike. So maybe my theory isn't a theory at all, but I do think her relationship with Quentin had slowly been disintegrating over the years and she was angry and bitter. She'd given him so much and she felt like she'd been tossed onto the scrapheap."

Belle nodded. "Why do you think she kept copies of the letters?"

I shook my head. "No idea. But just as well she did, else we may never have found the truth."

The new iPhone in my pocket buzzed. I reached inside, pulled it out and rolled my eyes. "I don't know why I let you talk me into getting this."

Belle peered at the screen. "You had better answer."

I curled my lip, swiped right and held the phone to my ear.

"Josie, darling. Where are you?"

I attempted an answer, but Finolla swept over my protestations like the force of nature she was. "Hurry up, Josie. The press are here and for some incomprehensible reason they want to take your picture."

I simultaneously disconnected the mobile and did a one-eighty back towards the church.

With her one good arm Belle swiveled me around. "Josie, you can't not go to your aunt's funeral reception."

"Watch me," I replied, eyeing the camera vans, wedged like Legos around the village green.

My eyes were drawn back to The Dirty Duck and the svelte figure of Finolla standing beside the stocks, beckoning me like a thunderous cloud. I let out a long breath and headed towards my conception of pure hell—a state that could be neatly summarized by the combination of two words: "Finolla" and "reporters."

I paused to let a magenta Rolls inch its way through the scrabble of parked cars. The car practically screamed of old money with a dash of pretentiousness in equal measure, so it was no surprise when the door eased open and out stepped a ruggedly handsome man with shoulder length dark hair and a rakish grin. The man was outfitted in a stylish polo neck sweater and wide-legged trousers, the latter accentuating his slim waist, the former his well-defined triceps.

The press, momentarily quietened by the arrival, swung as one into full force at the realization of who was before them. I had to admit the guy looked familiar, but it took Belle nudging my arm for me to put two and two together and arrive at four.

"Isn't that..." began Belle.

I held my breath and waited for the inevitable, as the world-famous Argentinian polo captain strolled towards Finolla, taking her dramatically in his arms.

"Well, cluck a duck," I murmured.

"Looks like those tango lessons really paid off," said Adam, appearing at my side and sliding his arm around my waist.

"I'm sure they're just good friends," I said, as Finolla threw back her onyx-colored funeral veil and kissed the Argentinian with a passion that even I had to admit did not look anything close to platonic.

"Woohoo, Josie. Over here," cried Finolla, coming up for air.

"Shoot me now," I muttered, as every camera focused in my direction.

"Go on, Puke, you might as well get it over with. I believe fame only lasts fifteen minutes, so don't fret too much," said Adam.

Gritting my teeth, I muscled my way through the multitude of Fleet Street's finest and took my place by Finolla's side.

"Darlings, thank you so much for being here," trilled Finolla, to her adoring press. "And of course you all know my fiancé, Santiago Garcia Herrera Fernandez, who was kind enough to take time out of his hectic schedule to help me as I deal with the suffocating grief at the loss of my beloved sister, Rose."

The press went wild, and the cameras exploded, while I stood as far as possible from my mother and her latest conquest without seeming impolite. Questions were yelled, suggestions were shouted and I gave thanks that I would walk away from this and *never* have to do it again.

I managed a full thirty seconds before I pulled away. I elbowed my way into The Dirty Duck and practically threw myself on the mercy of Petruska and an exceedingly generous glass of pinot.

I eyed Daisy nestled in the same darkened corner and indicated for her to move up, so I could take a seat.

"How come *you* got out of the family debacle with the fourth estate?" I said, tipping back my glass like a woman who'd crossed the Sahara.

"Remember, I've known Finolla a lot longer than you. I'm on to all her annoying, egotistical nonsense and besides, I was sitting at the back of the church. I took one glance at the press and made a bolt for it."

"Well, it's obvious which of us has the brains in this family," I said, draining my glass. I was about to return to the bar for another when the look on Daisy's face stopped me. I reached out and squeezed her hand. "You doing okay?" A stupid question to ask the sister of the deceased, while at their funeral reception.

"Fair to middling," said Daisy. "I wish to all get-go I'd arrived a day or two sooner. That I'd got to speak to her one last time. I feel like I didn't really know her, and she knew practically nothing about me and how my life turned out."

"Actually, that's not true."

"Whatcha getting at?" asked Daisy.

I reached into my handbag and brought out a well-thumbed paperback, featuring a meringue with a knife plunged into its side on the front cover.

"Where on earth did you get that from?" asked Daisy.

"Found it on Aunt Rose's coffee table the day after she died. I take it you *are* D. Braith? And look." I opened the book to a random passage and passed it to Daisy.

Daisy scanned the page and started to smile. "Rose always was one to make notes, on everything. Chalkboards, packed lunches, Dad's copy of the *Financial Times*. Ha, look at this one."

Daisy passed me the paperback and I read the note in the margin. I grinned. It was so typically Aunt Rose. Not mean, poison-pen letter Aunt Rose but full of the loving, caring Aunt Rose from my childhood. It read, *My sister is a legend.*

"Talking of Aunt Rose's notes, I received this through the mail yesterday." I pulled out a copy of *Musician's Monthly* with a picture of a kilted bagpiper on the front.

"What's this?" said Daisy. "Top six bagpipe tunes of all time? Tell me they're joking."

I shook my head. "Ignore the be-kilted one, if you can." I flipped through the magazine until I found the article I was searching for. "I called my neighbor Mrs Ackerman. I asked her to send me all the copies of *Musician's Monthly* from two years ago."

"You still have magazines from two years ago? What type of hoarder are you?" asked Daisy.

"Only these," I admitted. "And only because they were from Aunt Rose. Really I just kept them for the comments. After the whole thing with Quentin came to light, I finally recalled why he was so familiar to me."

"Why's that then?" said Daisy.

I pointed to the article titled "Quentin Young: Britain's Non-Child Prodigy." The article was only three or four paragraphs long, outlining Quentin's musical history, his inspiration, and his surprising emergence onto the classical musical scene with *Rosetta's Throne* after being unheard-of for the majority of his initial sixty-plus years. "Here, read what Aunt Rose wrote in the margins."

Daisy read aloud. "Couldn't compose his way out of a paper bag. Like all successful men, there's bound to be a successful woman behind him."

"She all but spelled it out for you," said Daisy, handing me back the magazine.

"What are you two laughing at?" asked Belle, arriving at the table with Philip in tow.

"Ah, nothing of consequence," said Daisy.

Philip pulled out a chair for Belle before addressing the rest of the table. "Can I get you ladies a refill?" Philip reached over and squeezed Belle's hand before raising it to his lips and giving it a kiss.

"Don't mind if I do," said Daisy, raising an empty pint glass. "Same again all around please, Curate."

Philip strolled towards the bar and I turned my attention to Belle.

"What?" said Belle, blushing.

"I thought you said you two were just 'partners in crime.'"

"We are. We were," said Belle, looking as bashful as one of the seven dwarfs. "And then when Philip was hurt I realized I may have had some previously unrealized feelings for him."

"I told you," I said, unable to disguise my delight. "I told you there was something going on between the two of you. You don't spend ten years teaching middle school without knowing the signs of young love blossoming."

"Young love? Does the clergy approve of such debauchery?" asked Philip, plonking one cranberry juice with umbrella, one sploshingly large pinot and two pints of stout on the table.

"We're talking about Adam and Josie," said Belle, turning the tables. "Rumor has it you went out on your first official date last week."

I turned to face my aunt. "That was supposed to be a secret," I said to the only person who had known about the clandestine date.

Daisy shrugged. "What can I say? Magna wheedled it out of me using a hearty bacon butty and a couple of tasty cinnamon buns. Lumme, that woman can cook. Besides, I'm sure she would never—"

"The woman will have shouted it from rooftops," I finished, laughing.

Daisy gave this some thought. "You may have a point. But it was worth it."

"Who shouted what from the rooftops?" asked Adam, joining the already crowded table. I scooted around to give him an ounce of room.

"That you and Josie are an item," said Daisy, in her usual blunt but endearing manner.

Adam cut his eyes to me. I shrugged.

"So, Daisy, what are your plans? Will you be staying on in Milkwood until your book's finished?" I said, subtly changing the subject.

Daisy drained her glass. "I most certainly am. How about you, Josie? You going to keep me company?"

I stared at Adam, who was studying his pint glass most attentively. Over the past two weeks I had felt more at home than I had... well ever. Languid days were spent lazing in the garden, enjoying wonderful home-cooked meals courtesy of Peter, and playing board games with Belle and Philip during the evenings. As summers went, it was pretty fabulous.

On top of that I had taken on more students and was hopefully instilling in them a love of classical music. I had never been happier. Yes, my home was in the US and, yes, my full-time job was in Austin, but right now my heart was firmly and truly in Milkwood.

Adam reached across the table, took my hand and gave it a squeeze.

I smiled. "Actually, I think I might stay."

THE END

MEET SAM BOND

Sam Bond is the best-selling, award-winning author of *The Puccini Connection* and the *Cousins In Action* series.

Sam was raised in a small village in England before moving to the States twenty-five years ago. When not writing you can find Sam behind the lens of a camera, playing Chopin, or reading one of the many books suggested by the two book clubs she runs. Sam has also been known to make a half-decent shepherd's pie and lives in Austin, Texas with her two daughters and a dog named Sausage. The Puccini Connection is the first book in The Milkwood Murders series.

CONTACT SAM

Readers are welcome to contact Sam at the following
e-mail: boundpublishing@gmail.com
Or find her on Facebook at 007BondSam

ALSO BY SAM BOND

Check out Sam's award-winning middle grade series for children aged 8-12. All available on Amazon.

Operation Golden Llama - Cousins In Action Series - Book 1

Operation Tiger Paw - Cousin In Action Series - Book 2

Operation Jewel Thief - Cousins In Action Series - Book 3

Operation Pharaoh's Curse - Cousins In Action Series - Book 4

Operation Dude Ranch - Cousins In Action Series - Book 5 (Prequel)

REVIEWS - DO YOU HAVE A SEC?

Dear Reader,

If you have an extra five minutes, please consider leaving an honest review on Amazon. Reviews help to spread the word, boost sales, and give the author a warm fuzzy feeling knowing readers, other than my mother, appreciate my make believe world. Just a couple of sentences will do. Thank you.

Sam

TAKE A SNEAK PEEK AT THE NEXT MILKWOOD MURDER.

CHAPTER 1

T ake a left," said Daisy.

I angled the steering wheel towards my aunt.

"No left!"

"This is left," I replied.

"Oh! Then I guess I mean the other left."

I took a breath. "So just to clarify, you mean 'right'?"

There was a mumbled ascent as I eased on Jenny's brakes and attempted to find reverse. There was no fear of anything going into the back of us. I hadn't seen so much as a car, truck or perambulator in a good ten minutes. All I'd seen was cows, hedges and the odd cottage and by odd I really do mean odd. The last abode we'd passed had a dead crow hanging claws up from the gate post, and the cottage before had been painted Pepto Bismol pink. Not a good color in even the smallest of quantities; utterly horrific on a three bedroomed semi.

I hung a right. "Are you sure, we're going the right way?"

Daisy turned the map ninety degrees and then another ninety. "Not entirely, but I've a pretty good sense of direction."

"You just told me to turn left when you meant right," I pointed out.

"Details," said Daisy, who was currently engulfed by Northern Surrey.

Daisy's head emerged from behind the increasingly crinkled map. "Was that Bumble Bottom?"

Once again I hit the brakes and seeked the elusive reverse on my circa 1980s Citroen 2CV. Unlike most cars, 2CV's have an interesting, read challenging, gearbox. My ability to drive Jenny was improving, and transferring from first to second was finally becoming manageable, however reverse was still fraught with frustration. Ramming my foot on the clutch I wrangled the contrary machine into reverse with just the slightest crunch of gears.

Daisy shuddered.

"Don't say a word," I said, "else you can drive."

"Then we'd *never* get there." Daisy had attempted to drive Jenny only once since she'd moved in with me. She had made it roughly three meters before proclaiming the car a fiend of nature.

Jenny kangarooed backwards, as I wound down her window in order to study the wooden signpost lurching drunkenly across the lane. "Yep, that's Bumble Bottom."

"Then it's the next one," said Daisy, avoiding my eyes.

I took a deep breath and counted to ten. I had been living with my aunt for the past three weeks and really enjoyed her wit, her enthusiasm and her charmingly wonky Viennese cupcakes, but her sense of direction was appalling. Of course, I knew I should give in and purchase a GPS like any other sane person, but my aversion to all things technological was at best—charming, at worst, and according to my sweet, darling aunt, butt-achingly annoying.

Still I soldiered on. A lone stand out in a world of sellouts— remaining determined to stay as far away from technology as possible. Yes, I had broken down and acquired an ancient (my friend, Belle DeCorcy's words not mine) iPhone, but in my defense it *was* an iPhone, regardless of its age. And it allowed me to connect with the handful of people (okay there were six, so make that two hands) I had deemed worthy enough to receive my number.

"It's the third on the right," said a deep voice.

I swiveled to see Adam Ward, lounging across the back seat, his arm draped languidly over the well-worn leather, his legs stretching from one side of the Citroen to the other.

"Did you use your cellphone?" I asked, my eyes narrowing.

Adam's face creased into a smile. "Might have done."

I negotiated Jenny into gear and we rambled down the narrow country lane. When we had set off from Milkwood, twenty minutes earlier, it had not been the most glorious of summer days, but it had been devoid of downpours and fog, two things that looked more imminent the closer we approached our destination.

I counted off two roads before angling onto the third, and seconds later I eased Jenny into the village of Morton-under-Lamb. Morton-under-Lamb consisted of a dingy looking Spar, a dodgy looking pet store, and a shop that might be used as a last resort to buy a distant aunt a forgotten birthday present. A very distant aunt. There were several other buildings, most boarded up, and I could see the outline of a well-known high street bank that had long since departed for more profitable shores. Immediately I gave thanks for the bustling village of Milkwood and its plethora of vibrant, successful businesses.

Two minutes later we had rumbled through downtown and entered a more prosperous-looking area. Larger, better kept abodes lined the road but, nevertheless, it was pretty slim pickings.

"Take a left at the pub," said Adam.

Glancing up, I saw a half-dilapidated sign swinging off kilter on its hinges. The sign proclaimed The Miller's Arms, and portrayed a ruddy-faced farmer in a white smock flexing his muscles. The sign had obviously been commissioned several decades before, but the flush pink of the farmer's cheeks gave it a quaint quality indicative of long ago England.

Giving directions purely by naming the pubs en-route was particularly unique English past time and an idiosyncratic quirk that I had missed while living in the States. As a child, there had been many times when my father had rolled down the car window and been given directions that consisted of 'take a left at The Kings Head, a right at The White Horse and, you've gone too far if you reach The Royal Oak'. Alas those days were ending, as more of Britain's pubs hung up their bar towels and retired their dart boards. A result of the smoking ban or just a shift in social habits? It was hard to tell, but it was impossible to ignore the plethora of pubs that had shuttered their windows and been turned into apartments.

One couldn't help wonder how long until The Miller's Arms suffered the same fate.

I swung Jenny left and up a slight incline. Here the houses were larger, no longer hugging the road, but set further back, with gardens overflowing with various types of horticulture. I was horrible with flower names. Of course I could identify the basics like crocus, tulips, daffodils—but those were spring flowers, a season that was well behind us. Other than roses and delphiniums, summer flowers were identifiable to me only by color, as in—that pink flower by the haystack or, that yellow bush by the stile. I mentally added 'learn to identify English flowers' to my ever growing list of things to do before I returned to the States.

"It's this one on the right," said Daisy, folding the map in two, then three, and finally in four, before stuffing it under the passenger seat.

"You sure?" I asked, leaning forward to survey the boldest house on the neat cul-de-sac. The house was brick, symmetrical and void of character. No English country garden lingered here, in fact the owners looked like they'd gone to considerable trouble to keep the front garden as utilitarian as possible. Two oversized gates book-ended east and west with a four feet tall brick wall, connecting the two. The entire garden had been paved in muted orange slab, the only greenery being two shoulder high topiaries sculpted into symmetrical balls erect, like guardsmen, each side of the wide front door.

"Pull up by the front, why don't you?" said Daisy, pointing towards the wrought iron gates.

"Erm!" I said, realizing that none of the other guests had taken such liberties. "I think I'll just..."

I maneuvered Jenny past a plethora of cars until I found a spot between a battered Corsa and a neon-colored VW bug. I said a quick prayer that I would be able to locate reverse and, my prayer answered, I neatly backed Jenny into the compact space.

Applying the handbrake, I opened the door and joined Daisy and Adam on the pavement. There was no point in locking Jenny. I kept nothing of value inside, and had chosen not to bring the removable stereo system, my choice of music being nowhere near compatible with either Daisy *or* Adam—Daisy being a diehard Motown fan, and Adam appreciating bands I didn't even recognize the name of.

It was a dull, miserable day, and I felt a swift breeze around my ankles, making me wish I'd worn a pair of jeans instead of my current short-sleeved summer dress

"Ready?" said Daisy, halfway up the drive.

"As I'll ever be. Remind me why I agreed to come with you?"

Adam fell into step beside me, slipping his hand into mine. It felt warm and firm and my heart did a little jig as I thought about how happy I was.

"You know I get nervous in social situations," said Daisy.

"You do?" I asked, not giving much credence to such a ludicrous idea. My secret aunt had turned out to be fun, witty and an amazingly decent baker. She got on well with Peter, my lodger and, when she wasn't whipping up some exquisite chocolate concoction, was busy penning a cozy murder mystery set in the fictitious village of Plumpton—which was what I was going to become if I didn't stop eating her coconut macaroons.

"*Do* you get nervous in social situations?" I asked.

"Nah, not in the slightest, I just didn't want to drive. Believe me, this is going to be at least a four-beer party, maybe five."

"Now we're getting to the truth," said Adam. "And what about me?"

"You're just here for eye candy," said Daisy, grinning.

Adam shrugged. "I can live with that. Remind me, how do you know this woman?"

"She's a writer buddy. Chairperson of Writer's In the Rough," said Daisy.

"Writer's in the what?" asked Adam.

But Daisy had moved on, pointing towards a note attached to the door.

"'Come on in,'" read Daisy. "Right you are, then." Daisy muscled open the door before stepping aside to let Adam and I enter.

The three of us emerged into an airy hallway and stopped dead. At the end of the passageway were two figures silhouetted against a hulking American fridge. Two figures that seemed to be partaking in an almighty row. In fact, they were yelling so loudly I was surprised I hadn't heard them back in Milkwood.

"You're such a cow! You think you can control me, but you can't," yelled a dark-haired boy.

"And you're a stereotypical disillusioned teenager," shrieked the woman, pushing a finger into her adversary's chest.

"Stop blaming everything on my age."

"But it's *true*, darling. Everyone knows teenagers are utterly impossible. You're just fulfilling a time-honored cliché."

"And stop calling me darling."

"But poppet!"

"That's even worse. My name is James. You should know it. You're the one who bloody well named me."

"Language now, sweetums," said the woman, placing a tentative hand on his arm.

"Piss off, mum," replied James, flinging her hand away before barreling out of the kitchen, and down the hallway towards us.

We parted like the proverbial Red Sea, as the stormy-faced teenager thundered past and clomped up the stairs.

The woman turned to follow, but paused as a man wearing an apron covered in cats entered the kitchen and spoke.

"Leave him be. Honestly, Delia, do you always have to get the knife in? You're going to push him too far, one day, and then what will you do?"

"Don't be so idiotic, Jeffrey," said Delia. "You really are such a silly little man. James *cannot* do this to us and he *won't*. Not if *I've* got anything to do with it."

Jeffrey's voice became stern. "For God's sake, Delia. Stop. First Toby, then me and now James. Will you not be happy until you've ruined everyone's lives?"

Delia was about to speak, but Jeffrey grabbed hold of her shoulders and held on tight.

"I'll tell you now, be careful, because we've just about had enough." And with that Jeffrey turned and retreated from view.

"Well, that was awkward," said Daisy, eyeing the front door as means of escape.

"Yeah. Maybe we should..." But before I'd a chance to finish my sentence Delia turned and swished towards us.

Delia's face was attractive and welcoming and, if I'd only just walked in, I would have thought her the most delightful host, ever.

"You must be Daisy's talented niece," said Delia, grasping my hand and giving it a hearty shake. "Delia Frogmorton at your service."

Honestly, it was as if the previous two minutes hadn't even happened. It was obvious that our hostess could turn from Hyde to Jekyll in seconds.

"Josie," I said, trying to extract my hand from the woman's bony palm.

"And who do we have here?" asked Delia, running her eyes up and down Adam like a violinist eyeing a particularly fine Stradivarius.

"This here is Adam Ward," said Daisy. "He's Josie's better half."

I started to object, but realized she was right. Adam and I had been officially dating for three weeks and, for lack of a better word, he was my boyfriend, partner, or whatever people called being in a relationship these days.

Adam stepped forward and grasped Delia's outstretched hand and gave it a downward tug.

"Aren't *you* a lucky girl," said Delia, winking in my direction. Turning her attention back to Adam she added. "Charmed."

Delia was a tall woman in her fifties. She was slim built, with highlighted, wavy hair. She wore a tight-fitting turquoise top and low slung jeans that hugged her non-existent curves. Four inch strappy sandals completed the outfit. She looked modern and smart and, with the exception of the height of the heels, appropriately dressed for a Sunday afternoon BBQ.

I was wearing one of my new summer dresses, while Daisy wore a linen tunic with matching trousers. Her hair was pulled off her face and little curls of grey danced jollily around her heavily ear-ringed ears. She looked comfortable and happy and I reminded myself, once again, how lucky I was to have her in my life. Adam wore what he always wore when he was off duty: jeans, a grey V-neck tee and a smile. Adam wasn't handsome in the traditional sense. His nose was a little too wide and his lips a little too thin, but he had a confidence about him that men admired and women desired.

Adam retrieved his hand and inhaled deeply. "Do I smell burgers?"

"Where are my manners," said Delia. "Of course, go through. Mingle. I must just check on James."

"Is that wise?" asked Daisy, never shy on opinions. "He seemed a little put out when he passed us in the hallway."

"The boy's just finished his 'A' levels," said Delia, as if in explanation for her son's bad mood. "He's a little tetchy."

Lord, if that was the definition of 'tetchy' then I was a monkey's aunt — tail and all.

Delia continued. "Been offered a wonderful place at Durham—going into pre-med. It's one of the best universities in the country, don't you know? A doctor in the family—just imagine!"

The door at the top of the stairs slammed so hard the entire staircase reverberated. Delia didn't seem at all bothered, which made me wonder if this was a regular occurrence.

"You know teenagers!" said Delia, airily. "One minute they hate you, the next they're crying for their mummy."

I had never mothered a teenager, but I had taught several hundred of them as a music teacher in my adopted hometown of Austin, Texas, and had never known this to be true.

Delia headed up the stairs and Adam and I followed Daisy down the hallway and into the expansive kitchen. It was all mod-cons in this neck of Morton-under-Lamb.

I admired the blue Aga, the deep farmhouse sink and miles of soapstone countertops littered with gardening and swimming pool catalogs. Obviously, the Frogmorton household was doing well for itself. Weaving through the conservatory I sidestepped several rattan chairs, before stepping into the pristine garden beyond. Well, pristine other than the motley crew that filled it.

To be honest, for a garden that was full to bursting, it was surprisingly quiet. Groups of twos and threes mulled under a yellow and white striped canopy, while a crowd of four huddled by the wishing well. There must have been at least twenty-five people residing in Delia Frogmorton's garden, but the sound level hovered around pianissimo.

I gazed around in awe. The front garden may have consisted of a sea of paving stones, but the back more than made up for it. As far as the eye could see was a riot of color with deep perennial borders, an ornamental pond and a whimsical summer house nestled between a cluster of apple trees.

Closer to home was a crazy paving patio hosting an oversized grill from which came the source of the aroma. I observed the grey-haired man in the cat apron, who was currently venting his anger by flapping a copy of *The Times* in the general direction of a plethora of sorry-looking burgers and hot dogs.

Don't get me wrong, there are certain food groups the British excel at. Fish and chips springs to mind. Shepherd's pie, traditionally made from the leftovers of a lamb roast, was another favorite, plus the humble curry—a welcome addition from our Asian friends. In fact, it was hard to believe that chicken tikka masala had arrived on these chilly shores barely seventy years before. Nowadays, it was practically de rigueur after a skin-full at the pub to traipse down your local curry house, although, to be honest, at that time of night, it was more likely to be requested with chips than rice!

Yes, the British excelled in many culinary dishes. Alas, the humble BBQ was not one of them. Having spent my last twenty years in Texas I considered myself, not an expert, but at least able to discern my brisket from my pulled pork, my ribeye from my sirloin, and not once had I ever served chili containing beans—something Texans had surprisingly strong opinions on. Even to a sturdy Brit, this array of burnt offerings could not possibly look appetizing. Could it?

"Grubs up!" yelled Jeffrey, abandoning *The Times* for a pair of tongs.

All heads swiveled, and a gathering storm swarmed towards the charred wreckage. It was then that I spotted the young, blonde-haired woman waving enthusiastically in my direction.

Made in the USA
Coppell, TX
27 November 2020